TALES OF
TRAVELROTICA
FOR GAY MEN

EROTIC TRAVEL
ADVENTURES

TALES OF
TRAVELROTICA
FOR GAY MEN

EROTIC TRAVEL
ADVENTURES

edited by

BRAD NICHOLS

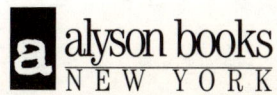

alyson books
NEW YORK

© 2006 by Alyson Books. Authors retain the rights to their individual pieces of work. All rights reserved.

Manufactured in the United States of America.

This trade paperback original is published by Alyson Books,
P.O. Box 1253, Old Chelsea Station, New York, New York, 10115-1251.

Distribution in the United Kingdom by Turnaround Publisher Services Ltd.,
Unit 3, Olympia Trading Estate, Coburg Road, Wood Green,
London N22 6TZ England.

Book design by Victor Mingovits

First Edition: August 2006

06 07 08 09 a 10 9 8 7 6 5 4 3 2 1

ISBN 1-55583-959-2
ISBN-13 978-1-55583-959-8

CONTENTS

INTRODUCTION

BRAD NICHOLS

DEAR TRAVELER:

Suitcases packed? Passport valid? Double-checked your itinerary? Got condoms? Good, then you're ready for your own erotic travel adventures. But for the rest of you, until you can plan your great escape, sit back with this amazing collection of "Travelrotica," a word I coined to best describe these erotic stories in exotic locales.

Our journey begins on the British Isles, and then, after a brief layover in Paris, we make our way through a dozen other European capitals and cities. From there it's on to the lush, romantic lands of Africa, the balmy islands of the Atlantic and Caribbean, to lusty South America and the distant Down Under and Far East, and finally to one last place that remains the ultimate in travel fantasy.

In J. Talbot's "Sleeping the Rails," a London tube ride turns into a different kind of ride for one sleepless young man. Check out "Pole's Foreskin," Michael Murphy's alluring tale of a traveler and the dancer he cannot resist. "Fernando" is the lucky recipient of two lovers traveling throughout Spain thanks to John-Paul Batista, and in William Holden's "Going Dutch," the phrase takes on a whole new meaning. Finally, blast off with T. Hitman's brave "Comrades."

So, armchair travelers, settle in for a long flight of fantasy that takes you well beyond any mile-high club. Discover what wondrous heights of passion exist in the world.

SLEEPING THE RAILS

J. TALBOT

THE LONDON TUBE is a soporific. Seriously, sit on the District line for an hour from the station Plaistow to South Kensington at say, nine at night and see what I mean. The sway of the carriage, the softly repeated "Mind the Gap" and the deathly quiet of the other passengers, all sort of lull you into a stupor.

It's good for me, because I'm something of an insomniac. I do my best sleeping on trains, which is probably why this trip to England has found me venturing out of London to Brighton and Leeds and Canterbury. Oh, sure, I love the Brighton Pavilion. It looks like a pleasure palace, somewhere a Georgian or Victorian man might have kept a harem of boys, all done up with eyeliner and gauzy pants. Leeds is great too, all gardens and tea. But it's really the trains I crave.

The British are so impossibly polite on trains, too. On the Metro in DC, or even the relatively clean T in Boston, the people will crowd on and fight for seats or smash up against you during rush hour. The tube can get that crowded, for sure, but it's usually orderly, and late at night, on the last two or three runs before it shuts down, the people never look at you, and hardly talk, everyone sitting with heavy eyes and clasped hands. They stare at the advertising posters above your head, or the floor of the carriage. Never at you.

Which was why it was such a surprise to wake up one night on the way back to my holiday rental flat and find him staring at me.

He was one of those young men you see all over in London, with shaggy hair in several different colors of blond and brown, wearing jeans that flared and a jacket that fit tight to his body. Bowling shoes and lots of jingly silver jewelry completed his look, along with a single, thin ring in his nose, not that silly bull-ring thing, but just threaded through one nostril.

His eyes were bright green.

Stiffening, I sat up and crossed my arms, frowning at him a little, but that only made him smile and move down three seats so that he sat directly across from me.

"You're not from here, are you then?" he asked. "American?"

I blinked, my mouth opening and closing before I asked, "How did you know? I might have been Australian or French."

"S'the white tube socks and trainers, isn't it? Couldn't be any-thing but."

"Oh." A tiny chain wrapped around his throat, a charm I couldn't identify sitting right in the little hollow at the base of his neck. I squinted at it.

"You want to see?" he asked, moving to sit next to me so quickly that I didn't have time to move away. He turned and lifted the little charm. It was a winged helmet.

"Hermes?" I hazarded a guess.

"Right. You know he's the god of motion." Then he winked. "And helping travelers sleep."

I blinked again. "What's your name?"

"Evan. Yours?"

"John," I replied. "I'm a writer." I said it like I needed an excuse to be in London. Like I needed something besides "tourist."

"Of course." Evan's lips curled into a half-smile as androgy-nous and enigmatic as the Mona Lisa's. "Is that why you sleep on the train? Because you're a writer?"

"No, I sleep on the train because I can't anywhere else."

The train clacked along. We stared at each other until the pleasant little canned voice announced "Blackfriars." Evan stood, swaying as the carriage slowed.

"That's me, then," he said, moving to stand just in front of the door. He gave me a look over his shoulder, his eyes twinkling in half light. "Are you coming with me?"

Was I? You bet I was. I slipped out just in time, my poor slug-gish brain almost making me too late.

"Where are we going?" I asked.

"To my flat. It's just on Upper Thames Street. Closer to Mansion House, I suppose, but I like the walk."

I followed him as he wandered, completely at ease, hands in his pockets. The streets seemed like a maze in the dark, at least to me, but he did have a point. You could walk almost anywhere in central London if you had the time. Given a good map it was one of my favorite things to do. For a moment I had a wild fancy that he knew that, and was amusing me. Or that maybe he'd missed his stop at the Mansion House station because he was absorbed in talking to me.

"So what do you write?" he asked, breaking my concentration on his ass. It fascinated me, almost boyish, even though it was clear he was in his mid-twenties.

"I uh. Mostly fiction, but I do some nonfiction travel writing."

"Yeah? I suppose that's why you sleep."

"I do," I agreed, following him up a flight of stairs once we finally got to his building. Six flights, in fact. By the time we got to the top I was panting a little. Londoners always walk my legs off.

"This is it. Not much, is it? But it's got all I need."

The tiny apartment had a clever Murphy bed, a double in fact and a kitchenette, as well as a sofa and entertainment system. It worked only because it was painfully neat, the spare ornaments and cheerful colors keeping it from seeming closed in.

"You have a great view," I said, looking out at St. Paul's Cathedral.

"I do," he agreed, standing so close behind me suddenly that his breath fanned my neck.

"I, uh . . . " I just couldn't seem to make my brain work all of a sudden. Back in my college years I'd been a wild child, picking up pretty boys at the drop of a hat. Now in my thirties I felt stodgy, cautious.

Evan didn't seem to share my reticence. His hands slid around my waist, clasping lightly over my belly, causing my muscles to quiver. I pushed back against him, his boldness creating my own. It was like we were feeding off each other.

His lips slid along my neck to a spot just under my ear. "Is this too forward?" he asked.

I just shook my head no and turned in the circle of his arms to take a kiss, to see if his pretty mouth felt as soft as it looked. It did.

I could imagine it all over me, on my hands and my chest and my cock, hot as hell. Evan smiled against my mouth like he knew, his fingers tracing my cheeks, stroking the back of my neck.

Still a little disbelieving, I tugged at Evan's tight jacket, wanting to see him before he decided he was making a mistake and booted me out. Utterly obliging, he lifted his arms and let me push it off, along with his shirt, let me trace the fine line of brownish hair that ran from his navel down to the waistband of his jeans. Stylishly thin, but with nice, lean muscles, Evan was hot enough to make me drool, make me want to touch every bit of him.

Laughing when I touched his ribs, Evan twisted away to shuck his jeans, his uncut cock heavy against his thigh. I love European men for that very reason. What, I'm shallow, okay? I reached for it, curling my hand around it, watching his eyelashes flutter as he moaned and pushed into my touch.

Then he seemed to remember I was there, all of me, not just my hand. He pulled at my clothes too, until we both stood there naked, and then he stepped close, rubbing against me. The feel of his smooth, lean body against my heavier, hair-rough form was just so damned good I had to kiss him again, hard, feeling his lips swell beneath mine, probably bruising right up. I love bruised mouths and fuck-starved eyes.

Our cocks brushed, his long and thin, the extra skin at the tip moving against me, mine thicker, shorter, weirdly naked next to his. Evan's fingers found them both, cupping just beneath, pushing them together, and I went up on tiptoe at the feel of it, at the pressure it put on my balls below.

"How do you want it?" he asked.

"I don't bottom," I replied immediately.

He gave me a smile that made my whole body stand up and take notice, all slow and sure and confident. "That's why you don't sleep," he said. "Let me show you."

"Suck me first, and I might."

That had him chuckling, but sure enough he dropped to his knees in front of me, grabbing my hips and turning me so I could see Wren's great cathedral out his window. Then all I saw was static as he licked at the tip of my cock, murmuring about how pretty it was before his lips closed over the head and sank right down, riding along the shaft like a tight, wet glove.

Gloves. I wondered if he had any condoms. That might be one way to get out of . . . oh God. His mouth. Those pretty lips stretched wide around me, and as I glanced down he stared up, his eyes hot for me, eating me right up. There's nothing sexier than a man looking you right in the eyes as he swallows your cock whole. Nothing in the world.

Evan used his hands on me, too, rubbing my thighs, my ass, reaching between my legs to gather up my balls. When he pushed at my hole I stiffened, but he just stroked the little ring of muscle, just tapped at it. Reminding me what I'd promised.

I rode it, letting him suck me, letting the pleasure rise up my spine as he worked me, up and down. When he went all the way down to the base, lips forming a seal with his hand as he pushed up, I lost it, coming so hard I saw stars. He didn't pull off. He just took it.

God.

"You ready to keep your part of the bargain, luv?" he asked, licking his swollen lips as he pulled off me.

"I pride myself on my honesty." I half dreaded it, half wondered if he could really make me fall asleep just by fucking me to exhaustion.

"Such a martyr." Evan's fingers circled my wrist, and he smiled at me as he rose, putting my hand on his cock.

I stroked him again, savoring the feel of him, before meeting his eyes. "Condom?"

"Yeah. Come on. Let's get comfy, yeah?"

"Comfy" ended up with us on the pull-down bed, a condom in Evan's hand, my cock making a valiant effort to rise again as he kissed me, touched me, made me feel fifteen again.

The lube ended up in my hand, and there was no mistaking the suggestive rise of Evan's eyebrows. How many times had I asked someone to get themselves ready for me? Fifty? A hundred? This felt like payback for all of them, and I was actually nervous as I popped the top and got two fingers wet.

"Nice and easy, luv," Evan said, petting my belly.

I only nodded, kneeling up to reach back, my breath catching as I touched myself, my fingers sliding along my crack to my hole, pushing right in. I just. Wow. It had been so long that I was immediately breathless from the pressure.

"Need some help?" The condom rolled right down over Evan's cock, and he reached for me, slipping one hand behind me to slide a finger in alongside mine. Fuck.

Oh, fuck that was hot.

Soon my hole was grasping at our fingers, open, ready, my every breath shuddering through me as I rode our hands. Pulling away, Evan pushed me so I topped back on the bed, and he pressed my knees nearly to my damned ears, the singing of my thigh muscles reminding me I wasn't fifteen, no sir, no how.

He stretched me as he slipped in, drawing a short, desperate cry out of me, making me sweat. My cock hadn't flagged a bit though, throbbing against my lower belly as he speared me, pushing in and in until I thought I might split from the pressure. Evan didn't stop until his hips sat flush with my ass, his forehead leaning against mine.

"All right, luv?" he asked.

I could only grunt my assent.

When he started moving, it rocked me to the core, my whole body shaking with the impact of each thrust. God, I hadn't been so fucking excited in years, and my legs finally unbent, wrapping around him, my hands pulling at him, getting him closer and closer.

Kisses bruised my mouth, pressed my lips back against my teeth as Evan pummeled my ass, thrusting harder and harder. When it occurred to me to touch my cock it was almost too late, hot drops slicking my entire shaft, not just the head, the length twitching wildly as I started stroking.

Evan's eyes widened like he could feel it around him, and he moved harder, faster, his hips punching against me until finally he cried out, coming hard, filling the condom in my ass. His fingers closed over mine right at his last thrust, pulling hard on my cock, and I shot a load of spunk between us like I'd never seen come out of me before.

We flopped like rag dolls, the sound of a boat horn out on the river suddenly loud, echoed by the bells at St. Paul's. I had to laugh.

"Talk about ringing in your ears," I said, still chuckling in that post-coital silliness.

"Shut up and go to sleep, John," Evan said right back, stroking my forehead, and amazingly, I did just that.

I slept like a baby, in a bed, for the first time in years.

The next morning Evan and I boarded a Eurostar to Paris. I slept on trains and in beds with him from Paris to Belgium, from Germany to Spain. When I woke up without him in Lisbon I knew it was over, but it was all right. My insomnia was well past.

I don't need the motion of a train anymore, not for sleeping at any rate. But every time I get on a rail line, whether the London tube or the Amtrak from Seattle to Denver, I think of Evan, the hot little avatar of a long ago god. He left me his little Hermes pendant.

I wear it every day. And I've never slept better.

LOVE IN ANOTHER LANGUAGE

BOB CONDRON

HE WOKE IN the night to the sound of the rain lashing against the attic skylight. He lay in the dark of an unfamiliar bedroom, in an unfamiliar bed in an unfamiliar land, and listened. It was a strangely comforting sound. Snuggling down under the bedclothes, he reveled in the warmth and protection they afforded him. Happy to be safely tucked up in bed while the storm raged elsewhere.

Somewhere in the distance, a crack of thunder. Then a second closer to hand. Behind his closed eyelids he could visualize the squall at sea and the warning beam from Whitby lighthouse, sweeping over the churning waves as they battered the North Yorkshire coastline. England, he remembered, was famous for its rain.

But no worries. The fisherman's cottage that he would call home for the next seven days had stood the test of time. It had first been carved into the rock four centuries earlier. And, though the back wall had been reinforced, and reinforced again, against the damp and the ravages of time until the house was two-thirds of its original depth, there was little doubt that it would last for centuries yet to come.

Suitably reassured he fell into a deep and thankfully dreamless sleep.

✦

ROBIN HOOD'S BAY out of season was about as sleepy a hollow as could be imaginable. It was one of the main reasons he'd chosen to spend the week there. That, and its proximity to the sea. He loved the sea; could lose himself for hours just watching the waves roll in. Timeless. Looking outward with nothing on the horizon but blue, he felt as if it could be any point in history; knew that men had seen this same unchanging seascape for century upon centuries past. It was a comfort. Not least because the past was where he felt most at ease and where, given the choice, he would have preferred to remain.

✦

"COMES IN QUICK, doesn't it?" The barman asked him. "The tide," he added, as clarification in the face of Bodo's puzzled expression. "What can I get you?"

"A pint of Bitter, please." It was only as he spoke that, Bodo realized, he himself had not spoken a word to anyone since the previous morning, and then only when he had stopped off for petrol on the drive over. As skilled as he was, he was hesitant about speaking English at the best of times. People usually remarked on his German accent and he was not at all sure if he wanted to get embroiled in a polite conversation today.

But the barman didn't remark about it. "Saw you through the window, down the hill," was all he said as his right hand worked the pump, filling Bodo's pint glass. "Best to keep wrapped up warm when you're out. The cold can be deceptive." He handed Bodo his pint and Bodo handed over his money. With a nod of thanks, he took his beer over to a table beside an open fire.

The pub was empty save for a couple of workmen in the snug out back. Bodo could see them sideways through an archway but their ripe dialogue was lost on him and merely drifted through as so much background noise. Bodo took a pad and pen out of his pocket and hunched his stocky body over the table in quiet contemplation; jotting down his thoughts, just like the doctor had prescribed.

"It's not always this dead you know?" It was the barman.

Bodo looked up, reluctantly.

"You should see this place in summer. Heaving! Fishing's at full throttle. Then there are the tourists. Gets packed out this place. Rushed off our feet."

Bodo smiled, nodded.

"Let you get back to it then," said the barman.

Bodo smiled, nodded.

He took a pull on his pint. Returned to his scribblings.

"You stopping around here or just visiting for the day?"

"I stop for the week. Little John's cottage."

"Oh, right."

Bodo tried again to put his head down.

"The name's Jimbo, by the way." Would the barman ever shut up! "Jimmy Cullen. James on Sundays. But most everybody calls me Jimbo."

Bodo put down his pen and picked up his pint. "And I'm Bodo. Nice to meet you, Jimbo."

"Bodo and Jimbo, eh? Sounds like we'd make a good pair of circus clowns!" Jimbo's good natured smile faded as Bodo's face remained blank. "Sorry, didn't mean to interrupt."

Oh, yes you did, thought Bodo. But he really didn't mind. He deserved time off. Wasn't that what the doctor also ordered?

A welcome respite. Practicing his English with a strapping young barman. He was forced to conclude there were worse ways to pass an afternoon. It was only as he walked back to his temporary accommodation that he fell once more into quiet reflection on his life. A life after Joachim.

Theirs had been a small and cozy existence. Neither one had felt the pull of the gay world outside the home they shared together in the suburbs of Berlin. A home in which, increasingly, a simple gesture—like an amused arch of the eyebrow or a certain smile—had spoken volumes. Bodo had been content. There had been no reason to foresee a life without Joachim. A life after Joachim. No reason to imagine he would ever find himself alone at forty-four years of age and facing an uncertain future.

There had been no reason to suspect that Joachim had a heart condition. He was fit. Sporty. Always active. So when the phone call came through, to tell him that Joachim had collapsed at work, Bodo had no reason to expect the worst possible scenario. But Joachim was dead before Bodo even reached the hospital.

And with this, always the memory of holding Joachim in his arms one last time. Of holding him and rocking him and whispering "Oh, mein Schatz . . . " over and over like a mantra. Of then returning home to an empty apartment stuffed full of memories. Everything he touched and everywhere he looked. Everything conspiring to further stupefy his mind. Incomprehensible. A bad dream. One from which he had yet to wake up.

It was the doctor who had suggested he get away from it all. No, not suggested—insisted. A gay doctor. Bodo knew he had his best interests at heart. Go away somewhere quiet he had said, sort your head out. Well, it didn't get much more quiet than this. And it was here he had come to sit and watch the sea roll in, have an English beer if and when he needed company, and make notes. Lots of notes. Looking for the answers within.

✦

THE SEA SHOULD give up its mysteries so easily. Over the next couple of days, he spent hours watching the ebb and flow. Unfathomable. The only warmth and respite offered by the pub. Increasingly so. Not that he had ever been a big drinker. No, it was all thanks to Jimbo and his welcome distractions.

"Why do you stay open?" Bodo stood at the bar on the fourth afternoon. The pub was empty again. Even the workmen seemed to have moved on.

"Well, you never know," Jimbo replied, as he pulled Bodo a second pint, "There might be a sudden rush of visitors."

"You do think so?"

Jimbo smirked. "You should pop in for an evening. Pub Quiz. We pack 'em in for that. Why, there was almost nine in last Wednesday night!"

"I only come if you give me the answers to the questions before. I hate to lose."

Jimbo grinned. He had a pleasant face. Ruddy. Open. Laugher lines etched at the corner of his eyes when he smiled. "And there's me, thinking you looked like the man with all the answers!"

"No." Bodo dropped his gaze, wrapped his hand around his pint glass. "I just do know about losing."

Jimbo burst his bubble without ceremony. Snorted, "Nah, you're just in need of a good fuck. Take it from someone who knows!"

They both laughed.

"Not so much opportunity around here, I think?" Bodo replied, dryly.

"Well you know what they say?" Jimbo winked. "Stranger things happen at sea." Another laugh. He turned his head and looked out of the picture window that faced down onto the bay. "Having said that—probably best to stay home tonight at any rate. Looks like we're in for another storm."

✦

AND JIMBO'S INSTINCT was not wrong. If there had ever been a night to batten down the hatches it was this particular night. The wind and the rain battered the shuttered windows of Bodo's retreat, leaving him grateful to be safe inside. He stoked up the fire and poured himself another large, stiff one.

Maybe Jimbo was right, he thought. Maybe he did need a good fuck, as he put it. Or maybe it was just the whiskey talking. Alcohol always made him horny. It was one of the reasons why he tended to avoid alcohol, for the most part, in any of its myriad varieties. Then came the obligatory apology to an ever present Joachim for even entertaining the idea.

Fact is, he was scared. He could hardly bear to contemplate the thought of launching himself onto the scene again. Not at his age. And not after all this time. It had never been his forte even in his younger days. Thankfully, Joachim had saved him from all that— for a time anyhow. Strictly speaking, they hadn't actually met on the scene—well not in the club but in the taxi queue outside. It had been raining that night too. It was the reason they had decided to share that single taxi. And fate took care of the rest.

It was getting late and the whiskey bottle was running low. If it wasn't already time for the pubs to have shut he might have even dared to venture out for a replacement, drunken oblivion seeming suddenly attractive and eminently preferable to unrequited lust.

Then came the hammering at the door. Loud and insistent and with the clear intention of being heard above the raging storm outside. Opening the door, Bodo sprang back in surprise as a figure in a rain-drenched, bright orange souwester and waterproof jacket barged past him and entered. After shouldering the door shut, Bodo turned to find Jimbo, souwester removed, dripping all over the carpet, and grinning from ear to ear. He produced a bottle of whiskey from under the folds of his jacket.

"Hoped I'd find you still up. Brought you your winnings." He brandished the bottle.

"Winnings?"

"Yeah, from the Pub Quiz. You won the star prize by default. No other bugger turned up either!"

Bodo was at a loss. "I don't know what to say."

Jimbo held the bottle toward him. "How's about: Would you like a drink, Jimbo?"

"Yes, of course. You want a big one?"

"Large one. Large sounds good."

Bodo crossed to the galley kitchen in search of a glass, saying simply, "And you should take off your wet clothing."

"I was kind of hoping you'd say that," Jimbo replied, as he popped the studs on his waterproofs. "But I better warn you, I'm soaked right through."

✦

DRESSED IN ONE of Bodo's old T-shirts and jogging bottoms and warmed by the fire and whiskey, Jimbo fell asleep on the sofa. Fell asleep in mid-sentence. He'd been regaling Bodo with his tales of life as a merchant marine. A life before the pub, and one he clearly thought fondly off. His dreams would be sweet. Rather than wake him, Bodo covered him with a blanket, turned out the light and took himself off to bed.

The storm continued to rage outside and, much to his chagrin, Bodo now felt wide awake. He tried reading—the latest yarn by Dan Brown. Dull even in German, he imagined. It was usually enough to send him off to sleep but not this night. So, eventually, he placed the book on the bedside table, kicked back the covers and let his hand toy with his sizeable if flaccid penis. An orgasm at bedtime usually did the trick. And it had been a while. His balls felt unusually full and in need of emptying and he set about the task with increasing enthusiasm.

He grew hard thinking of Jimbo. Stroking his meat as he thought of the young guy's bulge. A bulge that had been revealed when he had peeled off his sodden jeans just an hour or so before. Powerful thighs too. Firm, muscular thighs. Bodo was a leg man. And now he indulged his predilection, imaging running his tongue over those powerful thighs, inching ever closer to the sizeable bulge in Jimbo's tight, white briefs.

Joachim would understand. It was only a fantasy.

And his cock swelled in his fist. So hard now. Had not been this hard for some time. The purple helmet straining even as it shone. The piss slit leaking its welcome lubricant. He reached down to tug on his ball sac. Tugging his *Eier* with one hand, pulling his *Schwantz* with the other. His head arched back upon the pillow, his eyes closed tight, picturing Jimbo's package and his own tongue and teeth struggling to unwrap it. His feet flexing involuntarily as the rhythm of his fist increased. Lost in the intensity of the moment.

When had he become aware of Jimbo's presence? Jimbo standing in the doorway, silently watching. Their eyes met. Bodo froze in mid-stroke.

"Oh don't stop on my account," Jimbo grinned. "It was just getting interesting."

✦

THE STORM HAD finally subsided. And, in the subtle light that crept through the skylight, Bodo studied the face of the man who now slept beside him. Face to sleeping face. Stunned and not a little amazed, he watched a smile play on Jimbo's lips. Lips he had kissed. No, lips he had ravished and then some. Hungry for the comfort to be found there. Famished.

How had Jimbo known he was so up for it? When asked, all Jimbo had done was to tap the side of his nose and remind him he'd been in the merchant marines. Like that was answer enough. And they had laughed. It was great to laugh in bed. To laugh so hard it made the bed frame rattle. Made his heart feel light. Bodo had even laughed when he came and Jimbo wasn't fazed at all.

He just laughed along with every stroke, with every pulse, with every powerful spurt.

Bodo had almost begun to believe that laughter belonged to a previous life. His life with Joachim. But the capacity for laughter remained with him, just as the memory of Joachim always would.

It was, at the very least, a step in the right direction.

A SENSE OF WONDER

HENRY JACOBS

CHRIS HAD ALWAYS wanted to travel to Ireland. Something about the country beckoned him, enchanted his senses, and drew him to its isle. That was what he knew Ireland was called: the Emerald Isle. He imagined it to be a romantic, mystical, haunted place. A sensual place. A place that would enrapture him, cling to him with an earthy grip, and draw him into its safe and wonderful haven.

Ten years he planned to make the trip; finally, when he was in his thirtieth year, he did. He flew right out of Logan, into Heathrow airport in London, and from there, caught a connecting flight to Dublin. Ah, Dublin. The capital city of Ireland. The bustling, thriving hub. Or so he hoped it would be.

It was dark and raining when he arrived, a torrential downpour that sluiced down the windows of the plane, as he looked out on the runway beyond.

I'm here, he thought, with a deep feeling of satisfaction. Finally, I'm here.

He spent an hour or so in the confusion of the airport, a new country, a new culture, soaking up everything at its gateway. Other people swarmed about him. But he didn't notice anyone. He was here! He was in Ireland and in Europe! His first trip ever outside the States. It felt great. Awesome.

With a joyous gait in his step he left the airport, huddling beneath the portico outside, his eyes searching for a taxi. He spotted a line of them clumped together in the rain, engines rumbling, and ran over to the nearest one. Getting in beside the driver, he named a gay guesthouse (one he'd learned of from *Spartacus*). The driver seemed unperturbed—and soon they were pulling away from the airport entrance.

As they sped into the city, Chris leaned his head back against the passenger seat and, through the raindrops on the window-pane, eagerly stared out at a new and European city he was being thrown toward.

✦

DUBLIN TURNED OUT to be a disappointment. It was a marvelous city, somehow managing to be fairly large but also reminiscent of a small town, and he guessed the gay scene was fairly impressive (though small), but . . . somehow none of it was what he was looking for.

Where was the magic? The mystical awe?

He was just in a small, thriving city with a gay scene that wasn't that different from anything back home. It wasn't what he expected. Despite some beautiful old architecture, the city was too modern. Too busy. He wanted small, and though—by American standards—the city *was* small, resembling a large town, it was still bigger than he expected. He wanted secluded. He wanted magical. He wanted . . . a sense of wonder.

After a week in the city, and with a week of vacation still re-maining, he decided he wouldn't find what he was looking for in Dublin City. He needed to go somewhere smaller, more re-mote—and more *magical*.

Studying an atlas as he strolled down O'Connell Street, find-ing an Internet café and going online, Chris finally, after much tortuous indecision, decided on a small town in the county of Cork, down in the southern part of the country.

He packed up his suitcases and found his way to the train sta-tion. As he settled into his compartment, the train started with a groan and a chug and he began to feel optimistic. Maybe this small town would bestow upon him all the wonders he'd hoped to discover in Europe . . . in Ireland. And, if he happened to find a local guy willing to show him the sights, all the better.

As the train chugged out of the station, Chris felt hopeful.

✦

◆

FOUR HOURS LATER, the train arrived in Cork City (much smaller than Dublin but still too big for his liking). Chris made his way to the bus station and managed to find a bus to his destination. The entire train journey from Dublin to Cork had taken about four hours, and the bus journey to the small town in West Cork was another two hours or so.

It was still bright when he was on the bus and he felt a sense of awe staring at the scenery that flew past the windows. It was so dramatic. Jagged. Coastal. Beautiful. In fact, it literally took his breath away.

The bus pulled in at a tiny depot on the edge of the small town and Chris stepped down out of it with a hard-on.

He took a deep breath, inhaled the wonderful sea air, and looked up at the sky. It was blue with the darkness of night hinting at the edges.

He walked along the road into town, the darkness gaining on both him and the landscape with every step, and when he rounded one bend in the road, he came upon a scene of such beauty and wonder, he had to stop to take it in.

The road had rounded into a circular area that looked out on a wide expanse of sea, calm waters nestled in the mouth of huddled, dark hills. The sun was setting, its waning orange melting into the horizon. The calm waters were streaked orange and pink, and the sky itself was a miasma of colors—pink, orange, gray. Tendrils of cloud brushed its canvas and already, though the melting sun was still in sight, the vague silver silhouette of a moon was making itself visible.

This was definitely starting to feel like the place for him. Chris walked up to the edge of the water and felt like he was in Heaven. This was it. Here was the magic, the awe, the mystical feeling—and the sense of wonder.

He was still hard as he stared at the beauty in front of him and, reaching down, he grabbed the bulge in his jeans.

Now all he needed was to find a guy. It would be hard. *Spartacus* and the Internet had provided no information for any gay spots of any kind in this particular part of the world.

But it's a challenge, Chris thought wistfully, holding his manhood through the denim and betaking the masterpiece of beauty in front of him.

He stood at the water's edge (he wasn't sure if it was a river or a lake) until the very last of the light left the world and he was in total blackness.

A few silver stars salted the inky-black sky as he walked along the road into town, careful to keep to the edge (though no cars had passed in at least an hour), but the silver sliver of moon had hidden itself behind a mass of dark clouds, withholding its illumination.

Coming to the very edge of the town, Chris heard distant laughter and music. Probably coming from a good, old-fashioned Irish pub, he hoped, grinning to himself, happy and excited and almost completely content.

He entered the first pub he came to, a place called O'Malley's. It was a small, poky place, packed with a crowd of good-humored, drunken locals. He made his way through the crowd and asked the bartender where he could find a room. The barman—a grizzled pirate in his forties— informed Chris that O'Malley's was also an inn and named him a reasonable price to which Chris readily agreed.

The barman's daughter, a young blond in her twenties, showed him to his room, up several narrow flights of stairs. It was a tiny hovel from which Chris could hear all the boisterous noise from below. But he didn't care. As far as he was concerned, it was perfect. A perfect, romantic little haven.

After the barman's daughter had left, Chris chucked his two small suitcases and shoulder bag on the narrow, single bed and went into the adjoining en-suite bathroom, little more than a cramped closet with toilet, sink and shower.

He stripped and got into the shower, turning the knob as far to Hot as it would go, then stood there, letting the lukewarm (the heating was obviously on the fritz) needles of water wash over him, cleanse him, wash some of the ache and tiredness from his bones.

Naked, he emerged from the shower and went back into the bedroom. Opening the closet he found a full-length mirror on the inner door. He stood back and surveyed his naked form.

He wasn't too tall, hovering just under six feet, and he had shoulder-length natural blond hair. A strong face, with a chiseled chin, and piercing blue eyes—rather Nordic features, all in all. His upper body was well defined and muscled from regular trips to the gym, his legs were long, and his cock, even flaccid, was nicely shaped—thick, curved, long. He grabbed it and began to play with himself, teasing his cock into an erection, and then checked it out in the mirror. He was pretty pleased with what he saw. It was about nine inches erect, and uncut.

Hope I find some nice *Oirish* boy to suck on it, he thought, and then turned away from the mirror, found a towel, and began to dry himself.

He dressed in a pale blue shirt and old khakis, then left his room and walked down the several flights of stairs to the bar below. Crossing through the bar and its noisy patrons, he found a door that led into a small, circumspect dining room with a few tables and chairs.

Chris seated himself at one of the tables and took up a menu—a green shamrock under the word O'MALLEY'S on a brown background. The food looked pretty much the standard meat-and-potatoes he expected and that was fine for him. No cholesterol worries on this trip. He could burn it all off when he got back.

Hearing someone move up to his table, expecting the blond daughter, he looked up—and almost came right in his pants.

Standing next to his table was a guy. And *what* a guy. Tall (taller than Chris), wavy dark hair, broad shoulders, a five o'clock shadow on a handsome face.

"*Failte*," the guy said, a deep, masculine rumble of a voice that escaped full, provocative lips.

"E-excuse me?" Chris stammered.

"It's Gailege. Welcome. What can I do you for?"

Chris almost choked. With an unsteady hand, he reached out and took the glass of water that rested on the table, managed to bring it to his mouth without spilling, and took a long gulp.

Realizing he was acting like an idiot, a blundering yank with a schoolgirl crush of all things, he put the glass back down on the table, made a conscious effort to get control of himself, and said: "Er—what do you recommend?"

"What?" The hot waiter looked at Chris as if he were an alien species, his eyes—brown pools—a tad suspicious.

"What food do you recommend?" Chris asked, hearing a much deeper voice than his speaking. "Any specials?"

The waiter considered for a moment. "Specials?" He shook his head. "No. But I can recommend the beef."

"The beef it is then," Chris said. "Sounds great."

Thank God I gave up that vegetarian phase, he thought wryly, then realized his eyes had dropped to the waiter's crotch. In horror, he jerked his head back up and looked into the waiter's face. Had he noticed?

The waiter studied Chris a moment longer, a look of bemusement on his handsome face, then said: "Will there be anything else . . . *sir*?"

"A G-Guinness," Chris managed.

"Of course. All our Americans order Guinness." The waiter turned and left. His ass was a tight rock in his black pants.

Chris took another drink of the water. *Will there be anything else . . . sir?* Was there something in the way he'd said that? Something provocative, teasing?

No way, Chris decided. Just my wishful imagination. And better tread carefully. Small country place like this. No good causing any homosexual rifts.

But Chris wanted the waiter. He wanted him badly. As he sat there, waiting for his dinner, his cock throbbed and his mouth watered, and he realized that if he didn't release the tension soon, he would burst.

Trying to turn his thoughts to other things, he looked out the window to his right. But it was dark. And raining again. Nothing to see. Sighing, Chris drank the rest of the water in his glass. From the closed door to the bar, he heard hoots and whistles. He tried to think of the place he was in, this remote little corner of the world, how romantic and magical it was—but his mind kept straying back to the waiter. His muscled arms, with their black hairs. His full lips. His raven-black hair. His slim, toned body—what it must look like beneath that black shirt and dress pants. What his cock was like . . .

Stop it, he told himself, or you'll have an accident.

His own cock was still erect, still throbbing. Making an effort to exert some control on himself, he licked his lips, and studied the menu the waiter had forgotten to take with him. The green shamrock. How very Irish. He was in Ireland!

He heard the creak of a door and looked up, seeing the waiter enter from the kitchen, a tray in his hands. He walked over to Chris's table and put down a foamy, frothy pint of Guinness, black with a white head. Then a plate on which two big pieces of beef, some carrots and a few potatoes were just about visible under a sea of gravy.

Chris quickly thanked him, then scanned his shirt, looking for a nametag, needing to know his name. But there was none.

"Enjoy your meal," the waiter said. The deep, masculine voice. But a lighter lilt in there somewhere too. An Irish accent? A Cork one?

Before Chris could reply, the waiter had disappeared, and he was left alone with his dinner.

✦

THERE WAS NO more sign of the waiter. Chris ate his gravy-saturated dinner and drank his Guinness (foul stuff, no different from the pint he'd tried in Dublin), then went looking for someone to pay—the waiter hopefully. All he found, though, was the blond daughter, who told him the meal would be added to his bill.

With a sigh and a few heavy steps, Chris made his way back up to his room. He felt depressed. Suddenly the little room no longer seemed romantic or quaint. It was oppressive, confining, like a coffin.

Chris undressed and, wearing just Jockey shorts, got into the single bed. The mattress groaned and creaked in protest. Chris lay his heavy head upon the pillow. From downstairs, the pub sounds—laughter, talk, and music—floated up. He felt lonely in the dark little room. A splinter of weak, yellow light slid under his door from the hall outside, and from a part in the curtains, weak moonlight arced into the room.

Getting out of bed, Chris made his way to the window, pulled

the curtains apart. It had stopped raining. He opened the window and leaned out into the cool night air, raising his head to the
sky. The shaving of silver moon had revealed itself again and now
floated on the dark, cloudy sky.

Leaving the window and curtains open, Chris got back into
bed. Beneath the sheets again, he began to think of the waiter
and he slid his hand down, cupped his bulge through the white
silk of his Jockeys. He was hard. And precome had made his
Jockeys wet; they stuck to his bulging pride.

He thought of the waiter as he began to tug on himself. He
let out a groan. Or so he thought. Then he realized it wasn't
him—but the door to his room.

Startled, he sat up, whirled around.

There, framed in the door with the light from the hall, was a
tall, dark silhouette.

"Just wondering if you needed anything, sir?" The masculine
voice with the lilt.

Before Chris could even begin to answer, the waiter moved
into the room, shutting the door behind him.

Darkness devoured the small space.

Chris heard the waiter's steps as he crossed to the bed, the
moan of the mattress as he climbed on.

And then he felt him, right next to him.

"Move over," the waiter said.

Chris obeyed, sliding over in the small bed until his companion was lying next to him.

"What's your name?" Chris said.

"Jeremy," the waiter replied. "We have to be quiet. The bar's
closing soon and I don't want my father and sister to hear."

Chris realized he meant the grizzled pirate that owned the
place and his blond daughter. Strange, Chris thought, he looks
nothing like either of them. Then Jeremy began touching him,
rubbing his strong hands up and down Chris's body. Chris quickly followed suit, forgetting his thoughts, tugging the waiter's
shirt from his pants, sliding his hand up his torso—then down,
cupping the impressive bulge in Jeremy's pants.

"I want to fuck you," Jeremy said. "I wanted to fuck you all
night."

"I thought you thought I was some dumb Yank," Chris managed between breaths.

Jeremy didn't reply. He flicked his tongue into Chris's earlobe and Chris sighed and moaned, his erection throbbing as Jeremy roughly tugged on it, repeating: "I want to fuck you."

"Yes, fuck me," Chris gasped.

Jeremy sat up in the bed and began to undress, throwing his clothes onto the floor. Chris only made out a few blurs in the darkness as the moon had hidden behind the cloud again.

"Is the door locked?" he asked Jeremy.

"Yes," Jeremy whispered, then reached down and tugged Chris's Jockeys off with a snap. "Turn over."

Chris rolled onto his stomach and felt Jeremy's weight against his back. Then something hot and wet slicked up and down his spine. He didn't know if it was Jeremy's tongue or cock—and didn't care which.

Jeremy roughly shoved one finger into Chris's ass. Chris hissed in pain and muttered, "Easy." But Jeremy wasn't listening. And he obviously didn't want to take things easy. He sucked three fingers into his mouth then shoved them up Chris, opening him roughly.

Chris was too turned on to object anymore to the pain and decided to grit his teeth and bear it. Then Jeremy entered him. Wow, he was big. Huge and bulging. Chris almost came as Jeremy entered him fully.

As Jeremy fucked him, Chris bucked beneath him, their breathing and gasps coming in rhythms.

"Don't worry," Jeremy said at one point. "I won't come in you."

"Good," Chris gasped in reply. "I want to swallow you."

Jeremy fucked him for several minutes, then pulled out, turned Chris around, and began to kiss him. Their lips scraped against each other's roughly, sucking, biting, tasting.

Then Jeremy had Chris in his mouth and was sucking him, moaning in pleasure as he did so. Chris reached up and twisted one of Jeremy's nipples. Jeremy struck him across the face—but not too hard.

Chris shoved Jeremy away. He rolled to the end of the bed and

Chris moved down on his knees, fell on top of him and began to kiss him, then began to slide down his body, licking his chest, stopping briefly to bite one nipple, moving down further until Jeremy's cock was against his face. It was thick and curved and very long. Chris took it all in, in one gulp, and slowly began to suck it, up and down, moving slowly, letting Jeremy's juices run down his throat. And then Jeremy bucked and came, his load flowing into Chris's mouth and down his throat, Chris swallowing.

A few minutes later, Chris got on top of Jeremy and stuck his dick in the waiter's ass. Nice and tight. He fucked him, hard, and Jeremy loved every minute of it. Until Chris couldn't hold it anymore and pulled out, spurting his come all over Jeremy's back.

They lay next to each other, breathing hard, not touching, not talking, for a long time after—maybe half an hour, maybe an hour.

"We didn't use condoms," Chris said finally, his voice, though lowered and whispered, slicing through the quiet night air like a knife. "I know we didn't come in each other but I did swallow you."

Jeremy just laughed. "Take it easy, man, ok? I'm safe. And sometimes you need to take risks."

Chris didn't reply. But he did worry about it for several more minutes—until he realized there was nothing he could do at present. It had been a mistake not to use condoms. But it had been great. And sometimes you *did* take risks. Especially on vacation. He decided not to worry about it until he had to—if he ever did. Before he knew it he had drifted into sleep.

✦

CHRIS NEVER SAW Jeremy again. He awoke the next morning to find the bed a mass of tangled, sweaty sheets—and empty.

After he had showered and dressed and seated himself in the dining room downstairs, he hoped against hope that it would be the hot waiter who took his order. But it was just the blond daughter.

After he'd finished his morning coffee and full Irish breakfast fry-up, Chris decided to question her.

"Your brother?" he began. "Jeremy?"

She looked at him sharply. "Sssh," she cautioned. "I don't want my father to hear you." She looked anxiously over her shoulder. But there was no sign of the pirate. And the bar was closed and quiet.

"So . . . you know then?" Chris whispered to him.

"I know everything," she responded with a hard look. "My brother left town this morning. Due back to the army."

"The army? He's a solider?"

"Yeah. Works as a waiter sometimes to help us out, when he's on leave."

Chris felt turned on by the soldier thing but heavy in his heart at the thought that Jeremy was gone.

"When's he coming back?" he asked, calculating quickly in his head how many days he had left on vacation.

"Not till next month. And you'd better clear off. My father and some of the locals get wind of what you are, you might be in trouble."

They stared at each other for a time, Chris thinking: Jesus, what a cliché. Fucking homophobic little town.

But he decided the blonde daughter was probably right so he paid his bill, packed, and left.

He spent a while looking around the little town, then caught a bus back to Cork. He'd try it out, try the gay scene there. That would mean he'd experienced Dublin, the small town, and another city too, by the time he got back home. But he'd already gotten what he'd come to Ireland for. A sense of wonder. And some mystery. And a solider-cum-waiter called Jeremy who he'd spent one amazing night with.

As the bus pulled into Cork, Chris was hard. He'd gotten a taste of an Irish guy. And he suddenly realized he wanted more. Maybe one in Cork, and another in Dublin before he caught his flight back to Logan.

Grinning, happy, Chris got off the bus—and started for the nearest gay bar. The waiter had given Chris a sense of wonder and he wanted more. There may only have been a few days vacation left—but he was going to make the most of them.

THE BEACH AT NICE

NEIL S. PLAKCY

DUSK WAS FALLING as I strolled the sidewalk next to the Promenade des Anglais, the highway that runs along the beach in Nice. Ahead of me, where the road curved around a hill toward Monte Carlo, I saw the streetlights wink on in sequence, new pearls being added to a faraway strand. To my left traffic whizzed by, while to my right, the ocean lapped against the pebbled beaches—Le Neptune, Le Sporting, Le Lido.

I was just twenty-one, spending the summer after my college graduation in a tiny studio apartment a few blocks in from the beach, where I struggled to write a novel—one I only felt I could get out by leaving behind the people and places I was writing about. By the end of my fourth week, I had about fifty pages, but I was desperately lonely.

I told myself that by walking along the beach at dusk, clasping a box of Dunhill menthols conspicuously in my hand, I might make a friend or two—some guy would stop to ask for a cigarette, and we'd engage in conversation, perhaps moving on to a café somewhere for a drink. Deep down, I'm sure I knew I was hoping for more.

The first guy to approach me was a Moroccan, a skinny old man with a single gold tooth. I shook my head and quickened my pace. Though I walked all the way down to the base of the chateau, past Vieux Nice, almost to the port, no one else approached me, and by the time I turned around it was dark.

The thudding of my heart eased as I admitted defeat. I was passing the Opéra Plage, on my way back to my tiny studio, when a deep, accented voice said, "Ah, Dunhill. I see you have good taste."

I looked over to see a slim guy, just a few years older than I was, with coffee-colored skin. He wore a T-shirt that read "University of Princeton," dark nylon running shorts, and flip-flops. "Would you like one?" I asked.

"*Mais oui*," he said. I opened the box's flip top and held it out to him. He picked one out, and placed it in his mouth. His grin was so sexy that my heart started to race again. I lit a match and held it toward him, and he cupped my hand in his. My whole body shivered, and he said, "Do not be nervous, *mon ami*."

"Just a cool breeze." I lit my own cigarette, and we began to stroll together, beside a line of stately palms. Only the occasional passerby, hurrying somewhere in the gathering darkness, shared the pavement with us.

"I am Hassan," he said. "What is your name?"

"Neil." I paused, trying to think of something to say. "You speak English well."

He shrugged. "In my country, I study in school. My French much better."

We continued to chat as we walked, and at one point, when we were laughing, Hassan reached over and put his arm around my shoulders. The salt air, the menthol cigarettes, and something spicy in his cologne combined to make me feel a little dizzy. As we passed the entrance to the square where they held the flower market, the *marché aux fleurs*, Hassan said, "You like to go somewhere with me?"

"Yes, please," I said, and the way my voice cracked caused him to laugh, and to lean over and kiss my cheek.

I wasn't a virgin, but my only sexual encounters had been fumbling mutual jerk-off sessions with other college guys, and once when an older man took me into a men's room at the train station in Philadelphia and gave me a blow job, while I waited for a train.

The promise that the evening suddenly held got my pulse racing and my dick hard. I worried that it was tenting out my shorts, but knew if I tried to rearrange myself I'd only call attention to it. Hassan steered me down one narrow street after another, past shuttered shopfronts and darkened churches. Occasionally we passed other people, mostly other North Africans, hurrying over the uneven cobblestones. In bits and pieces, I learned that he had come to France as a teenager, to study engineering, but then something had happened with his school or tuition—I wasn't sure which—and he had become a waiter. Now he was saving his money to open his own restaurant one day.

The air was rich with the scent of stews and rotisseries, and I heard snatches of French pop music floating out of open windows. I saw street signs hung on buildings, but didn't recognize any of the names. Occasionally we ducked down alleys so narrow that Hassan had to walk in front of me. Finally, he stopped before the door of a café.

"You like this place," he said. "We know each other better here."

Yes, my body said. Yes, I very much want to know you better. He led me into a smoky room, to a tiny table in the corner. "You will like a beer?" he asked. I nodded, and he raised two fingers to some unseen waiter, who appeared a moment later with two bottles of Kronenbourg. Fumbling with my wallet I pulled out a couple of notes and handed them to the waiter, who returned a few coins to me. I left them on the table and turned to Hassan.

Arabic pop music played in the background, and as I looked around I saw all the other customers were male, in pairs or small groups—almost all Arab. Under the table, I felt Hassan's hand on my knee, and I turned to him and smiled. He leaned forward and kissed me. His lips tasted of olives and cigarettes, and very quickly they parted to send his tongue darting toward me.

Finally, our lips broke apart, but Hassan kept his eyes focused on mine as he reached down for his beer. "You are good kisser," he said, smiling.

"You are very easy to kiss." He ran his fingers lightly up my thigh as we snuggled next to each other, drinking our beers and smoking more Dunhills. I asked him what kind of restaurant he wanted to open and he said, "Very romantic. To look like my country, to serve the food of my country, but refined, like in Paris. And I have only handsome waiters!" He winked at me.

"Oh, like yourself," I said.

"It is my name," he said. "In Arabic, Hassan means beautiful. You think I am?" His fingers continued to caress me, casually passing my erect penis, though he gave it no notice.

I decided it was time for boldness. "Well, so far I have only seen you with your clothes on. You have a handsome face, but as for the rest . . . " I gave him my best Gallic shrug. For good measure, I rested my hand on his thigh.

He laughed. "Sadly, I have many roommates. It is nowhere private for us to go."

"I have an apartment," I said. "I am alone."

"Ah," he said, taking my hand and placing it on his own very hard penis. "You are alone no more."

I thought I had never heard more romantic words. I stood up quickly, knocking the table over, though Hassan caught it before the empty beer bottles tumbled to the floor. "If I give you my address, will you take me there?" I asked.

He stood, and bowed a little. "It will be my pleasure."

Oh, no, I wanted to say. It will be pleasure for both of us. But instead I told him the street address of my little studio, and he led me out of the maze of narrow streets until we reached the Place Massena, where I recognized my surroundings and took over the lead.

My head warred with my groin for blocks—I was taking home a stranger, a man I'd met on the street, whose last name I didn't even know. But he was handsome and sexy, a great kisser with a dynamite smile, smooth skin—and a hard-on that matched my own in intensity. What the hell—I had little money and nothing worth stealing.

"You have—how you say—*preservative*?" he asked.

I was baffled until he made the motions of ripping open a package and rolling a condom down over a penis. "There is an all-night drugstore on my corner," I said.

He knew just what he wanted, handing me a box of condoms and a tube of lubricant. I paid the expressionless female cashier, from whom I'd purchased aspirin the day before, and she paid no attention to my giddiness.

Upon entering my building, I had to press a button for the single lightbulb over the staircase, and hurry up the steps to reach my door before it winked out. Laughing and bumping against Hassan, I didn't move quickly enough, and we found ourselves halfway up the steps in total darkness.

"Mmm, sexy," Hassan said, wrapping his arms around me from behind, and pressing his hard dick against my ass. He nibbled my neck, and I melted. It was so hard to move forward, to climb those last stairs in the dark, because I never wanted to leave his embrace. Even though I knew what joy awaited us when we got into my room and stripped our clothes off, I didn't want that moment to end.

But he pushed me forward, propelling me with pelvic thrusts; and giggling, we mounted the last stairs and I fumbled the key into my door. It was a single room, with a tiny kitchenette adjacent to the door, a queen-sized bed, and a wardrobe. Tall French doors opened to a railing overlooking the street, and because I'd left the drapes open, moonlight flooded the room.

Hassan was still behind me. I heard him kick the door closed, and then his hands had reached around to open my shorts. When he had them unsnapped, he pushed them, and my boxers, down to the floor. I was leaning against the side of the wardrobe with him behind me, his body pressing against mine. I heard a series of small noises, which took me a while to identify—the tearing of the condom package, the squirt of the lube.

Then I felt something cold and liquid against my asshole, and I shivered. "I know, it is cold," he said. "But I make it warm for you."

He nuzzled my neck, and with his left hand he reached around and under my shirt to fondle my left nipple, stroking it until it was a hard nub. I was focusing on the pleasure of that fondling until, with a stabbing pain, his stiff dick invaded my ass. I bit my lip to keep from crying out.

I had never been fucked before, and the sensations overwhelmed me—the cold, greasy lube, which warmed up just as Hassan had promised, the fullness of having his dick inside me, the pain as he stretched my chute and then the waves of pleasure that overtook me as his cock head reached my prostate. I held onto the wardrobe, and he fucked me with ever greater intensity, until with a last massive stab I felt his come fill the condom's reservoir.

"I want to fuck your ass since I see you on the Promenade," Hassan said. "Is just as sweet as I think will be." His breath was hot on my shoulder, and as his dick dropped out of my ass he reached around to massage both my nipples again. Then he turned me around to face him and we kissed in the moonlight.

We both stepped out of our shorts, which had pooled around our feet, and kicked off our shoes. I lifted his T-shirt above his head and stopped to admire his body in the silvery light. He had strong shoulders and biceps, and his body narrowed to a tight V at the waist. There was just a dusting of hair under his arms and around his now-limp dick.

My dick, however, was still rock-solid. Gently, Hassan unbuttoned my shirt and let it slip over my shoulders to the floor. He moved me backwards, to the bed, and had me lie down on my back. Then he began kissing my right foot.

"Hassan," I said. "My dick, not my feet."

"All things in time, *mon amour*," he said. He massaged the instep of my foot as he kissed, then worked his way up my right leg. Finally, his head approached my groin, and my body braced for his mouth on my cock. But no! He went back to the left foot and started his way up that leg.

And then it was my right hand, all the way up my arm and down my torso. Then my left hand. It was the most exquisite torture—every nerve ending in my body was tingling, and by the time he did actually touch tongue to penis, I felt I was ready to explode.

But Hassan knew his way around a penis. He'd suck for a moment or two, but as he felt my interest rising, he'd back off. Suck, and off. Suck, and off. I think I was crying and pleading by the time he actually took my shaft down to the root, and I came in spurts down his throat.

I'd never felt so overwhelmed by a sexual experience before. A quick blow job in a men's room, or jerking off with a boy as inexperienced as I was, just couldn't compare. Hassan was a master.

He got up to dig my Dunhills out of the pocket of my shorts, and I watched the arch of his body and his ass in the moonlight. It reminded me of one of those marble statues, the musculature caught at a moment of strain. He brought the cigarettes back to the bed, and lit one, which he handed to me, then another for himself. We lay there together, our bodies touching at a dozen different places, and smoked.

Outside my open window, the noises of Nice at night drifted by—a motorcycle, a faraway siren, the sound of the street-cleaning machine. Somewhere a woman laughed. I fell asleep then, breathing deeply of Hassan's scent.

When I woke in the morning, he was gone. The light was too bright, and the bedsheets smelled of stale smoke and semen. My ass was gooey with lube and my dick was hard, a remnant of my nighttime dreams of Hassan.

I was sure he'd taken my wallet and passport. I'd been stupid and horny and kicked myself. I wanted to cry but I choked back the tears. I was a grown-up; I had to live with the consequences of my actions. I got out of bed and walked to the kitchenette.

There on the counter was my wallet—passport and money intact. The pack of Dunhills was nearly empty, but next to them was a note in perfect, careful penmanship. "Opéra Plage, tonight at seven," the note read. "No *caleçon!*" The only signature was a quick scribble that was easily recognized as an erect penis.

I scrambled for my French dictionary. *Caleçon*, I discovered, meant underpants.

I fell back into the bed. The scents which had seemed so sour were sexy once again; I buried my head in the pillow and drew a deep breath of Hassan's aroma. My ass felt juicy and lubed, ready for him to penetrate once again. I closed my eyes, reached for my dick, and slipped into a pleasant daydream, hoping that the time would pass quickly until seven that night, when I would meet Hassan again.

INFIDELITY IN THE CITY OF LIGHT

MICHAEL HUXLEY

HE RAN HIS hands beneath my shirt, up my torso, over my head, along my upraised arms, past my fingertips. The shirt fell to the carpet. He said, "Nice tattoos" and shifted his glance to my pectorals. He pinched my nipple rings—gently. "So *many* nice surprises," he continued. "You are beautiful beyond compare, James," he concluded, appraising me, stripping off his tee. I drew his partial nudity into my arms. Our tongues intertwined. Our zippers distended. I ground my mounting arousal into his and thought: *Ah, infidelity . . . . How will Adam react?* For no way could I have seduced a man such as Alain Marquis and not informed my lover after the fact.

Adam: *my lover.* After more than a year together that label still sounded foreign, as a lover was the last thing I, raised to prioritize accomplishment above conjugation, had been seeking at the time we met.

I was alone in Paris—a city I knew fairly well—to do research for my novel-in-progress. Adam, concluding a major investment negotiation back in Los Angeles, was scheduled to join me for my last week. *Adam and James*, I pondered while cruising the boulevard, cataloguing the subtle nuances of everyday Parisian life that no library or Web site could provide. *What a complicated and obsessive convergence we have become.*

And then there was Alain, ascendant nova of the independent French cinema: reposed on the mattress before me, taking me *down.* And I: ecstatic between renowned sculpted lips. On the verge, many thanks to Alain's ability to generate pleasure in such unremitting measure. Hell, I knew thirty seconds into his blowing me that he loved me.

The French, dare I say, would exchange their souls for an exceptional cheese, or love.

I took Alain's succulent head between my palms and, in an effort to forestall orgasm, whispered: "Alain . . . stop . . . . "

✦

IT WAS NINETY minutes earlier, at the café la Marronnier in the rue des Archives, that Alain entered my gravitational pull. A chilly summer's day, intermittent showers had given way to partial sunshine in the afternoon. In small cars, on motorcycles, bicycles, Rollerblades, and thousands on foot, humanity was omnipresent, traversing at large the damp, narrow streets and even narrower sidewalks that constitute the very gay crotch of le Marais. After a morning spent moved to tears in the van Gogh room at the d'Orsay, I'd ambled through les Halles, half-looking for the perfect leather jacket—to no avail. I slogged past the Pompidou into le Marais, closer to the apartment I'd rented in the rue des Tournelles. I needed a break from walking; I needed a coffee, so I stopped at la Marronnier along the way. How fortunate to have acquired an outside table just being evacuated by two most attractive gentlemen, whose admiring glances in passing did not escape my notice.

I settled into my primo observation perch and lit a cigarette. On the sidewalk, in the street, at every table: gorgeous men surrounded me! *I fucking LOVE Paris*, I thought, just as the waiter, also adorable, arrived to take my order. Oh yes, I was in a mood.

"*Double espress, s'il vous plait.*"

Go figure, how I failed to spot Alain sooner, but he eventually caught my attention from several tables over. I recognized him immediately. An exquisite man, Alain Marquis was dressed in jeans, running shoes, white T-shirt, and the tough, short, dark brown leather jacket I'd hoped to find for myself. He nodded, which I returned as graciously as my murmuring heart would allow. Without breaking our eye contact, he spoke to his tablemate—an impeccably dressed older man who, dabbing his mouth with a napkin, turned to check me out. Alain's suggestive laughter, shared with his companion, preceded their rising from the table. He clapped his comrade on the back, kissed him good-bye on both cheeks, stuffed what I just *supposed* was a script into his backpack, and advanced toward my table.

Be yourself, James; just be yourself.

In scarcely accented English, Alain inquired: "Are you traveling alone?"

"Is it that obvious I'm an American?"

"Frankly, yes," he replied. "You are American perfection, despite your answering a question with a question."

"Thank you, but 'American perfection' strikes me as oxymoronic."

He grinned and said: "I like your hauteur."

"Would you care to join me?"

"Join you? Very much," he replied, taking a seat. "I am Alain."

"I know who you are, Monsieur Marquis."

"It's *Alain*, my friend. Perhaps later you will call me 'Baby,' eh?" He lifted a disconcerting eyebrow. "And your name is?"

"I'm sorry; it's James. James Sutton." I extended my hand but Alain did not take it; he kissed me—lingeringly—on the lips instead.

"*Je t'aime, James Sutton*," he whispered intensely. "*Je t'aime beaucoup.*"

I was taken aback by his outlandish declaration of love but managed a fairly steady "*Merci*" in response.

"So, you *are* staying alone in Paris, James?"

"Yes, until tomorrow evening."

"Where?"

"In the rue des Tournelles, 13, near the Place des Vosges."

"Excellent, it's close; we will stay there." He snagged a cigarette from my pack on the table. "And tomorrow . . . what? Your lover joins you?"

"*Oui*, but how did you—?"

"May I?" he interrupted, a Camel already poised between his gorgeous lips. "I adore American cigarettes."

"Please do."

"I'm too much, I know," he said with a shrug, lighting up.

"But in a world of not enough, I fit. You had other plans for this evening?"

"I promised Adam I'd have the kitchen stocked—we both enjoy cooking—but I dread going to the *supermarché*."

Alain, apparently amused by that, laughed to himself. He then proclaimed: "We will go together to *Monoprix*." Case closed, he changed the subject. "So, you're from California? L.A.?"

"You're good, Alain."

"You will discover exactly how good soon enough. Do you and this . . . *Adam* live together?"

I didn't appreciate his tone, but replied—truthfully enough: "I prefer to keep my own apartment just now."

"Fantastic. We will continue our affair when I go to L.A. in January to make my first American film."

"You're assuming a lot there, Monsieur."

"I'm good at that, no? You said so yourself. For example: do I 'assume' correctly that you hail from a wealthy family?"

I crushed my cigarette butt and tacitly replied, "No comment."

"You see?" he gloated. "I could go on and on. You're an artist, I suspect. You're politically liberal. You detest your current president, as well you should. Let's see, what else . . . . Of course your parents are divorced. You're closer to your mother—"

At which point I lost it: "Okay! I'm totally transparent! I get it!"

Alain laughed unapologetically. "All right James, I'm finished for now."

"Then let's get out of here for Christ's sake."

"I'd like nothing better," he agreed. "Are you on foot?"

"I'm surprised you have to ask," I replied with regained sarcasm.

"My bike is around the corner; we'll go to *Monoprix* first." That decided for me, Alain leaned into my face and growled: "*Je t'aime, James Sutton . . . . Mon dieu*, you are delectable!"

Thoroughly bemused, I left thirty francs on the table. Alain pitched his arm over my shoulder and led the way.

"So James, how do you know Alain Marquis? I am not yet well-known in the States."

"I don't know about that," I countered. "After it won the Palme d'Or at Cannes, *Possessors, Self-dispossessed* has become quite the rave. What a devastating film experience! I saw it when it first opened in L.A."

"Ah, then you already know how I look naked. I am not one to work out, like you."

"*Ton corps est* trés *joli, Alain.*"

"I'm glad you think so, but you can relax with the French. English was my first language; my *au pair* was from Denver. This is my bike." We mounted his understated Harley, the only Hog among the many motorcycles parked there. "Hold me tight," he advised, snapping his helmet secure. "Tighter, my love, until you can feel my heat. I move very fast!"

We sped through the market as well. Upon discovering that I'm a writer, he exclaimed that he "*must* read [my] work," that I "*doubtless* possess a unique vision," and thankfully left it at that. He selected two inexpensive wines he professed to "adore," and after checking out, off we flew to the rue des Tournelles, 13: Adam's and my not-so-little love nest.

Lovemaking precluded our putting the groceries away. After Alain removed both our shirts, after we kissed, he unbuttoned my loose-fit jeans and slid them to my ankles as he dropped to his knees. He exclaimed "Oh, *baby* . . . " at the revelation, and took me at once into his mouth. Such an instantaneous abstraction of masculine reality!

His wavy hair ran thick between my fingers. When I suggested we get naked, we stripped on the spot, moved into the bedroom, and took our aforementioned positions on the bed—where he resumed his superb nonverbal communication.

Close to the verge, I whispered, "Alain . . . *stop* . . . ."

But he did so only long enough to say: "We have all night, James; this is but an aperitif."

Being urged—and pleasured—so relentlessly triggered an unforgettable orgasm that I can only describe as razor sharp. Nor will I ever forget his streaking comeshot. Alain's Botticelli head lashed from side to side, as I held him securely in one arm and brought him to Scene One's completion in one take, with one hand.

I contemplated Alain's spent body in my arm, his eyes still closed in aftershock, and could not help but envy his natural beauty. All at once I felt overdressed in my tattooed and pierced nudity, so dramatically altered by weight training. *Beauty, and the concessions I have made to possess it,* I ruminated. *What is it about men's perception of beauty and its relevance to sexual desire? Men: Adam, all those before him, and now Alain. Is my youth to blame for the distinction I blur between love and objectification? Adam: Perhaps it is best not to become singularly invested at this point in my life.*

After lingering kisses, Alain insisted upon reading an example of my work. His extraordinary face lit by my laptop screen, smoking Camel after Camel, he chose not to comment until he'd completely finished the piece I'd selected, a short story entitled "The Re-creation of Adam."

"The world will be at your feet," he stated as if to confirm his worst suspicion. "'The Re-creation of *Adam*,' the God figure extending the flame to light the first man's cigarette: It's brilliant, James." He rose from the escritoire, walked to the bed, and sat down. He appeared to be staring at nothing, but much to my objective fascination, I witnessed his expression gradually shift from blank to apprehensive to aggrieved to agonized. "I am *nothing*," he whispered bitterly. "Do you have his photograph?" Indeed I did, a complete nude series I'd taken the first day Adam and I spent together. No way would I have traveled without them. "Show me!" he demanded.

He scrutinized the first few shots and snapped the folder shut. "It is clear you'll forget about me the moment he arrives."

"That's not true, Alain. Not now." I touched his head but he jerked away and, amazingly, pounded his fist into the mattress in a rage.

"I am *nothing* by comparison," he exploded. He swept his hands in the air above the photo file. "The man is Eros Incarnate! Masculinity Redoubled. He makes me love you more; but what am I? An *actor*." He threw himself back on the pillows and covered his eyes with his hands. "God, I detest life," he lamented miserably. "Get the wine, James. We will drink and fuck like dogs before bidding our hollow adieus."

I took the reins. "Look, Alain, I'll get the wine, but I've had it with the histrionics. You're the first man I've been with since I met Adam over a year ago. This is a huge risk for me. You're here because *I want you to be*, but . . . you need to get a grip!

"Did you read the goddamned story or *what*?" I continued. "Our relationship is very complicated; *Adam's* very complicated. He's not a happy man. He's haunted, disturbed. I've no idea what the future holds for him and me."

Alain, positively livid, shot up into a seated position and shouted: "*Every* man I love says that! Just when I think I'm holding happiness in my arms I'm shot with a cannon! *I* am complicated; *I* am disturbed; *I* am haunted. My life is a torment! *Now* can you love me?"

"Cut! That's a wrap!" I yelled back. "Give me a break. You have life by the balls."

He brightened in a blink. "'Life by the balls'? Tell me more."

I laughed dismissively and stood to exit the room. "Good god, I'll get the wine."

"You are very cruel, James. You laugh, but you don't know Alain Marquis . . . Wait! How dare you walk away! I'm prepared to forgive you! Where did you put the fucking cigarettes?"

"*Forgive* me!" I barked from the kitchen. "What are you talking about, *forgiveness*?" I reentered with the wine and two glasses. "I laughed because your comic timing is flawless. Here, drink this and just . . . shut up. *Please*."

"Oh, don't worry; I'll shut up," he said, affecting a wounded expression. He took his glass. "I can't talk about it anyway; it hurts too much."

Oh, brother, I thought. *If he weren't so goddamned stunning* . . .

A glass of wine later, Alain's joie de vivre was fully restored, as if his tirade had never occurred. We were making out frenetically, pretty damn worked up, when Alain started in: "James, I feel so much passion with you! Say you will be my lover when I go to L.A. Please say yes, come what may!"

"Yes, baby, yes!" I swore, further swept away than I imagined.

"Suck my cock, for just a minute—no, thirty seconds is better! *Ouais*, baby, tease me; I love it . . . . Oh, I *so* want you inside me, but I must first make a shit. No no, don't kiss me there. I *mean it*, James; I am not clean!" Alain latched onto my ear and whispered: "You want to be inside Alain, baby?"

"Shit, what do you think?"

"Tell me, then."

"*God*, yes!"

"*Tell* me what you want!"

"I wanna *fuck you*, Alain."

"*Mon dieu, je t'aime, James*; we'll spend the whole night fucking and fucking and fucking."

"*Alain!*" I lapsed. "*Moi aussi, je t'aime.*"

"Do you mean that?"

"*Yes.*"

He pulled away from our sweaty embrace, covered his face with his hands, and—burst into tears! "*Oh, mon dieu*," he sobbed. "You love me!" Astonished, I inquired if he were all right. "It's just that . . . I am so thrilled," he replied. And as suddenly as it had begun, his jag ceased. He kissed me fiercely then announced: "But I must now make a shit! I am very romantic, no? Do you have condoms?" Undaunted by his madness, I replied in the affirmative. "Then get them!" he commanded. He dashed into the bathroom without closing the door. A moment later I heard him say: "*Mmm*, my shit stinks."

"Then turn the *fan* on."

"No, I adore my odor!"

Keep me posted, my mind flashed while setting up the condoms and lubricant on the bedside table.

He flushed the toilet and reentered the room, beaming. "I feel *fantastic*," he swooned. He tugged his semi-erect masterpiece of circumcision and flopped on the bed next to me. There he languished: recumbent against the pillows, fiddling himself, his free arm relaxed upon a raised knee. The early evening sunshine streamed through the latticework on the balcony windows and played cubistically upon his body. I got hard just looking at him. How could such a babe, such a thoroughbred, have *not* achieved celebrity?

Alain reached for the lube, dribbled a dose into his palm, and began smoothing it up and down the pulsing proof of my fierce attraction to him.

"Jesus, that feels good," I muttered.

"What do you want from me, James?" he said, tearing open a condom.

"I wanna fuck you," I reiterated. (As if the degree of hardness he was rolling the condom down was not the answer, ipso facto.)

"And nothing more?" he uttered almost imperceptibly.

"What was that?"

"Nothing. So tell me: How do you '*wanna* fuck me'?"

"Lie on your back and raise your legs. Yeah." I lubricated, then mounted him, deaf to his subtle implication, eased through his gleaming circumference into unimaginable ecstasy. Alain caught his breath; his eyes snapped wide. I asked if I were hurting him.

"Yes, but don't stop. Does it 'feel good,' baby?"

"You can't imagine."

"What would make it better?"

"Nothing," I replied not altogether patiently.

"Don't lie to me!" he snapped. "What would make it *better* for you?"

His accusatory tone reduced me to squirming—within my own skin, within the condom, within Alain. "If I weren't . . . *hurting you?*" escaped my vocal cords.

"Love isn't just a 'feel good game,' James," he argued. "Love also involves pain, and it's *love* that I want. What is it that you *want?*"

Flabbergasted, halted motionless, I replied: "You scarcely know me, Alain."

"But I know myself; I know that love entails trust. *Je t'aime*, remember?"

I mouthed the words "I love you too," and resumed thrusting in response to some imagined necessity to meet nature's rhythm quotient.

Without warning, Alain's entire demeanor became charged with raw antagonism. He said: "You don't *love* me, James, but perhaps you will. I want you to fuck me like you've never dared to fuck a man before, little boy." I was stung he'd called me a little boy but opted to remain silent. Indeed, I picked up my pace even though he continued to hound me: "Does it 'feel good' to your cock, to your head, to conquer such a prize as Alain Marquis?"

"*Yes . . . both*," I literally *fucked* in response.

"But *not* your heart. No! Do not presume to kiss me! You 'wanna fuck,' right? So, fuck! . . . It makes you feel like a man?" he goaded. "To stay so nice and hard? Eh, little boy?"

"*Fuck* you, freak; you tell *me*," I snarled, nailing him twice, very hard.

"*Oh, dieu*. Two true moments! You *hurt* me you little fuck. Congratulations!"

"I'm not *little*, goddamn it!" Suddenly I *wanted* to hurt him, to make him *shut the fuck up*. Why was he provoking me? And why was I getting increasingly turned on? Questions unanswered, I rammed forward. "Does *this* feel 'little'? You want it *rough*? I'll fucking *show* you rough."

"Is that what you think I *want*?" he raved. "You say you're not little, but it will take more than your big dick to prove it, James. Yeah, *fuck* the lies, fuck *beyond* them, *ouais . . . .*" Leering at me, he raved on: "Face the absolute! You think you are God's Gift, but you're just a man. *Ouais*, baby . . . conquer, dominate, control, *fuck!* Make yourself 'feel good,' believe that you're able to love me, or Adam—that you love yourself! You needn't worry; I won't tell your mother who James really is. *Ouais, hurt* me . . . . Does my ass '*feel good*,' Jimmy? Are you *fucking* me yet?"

He dared to laugh, to call me "Jimmy!" When he added, with another spiteful laugh, "Oh, to think what *Adam* will say," something inside me snapped. I wasn't 'just a man.' I was gifted, loved, unique! *FUCK HIM*, I thought, vicious with unadulterated hump-rage, determined to slay him with my cock.

"*Yeah*, man," I began. "Your insides feel fucking *great*. You *like* that? How about *this*? Yeah . . . *take* it, you fucking whacko!" I was seething, thrusting the words viciously into him. "God *damn* you . . . You wanna be shot with a *cannon? No problem*. You think you know what's goin' *down* between Adam and me?" I imitated Alain's voice, snidely: "'*Je t'aime*, James; *Je t'aime!* He makes me love you *more!*' What a *crock*. . . . You don't love *shit*, except the stink of your own. *Fuck* you, asshole!"

I paused to examine Alain's face beneath me: It was thoroughly impassive with beatitude, which enraged me exponentially. "You're a hot commodity, *aren't* you, actor?" I sneered. "A real *sex* symbol. Well, I got you *nailed* against the mattress, *don't* I? Look at your cock. Yeah, like I'm not makin' *you* feel like a man. You're fuckin' *insane*."

His response, a soothing mantra, emerged as if from another dimension: "No, James, I am not insane, merely another fool. Fuck the lies; fuck beyond them in order to *reach* me, to become *us*. Hurt me in the process if you need, but do not settle for just . . . 'feeling . . . good.' You are afraid to face the absolute; you are afraid to fail, to lose yourself, but therein is found *the light*. Oh, *je t'aime*, James! Failure is best shared."

His face: My god, the joy it conveyed!

At precisely that way station, *I came to recognize* that Alain would be magnificent at thirty, at fifty, at eighty. That his ashes would sparkle, being cast into the Seine. I'd somehow acquired the courage to look beyond stimulation, beyond the frame-progressive artifice upon which Alain's beauty would be catalogued, and thus our coupling changed. We stopped talking, *lying*. He allowed our kissing to resume. My pace relaxed and I became oblivious to carnal mechanics as my ego dissolved into a heart of unmitigated ardor. What Alain had referred to as "facing the absolute" simply *was*, was sustained sans time's consideration, until it ceased.

Our eyes opened simultaneously. Although I had not been able to differentiate between the experience and its orgasmic conclusion—a phenomenon, come to find out, that he and I shared—all signs indicated that we both had climaxed: Our bodies glistened with sweat; his belly and chest were spattered with semen; my erection was fading within Alain, whose head I found gripped between my hands.

"Alain."

"Shhh. *I know*."

Inseminated condom discarded, my penis once again became my own possession as we attempted to deny the reality that time had resumed its relentless diminishment of our lifespans. Entwined within that bittersweet, parenthetical segue, we shared the failure that I can only hope bears some little resemblance to that which precedes and follows existence.

"*Je t'aime*, Alain."

"I love you, James."

I would most definitely, somehow, devise a space for Alain in my life.

We got up, shared a baguette with Roquefort cheese, a sausage, and demi-dried tomatoes. The strawberries were ambrosial. We drank wine, smoked cigarettes, and realistically forged plans for accommodating one another in our futures. Later, somewhat drunk by then, we wept a little—lamenting our lot as artists.

We discussed Adam, who assumed the mythology of being the first man ever betrayed, before I betrayed him again. Reversing coital "roles," Alain and I contented ourselves with "just feeling good," with searing orgasms experienced above and beyond the fine fucking itself. We'd earned that right, period. Yes, I'd fallen in love with Alain Marquis, and told him so repeatedly in both French and English.

We did not sleep in each other's arms that night. *Au contraire*, we did not physically touch at all. Alain Marquis and I remained two distinct entities, framed back-to-back within the same rectangle, unconscious and at peace upon a mattress in a rented space in the rue des Tournelles, Paris: not just the City of Light, but also the City of Love.

SOUVENIR OF FLORENCE

ROB MCDONALD

FIRST MOVEMENT (*ALLEGRO CON SPIRITO*)

I'D TRAVELED HALFWAY around the world from Australia to see him. All around Florence his almost faultless body graced billboard advertisements for Levi's jeans. Now he stood naked above me.

I circumnavigated his muscular thighs. My raised eyes gazed at his windswept curls, his taut neck, the indentation of his back, and his firm buttocks. They glanced at his raised upper lip. They roamed over his hard nipples, the cleft between his square pectorals, and the tensed muscles of his raised left arm. His relaxed but equally muscular right hand dwarfed his small penis, and I wondered how many socks were used to pad the jeans on the billboard.

My own penis pressed hard against my fashionable but painfully tight new Italian jeans, like a prisoner straining against a dungeon wall. I could no longer walk in comfort, and I halted beneath him.

I recalled the E.M. Forster story I'd read on the plane, about a young man locked eternally in an embrace with a statue of Priapus. Giggling, the young man fused with the phallic god into a new statue called *The Wrestling Lesson*. But unlike Priapus, whose erection had sent his fig leaf flying across the room, Michelangelo's *David* failed to respond, and in four languages a sign warned me not to touch.

"Oh, my God, Fred, will you look at that?" said a loud voice. "If I'd seen him first I never would have married you."

During my trance, a busload of guided sightseers had spewed into the Galleria dell'Accademia and assembled beneath the colossal statue. For a moment I wondered if she was talking about David or me.

"His dick's smaller than mine," said Fred.

Her eyes were locked on the statue. She was clearly talking about David. "He's confronting a powerful giant, Fred. He's just got stage fright."

I shuffled away from the tourist herd toward the *Prisoners*, the incomplete Michelangelo sculptures that, like me, seemed locked in a yearning to escape from intent into reality. "Tom," I told myself, "you're twelve thousand miles from your parents. Sex is legal here for consenting adults. It's 1972. Time for freedom, time for moving, time to begin. It's time for love and romance. Or at least for losing your virginity."

The sightseers milled around David. A singsong guide parroted a condensed version of Michelangelo's life. He told of the civic fathers' horror of placing such a sexy statue near the cathedral, but never once mentioned the sexual energies that inspired the artist's works.

Embarrassed at being turned on by a statue, I wandered ill at ease among the prisoners. My eyes kept returning to David, till his thighs were partially eclipsed by a tall, obese American with a loud voice and even louder checked Bermuda shorts. I lost my erection. It was time for moving, while my ball-breaking jeans allowed.

I bought a postcard, and followed Via Ricasoli toward the Duomo, planning to see Michelangelo's uncompleted *Pietà*.

The street teemed with handsome young Italian men, whose bodies were all restrained by skin-tight jeans. Last autumn, no Italian boy would have been seen dead in jeans. This season none could be seen without them. Even practicing heterosexuals toted nelly little leather handbags, because those thigh-grabbing pockets could not hold a flea's foreskin. I longed for a secret sign that would tell me which of the men were gay. But in Italy, men of all persuasions kissed when meeting and walked arm in arm. I had no way of telling.

I turned right at the Duomo, jetlagged, disoriented, and horny. The joyful, dancing surge from the opening of Tchaikovsky's *Souvenir de Florence* echoed in my head, but I felt like a wallflower at the dance. Where were the unrestrained, passionate Italian men that populated Forster's novels set in Italy? If I could only connect! Saving the *Pietà* for later, I dragged my tired feet toward my room, passing stalls chock-full of tacky souvenirs, including omnipresent replicas of David.

I remembered a school excursion from Woop Woop to Sydney, when I'd stood before a window of David Jones's department store with Rick, my best friend, goggling at a plaster copy of David. Shocked mothers of three had written letters to the editor, demanding a fig leaf to protect their innocent progeny from exposure to David's unabashed nakedness. Rick watched the reactions of people who stopped in front of the window, and made fun of those who were scandalized. I watched David and some of the men who stopped, while hoping Rick wouldn't notice what was happening in my loose, gray school trousers.

In Florence I was surrounded by thousands of miniature, stark-naked Davids but nobody batted an eyelid. I wished someone would.

SECOND MOVEMENT
(*ADAGIO CANTABILE E CON MOTO*)

I AWOKE, STILL jetlagged, unable to tell if it was morning or night. My room in the Pensione Bertoldo had no view. It didn't even have a window. By the light of the one surviving low-wattage bulb in a once glorious multi-branched chandelier, I tried to read *The Life to Come and Other Stories* by Forster, but the room was too dark. I inserted my postcard of David as a bookmark, and placed the book on the bedside desk.

Two dearer rooms at the front had a very interesting view. At this, the less fashionable end of Via Faenza, a few hundred extra lire bought not a view of the Duomo, but a picturesque nocturnal *tableau vivant* of bargain-price whores, who twitched their eyes at the twitches in britches of men on tight budgets.

Signora Bertoldo had interesting views too, and expressed them for no additional charge. She disapproved of my shave coat, which afforded a generous view of my legs. They offended her Catholic sense of decency. Forgetting I understood Italian, she complained to her husband every time I went to the bathroom about "*quello dalla vestaglia corta,*" the one with the short dressing-gown. "It's a shave coat," I wanted to explain, "not a dressing-gown. The weather's hotter in Sydney and we wear skimpier nightwear." But my Italian wasn't up to it.

My dick was. Again. The ubiquitous Davids and tight denims were getting to me. I removed the postcard from the book, and tried to wriggle out of my constrictive jeans without peeling the skin off my legs.

In the Galleria dell'Accademia, David was illuminated by a shaft of light from a massive dome, but in Pensione Bertoldo's spartan murk his privates were a shaft of dark. I could barely distinguish his distinguishing features. I closed my eyes and filled in the missing details from memory. A pent-up glob of come splashed beyond the bed onto the cover of *The Life to Come*, blanching the photograph of Forster's browbeaten stare; served the old bugger right for raising false expectations with his novelistic fantasies of hot-blooded Italians. Fearful of Signora Bertoldo's disapproving frown, I avoided a trip to the bathroom by toweling myself and Forster over the sink.

I escaped into light, and walked to a café near the Duomo. "Ciao, Rick," I wrote on the postcard. "Look, ma, no fig leaf. Having a great time. Wish you were here."

I couldn't think of anything else to say. I lay down the pen and flipped the card over. I missed Rick's company.

We'd been friends at school in Woop Woop from the first day of kindergarten. We both won scholarships that took us to Sydney University. He made it into medicine, and stayed with an aunt in Cremorne Point, in a piss-elegant house with a leafy view of the harbor. I studied music, and barely survived in a room in a decrepit Glebe rabbit warren dominated by a rooftop neon sign. We often met in the Union cafeteria, where, over coffee that tasted like dishwater, we talked about repressive Australian censorship laws and wished for an end to the regressive government which had kept Australia back for twenty-three years. Together we dreamed of traveling to Europe, which beckoned with promises of culture, a freer society, and coffee that tasted of coffee. But I traveled alone. After graduating, I won a scholarship to Florence, where I claimed to be preparing a thesis about Italian influences on the music of foreign composers. Rick stayed in Sydney, where he claimed to be studying the long-term health effects of university coffee.

I picked up my pen. "Haven't seen any opera or theater yet, although the prostitutes in Via Faenza, where I'm staying, provide plenty of live entertainment. Not that I can afford such luxuries on the scholarship money. Remember the banning of Leonard Cohen's *Beautiful Losers*? I bought a copy at a bookstall in Rome."

We'd laughed at Japanese tourists who expected to see kangaroos hopping along Pitt Street, but we'd been just as naive. I hadn't expected Luciano Pavarotti to belt out operatic arias in the street. I hadn't expected to see living replicas of David screw one another in the Piazza della Signoria. But what I saw disappointed me.

The day I touched down in Rome the streets swarmed with shrill busloads of shouting men who waved colorful flags. I thumbed through my blue guide, expecting to find something about a medieval festival, till I realized they were loudmouthed soccer fans. I spent my first night in the Albergo del Popolo's bar, where in jetlagged stupor I watched *Canzonissima*, a talent quest program that made Australian TV look good. In a magazine I bought to read on the train to Florence, I learned of threats to ban Bertolucci's new film. Censors insisted on the removal of eight seconds of butter-assisted sodomy from *Last Tango in Paris*. They wanted him to change the line "*Mettimi le dita nel culo*" to "*Non farmelo ripetere*." From "Stick your fingers up my bum" to "Don't do that again."

"How goes the Labor erection campaign?" I wrote. "Hope you soon find a cure for the current government, Medicine Man. Ciao, Tom."

It was time for moving, time to begin. I posted the card and browsed at the gallery bookstalls near Piazza della Republica. Two books caught my eye: English translations of Jean Genet novels that had been banned back home. Although not as stunning as David, the men on the photographic wrappers looked more enticing than the frowning Mr. Forster.

At the adjacent souvenir stall, an attractive American woman wielding a worn copy of *Europe on $5 a Day* scrutinized the gross souvenirs, while an effusive stallholder pitched his wares.

I bought *Our Lady of the Flowers* and *Querelle of Brest*. My eyes returned to the stallholder, whose jeans seemed designed to advertise all his wares without speech.

"This is the Duomo," he told her, "this is *The Birth of Venus*, this is Giambologna's statue of *Virtue Triumphing over Vice*, and this is *David*."

"David Who?" she asked.

He shrugged and grinned at me, nervously scratching his earlobe. He explained who David was, and suggested that while she was in Florence she should see Michelangelo's sculptures.

"Oh, I know him," she said. "He sculpted the Sistine Chapel. Can you tell me how to get to the Sistine Chapel from here?"

"Surely," he said. "Turn left at Via Campidoglio, turn right at Via delle Belle Donne, cross the big piazza, and buy a train ticket for Rome."

After her brain deciphered his message she left. With my limited command of nonverbal Italian, I tried to decipher his message for me. Tugging his earlobe, he seemed to be playing charades. Sounds like . . . Sounds like . . . What Italian boys do when their jeans are too tight for pocket billiards? Grinning, he ran his fingers down the back of a figurine. Sounds like . . . Sounds like, "*Mettimi le dita nel culo*."

"I'm Guido," he said.

"I'm . . . *Mi chiamo Tom*."

"I like Tom. That's nice. As in 'every Tom, Dick and Harry'. I like Dick too. You want to come for a ride on my Vespa? I show you the sights of Florence."

He handed his cashbox to the bookseller, who seemed used to the arrangement. "My boyfriend," he joked, as we sped past a semi-clad David on a billboard. We stopped and walked to the Piazza della Signoria to view another David. I clung to him tightly as he wove through the traffic to the Piazzale Michelangelo, where underneath a gargantuan David we viewed the Duomo through a thick haze.

In his bedroom we struggled with absurdly tight jeans, surrounded by cartons of Davids. And after forever I viewed his small, flabby cock. His jeans had been stuffed with a sock. Blue varicose veins crisscrossed his penis. His cassette player reverberated with the word "supersonic," pronounced like an Italian word containing a hundred r's, each of which had to be pronounced. An echolalic disc jockey motor mouthed over the top of Carly Simon. "You're so vain, you prob'ly think this song is about you. You're so vain. I bet you think this song is about you, don't you?" Where was the love duet between violin and cello from Tchaikovsky's *Souvenir de Florence*? Where was the soaring mad aria from *Lucia di Lammermoor*? Where were Forster's horny Italians?

I lay on Guido's bed, exhausted from the fight with my jeans, smothering Carly Simon's nasal voice by imagining Joan Sutherland singing *The Sweet Sound of His Voice Came to Me*. I tried to arouse him by kissing him. His stubbly chin prickled. His breath smelled of Nazionali cigarettes. I licked his flabby cock and he dozed off. I knew he must be tired from spending long hours at his souvenir stall, but this was ridiculous. I wondered how to excuse myself politely, but his arm around my shoulder prevented a discreet escape. Still jetlagged, I dozed off, too.

A persistent jabbing at my side woke me, arousing hope. But it was his mother poking me with a broomstick. "*Brutta razza di culattone*," she yelled. Several other rapid-fire curses got lost in translation, but the angry broom and frequent guttural repetitions of "*culo*" gave me a vague impression she thought I was a filthy rotten poofter, and that Guido should be at his stall earning money, not wasting precious electricity on reprobate recreations with randy foreigners determined to import their vices into Italy. She switched off the light and tensed her hand around the broomstick.

I shoehorned myself into my jeans, cursing Italian fashion as the fly tenderized my testicles. Guido, still naked, ducked to avoid the broomstick. In silent apology, he reached for a carton and handed me a statuette of David as a souvenir, while fending off his mother.

A frigid breeze from the river chilled me as I crossed the Ponte Vecchio, which provided a brief respite from the traffic and fumes. As I walked through cold, treeless streets toward the Pensione Bertoldo I missed the warm Sydney Novembers and the jacarandas blooming in the university quad. I missed Rick. Lost in thought, I lost myself in a maze of crisscrossing streets. Passing a tattooist's shop I noticed that among his designs, even he had an image of David. I looked at newspaper kiosks to find how the Australian elections had gone, and if anything had been freed or moved or begun. But Australia got mentioned in Italian papers only when someone got eaten by a shark.

When I reached the *pensione* I found Signora Bertoldo had switched off the central heating to save money. I put my two novels on the bedside table. It was too cold and dark to read. It was still early and I hadn't eaten, but I huddled under the covers, singing, "Varicose veins, you prob'ly think this song is about them. Varicose veins. I bet you think this song is about them, don't you, don't you?"

THIRD MOVEMENT (*ALLEGRETTO MODERATO*)

AT THE END of the queue in the Olimpia self-service, her purplish blue rinse stood out like a Scotch thistle in the Boboli Gardens. In a grotesque pastiche of David, her left hand wielded an elegant Gucci handbag, while the right held a thermos flask emblazoned with a map of Australia. I hadn't heard from anyone at home since the elections. I thought of asking her if she knew who'd won but relented, and joined the queue in silence behind her.

She peered at each bain-marie like an entomologist striving to identify a rare breed of cockroach. She turned and asked, "Do you speak English?"

I said nothing. But my blue guide gave me away.

"Of course you do. Do you speak Italian too?" she asked.

I nodded.

"Oh, you're a godsend," she quavered. "It's ridiculous. My husband was Italian but I can't put two words together. My name's Beatrice, but everyone calls me Bea. Can you explain I want some of that minestrone in the thermos to take home to my son? David's at home in bed with a stomach upset."

I reluctantly introduced myself and translated as well as I

could. I had no idea of the word for "thermos" or whether it was correct to use "*fiasco*." I soon knew it was. The thermos exploded. Its liner disintegrated into hundreds of silvery shards and soup gushed over the floor. I watched in disbelief at her futile attempts to soak up the mess with a Gucci handkerchief, while restaurant staff ran for a mop. I resolved never again to carry my blue guide in full view. Next time I'd pretend to be Bulgarian.

The staff, assuming I was with her, packed takeaway dinners for us all. Unable to stay and look the staff in the eye, I agreed to share a meal at home with Bea and David. They were renting an apartment near the Duomo.

During the short walk she told me her life history. Her husband had migrated from Italy to Australia and made his fortune importing *bombonierae*, the gewgaws Italians give to guests at weddings, christenings, and other festivities. Since his recent death, she'd dragged her Italian-speaking son out of university to help run the family business.

"I normally wouldn't eat at a cheap restaurant like that," she said. "But with Italy threatening to go communist, and Australia already heading that way, I'm spending all my money on fashion before they nationalize Via Tornabuoni."

I grinned from ear to ear. Australia gone communist? Not likely, and I couldn't see Whitlam nationalizing Italian fashion houses, but Labor must have won the election. It really was time for freedom, time for moving, time to begin.

"What brings you to Italy, Tom?" she asked.

"I'm over here to prepare a Master's thesis on Italian influences on classical composers. I study music at Sydney University."

"What a coincidence! David studied engineering there." I assumed she meant *her* David. "It'll be good for you to get together. He's been a bit lonely with just an old biddy like me for company."

Oh, yes, I thought. I can see him now. Slide rule hanging from the cords, sly drool on his face, and one of those gross engineering students' T-shirts with a picture of a woman's boobs on a beer tankard.

Their apartment was airy and light, and the central heating worked. My eyes bulged from their sockets. David sat on a sofa listening to a cassette, and looked perfectly healthy. He looked perfectly perfect. He was listening to Carly Simon's *No Secrets*, but I could be tolerant of foreign cultures.

"This is Tom, David," Bea said. "He's from Sydney too. I've just had the most embarrassing accident with the thermos, but they've packed us some food in boxes. How do you feel?"

His eyes locked on mine, and his perfectly sculpted hands missed Bea's proffered dinner box. "I feel fine now."

His physique, like his namesake's, was impeccable. Fitting him like a second skin, but looser than dictated by Italian fascists of fashion, were a pair of bell-bottom flares. A short-sleeved body shirt highlighted his square pecs. A tattooed butterfly on his right upper arm moved toward me. I was relieved I was wearing my looser Australian Leisuremasters while my tight new jeans were at the laundry. My hand moved toward his and so did my inside leg.

"If you're sure you're all right, I'll leave you two to get acquainted," she said, "and heat up my meal later. I want to go back to Ferragamo for some shoes before they close. I'm sure you'll enjoy one another's company more than mine."

"I'm not sick," he said after she'd gone. "I just couldn't stand another fucking art gallery or fashion boutique or *bombonierae* manufacturer, so I told her I was. There's nothing wrong with me at all."

There was nothing wrong with him at all. I was disappointed that he knew nothing about art, but I knew what I liked.

"So what do you do if you don't like galleries or shopping?" I asked as we ate.

"Listen to music. Go to the movies sometimes. Have you seen *Last Tango in Paris*?" he asked, eyeing the unused sachet of butter provided with my spaghetti.

"I tried to see it when it opened but it was packed," I said, "so I ended up seeing *No Sex, Please, We're British*."

"Doesn't sound much fun. Do you want to see *Buttered Buns in Florence*?"

The sex was quick and primal. His tattoo rippled as he unbuttoned my shirt. I pulled his over his head. With my jeans only halfway down, he unwrapped the butter and spread my cheeks.

He pulled us to our feet and pushed me against the window. I think there was a view of the Duomo. I can't remember. I winced as he entered me. Pain and pleasure mingled and rushed through my body.

"You're hurting," I yelled. "You're too big. *Adagio. Meno mosso.*"

My legs trembled. He withdrew and pushed me to the floor and entered again, *rallentando.* The tempo was more *allegretto moderato* than *adagio,* but the slower speed was more comfortable and pleasure started to outweigh the pain. I stared ahead at the floor in front of me to concentrate on the pleasure.

Someone knocked at the door. "David," Bea called, "can you let me in? I've forgotten my credit card and keys. It's one of those nights."

He pointed to the bathroom and whispered, "*Presto.*" As he withdrew I shot *prestissimo.* From the bathroom I saw him dragging up his flares and frantically mopping the mess with a paper dinner napkin.

"Don't go into the bathroom, Mum," he told her. "Tom's taking a shower. The fleapit where he stays doesn't have a decent hot water system."

"You can come here whenever you like, Tom," she called. "Don't wear those trousers tomorrow, David. You've spilled butter or something on your fly."

He winked when he showed me to the door. "You can come whenever you like," he said. I walked sideways like a crab in case any other spillage met Bea's fashion-conscious eye.

I came every night. Bea left us to get acquainted while she shopped till she dropped. The sex got better as I learned to relax. Eventually, even Carly Simon's voice caused me no pain.

I was in love. I had to tell someone. I wrote letters to both of my parents. For Rick I bought a postcard of the statue of *Virtue Overcoming Vice.* A naked but modest female Virtue looked away as she grappled with the muscular, male, and naked Vice. "I've fallen in love, Rick. Seriously. He looks more like the guy on the bottom than the woman on top. Although on the bottom is not where he prefers to be. Got you a souvenir, courtesy of another pleasant acquaintance. He doesn't have a fig leaf. Neither does the souvenir."

Eventually David and Bea had to leave on a business trip to Pescara then return to Sydney. David promised that when I'd finished my thesis we'd meet again in Sydney. My thesis was far from finished, but I planned an early return home.

The day before they left I headed for the tattoo shop. "*Sulla natica destra,*" the tattooist repeated unsurprised, as if people always asked for David to be inked onto the right buttock.

It was like losing my virginity all over again. For a minute I felt a painful hot scratch, then I got used to the sting and relaxed. The fatty ointment felt like butter. I was glad to be lying prostrate, in a position that concealed my arousal.

I hurried back to the *pensione* to change for a goodbye dinner with David and Bea. The bandage on my bum demanded looser trousers. My tight Italian jeans could conceal no surprises, and I wanted to surprise David in the shower after dinner.

We caught a taxi to a restaurant in Maiano, overlooking the city.

"I don't think David wants to go to Pescara," said Bea. "I think he's fallen in love with Florence."

"Florence Who?" I quipped.

Bea giggled. "I hope there's not a Florence Anybody. We're supposed to meet his fiancée in Sydney at the end of the month. Her name's Angela."

I coughed on the Chianti. "I didn't know he was engaged."

"I'm surprised he didn't tell you."

"I'm a bit surprised myself."

The night seemed endless. The balcony where we ate offered a view of the lights of Florence but I saw only the black sky. At last Bea went to the "little girl's room" and I had time alone with David.

"Be realistic," he whispered. "Mum can't run the business on her own. She doesn't speak the language. Can you see a couple of queers selling wedding gifts to Italians in suburban Sydney? You know how uptight Italians get about these things. It's bad for business."

"Fuck business! You promised we'd get together in Sydney."

"We still can."

"Oh, shit! Divorce Italian style. I'm sorry. Forget it."

"I love you. I really love you," he said. But he sounded like a badly dubbed Italian movie where the lip movements don't match the words.

His tattoo rippled as he reached for my arms. I slipped free. I wanted to grab a pistol and shoot him in the balls. He never saw my tattoo. I never saw him again.

I walked all the way down from the hills into Florence, leaving David to explain my disappearance, and reached the Pensione Bertoldo in the middle of the night. I had to ring to be let in. Signora Bertoldo's frown told me she would gladly shoot me in the balls.

She fetched me a newly arrived postcard. It featured the almost completed Sydney Opera House. There was still some scaffolding, but the building looked ready to sing. The card was from Rick. "You stupid bloody queen!" he wrote. "Why didn't you tell me? I was in love with you, you bastard."

I was gobsmacked. Why hadn't *he* told *me*? I'd known Rick as a friend who'd give me the shirt off his back. I'd never noticed once that he wanted to take off everything.

FOURTH MOVEMENT (*ALLEGRO VIVACE*)

THE RETURN FLIGHT was the longest journey I'd ever made. I'd traveled halfway around the world for a ridiculous, indelible souvenir of Florence. My thesis was incomplete, and I wondered if I'd ever finish it. The words of a tacky song called *Souvenir of London*, made tackier by faulty earphones, seeped into my brain. "Bought a souvenir in London. Got to hide it from my mom. Can't declare it at the customs. But I'll have to take it home."

No worry about hiding my Florence souvenir from my mum. Or my dad. Not a word since I'd written to tell them who I was. I had nothing to declare at customs except my own idiocy. The undeclared banned books were tucked discreetly into my uncompleted thesis.

Explaining my undeclared artwork to Rick, or anyone else not named David, was another thing. I mentally composed a classified for the *Sunday Review*. "Male art lover, 24, seeks discreet dalliance with similar. Must be named David."

I stepped off the plane into sunshine and warmth. A friendly customs officer barely looked at my luggage. Beyond the customs checkpoint, a smiling woman handed me a sample bag promoting the opening of the Sydney Opera House.

Beyond the smiling woman was Rick, who leapt into my arms. His hippie hair and beard were gone, replaced by a spiky rooster cut and a clean-shaven chin. We locked in a bear hug and I can't remember what he wore.

"You're staying at my place, in my bed. That's an order."

"Won't your aunt freak out?" I asked.

"Hardly. She's off to the Opera House opening tonight with her lady friend. She says you're welcome. I couldn't get tickets for us but we can watch the fireworks from the verandah."

As he drove over the Harbor Bridge I opened my daypack and produced the novels I'd smuggled in. He laughed. "Thanks, pet, but I've already read them. Things have changed while you were away. I got them in the book department at David Jones."

"Next you'll be telling me they've legalized sex," I said.

"Not yet, but it'll happen one day. You're not gonna keep me waiting till then, are you?"

The verandah had a panoramic view of the harbor. Lights from boats of every shape and size dotted the water. Tchaikovsky's *Souvenir de Florence* was playing on Rick's stereo. The fragrance of frangipanis, jacarandas, and sea spray rose from the garden below, and commingled with the faint smell of his sweat beside me and then behind me.

The fireworks began, and I could feel his firm body pressing against my back. I tensed as he unzipped my jeans.

"What's up, pet?" he asked. "You're as tense as a Christian Scientist with appendicitis."

"Nice one, Rick."

"I stole it from Tom Lehrer."

"I've got another souvenir of Florence."

"Oh, shit! You got the clap."

"No. A tattoo."

"Where? Where?" he said, lowering my jeans.

"I thought I was in love with a guy called David."

His hands roamed over the tatt and he laughed. "You look good enough to put in David Jones's windows."

His hand roamed down and across, then he stopped in a burst of laughter.

"I just had a horrible thought. What if he'd been called Ernest? Can you imagine coming home with 'Ernest' tattooed all over your bum? I could never love a bum called Ernest."

We doubled up with laughter. I tripped on my jeans, now hanging loosely around my knees, and collapsed onto the floor. Giggling beyond control, he fell on top of me. Clothing flew in every direction and our bodies fused in our own version of *The Wrestling Lesson*. His tongue sandblasted my ears then my nipples, and moved slowly southward.

He rolled away in another hysterical fit of laughter. "Oh, God! I just had another horrible thought. What if you'd fallen in love with a drag queen called Miss Lucy Honeychurch?"

We burst into laughter and rolled locked together across the floor. The night sky erupted with more fireworks, so we stood up to watch. He circumnavigated my imperfect buttocks and reached his tongue into my ear.

"So tell me all about this David," he said.

I turned to kiss him and said, "David Who?"

He stood behind me while we watched the firelit sky. I could feel a firm pressure on my naked buttocks and his hands twisting my nipples. The sky exploded in a fiery coda over the Opera House and the water, as he exploded inside me. I groaned with pleasure as cascading shards of light lit the harbor and fizzled into specks that resembled more small boats.

The record had stopped, and the arm hissed in and out of the turntable center, but neither of us wanted to move. It was good to be home, where I'd never been. It was time for not moving. Time to begin.

GIVE

CARY STEVEN

I AM GOING to skip the preliminaries. Like why I left—a long story—and how I got here. This is what matters: I've traded one constriction for another. This bed is impossibly narrow, the sheets too tight, shoveled under the mattress by what must have been the strongest arms. I barely fit, and I am small. The room is dark, darker than any American room; the light above the bed austere, unused to picking up the highlights in whorls of red-blond hair, like the ones pushing against my wrist, smuggled down the length of my right arm. My writing arm.

I am writing in bed, in Bologna, the Red City. Red because its politics were red once; red because its roofs still are. Because the first time I came here, the first time I really came, a friend of a friend pushed up the thin cotton shirt I was wearing, up over my nipples, up through more hair than any guy my age has a right to have, some shade of wiry bronze. He placed his thick fingers in the midst of it and said: *Rosso.* Red.

I didn't correct him. Later, when it was almost morning and we were in the backseat of a car, our friend driving, someone else shotgun, it was my turn to lift and place, bury my fingers, smaller, more fragile, below his belt, undone, in the fur out of which his cock arched up against his sweater, greasing my hand with the stink and the slick of a long day, the longest day. My willing hand. His black hair, which I had seen; his red, wet head pouting in its cowl, which I had not. Careful of the dark, of how fragile a cover it gave us, I looked out the window at the red roofs gone black, as if I weren't tugging the skin down to the base of his shaft and sliding it back up again; as if I weren't waiting for his hand, which was on my thigh, to press into me and let me know that my hand, now curved around his head, around what I could only imagine as its viscous, open flare, that my hand would make him come.

I smuggled a fistful of it, still hot, to my mouth, and when I swallowed I swear I glowed as red as the dash, as the city outside the windshield, red and almost stirring, warm for the first time in years.

That was years ago. My fist has had a lot of practice since then. Mostly my own cock, my own come. No one has held me as tightly as I can hold myself. No one has kept me as warm. This bed, its compression, could teach some guys I know a thing or two.

It is cold in Bologna this time of year. I am not here for sweltering sun. I am here because this city coils around me, and I need its noose: the rules of hospitality, the enforced socializing, the canons of fashion. An imperative: you must. I must.

This afternoon I was sitting on the cold steps of San Domenico, the unfinished façade too big, too blunt: a warehouse still under construction, a gym rat's torso. I was sitting on the steps, getting my bearings, wondering if I should walk up to the university and watch the panhandlers with their dogs, the African peddlers of plastic tchotchkes, the students who, eight years or so into college, were still far from finishing.

I like how long in the tooth Italian students are. Women barely younger than Anna Magnani wear their pink and turquoise Invicta bookbags from middle school. The men, conservatively overdressed, wool sweaters over button-down shirts, never fail to strain the seams of their jeans. This is, I'm not kidding, the country of cock. A constant swell, just to one side of a worn, infinitely distressed fly; a constant summons.

I decided to answer the call. I pushed my boner down—how did that happen, with cold marble so close to my balls?—and turned to walk up Via Zamboni, toward the university. My face, I imagine, was worn red, redder than usual, by the scrape of past desire and the all-too-present chill. But then, as sudden as you'd imagine, the other side of Piazza Maggiore was eclipsed by an oversized, tarnished belt buckle—was it an eagle?—and I felt a hand on my shoulder, insistent through my down jacket, through my wool turtleneck sweater, and even the flimsy wifebeater I'd already been wearing for two days: down to the skin, to the bone. A gesture, a grip, that I wanted to respond to as I'd responded hundreds of times in the past: haul the beast out, plant my face around it, suffocate. Swallow.

Five exposed buttons on his fly caught the sunlight. I didn't know the sun was out. The hand moved up the side of my neck, through the scruff that had grown there in the last month, over my right ear—which it pressed against the side of my head—fingers wrapped around the back of my skull. Then a face, level with mine, thick stubble on high cheekbones, down a long, thin neck, into dense tangles of hair poking from the splayed collar of a pale shirt. More sudden, though, was the smell of him: cigarettes and sandalwood. The press of his fingers against my neck was simultaneous with this quick inhalation and acceptance: yes; I must. This is strictly necessary.

Then I focused, breathed out. Marco. No one in particular, and all of a sudden the only person in the world. The guy who had been in the front seat, that night when the red roofs were black and my mouth was full of a stranger's sperm. Not a stranger, really, but estrangement has a way of happening, distance breaking in and breaking down.

"Marco."

"What," he asked, but there was no use answering, no need to, "are you doing here?"

This is what I said: that I had felt compelled to trade one kind of cold for another; to leave my small college town, its gunmetal sky and thin-lipped, thick-skinned people. That I had been overwhelmed by heat, so hard upon that unremitting frost, so I'd chosen someplace just as frozen, but someplace I could bury myself in. "I need," I said, "to bury myself for a while."

His eyes flashed, so dark and clear that it couldn't quite be called light. Infinitely lucid, infinitely firm, my head still held in his grip, he said, "Come."

And I did as I was told.

Here is all you need to know. Marco was still a student. His nose jutted out from his face like an Alitalia logo, a plane's tailfin in reverse. He had a thin blue circle at the crest of his right ear, and as we walked, each time the sun caught the blue, I winced as though I'd just tasted cold steel. You can laugh, but synesthesia happens. He growled when he spoke, his voice worn away by too many cigarettes and too many late nights talking—about what, I wondered? About love? I had forgotten these things. These things: they deserve a better tense than the past. His nose still juts; his Adam's apple still dives under his throat, under the dense black tangle at its base, and stabs back out with every swallow and every liquid moan.

Let me put it this way. We walked up three flights of stairs to a dim, oversized hallway that smelled like chlorine. He wrestled with the lock on the door. His shoes were scattered just inside. "*Permesso,*" I said as I crossed the threshold. A necessary formality: permit me. Let me in.

He made tea in a small clay pot, a Chinese rooster. His wrist slid out of his shirt as he lifted the pot to a low, red cup—mine— and tongues of nearly straight, nearly black hair lapped up against the bone. A thin vein of pale green tea slid down between his thumb and forefinger, tongue against tongue.

"I am," he said, "lucky to have found you." Thick curl of lash as his eyelids closed and opened again. He explained. Yes, he remembered that long ride home, all those years ago. Yes, he was still involved with the driver of that close car, the night of the close call. They lived in separate cities, broken and bound by that distance. Open. "It is—*come si dice?*—unresolved." And he blew across the top of his tea and took a fast, hard, brave gulp before setting the cup back down. His eyes, all this time, even when he was drinking, never left mine. His pupils were enormous, radiantly empty, as if I could curl up inside them.

He curled two fingers around a sugar bowl and looked away from me, toward the table. "And you? Where is your life going?" Now, folded into this bed and this darkness—what if, I'm shocked to think, it turns out that I am inside that inviting, fathomless eye?—I think he said *how*, not *where*, but that is what I heard, and this is how I answered.

"I am," and then I corrected myself, "I have been happy." I explained. I had been lucky to find a job, even in such a small, sexless town; lucky, at not quite thirty, to be paid to teach and write and travel. I had taken pleasure in that freedom. Lately I felt less free. Or free, perhaps, in the wrong ways: free to buy a house, to buy into the life of houses. Free to lock myself behind a thin wooden door, a screen of snow-covered trees, and forget the world, forget myself. Buried alive and alone, untouched, unscathed. I wanted a different kind of burial.

This is what I wanted to say but what I did not say: bury me. Wrap me up in that pale shirt which, even now, is drawn up in thin folds under your arms; wrap me up in the dry, hot smell and pulse and stretched skin inside those folds. Hold me close and let me fall.

I said that I, too, was unresolved.

Marco pushed aside his tea, and he smiled from the left corner of his mouth. He pushed his chair back across the tile, stood, and walked over to where I sat, immobile. His hand, then, was suddenly in my hair again, pressed to the bone. Strong. Deliberate. Slowly, forcefully, he crushed my face into his abdomen, held me there between flesh and fabric, touch and smell: I closed my eyes, and beneath his shirt I could feel the plane of muscle that, I knew, only ended in other muscle. I closed my eyes, breathed him in, and craved nothing more than the slow climb down that knotted rope.

That is how it seems to me now. Then, I think, I mostly wanted to cry. To say the plain words I never find the room to say in anyone's arms, the plain words those arms are so rarely equipped to receive. Here. Now. Yes. Everything.

"Come," he said, and I was back out in the world again, back in the kitchen, and he was walking away.

I followed him to a room barely large enough for a twin bed, three bookshelves, and a desk. There was no chair at the desk. Marco was sitting upright on the edge of the bed, his hands flat on his knees, waiting. Gray, late light threw only the most tentative shadow across the tile, itself gray and slightly luminous. Where did I belong? The bed was too narrow for us to sit side by side; the desk was covered in clothes.

"Come," he said, and he placed his hands on either side of him. He pushed himself back. Where was I supposed to go? He opened his legs. Even the weak light from the window was able to find the buckle and the buttons on his jeans, to set off a play of shadow across the worn denim against which his thighs shamelessly stretched. Not just his thighs.

I approached him slowly and, when my shins were dangerously close to brushing his, I bent toward him, toward the sharp line of his jaw, and I opened my mouth, ready for stubble and bone. To start with a kiss: this is the oldest ceremony. I placed my hands on his shoulders. Something in me tensed—something, or lots of things. Was there, I found myself thinking, some silver string of nerve linking my mouth to my asshole? I had forgotten it was there.

"No," he said, and shook his head. His hands moved to my hipbone and turned me around. I let myself be turned. I wedged myself into the thin space between his legs, the room he'd made for me. Then, inevitably, Marco's arms were around me, and his legs hemmed me in, and it all happened with such a slow vehemence that I knew that I was there and that I was not leaving. I reached back to touch his face, to make sure that there was a face behind these limbs.

"No," he said again, and one arm released me just enough to grab my hand, to press it against my chest and lodge it there. "Not yet." And then his mouth was on my neck, immobile, hot and lingering, and his nose was at the pulse point under my left ear, against that tense subcutaneous cord. I was just as unmoving. His heart was throbbing through my spine—or was that his cock? He bucked his hips up into the seam of my jeans and I had my answer. Both.

He held me like that, in the unresolved space between his heart and his cock, for ages.

This is what you want to know: on the other side of that interval, he turned me around and tilted his head back and pushed my mouth into his collarbone. My blind hands stumbled inside his shirt, clutched the tangle of hair around his navel; I pressed my left thumb into one of his ribs and heard him moan. He grabbed my hair and pulled my face up to his, and when his mouth closed on mine I swear I thought I was all tongue and teeth, pulsing muscle and resistant bone: my breath came faster; I wanted more.

I tried to push his shirt up over his head, but it was too tight;

I tore at the buttons. He let me tear at them, let me wrestle the sleeves from his arms. I inhaled him right where a white tanktop, whiter than mine, sliced across his sternum. He smelled like fall: brown grass, dead leaves, smoke in the air. My tongue left a trail across that landscape. There were pieces of him—stray hairs, scattered leaves—stuck to my tongue.

He didn't let me get farther than that frayed edge. It was a quick revolution, and before I knew what was happening, I was on my back, and hey, that was his tongue, not mine, clattering around in my mouth, and that was his hand sliding down under my ass, and my hand was fluttering around his waist, not uncertain so much as in suspense. He ground his dick through two layers of denim against the inside of my thigh, up over my belly, back down again. I pulled him even closer, if that was possible, and my hands slid beneath the denim, found another fragile layer of fabric drawn tight over his ass. I grabbed what I could. What was I wearing? Something white, I remembered, that would soon be full of sperm if we didn't get out of these clothes, these degrees of separation.

We weren't talking, but suddenly I felt his throat hum beneath my mouth and he was, I'm sure of it, speaking into me, talking through my mouth, and I pulled back and looked at him and said, "What?"

He breathed. "*Ora*. Now."

You can imagine how I tried to unbutton his fly, how I wanted nothing between us but our skin and our fur, red and black, slick with sweat and whatever I could smear from my mouth, whatever my dick would gladly drool. You can imagine how I wanted to say no and then say yes, to feel the slide of elastic down my hips and the snap of latex and then, with the same slowness, the same vehemence of his hand, to feel him open my hole with his cock, to feel his mouth suck me in and choke out that little death rattle, straight into the clenched center out of which the rest of me spirals. You can imagine how I wanted to lick my sperm from his skin.

This is what happened instead: he held our hips absolutely still, one hand at the small of my back, the other beneath my ass. We were frozen like that, on the brink, immobilized. He would not let us move. Our cocks were throbbing; our breathing did not get any slower. He locked his eyes on mine; he bit my lip; he shoved his tongue in as far as it would go. And when he stammered, "*Dài*," *come on*, and he drove his crotch into mine, holding me so tight I could never come loose, his eyes lost their focus, and his throat caught, and in that instant his dick heaved up inside his jeans, and I felt something shoot out of him, and I scraped my teeth against his cheek, and I came.

Dài comes from the verb *dare*, to give. It is a command. I am not sure what I can give, not sure what that means. But after the spasms had stopped, and it was just his body, still nearly dressed, on mine, and the curl of his bottom lip had somehow sunk into the side of my mouth, I noticed this: that his arms, beneath me, refused to uncoil, refused to let me go. I know what refusal feels like, but I have never known this kind, the kind that holds on.

That was a little while ago. I will turn this light out soon. If I close my eyes, I can see quick flashes of red. I should close my eyes. Beside me, Marco is sleeping. Later he will wake me up, and maybe I will give.

MY BEST CUSTOMER

ERASTES

"AND SEE TO the horses' feet before you go drinking with your friends," my father's voice caught me up as I made my way across the yard. "I have more tours arranged tomorrow than the rest of the week."

"And you don't want one lame horse to spoil your takings," I muttered in unison as he finished the sentence I'd heard a hundred times that week. I grumbled to the horses all the way through my chores; horses were wonderful things, they listened and listened and didn't interrupt. However annoyed I was at having to manage the stable single-handed since my father's accident, I did the work diligently, made very sure that no little stones were lodged between the shoes and the hooves, fed, watered, and bedded them down before sluicing myself down and running to meet my friends.

We always met in the same bar and, as I slid into the wooden booth, accepting the lager they had ready for me, I was greeted with shouts and accusations of neglect. Marco shouted at me over the din, "We had bets that you wouldn't get here tonight. I told them you wouldn't let us down, that Friday couldn't start until you came. I won!" He waved a handful of lira at me. "Your father no better?"

"The doctor says he should not move for another week," I said sourly, wondering if I would be able to catch up with their jollity, "so I have another full week of driving the pale and the rich around, at least."

Christoph grinned at me. "Beautiful rich, English ladies!" he said, holding his glass up for a toast. "You are lucky, Marco, lucky!"

"Yes, but he sits with his back to them, you idiot." Paulo

laughed, topping up my glass. "It's not as if he can sit and ogle at them all day."

"Nevertheless, it's a job I'd like, sitting on my ass all day and escorting the beautiful ladies to every museum and gallery. I apply for a job now, Marco, when you take over the business."

I laughed along with them, but I didn't reply. For one, I wanted to get as drunk as they were, and I didn't want to tell them that when my father did die, I wouldn't be taking over the business, I'd sell it and head for America. That's where the opportunities were. No more pleasure trips for English nobles and spoiled rich Americans; I planned to start a hansom cab business and line my pockets with gold.

The night passed as all nights with my friends did. A lot of drinking, a little boasting, a great deal of flirting with barmaids before we rolled into the red-light district and split up. I lied, saying I needed an early night, and made my excuses, and as usual they were all pretty drunk so they didn't really care one way or another. Some nights I had actually pretended to enter one of the whorehouses and sneaked out when they had passed on. They didn't suspect that I wasn't interested in women.

They'd never suspected. They were all amorous Italian boys; they thought about women all of the time, the local girls, the tourists, the barmaids. I hardly had to pretend anymore; they just assumed that I went along with them, like I did for everything else. But I didn't. It had been many years since I'd discovered that I didn't feel the same way. Since school, when I had fallen in love with Fr. Visconti, with his huge brown eyes and eyelashes—which were the thickest I'd ever seen—and I knew then. Knew I wanted to kiss his eyelids, to touch that skin. My cock reacted to men, and you couldn't argue with your cock. I'd learned to pretend otherwise, that's all.

Next morning my head was aching from the beer of the night before, but I slid out of bed at cockcrow and got the horses ready. I backed them into the traces, attached the harness, and tied them up before getting into my livery. That livery was the only thing about the job I liked. It was black with silver epaulettes, my father's conceit, and had cost a week's takings. But it was worth every penny. It made the tourists notice us—I heard them asking the tour guides for the "smart carriage with the black and silver uniforms"—and my uniform fit like a glove. The short jacket accentuated my broad shoulders and narrow waist, and the high-waisted trousers fit snugly over my hips and ass, showing off my long legs as I climbed on and off the driver's seat. I had made many a young signorina giggle with her friends behind their fans. With a final look at my appearance from behind, with the smuggest of grins, I slicked my black curls with some water into some semblance of order and clambered up onto the front of the carriage.

I didn't have a booking until ten, but I drove into the hotel district just after eight. Not a lot of my colleagues started this early, but I knew the tourists, they liked to start their pilgrimage around the city's art early and I usually got lucky by just being in the right place at the right time. That morning was no exception and being early paid off. The doors to one of the hotels opened and a fair-haired man emerged, holding the door open for a young lady and an older lady, both in voluminous skirts. I sat up straight as a ramrod, knowing that my rig looked cleaner and brighter than any of the others, and I wasn't disappointed as the man gestured to the porter of the hotel and I was called forward from the waiting line.

Leaping down from the seat, I unlatched the steps and waited for the gentleman to see his lady into the carriage, but the girl stopped and looked pale. She spoke words I didn't understand, and the older lady and the man chattered for a moment or two, then the two ladies walked back into the hotel.

The man watched them go, with a strange expression on his face, then surprised me by stepping into the carriage. The porter ordered me to take the man to the Vatican and wait for him. I was hired for the day. I tried to explain I had bookings, but the porter spoke to the man and a price was agreed upon that more than covered my lost bookings, so I drove away with a grin.

The day was the easiest I'd spent, the easiest money I'd made. I'd never had a customer all day before, and certainly not one who was so silent. After the Vatican, he visited the Forum, the Coliseum, the catacombs, all the normal spots, but at most of them, he didn't even get out of the carriage. It was as if he was checking them off in his mind, like a lot of tourists seemed to do. He ate lunch in a sidewalk café, while I fed and watered the horses, and it was unnerving that every time I looked over at him, he was looking over at me.

He was very tall, broad and muscular and very pale, the sort of paleness that I had always been scornful of, but his face was fascinating. Eyes that slanted upward like a wolf. His hair was shining and sandy, very short, unlike my shoulder length curls. But his mouth entranced me. It was wide, with slim lips, redder than I'd seen on a man before, and he was always smiling, as if sharing a secret with no one.

The lamps were being lit along the Via Appia as the day drew to a close. I looked forward to getting home, or perhaps coming out again with the small buggy to take couples to the theater. My passenger spoke to me in stilted Italian, and named a hotel I'd never heard of, in a street that I knew, in an unfashionable part of the city. I turned to look at him in surprise to find him sitting on the seat nearest me, and in the dusk his hand had moved to my ass, leaving me in no doubt of his intentions. His daring, and his beautiful teasing mouth made my decision, and I nodded at him, my cock stirring in my pants.

My mouth was dry as he paid the concierge and led the way through the narrow corridor. My heart was beating so loudly that I thought he must hear it, but he made no sign; simply opened the door to a room at the end and waited for me to enter. I hesitated for just a second, but he held out his hand, as if I were his lady, and pulled me in, gently, closing the door behind us.

In a second he had pulled me into his arms, his mouth against my neck, rough and prickly with stubble and muttering words I didn't understand, his voice hoarse and muffled. His hands pulled at the fastenings of the jacket, not managing them, so I took over, while his hands slid around my waist and over my ass, cupping my cheeks and pulling me up and close. He was as hard as I, and the feel of his erection through cloth made me gasp with surprise. I had made this beautiful man hard. I had given him that pleasure. He wrenched the jacket from me and dropped to his knees, sliding his hands up inside my vest and kissing my stomach as he unbuttoned my pants.

I was startled; I hadn't expected this. The one other experience I'd had had been rough and brutal: an alley, another driver, and hard callused hands on my cock while he pounded my ass, scraping my face against the bricks, giving me bruises I had to explain away at home. As much as I wanted this man's cock inside me, his hands on me, I did not expect this gentleness, this worship. As he pulled my pants and underpants to the floor I attempted to kneel with him, but he was too fast; he swallowed my cock to the root like a man starved, his eyes closed, his pale lashes fluttering on his cheeks, and I cried out in utter joy, as I came so quickly that my cheeks burned red with shame. He shamed me further by sucking down my seed, his eyes still closed, his nose buried in my dark curls, then suddenly he stood and stepped back, leaving my cock cold and my knees weak.

I gathered my mind in embarrassment and bent to pull my pants back on, thinking he'd want me to go, but he laughed, drawing my startled glance. He closed the distance between us again, picked me up easily in his strong arms, and literally threw me onto the bed. I was tangled up in my clothes, annoyed at being so manhandled, and swore at him, but his smile didn't falter. He pulled my boots off, kissing the insteps of my feet, doing such things I'd only heard of my friends dreaming of doing to their lady loves. Gently he removed my clothes and then stood to disrobe, almost teasingly, never taking his pale blue eyes from mine. His skin was like porcelain, his broad chest free of hair, his hips ridged and high, and his cock saluted me, long and slender with a delicious curve. He didn't move, but stood there, drinking me in with his eyes until I blushed again and he laughed. "*Prego*," he said, with an appalling accent, nudging his hips forward.

I'd never done what he was asking me but I had long wanted to, so I crawled toward him and sat on the edge of the bed, taking his cock in my hands, pulling the hood back and touching the tip of it with my tongue. My eyes flickered upward to gauge his reaction and saw his eyes close in pleasure; Thus encouraged, I licked again and again, learning the shape of him, lapping from root to tip, loving the unusual taste, musky salty but not unpleasant. Remembering what he'd done to me, I sucked his cock into my mouth. It was too long to take in completely but I did my best, my hands gaining confidence, daring to smooth over his flat belly and reaching up to explore his chest. As I touched his nipples, deep groans rumbled in his chest, so I rolled them gently in my fingers, knowing how I liked that when I brought myself off at night.

He pulled out and lifted me again, placing me back on the bed, and gestured me to roll over, which I did. I waited for him to breach me, spreading my legs as wide as I could. He slid down, his lips ghosting over my shoulders and back as he went. I started in shock as I felt his hands on my ass, pulling my cheeks apart, and then felt the slick wetness of his tongue laving my cleft. My cock responded with a jolt—as if it were directly connected to the flesh he was licking and kissing—and I cried out to God as I felt his tongue enter me. It was nothing I had experienced, nothing I had ever expected. It seemed wrong, but so utterly delicious that I never wanted it to stop. He had me thrashing on the bed, biting the pillow to stop myself from crying out too loud, before he replaced his tongue with one finger, then another, stretching patiently, all the time talking to me in English. Hardly any of it I understood, except "beautiful," and "yes."

Finally, when I thought that I would destroy the pillow with my teeth, I felt his cock, warm and blunt and damp as he rubbed it up and down my cleft, and I pushed back in happy encouragement. He wrapped his arms around my hips, pulling my ass up, and slid in, inch by inch, groaning and grunting. It burned a little, but as gentle as he was, it felt so good. I could feel the drip of his sweat on my back. I was so eager now that I wriggled like a fish on a hook, I wanted him to fuck me so badly. He obliged, so slowly at first I thought I would die from it, but gradually building up speed until I could feel his balls slapping against my own. I was gasping in counterpoint, waves of pleasure building from groin to stomach in fluttering spasms and back again to center in my tightening balls. He grasped my cock and stroked me in a steady rhythm to match his as I propped myself up on my elbows and rose to meet him with every thrust. I knew he was close as he would stop suddenly, then push once, twice, three times with a "mmmm" that melted me somewhere inside. He seemed happy enough to do this forever and my cock and ass were not arguing. This man could have anything he wanted, he could stick that glorious rod anywhere he liked if it gave him pleasure.

He fell forward, kissing my shoulders and neck, and pumped full-speed, jabbing at me with his hips, doing something new, something wonderful that made my balls explode, spattering the bed, his hand, and the headboard with my come. I collapsed onto the bed, unable to support our weight any longer, and let him pound me, the mattress squeaking so loud that I was sure we would be arrested. He gave a guttural cry, which sounded like a name, and I felt my guts fill with his warmth, felt his cock twitch as it died inside me.

I was expecting him to get up, to get dressed, leave his little whore alone, with a fistful of lira, but he didn't. He gathered me in his arms and kissed me for the first time, his mouth warm, salty with the remnants of my seed, his tongue as gentle as the man himself. He ran his palms over my body, as if learning every plane, every curve. I'd never been kissed like that, and my cock even gave a half-hearted twitch which I knew it didn't really mean.

Then he pulled away and said one word in Italian. One word I understood. "Tomorrow," he said.

And I nodded.

THE ACROPOLIS OF LOVE

JOHN SIMPSON

HERE I SAT in first class listening to the landing instructions over the loudspeaker as we prepared to land at Athens International Airport, feeling as excited as a nine-year-old boy on Christmas morning. My plans revolved around seeing all of the usual tourist attractions in order to take in all of the history of this great world-class city. I had waited a long time to take my vacation to Greece, a place I had always dreamed about. I had heard the land was beautiful, full of history and good looking Greek men. I'm not quite sure what intrigued me the most: the history or the men!

As I cleared customs and immigration, I hailed a taxi and asked to be taken to the Divani Caravel Hotel in center city Athens. I chose the hotel because it was near embassy row and the city's main square. From there you could see the changing of the guard for the Greek parliament.

The young bellboy who took me to my room was typical of the Greek look: black hair, dark features, and a refined youthful face.

"If there is anything I can do for you while you are here, please let me know," Demetri said in almost flawless English.

I tipped him, smiled, and watched his ass as he left the room, smiling as he turned to close the door. If that was the ass of a typical Greek boy, I was going to love Athens! I unpacked and lay down for an hour to take a short rest before venturing out into the city. I wasn't the least bit hungry, at least for food. I drifted off to sleep thinking of Demetri and what it would be like to share my bed with him.

✦

I WOKE UP over two hours later, got up, showered, and went down to the restaurant to have something to eat before my first sojourn into the city. The waiters in the hotel restaurant were as handsome as the bellboy, and my server got a nice tip for his attentive service and smoldering good looks. I finished and headed out on my own, preferring to walk rather than take a taxi or bus. Since I was near the square I headed there first.

The main square was packed with people enjoying the warm weather in the early afternoon. Men walked in pairs and singly and women sat along the short concrete wall eating their lunch. The tourists stuck out like a sore thumb as their dress was different and their heads were constantly swiveling to take in all that could be seen. One thing that could be said of most of the men was that they loved wearing black pants or jeans. Everywhere I looked I saw tight butts wrapped in black material. They looked fantastic and since I was not hard on the eyes, I got my share of looks. At twenty-two with blond hair and blue eyes, it wasn't hard to be noticed as being different from the sea of black hair and black eyes. As I sat on the wall a young guy about nineteen sat down beside me and started to talk with me.

"Hello. You are a tourist?" he asked.

"Yes, I'm David, from America," I replied.

"Hello David, I am Feodras, I am glad to meet you."

"Feodras, what an interesting name," I replied. "What does it mean?"

"Nothing special. It only means 'stone or rock' in Greek."

Feodras was very good-looking and like the others, was dressed in black pants and a white shirt open three buttons down to reveal a nice light covering of chest hair. He had a naked sex appeal that was hard to ignore.

"So, you are staying in a hotel here in Athens?"

"Yes, not far from here actually, the Divani," I said as his eyes wandered over my body, coming to rest on my crotch.

"Maybe you would show me your hotel room some time," he said with a smile that left no doubt in my mind that he was looking for more than polite conversation. I was horny and here was a chance to make it with my first Greek man, one who was incredibly handsome. The lustful look he now had in his eyes was overpowering and left me no choice as to what my answer would be.

"I would love to show you my room, when you have the time," I replied coyly.

He grabbed my hand and pulled me to my feet, heading toward my hotel. "I have time now," Feodras said with a smile. "You have certain things in your room or do we need to stop in what you call a drugstore?" he asked.

Of course he meant protection and lube. "Yes, I have what we need," I replied openly as there was no longer any need to hide our intentions. My heart raced as we neared the hotel, with a sexual lust burning in my throat and groin. Here I was, with an extremely beautiful Greek man, headed toward my hotel room to have sex on a warm afternoon. This was the stuff that fantasy was made of and yet I was going to live it.

As we passed the front desk heading toward the elevator, the desk clerk looked at us and smiled and wished us a pleasant afternoon as if he knew we were going to go fuck our brains out. It made me wonder if this was a sight he was used to seeing or if Feodras was regularly seen here at the hotel in the company of male tourists. We passed Demetri in the hallway and he and Feodras exchanged greetings in Greek.

"Do you know him, Feodras?"

"Yes, we used to be lovers last summer."

As the door to my room closed, Feodras turned, grabbed me, and smothered me with a long passionate kiss that included plenty of a tongue that seemed to be searching for gold in my mouth. He literally took my breath away. He moved us toward the king-size bed and pushed me down onto it, once again kissing me with all his passion. He then went to my neck, kissing, licking, and nibbling as he smoothly unbuttoned my shirt and opened my belt. He then pulled my shirt up and off my shoulders and smiled, looking down on my pecs.

"You are as well-built as I thought you would be," he said. "Now let us see if the rest of you matches your beautiful chest."

With that he pulled off my shoes and socks and unbuttoned my jeans, pulling them down, my Calvin's traveling with them, revealing a nice American dick in all its glory. He flung my pants and underwear across the room and slowly removed his shirt, smiling all the time while staring at my prick, which became engorged at the intensity of his gaze. His chest was well-defined, with a light covering of black hair between his pecs leading to a treasure trail that went beneath his belt buckle. I was rock-hard watching him drop his pants, revealing a very European style of white underwear that showed off his basket with perfection.

I sat up and reached for him and pulled him toward my face. I wanted to drop his shorts so I slipped my fingers into the waistband, and as I rolled them down over his tight ass, a nice cock was revealed with two large balls hanging low, nestled in a patch of black pubic hair. I turned him around to set sight on what I knew would be a breathtakingly beautiful ass, and I was not disappointed. There, directly in front of my face, was the magnificently sculpted ass of a nineteen-year-old Greek male. My mind flashed back to all of the stories of ancient Greece and what the social norm was regarding such a beautiful youth.

"Incredible, Feodras. Your ass is beautiful—it takes my breath away."

"David, it is yours to enjoy for this moment in time," he replied.

I turned him around once more and found his cock fully erect at about eight inches. It too was beautiful and I immediately went down on it, taking it all the way to the base. As I slowly withdrew his cock from my mouth, a soft moan escaped his lips. As I slowly went down on him again, I fondled his voluptuous balls with my right hand while stroking his magnificent ass with my left. Feodras ran his hands through my hair, moaning and sighing with delight as I sucked harder, wanting to give him the best blow job he had ever had. Finally Feodras started to pump my mouth, shoving his cock all the way in as his balls bounced off my chin. I felt the juices in my own balls start to churn as the sexual heat was turned up quickly with this face fucking action.

I pushed him back far enough so that his cock fell out of my mouth. I moved him around onto the bed and lay back myself. At this, Feodras cupped my balls and started to lick my shaft. His tongue moved ever so slowly over the head of my dick, around the head and down the underside. He then took each ball, one at a time, and sucked gently on them, which drove me wild. His tongue went below my balls to that very sensitive strip of skin between them and my asshole as it probed the area skillfully. At this point, I wanted him to go all the way and eat my ass out as it quivered at the thought of his beautiful face buried deep inside. As if to read my mind, he lifted up both of my legs and pushed them back and over my shoulders, exposing my asshole to whatever he had in mind.

I felt his burning hot tongue lick each of my ass cheeks, working slowly toward my crack. Once there, he licked up and down the crack, soaking the area with his saliva. When I could not stand it any longer, I urged him to eat my ass out.

With that command, he spread my ass cheeks wide apart and drove his tongue deep into the recess of my ass, sending me into a frenzy of lust and sexual pleasure. After seeing my reaction, Feodras swung around on top of me with his cock hanging over my mouth and bent his head over and back into my butt hole where he continued to lick, nibble, and eat my hole while I stared up at his magnificent cock and balls. As he continued to eat away, I took his hard cock into my mouth and started to suck it as earnestly as he was eating. Just as I thought I might come from the outstanding rim job I was receiving, my momentum was interrupted by a knock on the door. Feodras removed his tongue from my ass and rolled over onto the bed. My legs dropped down and I yelled at the door, "Who is it?"

"Room service, sir," came the reply.

"I didn't order any room service, please go away!"

"But sir, the other gentleman did order room service," the disembodied voice said.

I looked over at Feodras with a questioning look on my face and said, "What the fuck is he talking about?"

"I'll get the door, David, just you stay hard," he replied with a leer.

I was becoming alarmed at what might be happening when the door opened and in walked Demetri, with a big smile on his face and a bulge in his pants. I looked at Feodras who also had a huge smile on his face.

"When we passed in the hallway, I told him to join us in twenty minutes. You don't mind, do you?" he asked.

I could not believe my eyes as Demetri swiftly took off his clothes and revealed an even larger cock and tighter ass than Feodras had displayed.

"No, I don't mind. I really wanted to see that nice ass of yours, Demetri."

Demetri knelt down beside the bed, bent his head over, and started to suck my now limp cock back to its former state of a couple of minutes ago. As Demetri continued to give excellent head, Feodras climbed up onto my chest, shoved his cock into my mouth, and started to face-fuck me once again. The sensation was incredible as Feodras slowly rocked his cock in and out of my mouth while twisting my nipples ever so nicely. I was once again in pure lustful glee as these two beautiful Greek boys worked my cock and mouth together. Feodras grabbed the back of my head, lifting it up slightly, and started to slam-fuck my face, running his cock in and out of my mouth at an ever quickening pace. Demetri had switched to licking and sucking on my balls while jacking my cock with his hand. I felt an explosion of come starting to work its way up and I gave a signal to stop to both boys.

As I lay there for a few moments to let myself cool off a bit, Demetri started to suck Feodras's cock as I stared at Demetri's beautiful ass. I wanted to fuck Demetri as much as I wanted to fuck Feodras. I was pretty sure that Demetri was a bottom, but was uncertain about Feodras. I finally reached out and started to play with Demetri's ass, including massaging his asshole. He reacted instantly by grinding his ass into my finger as Feodras smiled and nodded at me as if to say, you got it!

I wanted to suck Demetri's cock as well and got on my back and wiggled my way between his legs as he sucked Feodras's cock. I started by licking and then sucking the balls that hung in my face like two ripe plums. They had a salty taste from his working his shift and then coming to the room. I finally went down on his big dick and sucked with a hunger for cock that was reaching a critical point with me. When I pulled off his cock, I turned over and went for Feodras's balls and licked them as Demetri continued to suck his cock. This drove Feodras wild and not soon after, he threw us both off his cock and balls.

Demetri then turned me onto my stomach and buried his face in my ass and ate me out as well as Feodras had done just minutes before. I moaned and found myself drifting off to that place of ecstasy that only getting my ass eaten out sends me to. I felt Demetri's tongue stop and felt it replaced at once by Feodras who continued the eating job that was bringing me so much sexual pleasure. My cock was rock hard underneath me and I wanted to come so badly. After a few moments, I felt a finger slide up my spit-soaked ass and felt my prostate being massaged by Feodras. I was truly in heaven at the touch and feel of Feodras so far up my ass; it made me want to get fucked by the entire Greek army.

"Do you like this, David?" he asked

"Yes, and I am a top!" I exclaimed in delight.

"Would you like me to make love to your beautiful ass with my cock?"

I didn't even have to think for a moment when I answered, "Hell yes, please!"

With that I heard the ripping open of the condom package and turned my head to see Demetri putting on the rubber for Feodras. Demetri then got the lube and poured some on Feodras' cock as well as a glob on my asshole. Demetri worked the lube up my ass and I squirmed with the pleasure of the sensation.

Feodras rolled me over on my back and lifted my legs up and over my shoulders once again. He then gently placed the head of his dick at the entrance of my well-eaten ass and began to push. It didn't take much, as I was well primed for a good fucking. It wasn't long before I felt Feodras's cock slide past the hole and up my ass by at least eight inches. It felt incredible! Feodras started to fuck me slowly at first, while looking deep into my eyes. His beautiful black eyes were twinkling with pleasure as he rode my ass, making me his bitch for an hour. I felt his balls slap against me each time he drove his hard cock into my seldom-fucked ass. Demetri sat next to us and then swung around and dropped his cock into my mouth so that I was getting fucked both anally and orally at the same time.

I could not believe the multitude of sensations that were coursing through my body. Feodras was able to hit my prostate gland with each thrust as Demetri drove his cock down my throat in unison with Feodras. Finally Demetri pulled his cock out and lay next to us, watching my expert fucking by this Greek god. I heard myself saying to Feodras, "Fuck me, fuck me hard, Feodras, and slam it into me stud, please!"

With my urging, the pace of the ass fucking picked up speed and I felt a constant fast rhythm of pounding that I had just begged for. This went on for another five minutes, then all of a sudden he stopped and pulled out. He flipped me over and pulled me to the edge of the bed, lifting my ass up in the air. He drove his still hard cock back into my ass and continued fucking me like a bitch while standing and throwing harder thrusts from this new position. My ass was starting to tell me that the pounding was taking a toll as the tingling became a little more painful and a little less pleasurable, but still I took the pounding. I wasn't going to stop this man from getting what he wanted. He wasn't going to see this American begging for him to stop.

Finally, I heard him begin to moan louder and louder, with his breath becoming shallower and shallower, when all of a sudden he thrust his cock deep into my ass and held it there as he came, filling the rubber with his come. Feodras groaned and groaned as spurt after spurt erupted from his prick into my ass. Then all of a sudden he collapsed onto my back and we fell flat on the bed, as I listened to his heavy breathing in my ear.

Slowly, I felt his cock start to soften and as it did, he began its withdrawal from my well fucked ass until it popped out altogether. Feodras rolled over and I saw that the condom was full of bright white come, which actually leaked out onto his cock as he rolled the rubber off his dick.

"Now I know why your name means rock or stone. Your cock was as hard as a rock the entire time you were fucking and sucking me," I said.

"You are right, my friend, my cock stays hard until I tell it I am done with it for now!"

As Feodras sat down in a chair close to the bed, Demetri said, "Now it is my turn to get fucked, sir."

I looked at Demetri and smiled and said, "You're damn right boy!" I heard Feodras laugh as Demetri retrieved another rubber and the lube. I was still stiff myself, and Demetri put the rubber on my cock and lubed it up. He then put a gob of lube on his asshole and asked, "What position do you want me in?"

Having just had the hell fucked out of me, I decided to take the lazy route to coming and told him, "Ride my cock like a cowboy," as I pointed to my cock.

Demetri smiled and climbed onto my lap, easing his ass down on my cock. His ass was tight and I could feel the heat it generated as it surrounded my hard-on. He began to ride slowly at first and while doing so played with my nipples, which I truly love. I looked over at Feodras and found him hard again, slowly stroking his cock as he watched his friend ride my dick. As Demetri picked up the pace of his downward thrusts, he started to jack his cock and it was plain to me that he planned on coming all over my chest. I had no problem with that whatsoever.

As the pace quickened even further, I felt my balls starting to churn a load of come for what I knew would be an explosive climax. Demetri noticed that fact on my face and quickened his jack off pace so that we could come together. As he slammed his beautiful tight ass down on my fuck stick, I heard Feodras moan and saw him shoot strings of hot come into the air, which hit the bed and my chest. Demetri started to come all over my face and chest, and with that I blew my load up his ass. Stream after stream of hot come hit my face and chest from both Demetri and Feodras, as I felt myself continue to unload into the boy's ass that was giving me the ride of my life.

Finally, I was the last one to finish coming and I felt drained of all energy. Demetri pulled off my cock and it fell down on my stomach with a loud *twap*. I looked down on my chest and saw a sea of come, not to mention the come that was dripping off my face. None had gotten into my eyes, thankfully, and I saw Feodras throw a towel at me so that I could wipe off the rivers of come coating my upper body.

As I did that, Demetri rolled off the rubber that was still on my dick and threw it in the wastebasket to join the one taken off Feodras. Demetri then took a fresh towel and wiped down my cock and a couple places that I had missed.

When everyone was all cleaned up, we just smiled at each other. We were still naked and made a very sexy sight to anyone who might have caught a look at us. They were two very beautiful men and I would not forget them anytime soon.

"What can I say, guys, but thank you? What an incredible sexual experience you two just gave me. You both managed to hit all of my buttons and I could not have asked for anything else," I said.

As Demetri and Feodras got dressed, I continued to admire their beauty and cherished the gift they had given me. If I remembered Athens, Greece, for nothing else, it would be for these two men and this afternoon.

PRAGUE PASTIMES

MORRIS MICHAELS, JR.

HE WAS STANDING by the side of the old church on a street not far from the Old Town in Prague, just off one of the main avenues in the New City neighborhood. He had been to concerts in this church before and the last time remembered noticing the large rainbow painted on the door of the building behind it. There was no sign identifying what establishment was announcing its rainbow-hued presence and the door had been locked, at least on that prior occasion. *It must have been the year before*, he mused, *in the spring.*

He had been coming to Prague two or three times a year for meetings, going on five or six years now, but this was the first time he'd felt free enough to take some time for himself. Always here on business, he had always been too busy working (or so he told himself) and had never been able to get away for some more private moments in this most beautiful of fairy-tale cities. He had memorized the Old Town and the Castle areas like the back of his hand, always becoming the de facto "tour guide" for his colleagues who were in the city for the first time at their various meetings. Each time he arrived in Prague—that first view of the cathedral as the taxi drove in from the airport—always felt like he was "coming home." But for all his love of the Czech capital, he was always nervous about trying to go out by himself to the gay neighborhoods and pubs, afraid he would misread the various cultural signals that might be so different from those at home in New York—or might not, he had also always told himself—as well as misunderstand the languages used to negotiate any kind of tryst with one of the locals. Being gay in a foreign place was just too complicated. Alas.

The second time he had come here, he had tried to go to a small pub listed in the gay section of his tour book. It was described as a folksy, neighborhood hangout near the St. Agnes's Cloister by the river. He had set out after dinner, making his excuses to his colleagues and cutting short the usual after-dinner drinking at their favorite pub behind the Our Lady of Tyn Church (with its amazing towers, buttresses, and lacey stonework that made it look more like the fragile sculpture of a tree caught in an ice storm than a real, solid thirteenth-century stone church). He had taken the address and a detailed map, knowing that most streets in that part of town did not have street signs posted. He had gotten to the right vicinity easily enough but then spent about ten to fifteen minutes wandering, peering in the dark at both the map and the numbers on the buildings, getting just a bit frustrated, when he realized that he was standing right in front of the pub he had been looking for. On a back street, at the corner, it was a cheery beacon of light in an otherwise deserted-looking, dark, foreboding intersection. He went in.

It looked like any other friendly neighborhood pub. A handful of tables were occupied, mostly by men, in groups of two or three. The waiter behind the bar, who was wiping off the counter, smiled cheerfully, and said something he didn't quite catch. "One beer, please," he said, holding up one finger and looking around as he decided where to park himself. He figured he would just hang out, soak up the local atmosphere, and be glad to simply be in a gay place for once in his travels. He wouldn't refuse to talk to anyone if he was approached, but mainly he just wanted to sit and be here. Finally.

The waiter repeated himself, this time in English. "Sorry, sir," he explained. "We are closed." He shrugged, apologetically, and smiled again.

"Closed?" The visitor pulled himself up short. There seemed to be plenty of people here. What was going on?

"Yes, sir. Sorry, sir. Closed."

"Okay. Thank you." The man nodded to the waiter, noticed several of the patrons seemed to be taking all this in with a rather amused attitude, and left.

As he returned to the hotel, he tried to sort out what had just happened. He, a stranger, had entered a gay pub and had been immediately informed that the bar was closed. Had the fact that a stranger, someone unknown to the neighborhood folk, had intruded been looked on as a possible threat? Was this a leftover from the communist era? Had the waiter told him the pub was closed in order to protect the regular clientele? It also occurred to him that although there were patrons sitting in the café, the plates were all empty and most of the eating seemed finished. Even the beer glasses had only been half-full, at most. Although it seemed a little early, maybe the establishment really was closed for newcomers and the people there had all been in the process of finishing their drinking, paying their tabs, and about to head out into the night themselves. Either explanation seemed plausible.

On another occasion, he had used the Internet to get the address of a leather bar in Prague and had set out for it, up the hill past the Strahov monastery. But knowing that leather bars generally tend to be in dicey neighborhoods, and not comfortable enough with his few Czech words, he had decided to forgo getting lost in a bad neighborhood looking for a leather bar that might not even be there anymore. After all, he had been misled by Web sites announcing that the National Gallery's collection of medieval Bohemian art was up near the castle, next to St. George's Basilica, when in fact it had all been moved down to the St. Agnes's Cloister at least four years earlier. Even if he got himself to the right place on that dark, blustery Saturday mid-March night, who knew if the bar would even be there as advertised? Once again, he gave up.

But now, this time, finally he had gotten his nerve up to actually have a gay experience in this, his most favorite European city. He had looked up "gay Prague" in more than a few guidebooks and Internet searches and had compiled a list of about half a dozen bars, cafes, discos, bookstores, and a bathhouse that seemed to be up to date. He had taken spare minutes to locate the ones that were within reasonable walking distance of his hotel and to make sure he knew both how to get to them and how to get back to the hotel; given his terrible sense of direction, he relied on memorized routes and landmarks to navigate—even at home! He wanted to be sure he didn't get himself lost in the night, if he actually got up the nerve to try to visit one of the gay establishments he had so carefully researched.

But the bathhouse was open Sunday afternoons, as well as weeknights. The perfect solution! He could get there in the daylight and it would probably be no more than dusk when he came out. Whew! He heaved a sigh of relief when he realized that he would be able to get to the bathhouse, which the reviews said was quite a sex club, and would only have to risk getting lost in the daylight.

So here he was, next to the church on a Sunday afternoon, looking at the door with the rainbow stripes, which he now knew was the entrance to the bathhouse. He walked up to the door, pulled it open, and entered.

He found himself at the top of a short flight of stairs which he descended, then he walked down a short hall and turned left. There was the counter with the cashier and towels. The cashier was an older man, not much older than himself, but with a shaved head and rippling muscles clearly visible under his black T-shirt. A Czech version of Mr. Clean from the American television commercials of his youth. He caught his breath with anticipation.

"One, please."

He paid the cashier the price requested, only slightly more than what the guidebooks had listed, and was given both a lock and a towel and pointed toward the locker room across the narrow hall. The cashier, though of few words, seemed friendly enough and only gruff enough to keep the "line" moving. Other men came down the steps and up to the cashier's window, not in a steady stream but a fairly constant flow of individuals and small groups of two or three friends coming together for an afternoon of "exercise."

He found a locker in the locker room, put all his clothes into it, and locked it. He wrapped the towel around his waist, slipped the key on its rubber band around his forearm, took a deep breath, and walked out into the bathhouse proper.

He found himself in the bar area, a nice clean area with easy chairs and small tables around the edge of the room as well as bar stools along the bar itself. It was well lit, if a bit plain, and several chairs were occupied by men sitting in their towels and drinking. Several "types" were present—one older dark-haired guy with a goatee who was talking to a younger clean-shaven blond, a slightly overweight bald man smoking a cigarette, a muscular well-built student chatting with a thinner, hairier version of himself. Another deep breath. This afternoon looked very promising indeed.

Off the bar area was a whirlpool and two small rooms which served as sauna and a steam rooms. There was also a narrow staircase to his left. The whirlpool seemed full with a variety of guys, judging from the heads bobbing along the side of the pool. The water was deep and given the intense churning of the steaming waves he couldn't see anything below the occupants' chins. Although some of the guys had their arms stretched out along the edge of the pool, it was impossible to tell where the other guys' hands were or what they might be up to. A few men lingered around the pool, waiting for a spot to open up or taking turns in the steam and sauna rooms. Everyone had their towels on as they stood around, but whenever someone got up from the pool or someone else took his place, the towels were draped over racks and dicks and balls swung free—more than he had ever seen in one place before. Low-hangers or sacs pulled up tight next to the cock, as well as cocks thick and long or short and thin, were all tantalizingly within reach. He licked his lips with anticipation.

He went downstairs to look around. A number of small rooms were arranged in a long labyrinth of hallways, all of which led to one large room with a large screen on one wall. Porn was playing on the screen and a number of men were lounging on the bleachers opposite the screen. As the young farmers and lumberjacks cavorted on screen, discovering the joys of nature, the audience was also engaged in discovering a variety of joys: two guys were making out and fingering each others' nipples, one was bent over another's crotch and eagerly sucking, while one guy sitting off to the side was gently massaging his own cock and balls. Another stood by the doorway, taking in the whole scene at once, his pumped arms crossed over his thickly furry torso and his cock semi-erect as he carefully surveyed the panorama before him. The visitor went back upstairs, electricity racing through his body as he brushed against the man in the doorway. The man turned and watched the American as he climbed the steps.

He returned to the whirlpool area upstairs. One man, a "dirty blond" in his late twenties or early thirties and well built, was just climbing out of the water. Rivulets poured off him and splashed on the tile floor as he stood by the towel rack and dried his hair. Smaller drops slowly went winding down the muscular folds of his torso, finding their way wherever gravity pulled them, caressing the younger man's skin with pauses as well as sudden lurches downward. One drop hung suspended on the tip on the man's cock for just an instant longer than the American thought possible, then dropped onto the floor and exploded into a thousand smaller prisms. The man held the towel in one hand and casually walked past the American into the steam room behind them.

The American paused a moment. Did he want to follow the younger man into the steamy darkness or take his place in the whirlpool? Almost without consciously thinking it through, he found himself hanging his towel on the rack and climbing into the crowded pool. The steaming, churning water rushed up his thighs as he descended the underwater steps and steadied himself on the railing. The surging water sucked his balls down into their waves as he felt all his fear and nervousness melt into the comfortable-on-the-edge-of-too-hot water. He felt a tangle of legs or arms, he wasn't sure which, as he pushed against the waves to the other side of the pool, to the recently vacated spot he had his eye on. He managed to get there without tripping over any limbs and sat down.

The water raced up his descending body, burying him up to the neck like everyone else in the pool. The pulsating heat caressed him and he stretched out his arms along the edge of the pool, behind the backs of those next to him, as he stretched out his legs into the center of the current. The other legs ("Attached to which faces?" he wondered) which had parted for him to walk through again made room for him, this time enfolding his into the tangle of flesh and bone under the water. He closed his eyes, leaning his head back against the edge of the pool, and sighed contentedly. It didn't take more than a moment or two for one or two feet to begin to nudge his and for someone's toes to begin rubbing along the bottom of his foot. He sighed again, even more contentedly, and sank deeper into the water, just barely keeping his nose above the splashing water. He kept a good grip along the edge of the pool so as to insure he didn't slide completely under the water.

A hand began to cautiously caress his thigh, sliding gently up and down the inside of his right knee. Meeting no resistance, the hand became more daring, slowly working its way up his inner thigh, closer and closer to his crotch, and finally actually reaching his balls. The hand paused a moment, gently massaging the inner thigh next to and under his balls; nudging his torso forward ever so slightly, the American invited the hand to massage his balls as well, which it did with gentle gusto.

Opening his eyes barely a crack, he stole a look over to his right to see who it was that seemed to be taking such an interest in him. His effort to not be obviously looking, coupled with the steam and splashing of the whirlpool, made it difficult to discern the details of his suitor. From what he could make out, the man was about his age and had a goatee as well as a pleasant smile. And a pair of closed eyes. Both men were sliding deeper into their own world, even as they were surrounded by the others in the pool.

The hand continued to massage his balls and began to work its way up his increasingly stiff dick under the bubbling waves. The hand momentarily brushed the inner thigh of his other leg as well, but it was evidently too hard to reach or at an awkward angle because the hand quickly returned its attention to his now completely erect cock. Engulfing the organ in a fist, the hand slid up and down a couple of times and then paused.

The man looked over at his neighbor. The neighbor was looking at him now, as well, and continued to smile pleasantly. His eyes were blue, the goatee and hair a gentle reddish-blond fading into gray-white and the torso—what could be seen now that the neighbor was sitting upright in the pool—was in good shape, with a moderate covering of silky, dripping wet hair.

The neighbor spoke a word that the man couldn't quite make out, partly because of the foreign language, partly because of the thunder of the water in his ears, and partly because of the thunder of his own heart pounding. The man sat up as well. The neighbor just tipped his head toward the stairs, answering the questioning look on the man's face without a word. Both stood.

The neighbor's body was beautiful. Carefully sculpted, but not overdone, muscles gave a firm shape and contour to the flesh. The dripping hair was confined pretty much to the neighbor's chest, although he certainly didn't shave his body either. His butt was firm and round, pouring off water as the he stood. As the two men exited the pool, more than one of those remaining smiled knowingly as they witnessed men who spoke no common language, other than desire, go through the familiar dance of finding each other and connecting under the waves. Two more men who had been standing near the pool and who seemed to be locals who knew each other—as the man noticed they had been speaking together—entered the pool and took the two newly vacant spaces. The water swallowed their blond physiques as they laughed and collapsed into the current, their cocks already half-hard.

The neighbor seemed to have been to the bathhouse before. Grabbing their towels, he led the man directly to one of the rooms downstairs and closed the door. The towels, which had only been held in one hand by each of them, barely concealed the erections that had softened just a whisper since emerging from the pounding heat of the whirlpool. The neighbor dropped to his knees.

He took the man's balls and held them gently, admiring them. Then he slowly sucked one of the nuts into his mouth, looking up and keeping one eye on the man's face as he kept the other on his prize. As he continued to hold the ball sac, he scratched under the scrotum and with his other hand reached up to tug the man's nipple. Electricity ran throughout the man's body, bridging all these points of contact. He shuddered with delight. His cock sprang to full attention again, the blood surging through its veins just as it pounded in the man's ears. His attention to the man's balls intensified, shifting one into his mouth and then the other, followed by the first again. He nibbled the sac itself, the gentle nips and tugs of his teeth firing ecstasy to the man's brain. He even twisted his head and bit under the sac; the man bent his knees and pushed himself down onto that eager mouth, and the tongue darted along the edge of his asshole. This had turned into a better afternoon than he could have ever hoped for!

The neighbor's mouth slid forward again, then up, and began to lick the length of the man's dick. An occasional nip or tug on the head sent an extra ripple of delight up the man's back, and then the mouth descended, swallowing the dick in a single dive. A moan escaped the man's slightly parted lips, as he propped himself up by the elbows against the walls of the narrow room which, he now realized, didn't even have a bed or couch in it. The mouth began to slide up and down his cock, the tongue playing with his piss hole. Warm, wet saliva replaced the warm waves of the pool upstairs and the lips folded around the cock, as firm as any fist could have ever pumped it upstairs. The man's hips rocked forward involuntarily. Even if he had wanted to prolong the joys of the afternoon, he would have been unable to resist the call of nature to respond with the same eagerness of the mouth.

The neighbor's hands began to caress the back of the man's legs, gently at first and then more powerfully assisting the man's hips, helping him to balance as he rocked there in that narrow room, in the basement of a bathhouse off a side street in the most glorious, fairy-tale capital of Central Europe. The neighbor held the man's ass firmly but lovingly, pushing the man forward, gulping more and more of the cock, down to its hairy base. The neighbor's whiskers scratched the man's thighs in a delightful way, harder and then even harder. His hips rocked, one long continuous moan drawled out of him from somewhere deep within—exactly from where, he wasn't sure—and the neighbor's lips and tongue more greedily slurped up and down the muscular pole before him. His knees began to hurt but he didn't care. This nervous American man was one of the most delicious he had ever encountered in the bathhouse. A little moan of pleasure escaped from him as well, in spite of himself.

A familiar tingle began to rise in the man's balls. He pitched himself forward more forcefully, now grabbing onto the head of the man kneeling before him and pulling the mouth down his cock as the neighbor's hands pushed the man's ass forward. Pushing, pulling, moaning—and from inside now came the unmistakable surging, not of whirlpool waves, but of another steaming current that burst out of the man and down the neighbor's throat as they both rocked and moaned in unison.

It took a few moments for them both to regain their composure and to want to even begin to extricate themselves from the tangle of tongue and cock, hands, hips, and ass that they had gotten themselves into. The man finally withdrew his now spent cock from the neighbor's mouth, a thin strand of pearl-like, glistening come tracing the path of the man's cock in the air. The neighbor looked up and smiled.

"*Douche?*" the neighbor asked, in what the man now realized was a German accent.

"Yes," the man answered in English, nodding his agreement. The German stood. He took the American by the hand to lead him upstairs to the showers. Both were truly happy. And both hoped this afternoon might just be beginning.

POLE'S FORESKIN

MICHAEL MURPHY

WARSAW, POLAND. I found myself there at the end of a soccer tournament a few summers ago. That year I was a trainer for a Canadian college team and had the chance to travel with them when I replaced the regular guy. What a beautiful city! Reconstructed after the near-total devastation of World War II, clean new parks were set among restored churches and palaces that reeked of Poland's medieval history. Once a cultural center for Eastern Europe, it still retained much of that old world flavor. I didn't miss fast food restaurants and mini-malls in the least while wandering around the historic sites of a bygone age.

The Wisla River bisects the city, with the western section dominated by the Old Town and its Royal Way, lined with baroque and neoclassical palaces and churches. The Cathedral of St. John and the Palace of Culture and Science both had me suitably enthralled.

But tourism can get you horny, all that walking and then all those art galleries with men painted in all manner of dress and undress. Those medieval dudes knew how to paint a lusty male when they wanted to!

Training a bunch of college soccer players can get you horny too, but I made it a practice of not fooling around with the team. Besides, I was intrigued by the hot Poles all around me. Rich Polish vowels and consonants bombarded me, tantalizing with their unknown messages as the occasional hunky young sandy-haired Pole eyed me while commenting something unintelligible to his just-as-cute buddy. Was he telling his friend how much he wanted to fuck me? Or how he yearned to suck my cock? I could imagine all kinds of nasty things when I didn't understand a word of what was said.

I played the tourist for a few days, then went in search of some sign of gay nightlife.

I found it on a warm Saturday night. In the bowels of the warehouse district, beneath a busy nightclub with pounding Euro-disco music, I discovered an amazing backroom pub, with a maze of small bars, dim rooms, and even a dark room. Getting inside required passing a gauntlet of burly Poles who eyed me suspiciously, then smilingly admitted me after looking at my Canadian passport. Communism had fallen, but I had the distinct impression gay lifestyles were still tidily hidden behind an iron curtain.

As I passed the final pair of bouncer-guards, I once again experienced the little cock-rising thrill of having two hot men look me over, comment to each other slyly in a language I didn't understand, wink, and then pass me on. What had they said? They liked the bulge in my jeans? They wanted to suck me dry? My imagination was going wild by the time I pushed past the last set of doors barring my way into Warsaw's underground gay world.

Men were everywhere, dancing, cruising, and drinking. Awesome! I contented myself with wandering, being jostled and groped, and shouted at in a number of foreign languages, before I realized I'd hit the jackpot. Without intending to, I stumbled into one room crowded with jostling men surrounding a small stage where a spotlight illuminated a dancing, semi-nude male. The pounding Euro-rock beat vibrated through me as I took in the sexy figure who gyrated upon the stage a few dozen meters away.

The dude was young, and fucking cute. Already stripped down to a pair of clinging cotton underwear, his body was soaked in sweat, droplets flying from his muscled torso as he swayed and gyrated to the music. A thatch of thick brown hair above a wide-boned handsome face and lush lips added to his considerable allure. He danced well, seemingly oblivious to the crowd.

I arrived just in time as he completed his striptease within a minute of my arrival. With his eyes half-closed against the glare of the spotlight, he skinned down his cotton boxers and pulled them off over a pair of heavy construction boots. Now, except for those boots he was entirely nude!

I wormed my way up to the front. The dancer thrust his hips forward above the crowd, and we were treated to the sight of his long flopping dick, half-hard and swollen to a substantial girth. I stared at it in awe, and abruptly acute lust. He had a foreskin! The sheath of flesh half-hid his knob, the piss slit just peeking out of that rounded tip.

I was mesmerized by that cock as it flopped from side to side against his strong thighs while he danced. I had never seen an uncut cock in real life, or touched one. Apparently it was more common here in Europe than in my native Canada, but I hadn't been laid on my European tour yet. I was horny as hell. With this fantastic specimen flopping above me in all its glory, my own dick rocketed up in my jeans, eager for satisfaction. I think I actually moaned out loud, although the loud music would have muffled that unconscious sound.

Staring up at him, I thought I caught his eye. He seemed to notice me, although I wasn't sure he could see past the bright light illuminating him. Then, all at once his bobbing dick rose up a bit, still semi-flaccid, but definitely poking out from his crotch. That magical foreskin slid back partially, exposing more of the piss slit and head. A drop of fluid even emerged from that slit. I know I moaned at that steamy vision.

Still staring down at me, as if he really did see me, he did something that excited me beyond belief. He turned around, spread his legs, and crouched down, his head turned back to look at the crowd, and at me.

What a gorgeous ass!

Bent over, each of his rounded butt cheeks were clenched in perfect firmness. His butt crack was wide open, a scant trace of amber hair surrounding a crinkled ring of anal flesh. I gasped and grabbed my own crotch to massage my dick beneath my jeans. I'm sure no one in the crowd noticed; all eyes were glued to the spectacle above us.

This hot Polish stud then performed for us. All that went on before had been only a preliminary for the hottest scene I'd ever personally witnessed.

He flexed one arm across the lower part of his face so that his deep eyes stared back at us and his mouth was hidden. His smooth, broad back tapered down to that perfect butt and wide-spread thighs. His other hand appeared between his thighs to grasp his dangling dick and he began a leisurely stroking of the hanging appendage. The head of that lengthy fuck-bone was still half-hidden by the foreskin as it hung down below his full nut sac. But, as he began to rub it up and down, the foreskin pulled back and the shining helmet emerged. He was covered in sweat from dancing, but that glistening dickhead making its appearance shone with something other than sweat. A clear fluid coated the head, no doubt a liberal oozing of precome.

As he stared back at us, those deep brown eyes half-closed, he stroked his dick into a full erection, although he managed to keep it pointed down to the floor so we could watch it swell and pulse under his slow ministrations. His firm butt cheeks clenched and unclenched as he stroked his cock, and then even that small hole between them began to pulse in time to his cock's beat and the music.

What a show!

Crouched down with his thighs wide apart, he played with his fat cock for an exciting, gut-thrilling ten minutes. The foreskin slid back and forth over the shining head, which I found totally fascinating. I imagined my mouth on it, tasting it, licking at it, biting at the unusual flap of flesh. And I couldn't help but think of driving my fingers up that pulsing butt hole at the same time.

With his eyes still staring back at us, and his biceps flexed across his mouth, he eventually milked a load out of that amazing cock. The tempo of his slow, steady stroking didn't alter, until suddenly his dick expanded and stiffened between his fingers, his asshole clamped tightly, and his butt cheeks clenched while his balls tightened up between those beautiful thighs.

A rocketing geyser of come spewed out from the gleaming helmet of his cock, splattering the stage floor. I creamed my jeans a moment later. My own hand had been playing with my dick and that torrid sight had done me in. I was left moaning when the spotlight went out and the cute Polish dancer disappeared.

I roamed the crowded club for another couple of hours, searching futilely for that sexy Pole. Although I was still burning with lust, I rebuffed everyone who attempted to come on to me. I finally returned to my hotel room and jacked-off to the memory of that amazing dude.

I couldn't help but return to the same hidden club the following night. I was surprised that it was busy on a Sunday night; I wasn't certain it would even be open. It was quieter than the night before, and one could actually move around without constantly embracing a hundred strangers. I found the same room with the stage, but no dancer. I hung around there for a good half hour, and was ready to move on when I felt a hand on my shoulder.

I turned to confront the man of my dreams. There he was, the dancer from the night before. It was definitely him!

As I stared down into his hooded brown eyes, I was too stunned to hear what he was saying. I'm a tall guy, a tad over six-foot-two, and this dude was quite a bit shorter, probably only five-foot-ten or so. I gawked down at him open-mouthed, thinking about the sudden stiffening of my cock in my pants. I realized he was speaking.

I shook my head. "Sorry. No Polish. I speak English, and a little French."

With a concentrated effort I understood the young stud was answering me in English. He wanted to know if I'd seen his show the night before.

"You were standing in the front. I could not mistake you. Tall, handsome, and blond," he said, or at least I guessed he said. He may have been calling me a dog in heat for all I knew, but I decided to translate generously.

"You were awesome. I've never seen anything like that!" I gushed in rapid English. He grinned, straight white teeth around a pair of lush lips. How could it get any better?

He laughed, then spoke to me in his garbled English.

"Come with me. I know a place." He smiled, taking my hand in his. What kind of place did he know? I fucking prayed it was a place to have wild, hot sex.

He dragged me by the hand, his much smaller than mine but firm and strong, leading me through a crowd of men and a maze of rooms. At a dead end, we halted in front of a chain-link gate against a back wall of the warehouse building the bar was beneath.

"I will dance for you again?" He laughed, the loud Euro-music blasting even in this out-of-the-way nook.

I grinned and nodded my acceptance as I released his hand. Travel can be very liberating. No one knows you in a foreign land, no one has any expectations of you, and you may never see any of the people you run into ever again. You can do or say things you rarely would at home for fear of gossip—or whatever.

This is especially true in the sexual arena. I was horned up, and couldn't care less what anyone around me thought. Whatever my Pole wanted to do, I was up for it!

He smiled seductively and began to gyrate, pumping his hips and running his hands up and down his T-shirt-covered torso. Was that ever hot! I glanced around and noticed a half dozen other men passing in and out of the room, some looking our way, but most just meandering through. I looked back to see my new friend already stripping off his shirt, obviously intending to waste little time, which was fine with me. His tight-fitting jeans came off next. His underwear right after. He was naked in front of me in under five minutes of tantalizingly seductive dancing.

"I am Serge!" He laughed, leaning back with his hands entwined in the links of the gate behind him, his hips thrust forward and that incredible dick flopping up and down right in front of me.

"I'm Victor," I mumbled, my attention riveted to that uncircumcised meat bouncing around as he pumped his body in steady rhythm to the electronic music.

I reached out and touched it. Suddenly bold, blocking out mentally the men who were walking past, my entire attention focused on the hot young Pole writhing in front of me. When my trembling hand connected with that long Polish pole, its torrid heat shot right up my arm and into my lungs like an electrical shock. I gasped.

Serge groaned and said something in either English or Polish that I couldn't understand. It hardly mattered. He dropped down, leaning back with his hands above and behind him clutching at the fence. His thighs splayed apart, those same dark construction boots he'd worn the previous night his only remaining clothing.

His dick slowly swelled in my hand. I stared down at it as

my fingers moved over the head, playing with the amazing foreskin that stretched over the gleaming knob. It was silky soft, and quite strange to feel that foreskin sliding up and down. I rubbed my fingertip into the area around the head, feeling drops of lubricant drooling out of the half-hidden piss slit. I tickled that oozing slit, which had Serge groaning and thrusting his hips forward. As I played with his dick it grew stiffer. And fatter, and longer. The foreskin peeled back as the shaft expanded, but I could still move it back and forth, a totally nasty turn-on. I glanced up. Serge's deep eyes were half-shut, his lush lips parted and his tongue tracing them with concentration. He was excited, and he liked what I was doing.

I continued to stroke his stiffening dick, teasing the sensitive cap as it came out of hiding, and working the foreskin up and down. I could still pull that flap up and partially over the hardening dick, but as it grew ever larger it was less and less easy to do. I was spellbound by it, and totally got into stroking that Polish cock and pulling on that Polish foreskin.

"No one plays with it so good as you," Serge moaned in English I thought I understood. His head rolled from side to side as I continued to tease and tickle his bobbing boner. I guessed uncircumcised cocks were common in Poland, and not something that so completely fascinated most other Poles.

I moved in closer and slid my other hand down to his tight ball sac, squeezing the nads as I rubbed his drooling cock. He groaned louder, leaning forward into my hands while his fingers tensed above him, locked around the chain-link fence at his back. Emboldened by the look of pleasure on his face, I slid my hand farther back into the warmth of his wide-spread butt crack. I tickled the perineum lightly then found the puckered asshole right behind. He grunted and sighed as I teased at that opening in time to my fingers stroking his pulsing hard-on.

I was a little shocked to discover he wasn't only sweaty down there, but that he'd greased his hole with something, making it slippery and welcoming. His anal lips quivered and parted at the touch of my fingers, welcoming them inside. I dug two fingers into his asshole, stretching open that pulsing pit.

He gasped out something unintelligible, his entire body

wriggling and grinding as if still dancing, although now he was dancing around my hands working his asshole and his stiff Polish pecker.

That sexy foreskin slid up and down with my strokes, like a fleshy glove. I rammed two fingers deeper into his hot ass pit as I increased my frantic dick-stroking. He huffed and grunted and shoved his body forward, suddenly going rigid all over. Wads of come abruptly blasted me!

The sticky fluid shot in the air, landing on my bare arm right up as far as the biceps. Then it drooled out of his dick all over my hand as he shuddered and almost collapsed. His asshole pulsed around the fingers probing it as he orgasmed.

"Fuck my butt with your big dick, blond stud!" He growled, his voice shaky but his English clearer than ever before. His unsatiated desire was evident in the way his mouth hung open, his tongue still licking his plump lips. I was only too eager to oblige.

He turned around and leaned into the fence, raising his hands to hold on to it. He turned his head around and grinned at me, his thighs spread wide, his ass crack open and inviting.

Incoherent words urged me on. I didn't bother to attempt translating in my head. It hardly mattered what he said now. I knew what he wanted.

His own dick hung down between his muscular thighs, softer now and dripping come. The foreskin was slipping back over the purple, glistening head. I glanced around again, noticing that several guys had stopped and were watching. I didn't give a damn. I stripped off my jeans, almost tripping over my shoes in my haste. I stepped forward and pointed my very hard cock at the hair-ringed anal slot between my dancer friend's big, taut ass cheeks.

I lay my cock along his sweaty crack and began to rub it up and down his moist flesh. The knob poked at the pulsing rim of his hole and I held it there. The hole expanded as he shoved his butt back, as if he wanted nothing more than to swallow it with his puckered anal cavity.

That is exactly what he did. While hanging on to the fence with his hands, he grunted and grimaced as his ass lips parted and surrounded the head of my dick. He kept on going, taking the entire head inside his hot pit, and then sliding his rectal ring right down over the remainder of my fat shaft.

"YES!" He groaned in one loud unmistakable plea, the insistent music punctuating his shout.

I felt overwhelmed by the heat and tightness that gripped my cock. I was all the way inside him, right to the balls. He massaged my buried cock expertly with his anal muscles, grinding his ass back and then raising it up to let some dick escape, then sitting back down to get more inside of him.

I reached down between his spread thighs and grabbed hold of his dangling pecker. It was hanging there, swollen but not stiff. The hugeness of the dick up his butt may have been the cause, as well as the fact that he had just come. Anyway, I loved it. I could play with the foreskin, which totally excited me. I stretched it out, pulling it over the slippery, come-coated head, then slid it back almost to his tight balls. As he fucked his butt over my huge bone, I massaged his semi-stiff dick. It did swell slightly, but remained only half-hard as he fucked himself steadily. I pulled the foreskin up to surround my fingers with the unusual flap of stretchy skin. I totally lost myself in it, teasing his swollen but still-soft prick. It lengthened every time my own huge cock slid deep into his asshole as he fucked himself over it.

He danced over my dick, his clenched butt cheeks writhing up and down deliciously. I planted my feet wide apart and held my hips against him, allowing him easy access to my long bone. Both my hands were around his waist and down in his crotch playing with his half-hard prick and awesome foreskin.

I couldn't keep it up for long. I was so horned up and so excited by the bizarre situation, and by the feel of that massaging hole over my stiff meat, I felt the come boiling up and couldn't hold it in. With a loud grunt, I held my dick deep up his squirming butt and shot my load.

I yanked on his foreskin, stretching it way out, and that must have done something to him, because all of a sudden his cock began to pulse and spasm. Another creamy load of goo splattered out all over my teasing fingers. Even though his dick never got completely hard, he'd come once more.

I leaned into him, both of us clutching at the gate for support, our breathing labored, our dicks drooling come, his on my fingers, mine up his clenching asshole.

I came to my senses eventually, noticing there were men watching us. I slid my dick from his warm anal glove and reluctantly released that slimy foreskin I was still playing with.

Serge turned around and slid into my arms, his smaller body hard, tight and warm. We embraced in the semi-darkness of the room and held each other for quite a while. Passersby eventually ignored us.

We went out for coffee after that—European cities have a late nightlife—and it was almost dawn by the time we found our way back to my hotel. Once in my bed, I was keen to attack that sexy foreskin all over again. This time I explored it with my lips and tongue.

Serge and I found all sorts of ways to make love over the next couple of days. I was sad in the end to leave Poland, and leave Serge with the sexy foreskin and hot dancer body. I never understood much of what he was saying, and I'm sure he didn't really understand me either, but we communicated where it mattered the most. Cock to cock.

He promised to write, but never did. I'm sure he found another hot stud to play with his adorable body and dick. Oh well, I had the time of my life and no regrets. Ain't travel a blast?

GOING DUTCH

WILLIAM HOLDEN

THE SEAT BELT sign came on as the purser announced our descent into Schiphol Airport—in Dutch and then in English. This was my first vacation in a long time, and my first trip to Amsterdam. It was also the first vacation I had ever taken alone. Being in a relationship for five years, I had always traveled with my boyfriend. It took the two years since our breakup for me to feel comfortable again with being single.

As I made my way through customs and into the main area of the airport, the smell of marijuana grew stronger. I stopped, took a deep breath, and grinned. I had always heard about the high tolerance the Dutch community had for weed and hash, but I never thought it would be quite like this. Still, my first order of business was to find the currency exchange counters and then to locate a train that would take me to my destination. After many wrong turns, I finally boarded the right train. With my luggage in hand, I made my way through the narrow aisles until I found an available seat.

As I sat there, I started remembering my life with Steve. Maybe it had been my age—I was seventeen when Steve and I first met—but my long relationship with him was something out of a fairy-tale. Steve was beautiful. His swimmer's build and hairless chest were a definite turn on for me. Our sex was what most people would call vanilla, but to me it was always passionate and intense. It was just in the last year that things seemed to change. Steve became distant, always working until late in the evenings, never acting like himself. I tried many times to get him to open up to me, but the harder I tried the more distant he became—especially if I started to talk about how passionless our sex had become. Finally he decided to talk. He was leaving me. He had found someone else; someone who valued his ideas about a successful career more than I did.

As the train made one of its quick stops in Amersfort, I forced myself to stop replaying our last few nights together and tried to concentrate on the Dutch countryside. As I watched Amsterdam move closer, a sense of excitement suddenly came over me. It was a city famous for its gay scene—especially for its rough and sometimes exotic bars. This was my chance to do what I wanted: to be myself, and perhaps explore something new.

I gathered my luggage and stepped out into the fresh afternoon air. Outside of Central Station the city came alive. Its sights and sounds were foreign yet strangely comforting. From all directions I could hear the voices of people speaking languages I didn't know, and the trams, ringing their bells as they made their way around the city. In the distance, I could even hear the deep sound of one of the old clock towers, its music haunting, yet inviting.

I had spent many hours planning this vacation and decided early on that I wasn't going to "wimp out," that if I was going to do this by myself, I would do it right. With that mindset, I had booked a room in the leather district on Warmoesstraat. I had never really gotten into the leather scene, partly due to my boyfriend, but mostly because the idea tended to scare me a bit. I took a deep breath to calm my already shaky nerves, and following the map, began walking up the Damrak toward the center of the city. After a couple of blocks, I turned left to find the famous Warmoesstraat—a narrow street, not much bigger than an alley. The bars, tattoo parlors, leather and sex shops surrounded me in both directions. The smell of marijuana lingered in the air as I made my way through the mass of men, my suitcase wobbling behind me on the cobblestone street.

The hotel was just as described on the Web site. The building was painted black with dirty white trim. The large front windows were darkened as well and held the hotel and bar name in bold blue lights. The side door which led to the hotel opened up to a narrow set of stairs. I felt awkward as I made my way up the steps sideways with my hands loaded down with luggage. A man stood at the top with a smile on his face.

"You're handling yourself quite well on these stairs, but here let me help you."

"Thanks," I said, as I tried to catch my breath. I steadied myself and lifted a suitcase in his direction. His arms were large and muscular, and covered in dark hair. He wore tight blue jeans, which left nothing to the imagination, and a black leather vest which exposed yet another part of his body that was carpeted with dark swirls of hair. As he turned to leave, I noticed the seam in the pants was ripped, exposing the fact that he wasn't wearing any underwear. I stood there alone for a moment, wondering if I had made a mistake by coming here. I was definitely out of my usual scene and for a brief moment I thought about turning around and heading for the safety of my own home back in Atlanta. I pushed myself on, not letting the fear of the unknown overcome me.

"You must be exhausted from your trip?" He turned to look at me. "I'm Lars, I run the hotel and bar downstairs."

"I'm Joe," I said, as we shook hands. "Yeah, I could use a nap."

"Well, let me give you a tip for your stay here. If you can, I would sleep during the day, while it's quiet; because once things get started at night, it gets really loud and will stay that way till daybreak."

"Great, I'll keep that in mind." We performed all the necessary steps for check-in and then I was escorted to my room.

"We don't have any alarm clocks, but I'd be happy to wake you up; say around seven? That should give you plenty of time to get out and get some dinner before heading out for the night."

"Yeah, that would be great. Thanks." He handed me the key and left without another word. The room was small with the ceiling slanting down to the floor on both sides. The furniture was all black, along with the floor. The only color in the room was from the gray sheets on the bed and dark blue curtains hanging on the window. I pulled the curtains closed, undressed, and crawled into bed. Sleep came almost immediately.

✦

AS PROMISED, LARS came into my room to wake me up. I pulled back the sheets as he opened up the curtains. He turned and looked at my naked body lying on the bed.

"The Dutch boys are going to love you."

"What do you mean?"

"Most Dutch men are uncut so they get a little tired of the same old thing. They'll be all over you once they realize you're American and circumcised." He leaned over the bed and ran his hand over my soft cock. "Oh yeah, they're going to eat you up."

I stood up, feeling a bit uncomfortable with Lars's closeness, and tried to change the subject. "Speaking of eating, is there a place you can recommend?"

"There is one place I recommend to all my guests," he began to respond, as he continued to look at my nakedness. "It's a Caribbean restaurant on Reguliersdwarsstraat. It's a bit of a walk but worth it."

"Well I guess I better get showered and dressed." I headed for the bathroom hoping he would take the hint that it was time for him to leave. He did.

I had ordered several drinks before, during, and after dinner hoping the alcohol would loosen me up for a night out, but as I stood in front of the Cockring watching the men going in, I decided that I hadn't drunk enough. I lit a cigarette, inhaled deeply, and made my way to the front door, then up a couple of steps and into the bar. I showed my identification to the attendant and followed the other men through a darkened hallway that led to the first floor.

The room was smaller than I had expected, a bar stretched across the left side of the room ending where the dance floor began. Most of the men I had followed in headed to the back stairwell behind the dance floor. They disappeared into darkness. I noticed a few empty stools around the bar and took a seat.

The bartender was quick to respond to my arrival. "Hi, babe, what can I get you?" His eyes were a deep brown. They sparkled as the swirling lights from the dance floor crossed his face. His hair was black, shoulder length. His bangs fell across his forehead, just above his eyebrows. A day's stubble covered his square jaw line and ran down his neck. As I watched him watching me,

I almost forgot what he had asked me.

"Vodka-cranberry with a lime."

"You got it." He winked as he turned to make my drink. He began singing to the song that was playing, his hips shifting from side to side as the beat grew louder. I found myself staring at him. His jeans were low cut and fell nicely on his hips. I watched as he bent down to grab the cranberry juice. His gray T-shirt pulled up, exposing the head of a snake tattooed on his back. I quickly shifted my eyes down to my cigarettes as he headed back in my direction. He sat the drink down and leaned his forearms against the bar. I looked up at him. He was at eye-level with me. A half-smile crossed his face. He didn't say anything. He picked up my cigarettes, pulled one out and slipped it into my mouth. His smile grew. His left hand slid into the pocket of his pants and pulled out a lighter. The flame shot up, casting an orange glow across our faces. I took a drag and blew the smoke out. It encircled us as the beams of light tried to push their way through.

"Your first time in our city, isn't it?"

"Is it that obvious?" My face felt flush.

"Not to most people. But I've developed a sort of sixth sense over the years."

"I'm Machiel by the way."

"I'm Joe."

He took the cigarette from my mouth and placed it in his. I watched as his lips curved around the end where my lips had just been. My stomach started to churn, as I found myself wanting him. He leaned closer to me. His face inches from mine. He leaned to the left of me. His scent surrounded me. My pulse increased as I took a deep breath of him. I could feel his lips not quite touching my ear. "Well Joe, I've got to start cleaning up. I'm off in about thirty minutes. Perhaps I could show you around tonight?" He brought his face back around and stared into my eyes while waiting for a response.

"Sure." The word came out before my mind could stop it. I knew there was no turning back.

"Why don't you go up to the third floor and check out the dark room. You can't come to the Cockring without experiencing it." The tip of his tongue darted out briefly as he raised his eyebrows and smiled. "I'll come up and find you when I cash out."

I looked in the direction of the back stairs, then back at Machiel. I downed the rest of my drink and handed him the empty glass. He began wiping off the bar as I stood up and headed toward the back of the bar.

The stairs were narrow, lit only by a few dim bulbs. I reached the top and stood paralyzed as I stared into complete darkness. Sweat beaded up on my skin as my body trembled with fear and a newfound excitement. I could feel the dampness under my arms. I pushed back the fears and walked into the unknown.

The darkness engulfed me, shutting me out of the world I knew and into something unexplainable. I stood quietly waiting for my eyes to adjust. They never did. Without my sight, my other senses took over. I could feel the presence of others all around me. The heat of their bodies. The low whispers of pleasure. The warmth of someone's breath brushing against the back of my neck.

My heart jumped into my throat as I felt someone wrapping their arms around the front of my body. Warm, soft lips caressed my neck as the hands traveled across my chest. My cock stiffened in my pants. The boxers I had on gave no support as it continued to lengthen. I let the desire consume me, my fears faded away into the dark. My head fell back against his shoulder as he moved around and kissed my throat. His hand moved up to the side of my face and turned it in his direction. He kissed me, sinking his tongue deep into my mouth. I could feel his cock pressing into me as we continued to kiss. His free hand lifted my shirt and ran across the soft patch of hair covering my stomach. His fingers dug into my skin, inching their way into the waist of my pants. My knees became weak from the intense pleasure of this unknown man. He tightened his grip around my body to support me as he pulled his hand out. The grip loosened and before I could respond, the man was gone, leaving me once again alone in the darkness. I wanted to find him, to have his hands touching me again, but I knew there was no hope. I turned in the direction that I had come, and saw the faint glow of the stairwell. Darkened silhouettes passed back and forth. I walked toward the light, brushing against sweaty skin.

As I approached the door, I saw Machiel standing just outside.

"Looks like you had fun." His eyes glanced down at the bulge in my pants. "I bet the guy did too?" He smiled at me and winked. "Come on, there's a party I want to take you to." He grabbed my hand, interlocking his fingers with mine. I looked back into the darkness and wondered if that had been Machiel in there with me.

The night air chilled my overheated body as we made our way down the crowded street. Men wandered aimlessly in all directions. The sexual energy of the street filled the air, intoxicating those within it, and I was right in the thick of it.

We stood in front of Stablemaster. Machiel squeezed my hand. "You ready for this?" Before I could respond, he led me into the bar.

The inside looked just as the name implied—a large open stable. The walls, floor, and tables were all wood. A heavy smell of sweat and sex hung in the air. The men were in various stages of undress. Some stood around in their underwear and socks, while others wore nothing at all. The corners were filled with groups of men, kissing and stroking each other. The sexual energy I had experienced outside dimmed in comparison. We walked up to the bar. Machiel leaned over and kissed the bartender and ordered us drinks.

"Let's take a seat over here." Machiel motioned with the drink in his hand. "This place doesn't seem like much now, but in a few hours it will be packed for the jack-off party." He nudged me with his shoulder. "You gonna participate?"

"I doubt it." I smiled back at him, a bit embarrassed at my shyness. "I'm not much of an exhibitionist." I wondered how long Machiel would put up with my lack of experience.

"Me either, but it can be fun to watch those who are." He repositioned himself on the bench to face me. He turned my head in his direction. "There's something about you I just don't understand."

"What do you mean?"

"Come on." He lit a cigarette and looked at me questioningly. "You are fucking hot. You have to know that, yet in some ways I don't think you do. You give off this amazing sexual vibe, yet you seem so innocent."

"I'm just not that experienced when it comes to this kind of scene, that's all."

"Well, whatever your story is, I like it." He leaned over and kissed me. His lips felt warm and familiar, yet new and exciting. As I opened my mouth to his tongue, someone behind us grunted as he lost his load. The moaning and voices of approval echoed around us as someone else followed suit. We turned to watch as yet a third man came against a mirror, his come splattering the glass and wall. I continued to watch in amazement as more and more men gathered in a large circle in the center of the room. Machiel's hand moved down my leg. My cock responded to his touch.

His hand was large and covered my crotch completely. He tugged and squeezed with a strong, firm grip while still maintaining a gentleness about him. I turned my head in his direction and looked into his eyes. For the first time in my life, I saw pure, raw desire looking back at me. I had never seen that in Steve or anyone else, and until that moment, I didn't even know it existed.

"I want you," Machiel whispered to me. His eyes pierced my soul. I became lost in this strange and erotic world. After years of nameless sex for nothing more than pleasure, there was a world of power and passion that was opening up to me. He leaned in closer. "I want to give you everything you need and desire. To worship your body like no one else has."

His words alone did more to me sexually than any of the men could have done with their bodies. My body ached with desire for him, and still the fear of not being enough for him tightened in my chest. I didn't know how to respond. I was paralyzed by his eyes, lips, and voice. I could feel the heat radiating off his body, his scent becoming stronger. My pulse pounded in my chest with lust, desire, and need. The sexual tension between us was thick, suffocating.

"Will you be with me tonight?" Machiel asked. "Will you let me give you what you know you want?" He gripped my chin in his hand. "If only for tonight, let nothing else matter but you and me."

I couldn't take it any longer. I stood up, hoping my legs would not give out on me, and reached for his hand. We left the bar and headed up the narrow staircase next door. As we climbed the steps I could feel him watching me, wanting me. I fumbled with the key and finally slid it into the lock. Once inside, Machiel shut and locked the door. Before I could say anything, he had me against the wall, his tongue exploring every inch of my mouth.

His body felt heavy as it pressed me against the wall. He raised my arms over my head, and held them together with one hand. His mouth left mine. He moved down my neck and to my chest, kissing and licking my body through my T-shirt. He moved to the left, and licked the material under my arm. I let out a sudden gasp, as his teeth tore a hole in my shirt. His tongue darted through the hole, licking the dampened hair of my armpit. His teeth gripped the material and ripped the shirt open to my chest. His mouth covered my nipple. He moaned as he tasted my skin and licked the sweat off the hair on my chest. He looked up at me; our eyes met. Our breathing was heavy.

"Hang on," he said between breaths as he picked me up. He cradled me in his arms and took me to the bed. He straddled my body as his hands gripped the torn edges of my shirt. My body shook as I heard the material ripping. His strength and determination pulsed through my body. He pulled his shirt over his head. His soft, hairless body glistened with sweat.

He lowered himself to me, his mouth exploring every inch of my body. His tongue slid along the edge of my pants as his hands undid the button and zipper. Neither one of us said a word. Our bodies were all we needed.

My hips arched as he slid my pants down. He quickly removed my shoes and then my pants. My boxers left little to his imagination. He looked at me and smiled as he saw the length and thickness of my cock pressing against the material of my shorts.

I watched as he stood next to the bed and began to undo his pants. He kicked his shoes off. I could smell the warm leather rising from his feet. I gripped the headboard to keep myself from losing control. I wanted him to do what he wanted with me, with no interference of my own. His white underwear was swollen with excitement. He looked at me and smiled as he pulled them down.

His long, slender cock stood out in front of him. Folds of

foreskin pulled back to show the pink tender skin of his cock head. Precome gathered in the creases of his skin. I stared at his body, watching the heavy rise of his chest and stomach as he tried to steady his breathing. He lay down on top of me, the head of his cock slipping into the fly in my boxers. Our cocks met and rubbed against each other.

"You are the most amazing man I have ever met." His voice was soft and gentle. He lifted himself up with his arms. His hips began to move, sliding his cock in and out of my fly. He watched me the whole time, never taking his eyes away from mine. Our breathing grew heavy again. Sweat ran down Machiel's face; I leaned up and licked it off his neck. His salty flavors melted in my mouth.

"Let me be with you tonight. Let me give you what others never have." His eyes were soft and pleading. "Please, I need to be inside of you."

I smiled at him and shook my head. I hadn't any breath for words. The anticipation of having his cock inside of me was more than I could take. My body trembled. Sweat poured out of every gland on my body, until the sheets were damp against my skin. He gently tugged the condom from its wrapper and slid it over his cock. He grabbed a small package of lube from his pant's pocket and began stroking himself.

He moved off my body and removed my boxers. My cock bounced against my skin as he ran his finger over the shaft. He moved in between my legs and rested them on his shoulders. I watched his every movement, every facial expression as he brought the head of his cock closer to my tight hole.

He kissed my calves and legs as the head of his cock pushed through the tight layer of muscles. My entire body tightened as I felt it break through. He watched me watching him and slid another inch farther into me. He leaned down and kissed me and still he went deeper. He began rocking our bodies simultaneously in long, slow, swaying movements, pushing the last of his length inside.

"Oh yeah."

"Damn, that feels good," I groaned. "Please never stop fuck—" Before I could finish, he began thrusting himself back and forth into me. Our bodies, drenched with sweat, moved in perfect rhythm. Our breathing seemed to become one. I gripped the headboard as he leaned down and took my cock in his mouth while he continued to fuck me.

His cock pushed into me as his mouth pulled up on my shaft. Back and forth he worked me over, till I thought I would lose my mind. Spit and precome poured out of his mouth. He took me all the way down, the head of my cock pressing against his throat. He held me there, while he continued to slide his cock in and out of my ass.

He started to moan. The vibrations in his throat teased the sensitive nerves of my cock. His throat began to tighten then relax as his tongue moved up and down my shaft, squeezing more and more precome out of me. Still he held me at my full length.

I could feel the come building up in my balls. My hips moved up and down as he continued to suck me while his cock was deep inside. He couldn't talk but I could tell by his moaning he knew I was ready to come. His mouth and tongue moved faster over my cock, his moaning became louder as I reached my breaking point.

"Machiel!" I shouted, as the pressure mounted. Suddenly, the rush of pure pleasure swept over my body as I shot my first load into Machiel's mouth. He continued to suck, pumping more and more come out of my still stiffening cock. His mouth reached capacity as I shot for a fourth time. It ran out of his mouth and down my shaft.

He pulled my cock out of his mouth and grabbed my leg. He licked the come off his lips. His hips moved faster and harder, shoving his cock into me. I felt his cock thickening inside of me. I knew he was getting ready to come. He pulled out and tore off the condom.

"Oh yeah!" He moaned as he moved himself up to my stomach.

His cock was only inches away from my face. The piss slit began to grow and widen each time the foreskin was pulled back. My cock became hard again, watching Machiel pleasure himself. His body trembled. His moaning turned to a groan, his groan to a growl as the first round of his hot come exploded from his cock. It splattered over my face. The warmth of his come was like nothing I had ever experienced. He continued to stroke his cock and shot another load over my neck and chest.

He fell against me. Our sweat, spit, and come mingled together. He looked up at me and smiled. I brushed the hair from his forehead and smiled back. We fell asleep and didn't wake until morning.

✦

THE PILOT ANNOUNCED the initial descent into the Atlanta Hartsfield Airport, and my cock began to twitch as the thoughts of Machiel ran through my mind. We had spent some time together during my vacation but not as much as I had wanted. Machiel said that it wouldn't be fair to me. He wanted me to go out and experience more of what Amsterdam had to offer. The morning I had to leave, he walked me to Central Station. He kissed me one last time and before I boarded the train he handed me an envelope.

"Don't open it till you get back home," he yelled as I stepped up into the train.

I took the envelope out of my carry-on and decided I was home enough. Inside was a note, telling me he loved me, and a roundtrip ticket to Amsterdam asking me to come back and visit him soon.

FERNANDO

JOHN-PAUL BATISTA

YOU'D THINK THAT a world-traveling photographer wouldn't have anywhere to go for vacation. But I spend so much time living life through a lens that I find little time to truly experience the places I visit. I keep a journal of some of my favorite places so that I can visit them later when I have more time to explore. One such place is Seville.

I'd heard about a festival that they hold in April that was the highlight of the year. It revolved around bullfighting and, although I'm not a proponent of the sport, I was a proponent of partying. And this festival, I was told, is one party I didn't want to miss. It'd also give me and Elliott some much needed time alone. We were a few weeks into our relationship and it was still vaguely defined. I felt the trip would give us an opportunity to clarify some things.

We spent the first day walking the streets, taking in the festivities, and listening to the Flamenco bands weave magic with their songs. That's when I saw him: a young musician dressed in his traditional black flamenco suit and hat, singing and strumming his guitar.

He was a dark-skinned Sevillian with classic Mediterranean good looks. He was a few inches shy of six-feet tall and had a slim figure—smaller than the men I usually find attractive. He also had long, dark black hair which was drawn into a ponytail. I've never been too fond of men with long hair because I feel it tends to blur the gender lines. But with his dark, soulful eyes and strong, masculine features, I was willing to make an exception. As if sensing me staring at him, he looked my way and locked his dark soulful eyes on mine. For a brief moment, he seemed to be singing only to me. Then he smiled. My heart stopped and I drew in a sharp breath.

"What's wrong?" Elliott asked, snapping me out of my trance.

"N-nothing," I stammered. "I'm just a bit overwhelmed."

"Yeah, it is wild, isn't it? Thanks for bringing me." He gave me a tender kiss on the lips. "C'mon, I think the bullfights are about to start."

I dragged myself away, looking over my shoulder to look at the sexy crooner one last time. For the rest of the day I focused all my attention on Elliott and never gave the young Spaniard another thought. We had a great time, even during the bull-fight. And when we returned to our hotel room, we made love all night.

The next morning, I was awakened from my sex-induced slumber by the sounds of flamenco music rising from the court-yard outside our room. Whoever it was had a beautiful tenor voice and was a talented guitarist. He sang a song of unrequited love. As beautiful as it was, I would have preferred to hear it at a less ungodly hour. The clock by the bed read 8:00 which was way too early to get up when you're on vacation, especially after the long day and night that I'd had. I looked over at Elliott who was sound asleep. He could sleep through anything, especially after a long night of fucking.

Our room was on the second floor of a small, three-story, fam-ily-run hotel. It had the comfort and hospitality of home and, ap-parently, some very relaxed customs. I knew the only way I could get back to sleep was if I could reason with the fellow and get him to stop playing his music. So, I slipped out of bed, donned my robe, and headed for the balcony.

The musician was sitting on the fountain in the center of the courtyard. His head was bowed as he skillfully plucked out the intricate melody on his guitar. He must have heard me or sensed my presence because he stopped playing and looked up in my direction. I nearly fell over the railing when I saw him. He was the musician that I saw at the festival.

"I'm sorry," he said. "Did my music wake you?"

"No, I was already awake," I lied. "It is rather early, though."

"I like to play early in the morning before the city wakes up. If

I'd known we had guests, I would have gone somewhere else."

"It's okay . . . it was a pleasant start to my morning."

"Thank you," he said as he started packing up his guitar.

"So you work here?"

"When I'm not performing. My family owns this hotel; I help them whenever I can."

"That must keep you pretty busy." He nodded and started to walk away. "I saw you playing at the fair yesterday," I blurted out.

He looked up and considered me for a moment. "Ah yes, I remember you. You were with the redhead, no?"

"Yeah, that's me."

"You seemed to be enjoying our performance."

"I was . . . very much. I wish I could have stayed to hear you play some more, but the bullfights were about to start."

"Then perhaps during your stay here I can give you and your friend a private performance."

"Oh, I appreciate the offer but you don't have to go through any trouble for me."

"It would be my honor. I love to play for an audience, no matter how small."

"How about tonight, at dinner? Elliott would like that."

He thought about it for a brief moment. "Okay," he agreed. "Since you two are our only guests until tomorrow, I'll have my sister plan a special romantic dinner just for the two of you."

"Wow! Elliott will love that. Thanks a lot!"

"It will be our pleasure," he said. "I have to go now. Duty calls."

"Until tonight, then," I said and waved. He took a bow, waved happily, and left the courtyard.

I walked back into the room, chucked my robe, and climbed back into bed with Elliott. My sleeping beauty roused a little bit when I cuddled up to him.

"Who were you talking to?" he asked groggily.

I kissed him on the shoulder. "I'll explain later."

Elliott and I woke up around eleven and took a walk through the city. I'd been to Seville a couple times before, but it was El- liott's first trip there, so we stopped at every shop we passed. It was around five by the time we returned to the hotel. We showered and dressed for dinner. I told him to dress up because I had a surprise for him. I didn't even know the full extent of the surprise until we got to the courtyard.

By night the courtyard took on a romantic air of its own. Dozens of candles, placed in every nook and cranny conceivable (even floating in the fountain), cast a soft orange glow over the entire square. I saw the musician standing at the far end of the yard, near a secluded alcove.

He looked just as hot as he did when I first met him, dressed in his performance attire. There was an immediate stirring in my pants. I thought maybe it was a mistake to agree to this, but it was too late to turn back now. I took Elliott by the hand and led him to our private niche.

"Welcome Elliott and John Paul," the musician greeted. "My name is Fernando. It will be my pleasure to provide the music for your romantic dinner tonight." He took a seat on a stool by the table. His fingers tickled the strings on his guitar a few times and he began to sing.

"This is the guy I was talking to this morning," I explained quietly to Elliott. "I heard him playing in the courtyard this morning. After I came out to see what was going on, we struck up a little conversation. One thing led to another, and he agreed to entertain us during dinner."

"This is incredible. I don't know what else to say," he said, weaving his fingers into mine, "except I love you."

"I love you too," I confessed and kissed him.

I felt a little self-conscious with Fernando standing there, but he remained the consummate professional, pretending not to notice. A young woman—his sister I presumed—brought us our meal. The chef had prepared a special lamb dish especially for us; it was served with their best bottle of Manzanilla. While we ate and drank, Fernando continued to play his songs of love—lost love, renewed love, unrequited love, and even forbidden love.

Between the setting, the music, and the alcohol, I was getting pretty horny. So was Elliott, it seemed, by the way his hand was caressing the inside of my thigh and the bulge growing between my legs. We kissed passionately, groping each other under the table, not caring that we weren't alone. As a matter of fact, I was getting off on the fact that Fernando was there. Even though he didn't seem to notice, I knew he was watching.

As we continued to make out, Fernando's playing became sloppy. Eventually he stopped playing altogether.

"What's wrong?" I asked, dragging my lips away from Elliott's.

"I'm thinking the two of you would like to be alone now," he suggested, and stood up.

I motioned for him to stay. "Play one more song please."

He gave me a strange look, as did Elliott, but I was unwavering in my request. After a long, awkward silence, he sat back down and started playing another song. I leaned in to kiss Elliott, but he was reluctant to resume now that he was aware of our audience. But, with a little coaxing from my groping hand, he soon got back into the mood.

Fernando's playing grew more and more irregular as we intensified our coupling. It turned me on knowing that we were affecting him so strongly and I wanted to see how much he could tolerate. Not much, it seemed, because less than a minute later the music stopped again. I looked up, expecting to see nothing but the dust settling in the wake of his hasty escape; instead, Fernando was standing right next to us, holding his guitar in one hand and squeezing his crotch with the other.

"Why don't you give him a hand with that," I whispered to Elliott.

He answered my request with a confused and panicked look on his face. I gave him a reassuring nod. His hand then slowly crept up Fernando's leg until it displaced the musician's own groping hand. My lover fondled Fernando's tool as only he could, and I could tell by Fernando's groans that he enjoyed the feeling as much as I usually did.

I sat back and started playing with myself while I watched my boyfriend caress this stranger's package. I could see the hunger in Elliott's eyes—it was the look he used to have only for me. Oddly enough, instead of making me jealous, it only made me hornier.

"Take it out and play with it," I instructed.

"What if someone walks out and sees us?" Elliott asked.

"Dinner is over," Fernando replied. "No one will disturb us."

"Now on to dessert," I said.

A devilish little grin spread across Elliott's face that made my cock twitch. He popped the buttons on Fernando's pants and unleashed the musician's spicy chorizo from its tight confines. My sexy little redhead licked his lips and stroked Fernando's thick, juicy uncut cock—feasting his eyes on the hefty nuts dangling below it and probably wondering how much sperm he could coax out of them. Elliott loved to suck cock and he was quite good at it. He could easily swallow my boner whole; Fernando's super fat six-incher wouldn't pose much of a problem. Sure enough, Elliott turned his chair around, opened his mouth wide, and gobbled up that fat fucker.

"*Dios mio!*" Fernando muttered. His head rolled back and he let his guitar slip from his grip. It fell to the ground with a loud twang, but he was too engrossed in Elliott's blow job to care.

By then, I'd had enough of watching from the sidelines and decided to partake in the activities. Elliott was busy clawing and kneading Fernando's ass, trying to get more of that Spanish cock in his mouth. I slid out of my chair, knelt behind Fernando, and buried my face in his ass. His body shivered as I attacked his hairy asshole with my tongue. Fernando grabbed a handful of my hair and crammed my face in his ass while Elliott opened him up wide to give me better access. I lapped up his bung hole until he screamed.

I reached out for Elliott through Fernando's spread-eagled legs and groped around his body until I found his belt. After blindly unbuckling it and undoing his pants, I reached inside his boxers and fished out his cock. He sighed in relief as I released it and held it firmly in my hand. It was already slick with goo, just waiting for a tight hole to slam into; and I had just the hole in mind.

With my free hand, I tickled Fernando's pucker—just to test the waters. He didn't seem to mind, so I slid a finger in. That wasn't the first time he'd taken something up the ass—oh no. It was snug, but the way it gulped down my finger and twitched for more told me that he'd had some experience. I inserted another finger, spread him open a bit, and spit into his hole a few times. I worked the spit in with my fingers until I was satisfied that he was sopping wet.

I poked my head around the Spaniard's narrow hips. "You ready to poke this ass?"

Elliott let Fernando's dick pop out of his mouth. The feisty redhead looked me in my eyes, flashed that wicked grin of his, and replied, "You bet."

We both looked up at Fernando who was gawking at Elliott's huge prick. "No," he argued, "he's too big."

He closed his eyes and moaned when I slid a third finger into his ass. "I think you can handle it. Just be gentle with him, baby."

"You know me," Elliott said, grinning even wider.

I stepped back to let him take over. He stood up and positioned himself behind Fernando, who obediently bent over a chair and waited for the fucking to begin. I gave Elliott's cock a few quick sucks then aimed it at Fernando's opening. With one steady motion, Elliott slipped his dick into Fernando's ass. I almost bust a nut just watching the little brown bung hole getting stretched by my stud's white donkey cock. From the whimpering sounds Fernando was making, I imagined that was the biggest cock he'd ever taken up the butt. My baby was nice enough to give him a few seconds to adjust to the invasion before he started plowing his hole.

Elliott liked to fuck fast and hard, especially during the first round, and he was pounding the shit out of Fernando. Their thighs slapped together in thunderous claps that I'm sure could be heard blocks away. I listened to the rising sounds of Fernando's stunted groans as my boyfriend literally fucked him breathless; they were the unmistakable groans of pleasure.

I watched them rut around for a few minutes before I took notice of my cock throbbing for attention. It was obvious that Fernando loved being fucked rough, but I wondered if he would appreciate the fine art of throat fucking. There was only one way to find out.

I straddled the chair that Fernando was using to brace himself. Each time Elliott rammed his cock home, it pressed Fernando's face into my crotch. Finally, he steadied himself and started licking and sucking my nuts through my pants, darkening the gray cotton with his drool.

"You want some of this?" I asked.

He hummed approvingly and continued to chew on the bulge in my pants. I had to fight him off just to get undressed. I pulled my pants and boxers down to my knees. As soon as my cock sprang free, Fernando had his lips wrapped around it and was vigorously sucking on the head. Then he dove down and worked on my balls, rolling each one around on his tongue before sucking it into his mouth. Meanwhile, my dick rested on his nose and forehead, waiting to be serviced. As nice as it was to have my scrotum cleaned, what I really wanted was for him to shine my knob.

So I grabbed his ponytail and pulled him off my nuts. His mouth was already open and waiting, so I drove my schlong right down his throat. He choked and sputtered a little, but never put up any resistance.

I felt his tongue and throat working the length of my pole, signaling me to proceed. I pulled my cock out until just the tip remained wedged between his lips, and then drove the whole thing back down his throat. Elliott stopped fucking him for a while so he could watch the action on my end. Once I got a good rhythm going, he continued the onslaught on his ass. We rammed him in unison, filling both of his orifices at once.

After a few minutes of mutual fucking, I heard Elliott growling, like he always did when he was getting ready to come. He rammed his cock in to the hilt and started working his hips in a tight circle. I watched his face flush and contort, and listened to him growl through clenched teeth as he dumped what must have been a gallon of come deep into Fernando's bowels. As he came down off his high, I leaned over Fernando's body and gave him a kiss.

"That looked like a big one," I commented.

"Yeah, this guy's got a sweet ass. You should give it a try."

Fernando was still slobbering on my prick. I freed myself from his lockjaw and asked him, "You want me to fuck you?"

"Oh yeah, fuck me like your boyfriend did."

I was willing to accommodate his request. Elliott stepped aside and let me take the helm. He had thoroughly opened up Fernando's hole, that's for sure. I spread his cheeks apart and just slid right into his sloppy, come-filled ass.

"Fuck! How much spunk did you drop in here?"

"I couldn't help it," Elliott answered sheepishly.

While I started churning up the large deposit of spooge he had left for me, Elliott sat on the ground and once again indulged himself with Fernando's tasty cock. I told Fernando to straighten up so I could watch him get his prick sucked while I fucked him.

I'd grown familiar to the view of the top of Elliott's bobbing head, but this time it wasn't my dick he was bobbing on, or my fingers weaving themselves into his red locks, or my voice encouraging him. Goaded by the sight and sound of Elliott's noisy slurping, and the sensation of his jizz coating my cock and dripping down my balls, I wrapped my arms around Fernando and fucked him with short, powerful thrusts. I got that familiar tingling in my nuts and the pit of my stomach—I was close to the edge. Wanting Fernando to blow first, I switched to long, slow strokes to pace myself. Elliott knew what I was trying to do and intensified his sucking.

For good measure, I reached down and played with his balls. I felt them tighten up in my hand and I knew he was close. Elliott must have felt it too because he stopped sucking and started jacking that fat, Spanish dick. A few skillful strokes later, Fernando's body started convulsing and strings of gooey come erupted from his dick, splattering Elliott's beautiful face. You see that done all the time in porn videos, but there's nothing like seeing it in person.

That, combined with the sensation of Fernando's quivering asshole massaging my cock, was enough to trigger my orgasm. I added my own spunk to the huge load Elliott had already dropped. It filled Fernando to capacity and rivers of come came gushing out of his ass—Elliott was waiting, with his mouth wide open, to drink it all up.

I pulled out of Fernando's ass and slumped into a chair, exhausted but satisfied. Elliott leaned back and licked as much come off his face and lips as he could. I saw his cock bouncing back to life—ready for round two. He pumped it to fullness and gave Fernando another sly grin. Fernando, however, didn't want any part of it. He pulled up his pants, grabbed his equipment, and left.

"Now what am I going to do with this boner?" Elliott whined. I lifted my legs and invited him to deposit his second load into my willing ass.

The next morning, the sound of a Spanish guitar once again invaded the sanctity of our post-sexual siesta. This time it sounded like it was coming from outside our door. I dragged myself out of bed, threw on a pair of boxers, and walked to the door. I opened it, and standing on the other side of the threshold was Fernando. He wasn't wearing anything but his guitar, a smile, and an erection that pointed straight at me.

"Who is it?" Elliott mumbled from the bedroom.

"Room service," I answered, then invited Fernando in and closed the door behind him.

A STORMY ENCOUNTER IN SPAIN

JOHN HOLT

THE FIRST NIGHT was promising—but the rest of the holiday was turning out to be a bit of a nightmare. If I'd wanted lashing rain, freezing cold winds, and rumbles of thunder, I could have just stayed at home. When I got on the plane from Ireland to Spain, I was expecting hot weather, big sunny bursts of it, lots of alcohol, partying, and sex. I wasn't expecting to spend half my time cooped up in my (admittedly nice) resort apartment, watching badly dubbed episodes of *The Simpsons*, having a few drinks at the resort bar, and thinking about the stunning straight guy I'd met that first night.

I was pretty tired when I arrived in Malaga airport, as I'd caught a late flight out of Dublin. By the time I'd gotten a taxi and arrived at the resort in the small town on the Costa del Sol, it was getting late. But I decided to make the most of things. I checked into the resort, had a quick look around (it was nice, four-star), and then went straight to my apartment (small but luxurious), and dumped my luggage. I didn't waste time looking around the apartment, but had a quick shower and changed into jeans and a white shirt.

I stopped for one drink in the downstairs bar, a cocktail to get me in the mood, and left the resort. Though tired, I was feeling pretty good as I strolled down the main thoroughfare. There was a balmy breeze, warm on my bare arms, and though it was getting late, every place was hopping—bars, nightclubs, late-night cafes. Music flooded the streets, merrily drunken tourists staggered about, and the men were pretty hot, too.

I lit a cigarette, took a long drag, and checked my watch. It was already after midnight. But this was Spain, after all, I reflected, and most places wouldn't close until about 4 a.m. If my strength held up, and all the drinks I was planning on having didn't conspire with my tiredness to drag me down, I could have a few hours of fun. And hopefully a dabble of debauchery. I grinned at the thought.

I looked around, trying to decide on a place to go. I couldn't tell if any of the bars or clubs were gay. It was unlikely that any of them were. I'd probably have to go to Torremolinos for that, as this little town was too small. It was okay by me, though. I knew when I'd picked the resort that I'd mainly be using this place as my base, a nice place to relax and sunbathe during the days, and the bigger Torremolinos would be my draw most nights this week for the gay bars and clubs. But as I looked around, I realized that most of the places here in the little town were probably gay-friendly anyway. I'd try to have some fun tonight, have a few drinks, cruise the guys—but I knew the main attractions would come later in the week, in the much bigger Torremolinos.

I was trying to decide which of the bars to go into when I spotted him. It's difficult to describe just how magnificent he looked. He was tall (taller than me and I'm six foot) with dark hair that was being ruffled slightly by the gentle wind. He was wearing long shorts and a tight dark T-shirt that showed off his big muscular arms. Standing against the railing of the main street, smoking a cigarette and looking down at the dark beach below, he looked like some sort of god.

I wondered if he was a local. He looked Spanish and he seemed to ooze sex, like some sort of promise, from every pore. I immediately felt aroused. Hoping my erection wasn't too obvious, I decided there was no point in wasting time standing there looking at him. I might as well try to get talking to him. He might be gay. Life was short; seize the moment and all that.

And so I wandered over, leaned against the railing a couple of feet next to him. I looked down at the beach below. About a mile in the distance, my resort towered at the end of the beach, sixteen floors reaching to the dark night sky. The waves lapped gently against the shore and moonlight dappled everything in a silver glow. There was something strange about a beach at night, unnatural almost, but beautiful and romantic too.

I glanced surreptitiously at him. He didn't seem to be aware of my presence. Inhaling the sea air, I took out my cigarettes and, ignoring my lighter in my jeans pocket, made a show of searching for one, fumbling around in various pockets, shaking my head, an unlit cigarette dangling from my lips. He didn't notice me, not at all.

I sidled up a bit closer to him and, taking the cigarette from my mouth, said, "Excuse me. Do you have a light?"

He turned, looked at me with a touch of bemusement, something glinting in his dark eyes. He didn't seem to mind that I'd disturbed him. In fact he seemed pretty happy that I had. My cock stiffened a bit more, and then he smiled at me, a gleaming smile of two rows of perfect white teeth, and I almost choked on the flood of desire and longing that welled up inside me.

"Sure," he said, reaching into a pocket of his shorts. He brought out an expensive silver lighter and, cupping it in his hands, he lit it and brought the flame toward me. I put the cigarette in my mouth and leaned down. As the tip of the cigarette touched the flame, I risked a look at his lower body. Nice, flat stomach, ripples of muscle. A slight, appealing bulge in his shorts—but impossible to tell whether he too was erect or not.

"Thanks," I said, reluctantly drawing back. Casually, I asked, "Are you a local or are you here on holidays like myself?"

"Like yourself," he said. His voice was deep, and there was some sort of drawl there. I couldn't tell for sure but suspected he might be American.

Was there something knowing in his look when he said "like yourself," something implied there? I was probably just letting my hopeful imagination get away with itself but I was sure he had just flirted a little with me.

"How long have you been here?" I asked, taking a drag of the cigarette and blowing a blue-gray plume of smoke out into the night air.

"A week," he said, flicking his spent cigarette out onto the road and leaning comfortably back against the railing. "How about yourself?"

"Just got here," I replied. I took a breath. "Looking to have some fun tonight," I went on, trying to inject some meaning into the sentence, just enough to see if he was interested—but not enough to offend or freak him out. I was playing carefully.

"Me too," he said. "Been clubbing all week in Torremolinos. Thought I'd spend my last few days here, bit quieter." Despite his deep voice, there was definitely a twang there. Definitely American. From Texas? Somewhere southern, anyway. I was surprised as he had such dark, good looks. There was nothing fresh-faced and boy-next-door-type about him, which I guess I'm guilty of stereotypically expecting all American men to look like. But I guessed there must have been a touch of something else in his genes—Spanish, Italian, Latino.

He'd mentioned Torremolinos. A lot of gay joints there. But it didn't necessarily mean anything, as there were no doubt even more heterosexual clubs there. I took another drag on my cigarette, sucking the smoke down my throat, holding it for a minute, exhaling slowly. I was trying to do my sexy-macho thing but I probably looked more stupid than anything.

"Torremolinos," I said on the exhale. "Going to check it out myself, maybe tomorrow night. Anywhere you recommend?"

He was about to answer but then he paused. "Listen dude," he said. "Nice chatting with you. But I gotta go. Have a good vacation." And with a wave he was gone, crossing the street, leaving my life forever.

I hesitated a moment and then threw my cigarette and caution to the wind and followed him. I kept well back so he wouldn't see me. If he happened to turn around, I decided I'd just smile vacantly at him and duck into the nearest pub. I was hoping he was on his way to some bar or club. Then I could follow him in there, wait a few minutes, and then "accidentally" bump into him there, what a coincidence and all that, buy him a drink, see what happened . . .

I followed him down a couple of streets. Even from a few feet back, I could appreciate his fine form. He had a great ass, nice and round, which his dark shorts hugged flatteringly. I fantasized about what I could do to him, what he could do to *me*. Then, as I was hoping, he stopped outside a bar called Strands and went inside.

I hung outside for a few minutes, smoked a cigarette, and looked around. I was in a quieter part of the town, away from the oceanfront, and there weren't as many bars or clubs here. Strands was housed at the bottom of a small, narrow building. Cheesy pop music flooded from it. The name of the bar was written in looping, old blue neon across white brick. A couple of the letters had burnt out so the buzzing blue neon read: ST AN S. I laughed. It could have been called Stan's, owned by some guy called Stan, like a little pub in the Texan hometown my dream hunk may have come from.

I stubbed out my cigarette, debated on whether to have another or not. At least five minutes had passed. Maybe more. Better give it another five, I decided. I didn't want it to seem like I *had* followed him. I lit another cigarette and loitered outside Strands/Stan's. I tried looking in a window to see if I could spot him but the interior was too dark to see more than a few huddled shadowy shapes.

I studied my reflection in the dark window. I didn't look too bad, even if I did say so myself. I was in my late twenties and, as I mentioned earlier, I was fairly tall, six feet exactly. My body was lean, not skinny and not fat but a good middle balance, and toned as I regularly worked out. I had dirty blond hair, blue eyes, and big lips. A guy had told me once he got really turned on watching my big lips and mouth gulping down his cock.

Taking a final drag of my cigarette, I decided I'd waited long enough and I walked into the bar. It was so dark inside, it was hard to see much of anything. A multicolored little neon light was above each of the private booths along the far wall, but the lights didn't illuminate much. A few tables were scattered in the center of the room and tall stools lined the semi-circular bar, which took up most of the space.

I walked up to the bar and ordered a pint of lager and a shot of something. I glanced around while I waited for my drinks. I spotted him. He was sitting at the bottom of the bar. Looking very sexy. But unfortunately so was the blond woman sitting next to him, licking his earlobe.

Feeling a crush of disappointment, I drank both my drinks down in a gulp when they arrived and then left the bar and wandered back to the resort, no longer in the mood for drinking or cruising. The night had seemed so promising. All it had taken to ruin it was one bleached-blond woman.

Oh well, I remember thinking as I drifted off to sleep, the rest of the week will be good. Lots of drunken nights. Lots more guys.

But the rest of the week wasn't good at all. It started raining the next day, a torrential downpour that overflowed the resort's big pool, pounded against all the windows, drummed endlessly on the roof.

"I don't understand," I said to a waiter in the dining room on the second night of my stay. I was looking at the rain sluicing down the glass of the big picture window in one corner of the room. "This is supposed to be a beautiful sunny spot."

"It often is, sir," he responded in badly-accented English. "But sometimes we get these nasty storms out of nowhere." He paused. "I think it's a sign of the end of the world that it is coming." I just stared at him. I didn't know what to say to that. Then he smiled and said, "But not to worry, sir. It will be gone I am sure by tomorrow and the sunshine it will be back."

Whether the apocalypse was looming or not, it was still stormy the next day. Vile winds were causing a mini sandstorm down below on the beach and the sea was churning frantically. I sheltered under the roof of my balcony, smoking a cigarette as I watched the chaos on the beach. But then the winds got so strong I was driven back into my little apartment.

I spent the rest of that, the third day, watching badly dubbed Spanish and (for some reason) German-language TV shows. Familiar shows. But not one channel was in English. I listened to the rain at the windows, on the roof, the howling of the wind. I felt miserable.

That night I wandered down to the bar. I got drunk and listened to some old-fashioned jazz music. I chatted to the bartender, an elderly Englishman called Arthur who had moved to Spain twenty years earlier. He told me it was the worst summer storm they had ever experienced. Just my luck, I thought glumly, downing another drink. He said it would probably go on for several more days, basically my entire holiday. Depressed and drunk, I staggered back to my room and passed out.

It rained all day the next day. On the morning of the fifth day, with only a couple of days of holiday left, I woke up and almost screamed in fury when I heard the wind and rain. What a miserable fucking week, I thought as I made strong coffee and sat down at the table in the small living room, looking out at my balcony, the beach below, and the gloomy day beyond.

I'd spent almost a week holed up in this resort, watching bad foreign-language TV, reading an equally bad paperback crime novel, wandering the marble-floored halls of the resort, drinking at the downstairs bar, chatting to the resort staff. And nothing else.

A few times I'd been tempted to catch a bus or taxi to a neighboring larger town like Marbella to do some shopping. But the weather was just too bad. And besides, the resort staff informed me a lot of the buses weren't running because of the weather and apparently none of the taxis were reliable. All this meant that I couldn't get to Torremolinos any night for some action either.

Fuck it, I thought. I'm having one good night before I leave here. I can't let this week be a total waste. I made up my mind there and then over strong coffee on the fifth morning of my stay that that night, bad weather and all, I was going to somehow get to Torremolinos. I was going to some gay bars. I was going to drink. And, hopefully, with a bit of luck, I was going to get laid.

My mind made up, I felt better. I spent most of the rest of the day finishing the mystery novel I'd started the night before. It was better than the crime novel I'd read but that wasn't saying much. With the approach of evening, the stormy weather outside unfortunately didn't seem to be lessening. But my mind was still made up. I was going to Torremolinos tonight.

I had a shower, shaved, and spent some time trying to decide what to wear. I had a lot of options because, as I'd been slouching around the resort all week, I hadn't had a chance to wear any of the nicer things I'd brought with me. I finally decided on a long-sleeved navy top that was kind of silky and showed off my upper body nicely, and a pair of dark chinos. I put on my leather jacket and hoped I wouldn't get too drenched. After all, as I'd been coming to so-called "sunny Spain," I hadn't thought to bring a raincoat with me.

I had dinner in the dining room downstairs and then ventured into the bar. My old chum, Arthur, the English gent, was behind the bar. He advised me against traveling out that night but I told him I was going come hell or high water.

As I sat at the bar, though, drinking a beer, I wondered just *how* I'd manage to get to Torremolinos. The buses were definitely out, I knew that. I thought about it awhile but I couldn't come up with any great plan so I decided it would have to be a taxi. It would cost a lot but I'd hardly spent any of my week's budget being stuck inside, so I wasn't too worried about the money. The problem would be getting the taxi driver to go to Torremolinos. It was several miles away and the hideous weather would be off-putting. I guessed that if the taxi driver wasn't willing to go, all I could do was try to persuade him by offering him something extra, maybe double the fare.

I turned to Arthur and asked him what he thought. He agreed the buses were definitely out of the question. But he thought I'd be able to convince one of the taxi drivers to bring me by flashing some money at them. "Taxi drivers are greedy by nature," he said. "Particularly here."

Feeling better and more optimistic, I ordered another beer. I decided I'd check into a hotel in Torremolinos that night and not return to the resort until the next day. I'd probably be out very late and there was no point risking the weather a second time; it'd be much easier to return the following day.

A howl of thunder rumbled outside and the rain fell harder, shaking the tall French windows at one corner of the bar. As Arthur put a second cold pint of lager down in front of me, he gave me a raised-eyebrow look, as if to say: "Sure you want to go out there?"

I felt a bit doubtful, but once I got to Torremolinos all would be fine. I knew from checking around online that a lot of the gay bars were close enough to each other, and apart from maybe venturing to a couple of different ones, then back to a hotel, I'd be inside for most of the night. No worries. Or so I told myself. I knew it wouldn't be ideal, and it might be a bit tricky finding a hotel near the bars, but somehow I'd work things out. I had to. I'd been stuck in the damn resort all week, I needed to get out and see a bit of the world, even if that world was a string of darkly lit gay bars. Plus I had to have sex; I wanted it *and* I needed it. Find some nice Spanish boy or some big hairy Spanish guy . . . hmm. It sounded too tempting to let the weather, horrific as it was, stop me.

I was about to bid Arthur good night and see about finding a taxi when I suddenly spotted the hunky American from the first night. He was in one corner of the bar, using one of the Internet computer terminals that were set up for guests' use. My heart began to thud in my chest. I'd forgotten how stunning he was. Was he staying here in this resort? I wondered. All week long, I hadn't seen him around, not since that first night. I wondered where his blond girlfriend was.

I forced myself to turn around and face the bar because I realized I was staring at him and could go on staring at him for a long time. I ordered a third beer from Arthur. There was a large mirror behind the bar and I watched the American as I drank my beer.

I thought about going over to him, introducing myself or rather *reintroducing* myself. But what was the point? He was obviously straight. He'd been with that girl after all. What would he want with me? I looked at my own reflection in the bar. I looked good but probably not good enough to convert someone.

Suddenly going out of the resort into all that bad weather, all that rain and those gales, seemed like a bad idea. Why not just sit here, nursing my beer and staring at the American? I could only see his back, and who knew how long he'd be down here, but it was something. Just being close to him made me feel hot. I guess I was fantasizing that he would notice me, remember me, buy me a drink and then—

My thoughts were interrupted when I suddenly spotted him getting up from the computer. Shit, that was it then. He was leaving the bar and I'd probably never see him again. I was considering following him again like I had the first night when, to my complete disbelief, I saw that he wasn't leaving the room at all but was walking up to the bar.

Swiftly, before I could think of what to do or what to say, he was standing right next to me. He ordered a vodka from Arthur and sat down on the stool next to me. He glanced briefly at me and said, "Hey."

"H-hey," I gulped, with a lump in my throat that I tried to get rid of by swallowing a big mouthful of beer.

Arthur brought the American his vodka. I watched as he raised the shot glass to his lips and downed it in one gulp. He slammed it back onto the bar, like a character in a Western movie, and ordered another. This one gesture turned me on so much I nearly spilled my beer.

I decided to say something. He obviously didn't remember me. But here was my chance to say something, *anything*, to him. Faith and destiny (though I was too cynical by nature to believe in either) had thrown him back into my path two days before I was about to leave. Whether he was straight or not, I had to make some effort to . . . what? Well, I didn't know. But I wanted to talk to him, at the very least.

"Pretty nasty weather, isn't it?" I said in his general direction.

"Yeah," he said, not looking at me. Arthur put the second vodka in front of him. As he was about to drink it, he looked at me and said, "Hey, haven't I seen you somewhere before?"

Be casual, I told myself, and said, "I don't know. I'm not sure."

He drank his vodka. But he didn't order another one so Arthur retreated to a corner of the bar. The American looked at me again, studying me closely with his big dark eyes. "I'm sure I've seen you somewhere before," he said.

I was so happy he was just talking to me, I didn't think to reply; I just smiled at him. Then he slapped the bar with one big strong hand and said, "I got it. I remember. You asked me for a light a few nights ago. Right?"

"Oh," I said, playing dumb, "you're right. Yes, now I remember."

"Good to see you again," he said, sticking out his hand. I put my hand to his and he shook it roughly. "My name's Jeff," he said. "What's yours?"

"Adam," I said. He was still pumping my hand, his big one covering my smaller one.

"Good to meet you, Adam," he said, grinning. There was happy glint in his eyes. He stopped shaking my hand and slapped me manly on the back. "Let me buy you a drink."

Oh my god, I thought. My fantasy of a few minutes ago was actually coming true. He *had* noticed me, he *had* remembered me, and now he was buying me a drink. Suddenly this holiday seemed to be getting very good indeed. And to think I'd wanted to try to make it all the way to Torremolinos on a stormy night like tonight.

Don't get ahead of yourself, an inner voice warned me. Remember he's straight. He does seem happy to see you but he's just drunk and being friendly. Nothing's going to happen.

I ignored the voice and thanked Jeff for the drink. He bought me a rum-and-coke and one for himself. I sipped it, ignoring my unfinished third beer, and listened to him talk. About his girlfriend, mostly. What a fucking bitch. What a useless bitch. He went on like that for some time. He told me they had come to Spain together and had had a good time clubbing and partying, but the last few nights she'd refused to have sex with him.

"She said she was tired," he said. "Can you believe that? Bitch. I pay for a vacation for her and a good time. I spend a fortune on her and she doesn't want to have sex with me. I've been so fucking horny the last few days. And with this shit weather, I can't even leave the fucking resort and get some sun."

I felt a bit embarrassed. I was Irish and a bit of a conservative and not used to people telling me about their sex lives. I was used to having sex, and I was definitely used to wanting and thinking about sex all the time, but I just wasn't used to hearing strangers talk about it.

"That's fucked up," I said, though, to agree with him.

"You're damned right, it's fucked up," he said. "And that's not the only reason I'm mad at her. She's spent too much money. Totally maxed out our credit cards."

"That's not good," I said. It was all I could think of to say.

He went on a bit more about her, complaining, bitching basically. He also complained about her sister and boyfriend, with whom they had come on holiday. Then he stopped ranting and finished his rum-and-coke. He asked me why I wasn't finishing mine. I was about to answer when he said: "You know what I've got in my room?"

I swallowed some of the drink. "No," was all I could say.

"A great bottle of tequila." He smiled at me, flashing those pearly whites. He was amazingly attractive. I couldn't believe his girlfriend didn't want to have sex with him, regardless of his attitude or manners. I mean, he wasn't just hot, he was *Hot* with a capital H.

He was looking at me and I realized I hadn't replied to him. What had he said? Had he asked me a question? I couldn't remember. I'd trailed off into a bit of a fantasy world, imagining what I could be doing to him that his girlfriend wouldn't.

"Sorry, what?" I said.

"Tequila, man," he said. "This place is boring. Let's go up to my room and have some tequila."

He was inviting me up to his room already? Whoa, this was amazing. But it was happening so fast. Could I be dreaming or hallucinating? My mind was clouded by beer and rum. What was happening here?

"But what about your girlfriend?" I said through the haze of my thoughts.

"Sharon? That fucking bitch is out with her uppity sister and her prick boyfriend. Come on, follow me."

And suddenly I was following him, out of the bar, across the marble-floored lobby with all its potted palm trees, to the bank of elevators. I was at that giddy stage of drunkenness where I was still fairly sober but everything seemed so exciting, like the night could last forever and I could drink forever. And, amazingly and unbelievably, I was following this hot American to his room. I couldn't believe it.

I still couldn't believe it as I got into the elevator with him, got off on his floor, followed him to the door to his room. Was he really just inviting me up to his room for a tequila? Just tequila or something more? What if I made a clumsy drunken pass at him and he freaked out? Did he want to have sex with me because his girlfriend was holding out?

All these thoughts churned frantically through my head as I followed him into his apartment. His apartment was identical to mine, compact but deluxe. I was feeling great but anxious, horny but cautious: a mixed bag of emotions.

Like a flash-cut edit in a movie, I suddenly found myself sitting on the sofa in the living room with no memory of getting there. He was sitting beside me, talking about his girlfriend again. We were both drinking tequila. I looked at the bottle. It was half empty. There was a worm in the bottom of it. I hoped it was plastic. I looked down at my glass. It was empty. How much of the stuff had I had?

Jeff was saying, "She won't even give me a blow job. Can you believe it? She never has, says she never will, that it's not her thing."

Gone was my embarrassment at hearing him talk about his sex life. Maybe the drink had carried it away. I put my glass on the coffee table, got down on my knees on the floor, turned to face him, and said, "I'll give you one if you want."

He stared down at me for a minute. There was a look on his face that was difficult to interpret. I didn't know if I'd read the moment right, or if I had made a huge mistake. I figured it was probably the latter and, through the fuzzy layers of alcohol, I began to wonder if he was about to kick the shit out of me.

But then he said, simply, "Go for it."

I hesitated a moment, spluttered "what?" but then one of his big strong hands was on the back of my neck, pulling me forward, toward his crotch.

I was drunk and nervous and so stiff in my jeans it was painful. With shaking fingers, I pulled down his zipper, popped the top button of his pants. I reached in and felt his cock through a thin layer of underwear. It was very hard and throbbing. I pulled it out. Looking at it, I almost came right there in my pants.

His cock was a gigantic monster. At least ten inches. And it was uncut. It was also very thick, curving slightly to the left. A big, thick, uncut cock. I didn't waste time. I began to suck and gobble it, taking it all the way down my throat, nibbling at it with my teeth, stroking and sucking its shaft with my tongue.

Jeff clutched my head hard, kept forcing me down on it as I sucked him off. He groaned and said encouraging things like "fuck yeah" and "keep going" and "don't stop" and "suck it dry."

He came in my mouth. I felt him warmly erupting inside me

and I swallowed it, but some of his come trickled down my chin. When he pulled out of me, I mopped his come off my face with my fingers and then licked them. His spunk tasted so fucking good.

I thought there would be an awkward moment but there wasn't. He simply got up and went into the bathroom. I sat back up on the sofa. I still tasted him. I licked my lips. My own cock was bulging out the front of my jeans. I wondered if I should take it out and jerk off, or if that would freak him out when he came back.

I heard the toilet flush and a few seconds later he was back in the living room. He was completely naked. His cock was hard again, its big thickness jutting out. His chest was hairless and nicely muscled. Ropes of muscles coiled his big upper arms and strong thighs.

"Take off your clothes," he said, "and get on the floor."

I didn't need telling twice. I stood up and pulled off my navy top, then unbuttoned my jeans, pulled them down, and stepped out of them. Jeff looked down at my cock. I followed his gaze. My cock was narrower than his and not quite as long, about eight inches. But I thought it was still pretty impressive, even if it was nothing compared to his.

"Not bad," he said, and then he shoved his body into me, crashing me to the floor. We landed with a thud. He was right on top of me, a heavy weight. "I like you," he said and began to kiss me roughly, shoving his thick tongue deep into my mouth. I tried to tell him I liked him too but my mouth was full.

Outside a peal of thunder ripped across the sky, roaring like a lion. Blue-white flashes of lightning flickered through the room, distorting everything. Rain whispered and hissed against the glass of the windows and balcony door, shaking them in their frames, and showers of downpour drummed heavily on the roof.

I closed my eyes as he rolled me over on the floor. He began sucking and licking and biting my buttocks. My cock rubbed against the floor and I felt precome squirting out of it. I told myself to hold on, not to come, not yet.

Then Jeff was opening my ass, shoving his tongue up me, licking me out. It was great. I groaned and moaned in pleasure, rubbing against the floor, feeling more precome trickle out of my dick.

"I want to fuck you," he said.

"Yeah," I said. "Fuck me. Fuck me hard."

"I'll put on a condom," he said. "But I don't have any lubricant."

"It's ok," I panted. "Just fuck me."

As the storm outside built in intensity, and the sounds got louder and louder, Jeff began to fuck me. He fucked me so hard and for so long, I almost passed out. I heard growls of thunder, I saw flashes of lightning, I heard pounding rain. The rain in Spain, I thought wryly.

I opened my eyes. The room was dark. Then lightning flashed again and the room was full of white and blue light. Jeff's dick felt great inside me, he was filling me up. And I liked his heavy, warm weight on top of me. It was like we were in our own private little cocoon where nobody could find us in the storm.

My sphincter pulsed open and closed against his thick cock as it pounded inside me, going deeper than anyone else ever had. He fucked me hard, harder, harder still. I groaned and dug my fingers into the carpet. I almost screamed a couple of times.

And then he pulled out. He turned me over. "I want to come all over your cock," he said and perched over me. He took his thick cock in his hands. A long silver skein of precome hung from it.

"Yeah," I said, gasping in desire. "Come on my cock."

I held my own dick, jerked it off a bit, and then he came all over it. Big globs of come spattered all over my cock as I jerked it up and down frantically, using his slippery hot semen like lube. With a roar, I shot my own wad all over my chest.

He lay back on top of me. We were face to face. He kissed me briefly, and then we both lay there, panting and gasping, our come holding us together.

After a while he got off me and moved across the room. I lay there, listening to the storm and feeling wonderful. He came back with a pack of cigarettes and two glasses of tequila. He handed me a full glass and a cigarette. I didn't want the tequila so I put the glass down. But I wanted the cigarette. When I put it in my mouth, he lit it with the same silver lighter he'd lit my cigarette with that first night I saw him on the oceanfront.

We lay there on the floor next to each other, smoking and staring at the ceiling, lost in our own thoughts, not talking, just being next to each other and listening to the storm. I knew it couldn't last but right then it seemed like we'd be together forever. It was a moment I wanted to freeze in time.

After a while, he said, "Sharon's going to stay with her sister tonight like last night. I want you to stay the night."

"Ok," I said, and fell asleep.

When I awoke the next morning, I was in the bedroom. All I could remember was falling asleep on the floor. Jeff must have carried me to the bed. Did he sleep next to me? I didn't know but he wasn't here now. I sat up and looked around. The bedroom looked the same as the one in my apartment.

I got out of the bed and crossed to the door, put my ear against it, and listened. What if his girlfriend was back and out there? But all was silent. I stood there for a moment, naked and uncertain. My ass was sore and burning but the pain felt good because it was like he was still inside me.

I eased open the bedroom door. Like in my apartment, it opened right into the living room, which was empty. No sign of Jeff. The coffee table was empty. The ashtray and bottle of tequila were all cleared away. I couldn't see my clothes on the floor. I was about to leave the living room and go down the hall to the compact bathroom and kitchen, to look for Jeff, when something caught my attention.

"I don't believe it," I said aloud. Naked, I crossed the living room and went out onto the balcony.

The storm was over. The bad weather was gone. Bright sunlight warmed my skin and assaulted my eyes. I walked over to the edge of the balcony and looked down at the beach below. All was calm. The blue waves lapped gently at the sand. The beach was thronged with people, no doubt all of whom had been stuck inside like me all week long.

I smiled. This was the weather I was expecting when I came to Spain. I heard a sound behind me and turned around. It was Jeff. He was wearing a pair of shorts and carrying two mugs.

He looked so hot I felt my cock harden. He smiled at me, and then looked down at my cock and his smile widened. He handed me one of the mugs. I took it from him. It was coffee.

"I didn't know how you took it, so I made it black," he said.

"Black's fine," I mumbled, raising the mug to my mouth and swallowing a mouthful of the hot, bitter brew.

We stood there a moment, under the bright sunlight, looking at each other. I was still erect. I studied his body closely. His nipples were huge, I hadn't noticed that last night. He was tanned and buff. I couldn't believe my luck. The night before came flooding back to me and I smiled.

"Listen," he said, "when are you going home?"

I thought for a minute. What day was this? Then I remembered and said, "My flight's tomorrow night."

"Sharon, my girlfriend?"

I nodded. But I grimaced inside, hoping he wasn't about to start in on her again. This all seemed so perfect; I didn't want to hear about her.

"Well," he went on, "she's gone to Marbella with her sister for a few days. Do you want to hang out with me till you have to go home?"

I grinned. "Absolutely," I said.

This seemed too good to be true. The weather was brilliant and a hot, hunky American guy had fucked me last night, let me stay the night, and now wanted to spend the next couple of days with me.

"Awesome," he said and returned my smile. Then he put down his coffee mug, got down on his knees, and crawled over to me.

"What are you doing?" I said.

He didn't answer. He just took my erect cock in his hand and guided it into his mouth, then took it all in.

I groaned and leaned my head back as he began to suck me. Bright sunlight washed over me and I looked up at a clear blue sky as, for all the people on the beach below to see, Jeff sucked me off on his balcony.

After Jeff had finished sucking me, I dragged him back inside the apartment, shoved him up against the wall, and began sucking and biting those big nipples of his, while squeezing his cock

through his shorts. Then I got on my knees and sucked I
for a bit through the material of his shorts.

"It's my turn to fuck you now," I gasped, as I stood up and
turned him around, pushed him hard against the wall, and
tugged down his shorts, exposing that big round ass I had so
greatly admired the first night I'd seen him.

"Go easy," he said.

I did take it easy at first. His ass was nice and tight, virgin
tight. As I fucked him, I reached around and took hold of his
big, hairy balls, squeezing them tightly as I gradually increased
my speed and depth, plunging my dick in and out of his tight
hole. He roared in pain but told me not to stop. I fucked him
until he came, spurting strings of come all over the wall. I pulled
out of him and came myself, squirting my load all over his hot
ass, from which a little blood trickled—virgin blood.

I felt great. I'd broken him in. I smiled and kissed his neck
and we stood there for a long time, gasping, holding each other
against the wall. I had forgotten about the five days cooped up
indoors in the rain. Suddenly, this holiday was the best I'd ever
been on. And there were still two days of hot sex left! All thanks
to one stormy encounter.

TENDERLY, TANGIER

DAVEM VERNE

HE WAS TRACING Tangier when I met him, a dreamy young Moroccan, native to the many traditions of the Medina: kif, dirhams, Islam. I believe he imagined me a European, the colonial proprietor that many of these youths fear. My manners and habits should have been convincingly American, more than enough proof that this tourist would fall short of his ways.

In those last few days of 1956, Morocco was delivering its final blows for independence. Since the teens, Morocco had been divided into four: French Morocco, Spanish Morocco, Southern Morocco, and the International Zone of Tangier. It was a beautiful country, North West Africa, bordering the Atlantic and the Mediterranean. During these years, Tangier was a city and port on the Strait of Gibraltar and a mecca for mischievous tourists.

"How am I going to pay my taxes?" Ahmad Rashad bellowed to my party.

Our shoestring budget had landed us at the Villa de France along a well-beaten track. The hotel had long fallen to ruin: overpriced, cramped, and dingy. The little rooms each had a rocky mattress and a shower consisting of a bucket of water. At least the indigenous wall fixtures compensated with an Arcadian touch.

"Last year I was in all the guidebooks," the proprietor blasted at us, "and every day my hotel was full. This year my hotel's not in the book and I have no business!"

"Cool your motor." Gus wiped the heat from his brow.

A group of young men assembled, ready to whisk our baggage to our rooms. I found my eye occupied less by the hotel and more by this waiting staff. Each Arab youth wore a white gandoura with matching turban. Their uniforms were a striking contrast to our khakis and Oxford collars. My gaze grew suspect as I spotted the hunger on their faces. Coolies, wallahs, beggars; all they wanted was our money.

"Give us two rooms. That's all we need." Kip waved some green in Rashad's face.

"Na, Na, Na," Rashad complained. "Four Americans—four rooms. Four Europeans—four rooms. Four men—four rooms. No doubling up. I am a businessman, too!"

"Give him what he wants," Finch sighed, always giving in.

Gus turned to me.

"Its not the Taj Mahal. Think you can handle it?"

I shrugged and dug into my wallet. Rashad grabbed the bills with buttery fingers while squeezing my hand tightly. He clapped at the loitering youths and a feeding frenzy began for our suitcases.

"I suppose they'll want a tip on top of everything else," Kip complained. "Overpriced dump. Hey! My camera case!"

"You Americans are always welcome at the Villa de France! Tell all your friends! I will accommodate them, too!" Ahmad Rashad proclaimed as we were led through the narrow courtyard to the cluster of rented flats.

That night we smoked kif in pipes and savored Rashad's palate-pleasing delights, mostly lamb, served by the young waiting staff. We tried to exorcise them from our rooms, but they were incorrigible servants, loitering outside our doors for instructions and tips. I finally sent mine away with fifteen dirhams; Mjid had yet to return.

The other three, Yossi, Ami and Hassan, were pages to Gus, Finch and Kip, respectively. Since they couldn't be made to leave, we put them to use filling our pipes and stoking the lanterns. They knew little English, but spoke more French and Spanish.

Yossi and Ami looked like former shepherds, their physiques long and athletic and smelling vaguely of a goat. That Hassan had been a nomad was my foremost impression, for his eyes never wandered off Kip, as if waiting in the desert patiently. Kip protested the watchful intrusion, as it made him fearful of impending theft. I asked Kip how many times he had taken photographs of superstitious natives and that shut him up.

"*Si, si, asi es*," Yossi instructed Gus on packing his pipe. Yossi's lean hands and thin fingers were graceful at the art.

Wine and spirits of any kind were taboo in the port of Tangier. Liquor was consumed in private. So Gus had a stash of cognac handy in his valise.

I accompanied him back to his flat, hoping I might obtain a preliminary nightcap. The truth is, the presence of the three young men made me feel lonely. With my companions well-looked after, I was regretting the absence of my own servant, Mjid. Didn't he know I was only kidding when I brushed him off so quickly?

Yossi assisted with undressing Gus as I sat on a cushion. Gus was being stubborn with the cognac, so I lit some more kif.

"The local guest houses aren't built at exact angles," I observed openly, to no one's interest. "The labor in the desert use their eyes over measuring tools, creating an awkward sway to the interior."

Yossi held a flute up to his parted lips. His nose breathed in as he played a sweet song, enchanting our western ears with its melodic device.

"Here you go, buddy." Gus placed a few dirhams between he and Yossi. Yossi looked at me expectantly.

"I'm out. Mjid has my bank."

I reclined and swallowed the thick air.

"I read once that Moroccans don't like each other. They hate seeing one another naked and resent the one who might be prospering to another's advantage. Furthermore, there is no such thing as friendship between them. Only competition and ownership. Is this true, Yossi?"

"These Moroccans live for security," Gus replied. "That's why Moroccans love the Europeans, including the French. They make good paymasters for these little brutes."

I removed the pipe from my lips and inhaled the smoke hovering near my face.

A classical union was developing between my friend and the young Tangerian, an eroticism very natural to this region. Gus was practicing his colloquial Arabic, Darija, as he spoke secretively into Yossi's ear. He handed Yossi a few more dirhams and this made the youth increasingly grateful.

"Not for me," I professed. "These natives are genetically passive, inferior in my eyes. Living fossils of a weaker race. The world is my lebensraum; I am a tourist!"

Gus chuckled with his native youth. He kissed Yossi softly on the cheeks. Neither contested. Their discourse had ended. They were making embraces. My sunburnt friend held the dark youth closely that he could witness the soul behind the onyx eyes. Yossi shed his white gandoura. Beneath, his body was amply proportioned. Gus' hands, large and familiar with the conquering touch, made tender traces along each limb.

An act of male-on-male intimacy was occurring before me. It made me blush with anxiety. My companions had often spoke that this was a possibility in colonial countries, where sex was cheap and morality-free. That's why they chose Morocco and persuaded me to come; but I didn't expect it to be true.

Gus reclined on top of Yossi at the very corner of the mattress. They were crushing the springs. Gus weighed upon the youth with his heavy frame and placed his fingers at the crevice between two dark hips. The smallest hole parted as Gus made room inside the young man.

He rode the opening with the ridge of his forefinger. It was a tight ring, not the marrying kind, but a friendship ring that expanded as Gus forced his way deeper and held his stand. He packed his thumb up Yossi, breaking the cherry at the tanned thighs; with his other hand he caressed the brown boner that lay beneath the sheets.

Yossi murmured his compliance, sensing the affectionate security of his American lover. He held onto the sheet corners as Gus fisted him several times more. Yossi slipped into a trance and soon pocketed sperm into Gus' palm. This was the first time I had seen Gus act so tenderly and for the exclusive pleasure of someone else. How odd, since he was the hogging type.

My pipe was running on empty and I felt like an intruder. I neglected to refill it purposely. As the smoke faded, the cramped room filled with the scent of come. More was to follow. I said good night in French and let the crooked hallway tiles lead me to my dingy flat, where no one waited to greet me.

✦

THE NEXT DAY our troop decided to let our trusty guide-book recommend a path through the bustling city. Tangier was the business center of Morocco. And the crowded bazaar was a highlighted attraction.

We plunged into its frenzy. I quickly lost sight of my com-patriots through the thick smoke of roasting meat. Arab youths befriended me, willing to negotiate a trip. They surrounded me and led me through a fortress of walls as if into the African inte-rior. I implored them that I always traveled alone as I entered an arched threshold.

The Medina of Tangier was a world of wheels within wheels. This is where the opium of the Occident lurked. The narrow alleyways were smoky and half-lit. Houses encountered only through isolated tunnels fostered an impenetrable loneliness. Islam tempted, scintillating and deceptive upon the Arabesque faces and beneath the fluttering robes. Texture, depth and grain, it was a traveler's mecca!

I lost my way several times, purposely. It was fun at first, until the rugged surfaces mocked me. I spotted Hassan, Kip's nomad-ic companion. I called to him, but he made a menacing glance as he hovered beside a collapsing wall. He quickly vanished. Kip had probably frightened him with the shutter release, or a very wide lens. Another youth in baggy trousers, cloak, and turban jetted past me. He had short-cropped hair and a quiff over the forehead such that I mistook him for Mjid.

"Wait!"

I meant to follow the young man, maybe offer him some mon-ey, but he eluded my pursuit with long strides. Where was my indispensable servant? Still spending his easy wages, no doubt.

My solitary foray within the Medina was swathed by heat and dampness and teeming odors. I made footprints on African soil, but I wasn't alone. I adhered to my guidebook with religious determination. Somewhere near that corner was a restaurant es-tablished expressly for a foreigner's comfort.

Through a part in a wooden shutter, I was able to investigate a niche in the Medina. The Milk Bar, as it was called, was really an obscene play on words. It was founded by a European who, for mysterious reasons, fled into the Medina and never came out. Finch was there with his friendly servant Ami. The native bartender had retreated into his family chambers, leaving the enclave, a grimy, whitewashed parlor, for the visitors alone.

Finch was discrete by nature, while his Algerian-born guide smiled to the point of intimidation. I think this suited Finch. He drank a cool blend of soda and milk as Ami watched happily, remarking all the while of their next journey.

"Will you have another?" Ami urged in French.

"Nah. That did the trick. But I'll order one for you."

"*Oui, oui, s'il vous plaît!*" Ami begged with his hands, then prevented Finch from knocking on the wooden taifour between them. Finch frowned while his fingers were grasped by those of the dark youth. He was not a lover, Finch; he was a bit of the common steel worker at heart. But he held on to the tender grip like it was his last.

Ami had a woody for him inside his baggy trousers. Finch found it and tugged it gently beneath the table. The youth lifted his chandrisi and woolen djellaba in favor of the naked flesh. He parted his thighs for full view. Ami's skin was tender and taught. A washboard of caramel abs ripped beneath two well-proportioned breasts, round and athletic. His hips were lean and muscular, too, supporting a bulging crotch amidst dark, coyly hair.

Finch's thick thumbs crept down the chest to the tall cock jetting out from two dark balls. This tickled Ami. Finch wrapped his coarse fingers about the manhood, feeling its girth and texture. Carefully, Finch began to masturbate Ami who was giggling now upon the low taifour, his crotch propped up into Finch's face.

I thought that Ami wanted some milk, but now it seems he desired to *be* milked. He closed his eyes in prayer, the pools of deep brown disappearing behind two sensuous lids.

His head leaned back, exposing a small Adam's apple hanging inside a supple neck. Finch kissed Ami's neck as his hand jerked the youth. He kissed him most tenderly, biting the skin with his lips, making love to Ami's eastern flesh. Ami chuckled some more; only his brother had ever been this kind. Finch rubbed the lengthy circumcision and went down on his servant.

A taste at first, a lick, then a kiss. It looked sweet and smelled hot. He devoured Ami to the very base of his thickness. The olive cock vanished into Finch's pink lips and prodded the American's throat for depth.

Ami's body radiated of a dry sweat that filled the bar as his clothes fell off. The odor of naked youth was arousing Finch to consumption. Ami's white turban unraveled, revealing his boyish quiff over a wide grin. Unveiled, their lips met at last. The loose moisture spread over them and Finch kissed Ami's exposed brow and scalp.

In my usual combination of desire and detachment I thought, how charming, this desert Eros with his American consort. This would never be permissible back home, where women ruled. But far a field in the blistering heat of circumstance, men lost their reserve and remembered how to play schoolboy.

Ami pressed his manly prick further into Finch's clamped mouth. The cock slipped in and out, building momentum, banging inside Finch. Ami's movements were like a camel's, satisfying a nasty itch through the eye of a needle. The maddened stroke made Finch gasp. Desire was making him red with guilt. Ami's dick overwhelmed him. It insulted his moral upbringing. Finch's tongue cradled it nervously, easing the furious ride, but it grew inside him, bulging with desert juice and Arab blood and baking to a ready explosion.

Finch swallowed Ami's thick cock and held on, sucking hard, tasting the sour drops of precome seeping out. His face was so buried in Ami's quaking crotch that I could not appreciate the screech of joy as a liquid stream of come capped the olive head of youth and leveled an underground current of pure semen into my friend.

Ami laughed in blissful surrender. His hips pumped warm portions of milk into Finch before he collapsed his limbs unto the splintering taifour. Finch swallowed the forbidden flavor. He was shaking, my friend. The sleazy shithole of the milk bar had drugged him into submission. He was floating now inside a sexual slavery. He wanted more and sat back to wait until Ami could produce another bucket from the fount.

✦

IF I HAD a thread, like Ariadne did, I could guide Theseus through this hazardous maze and conquer the Minotaur of the Medina. The path through this narrow fortress was an ancient secret. It bewildered the unsuspecting pedestrian with its intricate web of towering walls. One's own shadow and footfalls seemed like the enemy's. Only the nationals knew how to trace an entrance and find the exit.

Mjid, where are you?

By midday, when I had finally given up on retracing my steps, I found Hassan lying in a dead-end alley. The alley was separated by four claustrophobic feet. He was lounging on a cart, the rascal, and playing with his black prick. The barest ray of sunlight reflected from a translucent pane of glass and subjected him to an intimate key light that dramatically tested his Moroccan features.

Kip had found him, too.

At one time, my travel mate had been a heavyweight champion. A Golden Glove, in fact. Kip even had the miniature gloves to prove it, chained around his neck. His tank top disclosed the large, muscular build of his youth. There was a famous boxer tattooed on one arm and Betty Boop on the other. He scraped a living training young men in his gym (and taking their photographs, too).

His camera spun gracefully in his hands as he hovered over the mischievous Arab. Close-up, medium shot, wide angle, hard focus; his fixation was becoming apparent.

Neither spoke. Hassan held his heavy cock in his hand and began rubbing it tauntingly. His palms and fingers were scarred and punctured from innumerable scorpion hunts. Kip went macro on them. The split fingertips, the callused skin, the sweat and oil. The camera went birds-eye to catch the cock peeking out, then hiding in the self-jerk.

Hassan pushed his hips off the cart to finger-fuck with his hands. His wry grin mocked his lover. The American's tank top tore off, revealing the hide of rippling biceps and pumped breasts. With the photo machine dangling beside his golden gloves, he lowered his khakis and stripped off his jockstrap. Kip's large, fat cock sprung out to engage them both by its alarming width. He hung over Hassan, dick and lens. The youth took the heavy prick and jerked his side-by-side, dark to light.

Kip clicked away.

The youth rested on his discarded turban and coyly lifted his legs over his shoulders. Kip bent down to face the crisp corridor of manhood. He captured the sensitive skin onto film: curly black strands dominating the male bush. But this ass was all shadow trickery. Kip ate the hole, feasting on the scent charming his lips. The nomadic youth moaned his approval. Saliva and ass juice dripped down the dark hips for Kip's last photo.

Resting the camera on its side and facing him, Kip leaned forward unto the desert opening. It split wide as his thick, roving cock pressed into it. The penis slit sifted in slowly, chewing at the ripeness and vanishing inside the bush of black hair. It soon arrived at a hot oasis. Kip's hard-on broke wide the opening, pink riding between hips of dark olive.

CLICK! The camera's auto-shutter released.

The American boxer began screwing the Moroccan quite hard. His was a coarse cock made of thick pig hide, immune to any exotic spell. Kip's curved hips, large and wide, stabbed his prick with fury, invading a continent and occupying the pre-civilized male pussy. With foreign savagery, he wished to colonize this local tramp. His dick-eye saw the tenderness of Hassan's interior, but screwed a throbbing boner with crude locomotion.

CLICK!

Hassan simpered through a contemptuous gaze. A tide line of come surged up against his will.

CLICK!

His stony heart melted and he sprayed his juice in clear spurts over Kip's chest, encouraging Kip to offend him even more. Kip's hairy groin planted a wicked cock box, bullying Hassan's ass chute and stroking the national with his American muscle.

CLICK!

Kip heaved Hassan in the air by the curve of his prick and spit a load of American seed with fiery force up the medina of manhood. Hassan shook at the crack and captured another load where no visible traces could discern, no thread could disclose, no wad uncovered.

CLICK!

✦

I RETURNED TO the Villa de France a wreck. I was horny and lost.

Already the vacant rooms were being rented out to new arrivals, a mixture of Europeans, Americans, and Canadians. Ahmad Rashad was doing what he knew best, clapping his hands and soliciting the foreigners with his flock of young, handsome servants. Had he opened his eyes instead of his wallet, he would have cried to Allah.

From the furthest corners of the civilized world these western vultures had gathered, a collection of moral primitives ready to feast on the last pickings of a waning colony. They neither loved Tangier nor hated her. They only smelled the carcass of death. The empire was in decay, but Rashad's business was picking up.

As I entered the lobby, I was warned that rebel activity was escalating in the city and that I should retire for the evening. But my flat was a scene of disorder. My personal belongings were scattered through the room and my postcards and souvenirs stolen.

"Come with me," a voice bid in French.

I turned around to face Mjid.

The youth was standing before me but in the dark; his smooth features melted my loneliness, though I remained suspect and cool. Mjid confronted me with his radiant eyes while displaying my passport in his hand.

"You are not safe. The Medina will be filled with spies by midnight. I am your only ally."

"But I am a tourist, not a diplomat," I rebuked, not a bit testy. "I gave you all I had before. You'd do better to arrange a new paymaster for your services."

"I will be your guide," Mjid nodded in earnest. "Tonight, no rate."

Mjid took me by the hand and led me swiftly through the International Zone of Tangier. He avoided the Medina. Colonized

Tangier was overwhelmed with the cry for independence. The fraternity of Islam was seizing the day. No place was safe.

"Stop there!"

A traffic official stood in the road, blocking our transit through the outskirts of town. He spoke to me in accusation, pointing to Mjid.

"Why is he with you? Why don't you send him away? You must come to the commissariat. It is against the law, but if you pay an acceptable fine, we could forget about it."

Like any apt guide, Mjid was in the middle of everything. Passports, kif, dirhams, bribes. He removed something from his burnous robe and slipped it into my hand. My money; all of it. I threw it at the guard, who vanished with healthy bills abounding.

✦

AFTER AN HOUR in flight, Merkala Beach was our final destination. The deserted sands stretched out before us; our footprints mingled in the tide. In the distance, we heard gunshots.

Mjid's face was swathed in blue moonlight as he spoke.

"We will stay here, for now. It is true, I ran away from you. You insulted me with your money. But I can no longer endure your neglect. If you cannot give me what I want, then I will take."

Before the creeping tide line, Mjid wrestled with my buckle until it snapped open. My cock rose to greet the gentle breeze as it was removed from my khakis. The penis stared at the uneven brow between Mjid's eyes as if it was looking at eternity.

Mjid kissed the head of my cock, tasting with his saliva an invisible drop of precome. He pressed it between his lips. I felt my shooter puncture the folds of his mouth and brush past his teeth. He swallowed me with heated intensity. My cock basked in the wet layers of his mouth where it reached the very end of its length.

We were doing the classical tango of foreigner and national. Mjid arrested my fears with a stream of licks, burying his head into my waist and squeezing my ass within his dark grasp. He cock-sucked me with hearty determination and bit my balls for some American honey.

Soon I was naked, my clothes scattered along the shore. Mjid was on top of me, a dark African creature feeding off my masculinity, seducing my ass cheeks with his sweaty palms and pressing his thumb where I was horny and tight. His silken face enraptured my dick, begging for fluid. He made a helmet with his tongue and strangled my cock head. The friction of his bite induced my seed to pop. I made no sound, but cradled his face to my groin, down to the root.

My prick submerged itself into his warm throat and coughed out a load from my locker. He teethed on the head for more. My swollen dick spit another nightcap, wet and gleaming across his lips. Mjid proclaimed his joy.

I turned away quickly.

I had fallen back on my promise not to get involved with the natives. With one fuck, I fell into his treacherous landscape. Though I had offended the principles of a seasoned tourist, I needn't keep up the pretense any longer. I was already ruined. If he had waited for me, then I will be *his* guide, into my own medina.

"Do this," I whispered softly. I lifted my right leg to my chest and leaned onto my left shoulder. He was on top of me. Squirming against the moist sand, I pressed my buttocks against his hardening cock.

In the damp breeze, Mjid wrapped his burnous cape over our free limbs. The cloth tangled about our legs. Within this blanketed hiding, Mjid found my hole by the lashing of his dick between my thighs. His circumcised head was enormous and wide as it kissed my opening. Mjid began impaling his sex into my ass. His boner slipped in smoothly without a complaint. Columns of ass juice swelled inside me nervously, indulging his manhood for a soft ride.

Under the crescent moon with gunshots crackling, my young servant found me an easy master and filled me with affection. Every concern I had before arriving in Tangier was washed away in the tide of his scent. Mjid's arms held me as his cock humped me and I fell deeper into his grasp. Yossi, Ami, Hassan, Mjid; they became one and the same, laying behind me, each taking turns pocketing their manhood in my hole and announcing their freedom.

Mjid took long to declare his independence. All of his flowers blossomed slowly. His trim waist rode me bareback, bucking and humping and ramming its length in, then slowing at the outfuck, long-cocking me for jism. I coaxed his prick with the butter of my ass, whetting his shaft as he packed my butt with his prick. It burned like fire, hot and snug, stroking my guts.

Suddenly, his body stiffened. The burnous was baking our desires. Mjid crammed his dick one last time into me and shot his load deep inside. His rich fluid heaved from two choked balls. When he slipped out, I could feel how hot and hard the screw had made him. And how tired.

It was nearly dawn when we awoke. Mjid took my hand to his lips and kissed me one last time. Then he stepped back.

"I must follow the traces of the sands that lead to my own destiny," he said, leaving me stranded on the beach. "Morocco is mine once more. We are free! Good-bye, American tourist."

I stood still as he vanished down the shore, a dark youth native to my dreams. Had he said those words before? Had he teased another American or European into submission, first by his absence, then by his scent? I had no answer. Mjid had guided me through more than Tangier that night. More than friendship or security could have known, we had gotten lost together, happily, far from colonial rule. And I, tourist, was conquered.

MASALA MASSAGE

LEW BULL

THE CLEAR, COOL seawater lapped gently onto the shore of soft white sand as Brad strolled alone along the palm-fringed beach. This was paradise as far as he was concerned: turquoise sea, white sand, green palm trees, and solitude. At no time in his life had he thought that he would be walking along such a tranquil, virtually uninhabited stretch of coastline.

He found the shade of a palm tree quite some way from the hotel, threw down his towel and rested there on the sand, watching the turquoise sea, which hardly seemed to be moving. In fact the sun blazed down and it too seemed hardly to be moving—it was as if life had come to a standstill. The locals on this Indian Ocean island seemed to follow the example of the sun and the sea, and they too seemed motionless. He had hardly noticed any locals on or near the beach other than the hotel staff who went about their various duties.

Brad pulled his T-shirt over his head to reveal a trim, muscular body, much like that of a swimmer, and then stepped out of his shorts to reveal a canary yellow Speedo underneath; then he stretched out on his towel. He lay there resting on his elbows, becoming hypnotized by the gentle ebb and flow of the sea's action up the gentle shore. He felt himself floating into a state of serenity when a foreign voice broke the magical moment. He turned his head slightly and next to him stood a tall, slim, young Asian man of about twenty-two years of age, with a sling bag over his shoulder, smiling at him.

"I am sorry to disturb you sir, but I wondered if you would be interested in having a massage?"

Brad was a little taken aback by this introduction, but he was neither adverse to a massage nor a friendly face.

"What is your name?"

"Goolam, sir," replied the young man, bowing his head as he said so.

"I'm very pleased to meet you, Goolam. My name is Brad."

Although Goolam was of Indian descent and had the usual dark hair of Indians, his complexion tended to be lighter than most Indians; in fact it might even have suggested that one of his ancestors had been white, but Brad was not about to ask him such questions.

"When you say would I be interested in a massage, where did you have in mind doing it?" asked Brad, smiling up at the young man.

"Right here on the beach. I offer a service to customers at the hotels," replied Goolam.

"But what about other people passing by?" questioned Brad.

"In this part of the beach you may have noticed that there are no people and you will have total privacy, and you are shaded from prying eyes that might be looking from hotel balconies."

Brad looked about him to secure in his mind the element of privacy and then at the young man's lithe body clothed only in a thin vest and shorts, and long fingered hands. Although Goolam's hands tended to look feminine, Brad could see that they were smooth but looked strong. Brad convinced himself that it would be safe and negotiated a price, which he paid and Goolam knelt on the sand next to Brad.

"You like a full massage or only a back massage?" enquired Goolam.

"Let's start with the back and see how you do," came the reply, and Brad flipped onto his stomach to reveal a muscular v-shaped back waiting for attention and a well-shaped bubble-butt tightly encased in the Lycra of his Speedo.

Goolam opened his sling bag and withdrew a bottle of oil from it, which he gently poured onto Brad's back. Although it was hot under the palm trees, Brad felt the coldness of the oil as it trick-led down between his shoulder blades and along his spine. He then felt the gentle touch of Goolam's fingertips as they spread the oil over his muscular back. Goolam's hands moved slowly and gently over the shoulder blades and slid down the spinal column, then back up to the shoulders again, very much like the gentle waves moved up and down the shore; it was as though Goolam followed the rhythm of the sea in his movement.

Brad could feel himself becoming more immersed in a tropical haze of relaxation as Goolam worked over the canvas of masculine flesh, kneading and caressing where necessary. He then felt Goolam's hands move to the top of his left leg and slowly begin a slow, sensual journey down its length over his well-formed calves until Goolam's hands reached Brad's Achilles and then began the return journey up to the firmly encased ass. The same movement was repeated a couple of times and then alternated to the right leg. All the while, Brad felt a warm, tingling feeling throughout his body as the young man's sensuous hands glided over his tanned skin.

Goolam's hands returned to Brad's back, pushing firmly on the deltoid muscles as the sun broke through the palm fronds creating shadows and light across Brad's back. After what felt like an eternity, the silence of the surrounds was broken.

"You want more?" whispered Goolam. "Or do you only want the back done?"

Brad groaned as he lay on his stomach. "Don't stop."

Goolam gently put his hands under Brad's shoulder as though to try and lift him, thereby suggesting that Brad flip over onto his back so that Goolam could massage his chest, stomach and the front of his legs. Brad eased himself over onto his back. As he did so he smiled up at Goolam serenely, showing the gratitude for what he was receiving from this young man's hands.

Goolam began on Brad's chest and shoulders, rubbing in the oil which he had gently poured onto Brad's heaving pectorals. His slim fingers caressed Brad's enlarged nipples seductively, causing Brad to thrust his pectoral muscles upward. Brad lay with his eyes closed, luxuriating in the pleasure that he was receiving. The strong hands moved to the sternum and lowered down to the diaphragm and stomach muscles. Goolam's fingers traced along the top of Brad's Speedo, as though combing the fine blonde layer of hair protruding from the top of Brad's costume. Goolam continued to work on Brad's stomach and chest for a while, then moved his attention to the thickly muscled upper thighs.

The palms of his hands slid from the outer side to the inner side of each thigh and as he did so Goolam's hand gently touched the firmly packed crotch of Brad's Speedo where the heavy balls lay encased in Lycra. Before starting to massage Brad, Goolam had noticed, with no small amount of interest, the size of the package that Brad carried in the front of his Speedo; however, Goolam was pleased with his actions, because he noticed a slight movement within the confines of the material. The outline of Brad's cock was becoming more defined and through the growing process, Goolam could make out the rim of the cut head of Brad's cock and its long stem going down to the heavy balls.

Goolam moved his attention to massaging the entire length of Brad's legs, working from the upper thigh down to the ankles and then up again, but each time ensuring that the tips of his fingers managed to gently rub against the taut material of the Speedo.

A gentle sigh emitted from Brad as each time Goolam's fingers moved up his legs toward his ever growing manhood and then slid back down toward the feet. A slight breeze blew up and the fronds of the palm trees rustled gently and the shadows moved across Brad's body. As the fronds rustled, so Goolam bent over Brad's stomach and gently blew across the thin layer of blonde hair protruding from the top of the Speedo. He noticed how Brad's cock throbbed when he did this and a small wet patch of precome began to appear near the top of the waistband where Brad's cock now rested. As he continued to massage Brad's legs, Goolam placed the tip of his tongue on the wet Lycra material where the head of Brad's swollen cock lay and gently flicked his tongue tasting the wetness, again causing sudden jerking throbs to occur. Goolam slowed down his massaging movements until there was no movement except for the lapping of the waves and the gentle rustling of the palm trees. He moved quietly from where Brad lay on the towel and slowly stood up, looking down at this Apollo glistening in the dappled light from the oil. Brad slowly opened his eyes and saw the smiling face of Goolam looking down at him.

"Don't stop. Why did you stop? That was so good."

"I have done what you have paid me for and I hope that you have enjoyed it."

"That was the most beautiful feeling I've experienced, but it feels incomplete. Please won't you finish it for me?"

Goolam smiled. "I would be most honored," said Goolam admiring the engorged package which now occupied the front of Brad's Speedo. He moved to position himself astride Brad's torso so that his legs were either side of Brad and he hovered over the throbbing Speedo. Goolam continued to massage Brad's chest and stomach and slowly lowered himself so that his shorts rubbed over the bulging yellow costume. Brad felt Goolam's crotch rub over his own and each time, his cock throbbed causing more precome to escape. Brad lifted his right hand and felt for the leg opening to Goolam's shorts. When he found it, he slid his hand in to search for Goolam's cock. He found a long, thin and hard piece of meat waiting to be fondled. He squeezed Goolam's cock hard and Goolam thrust harder onto Brad's crotch.

"May I sit on you?" asked Goolam, like a child asking for permission to do something.

"I'd very much like that," replied Brad, thrusting his cock upward.

Goolam stopped massaging Brad for a moment, rose from where he was sitting and searched his sling bag. Brad watched as Goolam found what he was looking for: a condom. He tore open the foil wrapping, pulled Brad's Speedo down allowing the waiting cock freedom from the constraints of the Lycra, and unrolled the condom seductively down the length of Brad's hard cock. Once he had completed this task, he slid his shorts down and stepped out of them, then lowered himself onto Brad's crotch.

Goolam took hold of Brad's thick, hard cock, aimed it at his ass entrance and slowly began to sink onto Brad's length. Brad could feel the tightness as he fought for entry, while Goolam's ass seemed to be resisting attack. Both men pushed against each other until finally Goolam gave in and sank, with a deep groan, onto the long awaited pleasure. He had pleasured Brad, now it was time for Brad to reciprocate. Brad thrust deeply when he felt the tightness strangling his cock, in fact he thought that he would shoot his load without much friction. Just as Goolam had been slow and gentle in massaging Brad's body, so he began a slow and gentle massaging of Brad's swollen cock. With his hands massaging Brad's nipples and his tight ass crunching Brad's cock between his sphincter muscles, Brad lay back and groaned in ecstasy.

"I don't know which is better, you massaging my body or my dick," said Brad, thrusting once more deeply into Goolam.

Goolam ground his ass around Brad's cock, sliding up to the tip of the swollen mushroom-shaped head and then just before it escaped from its confines, he would plunge down its entire length until Brad's balls slapped against his ass. Brad could feel the warmth that encompassed his cock which remained safely embedded in Goolam's tight ass, but he could also feel the nearness of his climax. He took hold of Goolam's uncut cock and began sliding his hand along its length, pulling the foreskin to its very tip and then sliding it all the way back to reveal the shiny head.

"You're getting me close," gasped Brad as Goolam once again slammed down on the nine-inch length.

"So am I," responded Goolam, increasing his attacks on the now sweating Brad.

Brad held tightly onto Goolam's waist with one hand and increased the speed with which he was stroking the young man's hardened cock, until Goolam's face took on a picture of delight and the young man fired the first of a volley of shots. Come shot across Brad's chest and he felt Goolam's sphincter muscle clamp even more tightly around his cock as though it was squeezing the life out of it. A second and third volley landed on Brad's stomach, at which point he couldn't contain himself any longer, and with a loud grunt he plunged deeply into Goolam's tight ass and proceeded to fill his condom with warm satisfying come. So intense was his deep thrust that Goolam almost fell over, but the sphincter never relented; in fact it felt as though Goolam's ass was draining every last drop of come from Brad. Long after both men had exhausted their supply of love juice, they continued to thrust and ride, not wanting either to part from the other and lose their binding connection. Finally, Goolam collapsed across Brad's chest, heaving deep breaths while the sweat from Brad's chest became absorbed in the material of Goolam's vest. Brad put his arms around Goolam and held him there for some time, without detaching himself. Brad could feel Goolam's ass pulsating and in doing so, it kept Brad's cock firm. It was almost as though Goolam wanted this to all happen again.

"I don't want you to pull out," breathed Goolam.

"I don't want to leave your ass at all," replied Brad, giving a series of gentle thrusts. "In fact I'm ready to fuck you again, but this time in the comfort and pleasure of my hotel room."

Goolam smiled a knowing smile, rode Brad's barge-pole two more times and then slid off, feeling the pleasure of having been impaled by this magnificent man, but anticipating what was still in store for both of them and the pleasure that they would give to each other. As they made their way back to the hotel, the tranquility of the beach, the sea and the palm trees added to the moment and the pleasure.

SIROCCO WIND

JAY STARRE

COLIN FELT THE hot, dry air whisper across his face, stealing moisture like some kind of ancient Berber demon of the desert. He had been told it was a sirocco wind, originating in the endless dunes of the burning Sahara, now reaching the cooler shores of the Mediterranean to the north where he sat outside a local coffee house in the pleasant lower section of Algiers.

Colin had just completed a tour of duty with the American forces in the Middle East and had delayed returning home for a brief holiday and rest in this famous North African city. He'd chosen it for a strange reason, or maybe not so strange. That reason, Mahomet.

Mahomet had been Colin's first boyfriend, or fuck buddy, or whatever label could be pinned on the intense but short-lived sexual relationship he'd savored in his freshman year of college back in Des Moines, Iowa.

Mahomet's parents were mixed, his father French and his mother Algerian. They had fled after Algerian independence in the early '6os like so many others, mostly Europeans. They had come to America, and Mahomet had been born in Des Moines ten years later.

Colin almost felt as if he could smell his long-lost lover in that dry sirocco wind. Mahomet had been a steamy lover, sensual and uninhibited, with deep brown eyes and a crooked smile. His skin had contained a bronze glow, as if emanating from within, and was hot to the touch. His long, brown cock had been so firm, and had seemed to scorch Colin's hand when he gripped it and pumped it to inevitable release. Colin remembered that, and the pain of being finally rejected by his friend who claimed he wanted to be free.

Free. That's how Colin felt that torrid Algerian evening. He was released from duty in the army. He had no one waiting for him at home, other than family he hardly spoke to. He didn't even have any real plans for how long he would stay in Algiers or Algeria before going home.

He looked up from his cup of coffee. The city rose from its bustling and modern waterfront to the twisted streets of the Old Town, the famous Casbah. The gleaming white of so many huddled African homes and businesses called to him. The lure was powerful. Dangerous, too, he'd been warned. He should hire a guide, he was told.

Colin spotted him out of the corner of his eyes. The sun was setting in the west, and slanting shadows framed him against a palm tree where he stood beside the wide boulevard, doing nothing, it appeared. Just standing, his eyes wandering over to where Colin was seated alone outside the Algiers café.

Colin stared. He knew it might be considered rude, but the French-built boulevard was wide and busy with traffic, a sort of impersonal barrier between them. The Algerian wore traditional dress, a flowing white-and-brown striped djellaba that billowed around his body in the rising breeze.

That sirocco wind. It galvanized Colin. He continued to stare, drinking in the stranger's appearance along with the remnants of his coffee. The Algerian was young. Probably only in his very early twenties, like Colin himself. His face was soft and round, with a trace of a beard growing beneath his chin line and neatly trimmed along his neck. His nose was the only sharp feature on a broad face. Lush lips formed a wistful half-smile. Wide-set brown eyes hovered under arching brows. He looked altogether soft, as opposed to bold or rigid. It wasn't a feminine look, but it definitely wasn't a hard, macho look either. Maybe it was the dresslike djellaba that flowed around him that lent him that aspect of seductive innocence.

The appeal of the young eyes that met his was instant, and Colin's cock rose up tight beneath his underwear and jeans. They stared at each across the wide boulevard. Then, slowly, the stranger's tentative smile broadened and he gave Colin a small nod. With a languid wave of his hand, he beckoned, smiled again, then turned and slowly headed up the intersection. Toward the Casbah.

Colin, his cock throbbing in his jeans, rose like a shot and raced to follow before the Algerian was lost in a sea of other djellabas. There were plenty of men dressed in western clothing, but the African kaftan was just as evident and the stranger not so unique he could easily be picked out among the throng.

Colin lost sight of him by the time he had crossed the busy street, and he instantly chose to follow the intersection up toward the Old City and the Casbah. Whether the tantalizing stranger could be found there or not, he'd intended on visiting that section of Algiers anyway. Now he had a goal.

Several times as Colin ascended toward the Casbah he was sure he caught sight of Mahomet. He caught himself thinking of the stranger as his old flame from college. They did look similar in a vague sort of way. Their wide faces, those deep amber eyes and thick lashes.

It was once he was within the twisting streets of the Old Town that Colin realized the sun had set and it was growing dark. He hesitated briefly. Was this dangerous? But there were loads of others walking around, or bicycling or driving where cars could negotiate the narrow lanes. It was busy, too busy for murder or terrorism.

Colin had served in the army. He had discovered he possessed a limited sixth sense for danger. He didn't feel any danger here. All he felt was the throbbing of his cock beneath his jeans, and that hot dry wind blowing around him.

Colin saw him!

It was him, standing at the entrance to another narrow alleyway, a cracked and dusty streetlight illuminating his djellaba, his distinctively soft features, and his bare head. There was that difference about him that distinguished him from many other Algerians. Those who dressed in the Algerian kaftan also sometimes wore the headdress of cotton or silk. He was bare-headed, for whatever reason.

Their eyes met again, now only fifty yards apart. The Algerian smiled, nodded and again raised a brown hand and waved laconically, almost diffidently, then he turned and slipped away up the darkened alley.

Colin was right behind him, his cock leading him on the chase. It might have been stupid and dangerous, but Colin felt no fear as he moved into the narrow alley. Dim light from a star-filled sky and the streetlight behind showed him the way and softly illuminated the lone man waiting for him.

They collided. Like two meteors from opposite universes, their bodies smashed together in the darkness, arms entangling and lips mashing together. No words uttered in that first sear-ing moment of connection were needed or wanted. No names to define or separate them into Westerner and African. Two young men, two hot bodies, two groping, lusting males with sex upper-most on their minds.

They kissed passionately, little mewls and moans escaping their clamped lips. Each had their arms wrapped around the oth-er, fiercely clasping the other's firm body against their own, as if now that they'd found each other, they would never let go.

One of Colin's hands seized the thin cotton material of the djellaba at the Algerian's side and pulled up on it. With greedy need, he bunched the kaftan in his hands, pulling up until the lower hem was in his fingers and he could slide his hand under the robe to search out the flesh beneath.

Colin snorted in air with a shock of surprise as he discov-ered bare skin. He had expected maybe European dress beneath, since he knew some men wore the djellaba merely over pants or even suits. But there was a hot, naked waist pressing against the palm of his hand. Colin searched lower now that he was under that flowing robe, and found more bare flesh.

The Algerian was naked under his djellaba! Colin's fingers traced the line of waist, then the rounded globe of naked ass. The feel of that hot skin seared his hand, momentarily dislocat-ing him as he recalled Mahomet's naked butt with perfect clarity. He reeled, snorting in air through his nose, teetering on his feet before the Algerian's firm embrace steadied him.

The moment was too intense for Colin to lose himself in mem-ories, no matter how bittersweet. He was here and now, in the arms of a young, eager Algerian who obviously wanted his body as much as Colin wanted his. Colin slipped his hand up between the Algerian's satin-hot butt cheeks.

Thighs moved apart and a little grunt escaped the Algerian's lips before he covered Colin's mouth with his own and pressed back into the probing hand. Colin inhaled a distinctive Arab scent, cloves, cinnamon, even perhaps the hint of fabled frankincense and myrrh. His fingers moved deep between the sweltering nether cheeks, searching until they found the puckered rim of a throbbing asshole.

The blond American moaned, sucking in tongue as he stroked that pulsing hole, tickling the lips and the heated entrance with an eagerness he could barely contain. He wanted to fuck this stranger! So fucking bad! He wanted his cock to go up that warm, palpitating hole and drill and drill and drill.

Warm thighs opened wider under the djellaba as the Algerian planted his feet back against the whitewashed wall of the alley and grunted deep in his chest. Colin began to worm a finger between the twitching anal lips while he sucked tongue and snorted air in through his nostrils. He could barely breath he was so excited.

His cock, erect and jerking, pressed into the front of the cotton djellaba, meeting another cock just as stiff and alive. Both male snakes thrust and rubbed against each other, the material of Western and Arab clothing the only barrier between their craved-for satisfaction.

Colin's right hand was buried between the Algerian's ass cheeks, pushing up the back of the djellaba. His left hand coveted the feel of flesh, and he pushed up under the front of the striped brown and white material, lifting up folds of the djellaba in the darkness to greedily hunt for the prize.

"Ummmnnn," Colin moaned as his hand discovered hot, hard cock. Now he had two hands busy working on the dusky Algerian's body.

Sounds in the alley barely distracted him from his exploration. Other men? Rats? Cats? Whatever it was, the sound moved off and they were alone again, wrapped in each other's moaning, grasping arms.

The Algerian ground his body against the hands probing it, while he took the liberty of sliding his hands up under Colin's loose shirt, popping a few buttons off in his rush to feel smooth chest and muscled shoulders. The hands were rougher than Colin expected, calluses on the palms from some kind of hard labor, and strength in the fingers as they kneaded and pinched Colin's muscles and then found his nipples and began to tweak and pinch almost painfully.

"You're as hot for it as I am," Colin gasped out, his mouth pulling away for a moment to stare down at the man in his arms.

"I am Mahomet," the stranger said in softly accented English.

Colin's hands froze for an instant. Mahomet. A coincidence? Fate? A common enough Arabic name, he had been told by his college lover. But this was almost too much.

Then a hand released his cock from the prison of his jeans, the zipper of his fly down and his pants and underwear shoved to his knees. Mahomet was just as eager for Colin's body, it appeared. But then, in the darkness, the soft voice spoke again. A whispered plea.

"Kiss me. Use your mouth on me. I'm clean."

Colin surrendered to the surreal moment, fate dictating his actions as much as desire. He understood what Mahomet was asking. Perfectly. With his hands under the Algerian's robe, he twisted him around and pushed him up against the whitewashed wall of the alley. Mahomet merely gasped and spread his feet obligingly, lifting his hips and rolling his sexy ass in a seductive wriggle.

Colin pushed the djellaba up to Mahomet's waist, revealing the sturdy brown thighs, hairless and well-muscled. Barely able to see in the semi-darkness of the alley, he peered at the ass in front of him as he dropped to his knees and spread it open with both hands.

Kiss me, Mahomet had begged. Use your mouth on me, he had whispered. I'm clean, he had promised. Colin's fingers dug into the satiny amber flesh of twin globes, spreading them to reveal the puckered hole he'd just been fingering. He could distinguish it once his pupils dilated enough to see in the night's darkness.

A hairless slit, a puckered sphincter between two solid butt mounds, calling to him. Kiss me, Mahomet had asked. Colin buried his face in the warm brown ass. His tongue snaked out, his lips clamped over the pulsing anal slot. He tongued and sucked and slobbered voraciously, totally out of control. He ate the Algerian's asshole with complete abandon.

Mahomet writhed against the wall, pressing back against the devouring mouth and invading tongue. His balls slapped against the blond American's chin. His cock, stiff and drooling, thrust into the bunched folds of his own djellaba. He bit his lip and closed his eyes, surrendering to the lips and tongue of the American stranger.

Colin revelled in the anal feast, squeezing and massaging the wide-spread butt cheeks as he wormed his tongue into the heated depths of the Algerian's anal slot. He felt Mahomet's body responding, squirming, humping backwards, emitting those incoherent moans. With the sixth sense he'd been experiencing all evening, he realized it was time to fuck the Algerian. Mahomet wanted it. He was ready for cock.

Colin reared up, his pants and jeans tangled around his knees. The hot brown butt was naked and spread in front of him, djellaba bunched up around Mahomet's waist. The ass writhed, eager for what Colin was about to offer it.

"I'm going to fuck you up the ass, Mahomet," Colin whispered.

It sounded strange to be saying that name again, but Colin let the emotional twinge flow through him and slip away. Just as his cock lurched forward to stab between the spread ass cheeks, a blast of that searing sirocco blew across them up the alley.

The wind incensed him. He thrust, much harder than he'd intended. His cock head, the fat knob thick and blunt, slammed into the spit-swabbed anal lips, stretching them apart as effectively as Colin's hands spread apart Mahomet's firm butt globes. Cock drove deep, buried in the scorching folds of Mahomet's insides.

They both cried out. Asshole pulsed around throbbing cock. The darkened alley echoed with their sharp outcries, then fell silent again. Colin focussed on the sweet sensation of that convulsing anus wrapped around his knob and half his shaft. He began to fuck, pushing a little deeper to the deep sighs of his Algerian partner, and then pulling out to even deeper sighs. Slowly, Colin fed Mahomet all of his cock, inch by fat inch, until their bodies were mashed tightly together, hip to hip, connected by pulsing, hard cock.

One of Colin's hands slid around Mahomet's waist and found the Algerian's stiff cock within the folds of the bunched djellaba. He wrapped his fingers around it and began to pump in time to his steady thrust from behind.

Mahomet spread his feet as wide apart as possible, lifting his ass and arching his back. He opened up to the deep fuck, his clamping sphincter relaxing and then enveloping Colin's cock in heated, moist acceptance. Colin's spit lubricated the way as the blond American fucked the dusky Algerian with slowly increasing speed.

They gasped and they grunted together as the fuck became more intense. Need rose up in both young men as their cocks surged with growing excitement. Colin's fingers wrapped Mahomet's dick with pumping heat. Mahomet's deep anus wrapped Colin's fuck tool with pulsing warmth.

The sirocco rose to blast them from the alley entrance. Heat on heat. Colin groaned. He couldn't hold back any longer. He felt, and sensed Mahomet's body tense, his asshole seizing Colin's thrusting pole. They drove together, ass cheeks slapping against hips in a final fury of hard fuck.

"I'm coming," Colin gasped out.

Spooge erupted from Mahomet's cock at exactly the same moment, drenching Colin's fingers as he pounded deep into Mahomet's ass from behind. Come rocketed out of Colin's cock head as he pulled out and sprayed the rounded cheeks of Mahomet's hot, writhing buttocks.

They orgasmed together, a climax of unusual intensity, come spraying and surging out of both sets of balls for several ecstatic minutes. Their heaving chests finally quietened, Mahomet's djellaba still bunched up around his waist and Colin's jeans tangled around his knees.

Finally they disengaged, pulling apart as they both covered themselves. The sirocco blew up the alley to waft across them a little more gently now, but with no less scorching intensity.

They looked at each other, less than a foot of space between their spent bodies in the narrow alleyway. Mahomet smiled first, broadly, his white teeth a splash of light in the semidarkness. Colin held his breath, awaiting the inevitable good-bye.

"Come with me. To my home."

Colin's breath came out in a long, emotional exhale. He smiled weakly. Freedom? This Mahomet wasn't claiming any need for that elusive state of being.

Colin reached out and took the Algerian's hand in his. They laughed together, moving up the alley into the Casbah. The sirocco blew against their backs, urging them on.

THERE ARE THINGS WHICH ARE HIDDEN FROM THE EYES OF THE EVERYDAY

SIMON SHEPPARD

PLEASE, TAKE YOUR time. Finish your mint tea. Perhaps you'd like another of these baklava? No? Well then, I'll have the last of them. I'm afraid I can't resist temptation.

My friend, there's a story I'd like to tell you. A story that may shed some light on what we've been discussing tonight. Perhaps it will help you deal with your . . . desires.

✦

LONG AGO, WHEN the Great War ended, a man found himself in Gibraltar, aimless and alone. (He'd lost whatever small family he'd had, whatever small faith had remained.) It was then he first heard rumors of the Magicians of Fez. A stranger in a café, a man he'd met on a train, a friend of a wartime acquaintance, each had mentioned a secret circle of miracle workers whose identities were unknown to any but one another. In clandestine workshops—some versions of the tale had them located beneath the winding streets of the city—they pursued investigations into the fabric of the universe itself.

Depending on who was telling the story, the Magicians of Fez were said to have power to transmute base metals into gold, or to read the thoughts of another, or to reshape matter in such a way that it was possible to walk through solid walls. Where they gathered, it was said, the night sky burned with the light of the sun.

Some even whispered that these sorcerers had gained power

over the very workings of life and death. An elderly man he'd met in Tangiers had pulled out a yellowed newspaper clipping and, claiming to translate from the Arabic, recounted the story of one Mohammed al-Lawati, a dyer of leather who had fallen to his death from a rooftop in Fez, but who, through the intercession of an unnamed passerby, had subsequently risen from the dusty street and walked off with no more than a scratch.

So, though not without mishap and misadventure, he made his way through Morocco to the Imperial City of Fez, in search of this underground cabal. It was not that rationality had failed him; he fully suspected that his myth mongering would prove futile. But, rootless as he was, he knew that even the wildest of fancies might distract him from bleak memories of combat and loss. As is often the case with those who think they have given up all hope, he set himself upon a quest which would have been meaningless if hope were truly gone.

He began to make inquiries wherever he went, follow every lead, no matter how unpromising. Each time, he would soon enough come to a blank wall. Like the endless horizon, the specter of the brotherhood fled always before him. The shoemaker knew nothing, but told him to ask the school teacher; the school teacher knew the name of a certain brassworker who'd know the truth of the matter; the brassworker, when found, professed ignorance but recommended making inquiries of the shoemaker.

However, it did not take him long to understand that, as a white man, an attractive young man with money, he might find all sorts of things in Fez, even if the Magicians eluded him. One afternoon (he'd only been in town a few days), a teenaged boy guiding him through the sun-washed souk pulled him into a blind alleyway and pressed his young body up against him. Though his only previous experience of sex had been with his late wife, with half-a-dozen loose women during the War, and with a miscellany of neighbor children long, long ago, he felt an undeniable, unsettling attraction to this brown young man.

Part of him was quite naturally appalled, but the boy's dark-eyed glance seemed to conquer his will. And the guide's hand quickly found stiffening evidence of his response. He leaned against a whitewashed wall, eyes closed, allowing his fly to be unbuttoned, feeling not danger, but a strange kind of safety as his hardness was exposed. The feeling of the young man's mouth on him was a delicious shock. His wife had never done this. One of the whores had, but her mouth was nowhere near as expert as this boy's.

He opened his eyes, looked down, watched his spit-slick, veiny cock being licked, swallowed down again and again by this ragged young stranger. As the guide took him all the way down his wet, warm throat, he closed his eyes again and with a sharp cry shot deep into the boy. He leaned against the rough wall for a moment, eyes still closed, dreading the inevitable haggling over the *dirhams* that would be demanded in payment for this pleasure. But when he opened his eyes, the boy had silently vanished.

Whatever guilt he came to feel after that was overwhelmed by a greed, a longing to find the boy and once again thrust himself down the beautiful young man's warm throat. In the mornings, wakened by the muezzin's cry, he would dress, gulp down a glass of syrupy mint tea, and go off to wander the streets of the city. He told himself he was on the trail of the secret magical brotherhood, but he knew he was always keeping watch for a boy with a beautiful face. A face he hoped he would be able to recognize.

Evenings often found him in a dimly lit café where Berber men would pass around smoldering pipes of sweet-smelling *kif*. One such evening, he was invited to a table where three elderly men sat, sipping lemonade from greasy, chipped glasses. The oldest of the three stared at him with his one good eye and told him the following story:

✦

IN THE NAME of the Prophet, this story is true (he began) for I have indeed been its witness. Once, not so very long ago, there were born twin boys. Abdallah was the eldest by just minutes, but he and Yakub grew up in very different ways. They both became sorcerers, but while Abdallah worked his magic for the forces of light, Yakub followed the left-hand path. While Abdallah became part of the holy fraternity of magicians, Yakub worked his dark magic in solitude. As the years passed, they became strangers to one another.

Then one day, Yakub appeared at the threshold of his brother's house. On the very brink of collapse, he barely managed to tell Abdallah what had befallen him. He had, in the course of his workings, conjured up an evil djinn which had turned on him, attacking the very roots of his soul. "And now I am truly damned"—with those words he fell down dead.

Leaving his twin brother where he lay in the dusty street, Abdallah rushed inside and returned with a scrap of parchment on which he had inscribed Yakub's name and a magical incantation. He placed the incantation between his brother's lips. His brother stirred, his eyelids fluttered. Abdallah drove a brand-new nail into the ground where his near-lifeless twin brother lay. This nail, you see, would nail down the djinn and keep him from repossessing Yakub's body and soul.

Abdallah bent over Yakub's prostrate form and kissed him on the lips. The parchment lay between the two brothers' mouths. As Yakub returned fully to life, Abdallah grasped the parchment spell between his own teeth and withdrew it from Yakub's lips.

With amazement, Yakub returned from the land beyond death. But he did not shower his brother with gratitude. Rather, he asked, then begged, then demanded of his brother the parchment that contained the wondrous spell holding power over Death itself.

At this, Abdallah held the parchment out before him and a dove swooped down and plucked it from his hand. Yakub became enraged. "How dare you so dispose of that which your own brother has asked of you?" And with threat and imprecation, he demanded that Abdallah call the dove back to him.

"Oh my brother," said Abdallah, "you still do not understand. The wondrous power you seek is truly all around you." He pointed toward the sky. And in the bright blue expanse there flew not one dove but dozens, then hundreds, then thousands, until the sun itself was hidden from view.

"But, since you insist," Abdallah continued, "I shall do as you ask." And he held out his arm. From the airborne thousands, a single dove swooped down and perched on his hand. It held the parchment in its beak. Abdallah took the parchment and held it toward his brother.

"Here is what you seek," said Abdallah. Yakub lunged and grabbed the parchment from his brother. It was blank.

✦

THE ONE-EYED MAN, having completed the tale, chuckled softly and sipped his lemonade. Despite repeated questions, he refused to say any more about the remarkable story he'd told. Eventually though, as the *kif* pipe made its rounds and the night grew deeper, the three elderly men consulted among themselves and then proffered an invitation. They would like to take him to a special sort of place, one they felt he might enjoy.

Following the three strangers through the twisting alleyways of the medina, he had to fight back waves of fear and suspicion, for it seemed they were passing the same corners, the same painted doorways, time after time. Would he be robbed and left for dead? Or were his suspicions the clouded workings of an intoxicated mind? Furtively, he slipped his wallet from the pocket of his trousers and hid it inside the waistband of his underclothes.

Just when his suspicions had reached fever pitch, his guides turned yet another corner and brought him to an unremarkable blue-painted door.

"Is this," he asked aloud, "where I can find the Magicians of Fez?"

He was told: "You'll have to decide that for yourself."

In response to an elaborate coded knock, the door swung open and they stepped inside. It was quite apparently a male brothel. A single leather hassock, decorated in gold, stood against a tiled wall of the dimly-lit room. A middle-aged man, eyes ringed in kohl, hair tinted with henna, entered through the archway carrying a brass tray holding a hookah and glasses of mint tea. The man served the visitors, clapped his hands, and was gone.

He took a sip of the sweet, hot tea. He felt not at all at ease. From the adjoining room, one hand-clap, then another, then a rhythmic beat. Two young men, naked and lean, came through the archway and started to dance. Slowly at first, then picking up speed, they whirled before him to the hypnotic beat. They came so close to him he could smell their bodies. He wanted to reach out to them. He wanted to get up and run away, forget about the Magicians of Fez, go back to the place that he once had called home. He wanted to find peace.

The clapping ceased. The young men stood still, very close to him, so close he could see the sheen of sweat on their dark pubic hair. He looked to either side; the three old men were gone. He was all alone in a tiled room in a far-off land, alone with two beautiful, naked men.

One of the dancers reached out and stroked his face. He tensed. The boy leaned over and gently kissed his tight-shut lips. The naked men were both upon him then, unbuttoning his clothes, stroking his chest, rubbing up against his stiffening crotch. He realized with a shock that his wallet, precariously hidden in his underclothes, had dropped out and been lost to him somewhere in the winding streets. Money, papers of identity he'd tried to protect were gone. But it mattered not. For all at once, he knew he had no choice but to give himself over to pleasure, more pleasure than he'd ever felt before. Two mouths found their way to his nipples, lips and teeth expertly stroking and nipping, till he felt so hot he knew he must surely be blushing.

He was naked. He was floating. He was on his back, being caressed by wet lips and warm fingers. He looked down. A naked stranger was straddling him, positioning himself over his hard cock, sliding down and up and down again. The other dancer kissed him, tongue pushing his moans back into his mouth. He didn't want to, not yet, but he exploded, exploded in the hot, soft ass of the young Moroccan. And went into a dead faint.

✦

HE AWOKE FULLY dressed on the bed of his hotel room. The morning sunlight was yellow as a lemon upon the white-washed walls. And somehow his wallet had found its way to the bedside table, all contents intact. It was as if the night before had never happened. When he went to open the door, it was locked from the inside.

He found his memories of the previous night troubling, not so much because what had happened was so unnatural, but because he had received so much pleasure. Never again, he resolved, would the seductive indolence of the tropics corrupt his soul. It was time, past time, to go home.

He soon found himself at the railway office, counting out a portion of his meager funds for the passage he'd booked. As fate would have it, though, an offhand reference he made regarding his failed quest brought an unexpected reply from the railway agent. If he truly sought the wonder workers of Fez, the agent told him, it was necessary only to go that night to a certain tent on the outskirts of the medina, near the Bab Bou Jeloud. The agent drew a map for him. The unbought ticket remained on the counter.

✦

WHEN THE BURNING sun had retreated and the Muslims had said their evening prayers, he took map in hand and made his way to the tent. This tent turned out to be a shabby, unpromising affair. In Arabic and several Western tongues, a sign hanging above its doorway read "The Melting Girl." A primitively painted picture showed a beautiful, near-naked woman, part of her body flowing into thin air. Could this possibly be the place he sought?

As if in answer to his doubts, a man neither old nor young, neither handsome nor homely, came to the door of the tent and silently beckoned him inside. There beneath the canvas, a single chair sat facing a curtained stage.

The nondescript man demanded what seemed an exorbitant amount of money. He tried to haggle.

"Do you wish to find what you seek, or will you let the matter of a few *dirhams* determine your fate?"

He reluctantly paid and took his seat.

The nondescript man vanished behind the stage. For several minutes nothing happened, nothing at all. He found his thoughts wandering back to the night before, to the touch of the naked men. His cock began to swell.

The tent went dark. A single lamp above the stage began to glow feebly. The curtains parted. A girl, probably no older than twelve but with a garishly painted face, sat in a chair, facing straight ahead. An unknown instrument played a sinuous tune. Bit by bit, the face of the seated girl turned into a skeleton, a grinning skull.

He was outraged. It was a cheap conjuror's trick. He had come all this way, paid all this money, to see a threadbare "miracle" produced by mirrors and shifting lights. He stood up abruptly. His chair collapsed noisily. The stage curtains clapped shut as the lights in the tent were lit.

"I demand my money back, all of it!" His cry went unanswered. He tried again, this time in heavily accented Arabic.

The nondescript Moroccan appeared from behind the stage. "Something troubles you?" he asked.

"You're damned right. I paid to witness real magic, not this shabby charlatan's trick."

"Ah, and you believe that you can find true magic simply by spending your *dirhams*?"

He was silent for a long moment. Then, calmed and crestfallen, he said, "No, of course not. I was a fool. I'm sorry to have troubled you. Good evening."

He knew then that it was a dead loss, that there were no men who could walk through walls, and that even if there were, he would never find them, ever. And that he would never be free of what he'd come to Morocco to lose, which was, after all, himself. He was defeated. It was time to go home.

He was nearly out the door when the nondescript man called him back. "Wait a moment. I believe that I can show you something else that will perhaps satisfy your needs. No additional payment will be required. Please, this way."

Having come this far, he could see no harm in doing as the Moroccan said.

He followed him behind the stage. From there, he could clearly see the mirrors and papier maché skeleton which had created "The Melting Girl." The ageless Moroccan drew aside a curtain and led him into a courtyard lit by lanterns of filigree brass. Beautiful carpets covered the ground.

Three young men stepped from the shadows. They were naked, their cocks erect. Startled, he recognized them: the guide who had sucked him in an alleyway, the two dancers from the night before.

He knew then what he needed to do. He removed every bit of his clothing and stood naked before the three. He was giving up every claim he had to his own misery.

The young guide walked over to him. He felt the boy's hands run down his torso, down to his cock, at first half-hard, then throbbing. The boy's hand grasped it tightly, squeezed hard. It was a beautiful sort of pain. He threw his head back, closed his eyes. The guide's thumb worked the head of his cock until fluid seeped from the slit.

Eyes still closed, he felt other hands on his buttocks, stroking and kneading his trembling flesh. Fingers made their way into his cleft, to a place no one was permitted to touch. But someone did.

Wordlessly, he lowered himself to the carpet-covered ground, crouching on all fours. He felt moisture lubricating his hole, felt a finger loosening the tight ring of muscle, felt a cock head pressing against him, firmly, insistently, until he let it in.

The slight pain passed quickly. He backed onto the shaft until it was all the way inside him. He'd never felt anything like it. So suddenly was he opened out, vulnerable, that as the hard cock began its long, slow strokes inside him, he felt the peace that had always eluded him. This was where he was meant to be, giving himself up to another man. In the alleyway, at the brothel, he'd allowed others to pleasure him, but had remained closed off still, his self-imposed barriers rigidly in place. Now at last, as he gave of his body, allowed another into his most secret place, his soul became open, free as air.

His entire life, he now saw, had been built upon oppositions, lines of demarcation. Himself or others. Pleasure or pain. What men did or what women did. His army or the enemy's. Now, at one mighty stroke, the barricades were broken. He'd crossed over into no man's land. And rather than finding a wasteland there, he found a world that was somehow whole. His burden of pain was so tiny beneath the infinite sky.

He opened his eyes. The colorful patterns on the carpet were moving, twisting, dancing before him. Arabesques. Dizzying arabesques.

He was wide open now, relaxed, all resistance gone. When one man had come inside him, another took his place. He knew there were three of them, but identities seemed meaningless as he lost himself in the dance of flesh. He shut his eyes again, and kept them closed.

At some point, he was on his back, ramrod strokes making his body shudder, when he shot all over himself, hot, sticky, running down his sides. He screamed. It was a scream of joy.

He felt a kiss upon his closed eyelids. He opened his eyes. It was the man who was neither young nor old.

"Perhaps the time has come. Look around you," the Moroccan said.

He looked around the lamp-lit courtyard. There were others there. Not just the three naked men who stood over him, smiling. There were many of those whom he had met in his search for the Magicians. The shoemaker, the brassworker, the teacher. The elderly man from Tangiers who'd read him the newspaper clipping. The railway station agent. There, in the corner—could it be?—the man from whom he'd first heard the rumors of the secret brotherhood. The two old companions of the one-eyed man. And amidst them was "The Melting Girl," who, head scarf removed and stripped to the waist, proved to be a young man of surpassing beauty, smiling the smile of an angel. All standing in the courtyard. All looking at him as he lay there, his own juices running down his body.

"What are they all doing here?"

"Can you not guess? No? Then perhaps I should show you who I am?" With that, the nondescript man passed his hand before his face. His features became fluid, shifted, resolved themselves into the face of the one-eyed man, the man who'd told him the story of the good and evil brothers. "You understand now, don't you? At last you see the truth. It is *we* whom you have been looking for. We who are men like you."

The one-eyed man continued, saying to him (as I now say to you), "Oh nobly born, this world is but a dance and we are merely dancers. Any meaning discovered in this dance, once grasped at, once written down on parchment, is doomed to vanish before our eyes. Thus mankind is fated to forever search for magic, and insofar as we search, we become that which we seek. True wisdom lies in knowing that the journey and the goal are one. Do you understand?"

"I think I do," he said. And perhaps he did.

The one-eyed man continued, "For truth is not our joy and truth is not our sorrow. It is merely a secret which we already know, though we may keep it hidden even from ourselves. But we shall never taste of truth till we let ourselves become that which we are, and indeed always have been, from the moment of creation. Though we are not this flesh, yet our flesh is all we have in this world. And so from the center of your being, come join us in the sweetly whirling dance of life."

"And the story of the brothers that you told me?" the naked man asked.

"It is all the truth. It all took place about a century ago. I did, however, omit one small detail. The evil brother, Yakub? That man who died and came to life, that man was I. Only when I surrendered my greed for immortality did I begin to live. I allowed the world to be what it is, no more, no less. And with time I truly learned, as you now also see, that there is a wondrous power all around us, if we are open to it, if we but have the open eyes to see." The one-eyed man looked toward the heavens.

He, too, looked up, following the one-eyed man's gaze. (Or rather, I looked up. For as you must by now suspect, that naked man in the long-ago courtyard, that man who found what he'd long sought, that man was I.)

The full moon, rising, filled the sky with its light. And there against the starry firmament, the form of one dove, then dozens, then hundreds, filled the nighttime sky.

A single bird swooped down, alighting on my heaving, naked chest. It had a parchment in its beak. I took the parchment. On it was written a single sentence: "Welcome to the brotherhood, o blessed one." And the dove flew up, rejoined its brothers, and the sky above Fez was filled with blinding light.

WADI BASHING

JACK STEVENS

SO PICTURE THIS. Gorgeous guy. Skin the color of dark honey. Eyes like melted chocolate. A smile that could stop your heart. And a perfect setting. Warm evening breeze and a sky full of stars. Blanket on the soft sand. No one around for miles—literally.

Trouble was, the sand was a desert in the middle of the Arabian Peninsula, and the guy was an Omani, citizen of a country that, officially, has no gay men. Even that blanket was standard Omani air force issue, just like the guy, and the Royal Air Force of Oman immediately court-martials any of those nonexistent gay men it happens to find in its ranks.

None of which stopped Faisal from being one of the most beautiful men I had ever seen, or did anything to soften the aching length of the cock in my trousers as I lay next to him that night on that sturdy, practical blanket under the glittering diamonds of the desert sky.

What had I been thinking?

Okay, so I knew what I'd been thinking. I had wanted to put as much distance between myself and Pedro as I possibly could. Traveling the world as a jobbing teacher of English had seemed such a great idea just over a year beforehand. There were always opportunities for short term contracts in colleges, schools, summer camps, and the like. And there were always guys willing to learn, or teach, so much more than just English. Like Jean-Phillipe in Paris, who'd shown me it wasn't just onions that could make a guy's eyes water. Or Pieter in Munich who'd put a whole new world of meaning into the words "German sausage." And Jan in Amsterdam who'd shown me that flour wasn't the only thing you could grind in a windmill. But then there'd been Madrid and Pedro, the swarthy muscleman who'd said he was a bullfighter but who'd turned out simply to be full of bull. He'd fucked like an animal but, in the end, had turned out to have the morals to match. And I'd fallen head over heels in love with him. Maybe I could have forgiven Pedro if I'd just found him with one of my students. But finding him with one of my students and the principal of the college I was working at, in my bed and using my lube and condoms as well, had all just been a bit too much to take.

So I had given up on my muscled Madrid matador and, in theory anyway, given up on men as well. "Try the Middle East," a friend had said one maudlin, drink-sodden evening. "You're not allowed to be gay out there."

"Or western," I'd said tartly. "I'm depressed, remember, not suicidal."

"I'm not talking about Iraq," my friend had insisted. "There are other countries in the Middle East you know, and many of them welcome westerners with open arms. Just not open gay arms," he'd added, "so there's no chance of repeating old mistakes is there?"

Like a fool I'd listened, and two weeks later I'd ended up in Muscat, ancient capital of Oman, as English language tutor for the Royal Air Force of Oman no less, which sounds slightly more grand than it actually is. And the very first classroom I'd walked into had been filled from wall to wall with breathtaking young Arab men in crisp military uniform, the testosterone so heavy in the air I'd barely been able to make it to my teacher's desk and sit down before my erection became too painfully visible in my light cotton slacks.

Twenty-two officer cadets between the ages of nineteen and twenty-five, all eager to learn the English that was essential for would-be pilots. Twenty-two fit, disciplined trainee top guns, lean as greyhounds, full of Eastern promise, and even among all of them Faisal had stood out. At night, back in my small room or *beht* on the compound, my wheezing, ineffectual old air conditioner set to maximum, I'd try to work out why it was his face I'd see in the dark, why it was his slim, naked body I'd imagine by my side, pulled in close, as I beat myself to a series of sweaty,

sticky climaxes. It wasn't the small, jet black beard and moustache: most of the lads had those, in spite of their relative youth.
It wasn't the tight glossy curls of his hair or the unmarred dark
coffee of his skin. It wasn't even the fact that he was the fastest
learner of all my students.

Maybe it was that smile. I'd been surprised at first how ready
to laugh my new students had been, how similar, once the barriers of language began to give way, our senses of humor were.
But Faisal was easily the most solemn of all of them, which made
his rare smiles so much more noticeable. I'd compliment him on
some well-expressed phrase or sentence in his writing or he'd
suddenly grasp some point of grammar, and there it would be,
like a flash of white lightning, so quick you might have missed
it unless you were looking for it. Or unless it was meant for you
alone.

And then there were his eyes, so dark and deep. He'd look up
at me from his desk while I was leaning over, trying to explain
some god-awful rule about subjunctives, pluperfects or other se-
mantic crap, and I'd have to stand up, to physically pull myself
back to keep from tumbling into their incredible depths. That
was what it felt like: like falling. Like falling in love. And I was
never going to do that again, oh no. Besides, it was impossible
here.

And then Faisal asked me to go wadi bashing with him.

"Is that like a euphemism?" I'd asked.

"A . . . euphemism?" and he'd put his head on one side, extending his neck so that my mind was momentarily flooded by
images of running my tongue down the length of it, from that
sensitive spot just behind the earlobe, down across the beat of
the pulse at the throat to the sharp edge of that tight military
collar.

I swallowed. "That's like when you say one thing instead of
another."

He frowned and I wanted to take his head between my hands
and gently smooth away the furls with my fingers. "Why would
you do that?"

"Because, sometimes, it might not be polite to say what you
really mean."

"And what did you think I really meant?"

I shifted uncomfortably. With most of the other cadets I might have begun to suspect they were taking the piss, but with sweet, earnest Faisal I just wasn't sure. "Y'know. Spanking the Monkey. Smacking the Pony. Playing the Pink Oboe."

Faisal regarded me with those fathomless eyes and gave that small, polite shrug that said he didn't know what the hell I was talking about. I got that a lot from him.

I lowered my voice, already uncomfortable at this discussion in the open at the RAFO compound. "Wanking," I hissed. "Jerking off."

For one horrible moment I thought he was going to ask me to explain that. After all, these weren't words we'd had much use for in class, but then his perplexed expression cleared and he gave one of those smiles, and I wouldn't have cared if he'd asked me to demonstrate what I meant then and there, just to make it all perfectly clear. (And there was a thought for that night's dreams! Me beating Faisal off on the pile of cushions and blankets that served for my bed, watching that oh-so-serious expression change, pass through surprise, puzzlement maybe, to a dawning delight before being swept away in open-mouthed, gasping abandonment as I pumped him slowly at first then faster and faster to helpless orgasm!) "Ah," he said, "you mean—" and he said something in Arabic that I couldn't catch.

"Right," I said, and I hoped it was.

"No," he went on, apparently completely unfazed. "That is not what I meant. I was asking if you would like to come out with me this weekend into the *jebel*, the desert, to see the *wadis*." He paused and regarded me steadily, almost as if he knew the effect those deep eyes of his had. "The valleys. They are . . . fantastic," he added. "Fantastic" was our word for that day. It seemed so appropriate right then.

My head spun. Back home, back anywhere in Europe, if a good-looking guy had invited me out for the weekend I'd have known exactly what he'd have been asking and just what we'd have been bashing before the first night was done. But out here? I looked closely at Faisal, as closely as I could without making the desire in my own eyes too obvious. His face was open, innocent. He really was inviting me out for some sight-seeing. Just that. Nothing else was possible. "Sounds great," I said, just a little hoarsely. A hundred and one reasons for not doing it ran through my brain. "Let's do it."

"Very good." Another small smile. "I will pick you up at your *beht* tomorrow morning at six. Good-bye."

"Tomorrow! Oh, yeah, of course. Good-bye." With typical military briskness Faisal was already halfway across the exercise yard before I'd finished my farewell, his tight little ass clearly outlined by the khaki cotton of his fatigues. Six weeks out in the Middle East and I still forgot that weekend here meant Thursday and Friday. I only had one evening to get ready. I turned and began to hurry back to my *beht*. So what exactly did you need to bash a *wadi*?

At six precisely, Faisal pulled up in one of the base's small battered jeeps that the cadets were able to commission for the weekends. To be honest, I was nervous. Me! I'd been sleeping my way around Europe and now I felt like a kid on a first date. It wasn't simply the prospect of spending the next forty-eight hours with the man I'd shafted every night in my dreams for the past six weeks. It was the sudden realization that this was the first time we had met in anything other than a classroom situation. What if he was very different? What if he was just the same?

He greeted me with the same simple formality he had used since our very first lesson, bundled my uncertainly-packed rucksack into the back of the jeep and held the door open for me so that I could climb in, before leaping in himself and driving us off. We had left the compound before anyone could see us, other than the MP on the gate, and at the end of his night's duty he was too tired to even note who we were.

I knew that to see Oman's real beauty you have to abandon its relatively recent roads and follow the dirt tracks out into the interior, but I still gasped in surprise when one minute we were driving along a perfectly normal stretch of highway and the next Faisal simply turned the wheel and we plunged off the smooth tarmac onto a pitted and uneven track designed, surely, only for goats. He looked across at me and smiled, and then actually laughed, and that, more than anything, reassured me that we were not in fact about to turn tire over axle and explode in a ball of burning diesel. As we drove on, and the trappings of modern roads disappeared somewhere behind us in a cloud of dust to be replaced by boulders, scrubby trees and bushes and all the rugged mountains that are Oman's true self, Faisal's smile grew broader, his laughter more frequent. "This is like where I was born," he shouted. I knew then that just as I was seeing the true face of this country away from the twenty-first century veneer of roads and buildings, so I was beginning to see the true face of Faisal, as the restraints of air force discipline loosened around him the further we traveled from the base. I wondered just how far he intended to travel.

For lunch we stopped in a small village, Faisal in his RAFO uniform chatting cheerfully and easily in Arabic to the shepherds and farmers in their traditional Omani robes or *dishdashes*. I tried to imagine my companion swathed in cool white robes instead of the impractical formality of a westernized uniform. What would it be like to embrace a man in a robe? How would you begin to explore the body within its folds? Would it be frustratingly awkward or erotically teasing? What was worn underneath, or would he be naked, and how did you begin to remove a robe? There was a laugh from one of the farmers, and I was sure one of them pointed at me before something rapid was said and there was another outburst of laughter. I knew then one more of a *dishdash*'s practical advantages: underneath one of those, no one can see when your daydreams leave you with a raging hard-on! Face burning I hurried back to the jeep. Faisal followed and by the time he'd jumped back in beside me I'd managed to spread a map over my lap to hide my evident tent. He was grinning but that could have been about anything. That's what I told myself. We drove off, and it was a good half hour before I could fold the map back up and put it away.

Night comes quickly and early at that latitude, so it wasn't many hours after we had left the village that we stopped at the foot of a sheer cliff at what Faisal said was a good spot. We made our camp and settled down for the evening. "Do you come here often?" I asked him, and then laughed at the awfulness of the cliché.

Faisal nodded, oblivious of my crassness. "As often as I can. When my duties allow."

I reached for my rucksack. "Do you often . . . take people with you?"

He looked out to the horizon, a line of scarlet and crimson now, deepening perceptibly as he watched, to purple and then black as the sun sank. "No," he said simply.

I fumbled in my rucksack, not really sure how he was going to take what I had there. "Look, I know you're not supposed to, and if you don't want to, and don't want me to, I won't be offended, but—" I held out the bottle of gin I had carefully wrapped in several towels.

Faisal grinned, an honest-to-goodness wide grin. "No one knows what happens in the *jebel*," he said.

"Is that an old Arab proverb?" I asked, unwrapping two similarly cocooned glasses, pouring generous measures and handing him one.

"It's an old Arab promise," he said and he raised his glass to me and we gently clinked them together as we looked at each other over their rims.

For what seemed like hours we lay on that blanket and talked about everything and nothing. My head was telling me to move away, keep a safe distance. My body was telling me to move closer, to lean my thigh against his, to accidentally brush my hand over his leg, his stomach. I lay there rigid, caught between the conflicting drives, my hands jammed firmly under my head to prevent them from wandering either to the sweet temptation of Faisal or to the aching demands of my rock hard dick. I gradually realized that Faisal wasn't moving either.

Faisal was very keen to learn about my home life and I was equally curious about his. As the time wore on though, it became increasingly obvious that there were very noticeable gaps in what we were asking and telling each other. As the moon rose and the level of gin in the bottle fell, I knew I wasn't going to be able to leave those areas unexplored. "So," I said, all nonchalance and innocence. "Do you have a girlfriend back home?"

He looked down at the glass in his hand. "No. In this country we do not have 'girlfriends'."

I tried to pick the bones out of that one. "Oh. Right. So, is it true that your wives are chosen for you?"

He laughed, but it wasn't as open a laugh as those he'd given earlier. "Sometimes. Or we may choose our own." He raised his glass, drained what was left in it and held it out for more. "I do not think that I shall choose a wife."

"Oh?" I gave the glass a hefty shot.

"In this country one must have, what do you call it, a dowry. That is very expensive."

I'd heard that. I also knew that as an officer in the Omani Air Force, Faisal would be comparatively very well off.

"And you," he said abruptly. "Do you have a girlfriend?"

My heart was pounding and my inability to think clearly was due to more than just the gin. This was a turning point. I knew it. I was pretty sure now that Faisal knew it too. I could play it safe—*should* play it safe—give the simple lie and say yes, there was this charming girl waiting at home for me who was going to whisk me off to a church the very instant I got back home and force me to give her babies. Or . . . "No," I said. "I don't have a girlfriend. I've never had a girlfriend." And then I shut up. And waited.

The heat of the day was gone but the night air was still warm, and on it I caught a hint of a rich, musky scent. Faisal. Arab men love their perfumes, often mixing them themselves. If this had been a musical note it would have been deep and resonant, intensely male. I'd caught hints of it during the day as we'd sat close in the jeep together, but now in the still glow of the night it seemed magnified, intoxicating, like a wine. I breathed deeply, drawing it into my mouth, my lungs. I turned my head to see if I could catch more of it. And Faisal was looking back at me, his head turned toward me too. "In this country," he said slowly, as if translating the words into English was suddenly difficult for him, "men without women sometimes turn . . . to other men."

Slowly he moved his hand, looking at me all the time, as if waiting for me to protest. Gently he laid it on top of my thigh, just as I had been fantasizing about laying mine on his all that evening. I continued to hold his eyes and said nothing. He sighed. I lifted my hand and gently laid one finger on his lips. The charge that ran along my fingertips, through my stomach and straight to my crotch was like nothing I had ever experienced before. Touching a man's lips was nothing! But here, the taboos were so much stronger, the charge that breaking them gave was so much more powerful. My senses swam with the heavy scent of him as I leaned in, cupped the back of his head with my hand, gently drew him into me and kissed him, my mouth filling with the sweetness of the figs we had just eaten, the bitterness of the gin as his tongue pressed in.

I'd thought our lovemaking would be frantic, clumsy even, Faisal eager but inexperienced, rushing to consummate it before the guilt of what he was doing overcame him.

It was not like that at all.

I don't know how long we had been kissing, our bodies pulled in tight against each other, arms and legs entwined, hands greedily moving up and down, over and around our bodies before I realized that his shirt and my T-shirt were both gone, thrown off somewhere onto the sand to one side, and we were pressed together, naked chest to chest. I broke free of his hungry mouth and pushed him back to see properly the dusky warm tan of his body, the dark nubs of his nipples, hardening in the open desert air, the strong black of the hair dusted across his chest, trailing in a thin line down over his flat belly into the promise that lay below his trouser line. I ran my hand over that soft skin, leaned in again and licked it, leaving trails of saliva across his ribs, his navel, reveling in the spiced salt taste of him, wanting to experience him with every sense I could.

Faisal arched, swung a leg round and over me and was astride my body, nuzzling me as I had him, dragging his lips and tongue over my belly, along my sides, working his way up to my chest, pausing to look down at me, then bending his head down to nip at the tender puckered flesh of my nipples with his bright white teeth. I cried out, instinctively going to fend him off but Faisal was leaning over me now, his hands gripping my upper arms, pinning me. Again he looked down at me, a question in his eyes. I said nothing but I let my arms go limp and Faisal leaned in once more and pinched and pulled at my nipples with his teeth as I gasped and hissed at the mingled pain and pleasure of it.

Emerging from that playful torture was like coming 'round after losing consciousness. I found Faisal still astride me but moved further back, sitting on my thighs, the buckle of my belt in his hands. With that solemn expression of his, as if he was unraveling some problem of English grammar, he undid the buckle and pulled the length of the belt from around my waist with a swift hissing sound, tossing it to one side. Both hands on my waistband, he moved further down, pulling my trousers as he went, until I was lying there under the night sky, naked except for a pair of white cotton briefs, already soaked and clinging to me from the sweet free flow of my precome.

Faisal lay back down at my side, stretched out, his hands behind his head, the invitation clear. It was my turn to remove his trousers, pausing only to push my nose into the dark heat of his armpits, to lick the hairs there, to drink in the male smell of him. The hair on his legs was as black as that on his head and chest, but stronger, more curly and wiry. As was the hair around his cock. All day Faisal had been naked under those trousers, and now his cock lay long against his belly, hard and thick and bloody magnificent.

I pushed my nose into his crotch and he cried out in a mixture of surprise and pleasure. The scent of him was hot and strong and I opened my mouth wide to suckle on his ball sac, to shove my tongue into the spongy space between that and his hole, grasping his hairy thighs with both hands to pull myself further into the dark warmth of his groin. Faisal bucked his hips, rubbing his crotch into my face and I moved it from side to side to feel the rigidity of his dick, like an iron bar, rubbing over my closed eyes, nose and mouth. With a sudden intake of breath, like a diver preparing to submerge, I went down on his cock, trying to take the length of it into my mouth. Faisal cried out helplessly again and I gagged, almost defeated by the size of what I had taken in but determined to take it all, to feel the veined shaft on my tongue, the engorged head way down my throat. I worked it hard, breathing heavily through my nose, and from somewhere above me I could hear Faisal groaning and shouting out something in Arabic, encouragement or curses I couldn't tell.

Gasping I pulled back, uncertain if the wetness running down my chin was from my own mouth or Faisal's come. He was lying back, both hands covering his face, panting as if he'd just run a race. Gently I prised his hands apart, and couldn't help laughing at the look of astonishment still plastered across his face. He frowned slightly, as if uncertain whether or not I was mocking him, but as I smiled down at him he understood that was the furthest thing from my mind. He smiled back and I kissed him again, and at the same time I twisted my hips, grinding the pulsing rock of my dick against his. His hands slid easily over my now sweat-slicked skin, down my sides, to my waist, round to the cheeks of my ass and into the waistband of my briefs, pushing them down and down. I shifted to make the removal easier then sank back down onto him, our cocks now both free in the open and sliding over each other, lubricated liberally by their own eagerness. He seized both of my ass cheeks with a slapping sound and pulled me hard into him even as he bucked and arched up into me and this time it was my turn to cry out in delighted surprise tinged with sudden alarm. I so did not want to come yet, but the burning pressure was building and much more rough handling like this and I was going to come a gusher all over him!

I pulled back, rose slightly on my haunches and turned Faisal over so that he was lying on his belly. I could feel his reluctance, almost resistance, but ignored it, succeeding, though his head and shoulders remained up, the muscles across the top of his shoulders tense ridges as he tried to turn and see what I was doing. I took a moment to look down the smooth length of his back, the clear valley of his spine, the perfect curves of his buttocks, with none of the ridiculousness of a western white tan line, the clean cut of the crack between them. My cock jumped and leaked more precome just at the thought of pressing hard into that tight crevice, working the cheeks apart, thrusting deep into his achingly beautiful body. I took his shoulders in both hands and gently kneaded them, marveling at the tenseness of the muscles beneath my fingers. Gradually, I felt the knots there lessen, and slowly Faisal's head sank forward and down onto the blanket as I massaged his warm flesh, moving down from the shoulders, past the lines of his ribcage, along the ridges of his backbone, down to the base of the spine and below that . . .

Faisal's head jerked back up and his hand whipped behind him, catching my probing fingers at the very top of his ass crack. He pulled himself up and round, the blanket getting caught up and twisted around him, until he was sitting facing me, still holding my hands. "Not that," he said quietly. "It is not right that a man—" He looked at my fingers in his hand but did not let go. "Not that."

"It's all right," I whispered back, and leaned in to kiss him. I felt the tightness of his grip on my hands loosen and then we were in each other's arms again, mouth hard on mouth, groins thrusting blindly into each other, and I knew now that there was no way I was going to be able to hold back the climax of this headlong passion for much longer at all. I turned and fell back, letting Faisal land on top of me.

He straddled me, knees on either side of my upper body, his cock jutting up and out over my chest and into my face. I reached for it with one hand and slowly stroked its length. He gave a great, juddering gasp and arched back until his face was turned directly up into the night sky, his eyes closed, as his thick cock pushed out even higher far over me. He moaned as he rubbed his hands over his own belly and chest, through the slick curls of his hair, over and over his dark nipples. My stroking became harder, faster, my fingers closed, or tried to close around his cock's swollen girth and I pumped him harder and harder. Faisal fell forward, arms out, taking his weight on both hands, the better to lean into my pumping, to pump back with quick, powerful thrusts of his hips. With my other hand I reached round him, smoothing my hand along his back, slapping at his buttocks. His face was over mine now, so close I could feel his short, sharp breaths, had to blink away the sting of his sweat as it dripped into my eyes, but his eyes were tightly closed, his gasps transforming to grunts as he moved closer and closer to his climax. My own cock was screaming for some hand action itself but by sheer force of will I kept that one hand that wasn't wanking Faisal away from it. I knew what I wanted to do before I finally jerked myself off, and I needed a free hand and exactly the right moment to do it. And that moment was coming now.

I knew it the instant I felt that brief moment of stillness, that fleeting second when every muscle in the body freezes before the irresistible surge of an orgasm smashes through your every thought and feeling. Without hesitating I brought my free hand up to my face, spat on its fingers, reached back behind him again and before Faisal could protest, before he could even see, blinded as he was to everything but his own, now inevitable climax, I slipped the two well-lubricated fingers into the crack between his buttocks and shoved them hard through the tight muscle ring, deep into his ass and up directly into the throbbing, pulsing center of his prostate. Faisal's mouth and eyes sprang open in shock even as gout after gout of thick white come exploded from his cock and rained down over my chest and face. His hands flew down to grasp my wrists but I shoved and pumped again and again and his orgasm showered down on me like a warm and very abundant blessing. I closed my eyes but opened my mouth and continued to jab, push and pull, and Faisal gripped my wrists so tightly they hurt, but did not pull me away from my working until every last drop of come had been forced from his heavily-loaded balls.

I lay there afterwards, waiting for him to recover from the stupor of his exertions, half fearful of what he would say, of how he would react. Finally he stirred, slowly sitting back up, moving carefully as if not certain that he had not been hurt in some way, not meeting my eyes. It seemed an age before he spoke. "It is not right," he said, "for a man—"

"Only a man can feel like that Faisal," I said softly but firmly. "Only another man knows that." I lay there, waiting, watching as the words sank in, as he sought to balance the custom and traditions of generations against the undeniable, primal sensations that had swept away every last vestige of reserve just minutes previously. I held my breath.

Faisal sighed. He nodded as if in answer to some voice he heard in his head. He looked up to me and he smiled, and his smile that night after our first lovemaking was the sweetest, happiest I had yet seen on him. And I knew then and there that it was pointless to deny it. I was in love with Faisal, and I knew he loved me. I shifted slightly and he looked down in surprise at my own sadly ignored erection, still raging, still unrequited, digging hard into his crotch. He reached for my cock with one hand, and as he did I reached for his other hand, pulled it to my face, opened my mouth and took two of his fingers into it. As I slicked them with my tongue I gazed into his eyes and Faisal smiled and nodded again, and I felt my ass thrill in anticipation.

Like I said, Faisal really was the fastest learner of all my students. And I had so much more to teach him as we bashed the *wadis* that weekend.

SUN, SAND & MAX

JAY NEAL

MONDAY, 14 DECEMBER

Hi Ron,

Well, this is the life! I now know, quite confidently, that I do not need a cake, or balloons, or presents, or a surprise party with drunken coworkers to celebrate my birthday properly. And after fifty years, I certainly don't need all the snow that I heard was falling back home. All I need for a perfect birthday was what I had this afternoon: a deck chair to lie on, a cruise ship to put the deck chair on, and some glorious Caribbean sun to shine on the cruise ship. Paradise.

My flight to Miami was without incident, which is about the best you can ask these days. The hotel last night was quite comfortable, and I had a delicious meal in their restaurant. There were only two other people eating. My waiter was cute and flirtatious, which enhanced my enjoyment.

Flying down the night before makes the whole enterprise so much more civilized. I went to bed when I felt like it, slept late, and still arrived early at the port to board the ship. They do let us on board early, in time for a light buffet luncheon, although we're not allowed near our rooms—or our luggage—for a few more hours. Those of us who planned ahead tucked a swimming suit into our carry-on luggage so we could make the quick change and get in some sun poolside before we weighed anchor.

One other thing I didn't need for a happy birthday was the band. There's always a combo on board, usually playing outside in the tiki bar to guarantee that everyone is having fun. I'm guessing that all the good ones were booked this week, which is how we aboard the *Caribbean Queen* got stuck enjoying the song stylings of this fourth-rate band. Of the three numbers they know, I've decided that "I Shot the Sheriff" just doesn't work that well on steel drums, particularly after the seventeenth hearing. One or two more and it may become "I Shot the Steel Drum Player."

I tried to keep my distance from the band by adopting a chaise lounge on the upper deck that ringed the pool. This also gave me a mezzanine view of the pool and surrounding deck, populated largely by undressed, mostly hairy men upon whom I might rest my eyes when my book failed to hold my attention.

I was just reflecting on how gracefully and succinctly the author of this crime novel had summarized my own proclivities: "What turned her on was a chunky build, good muscular definition, and an abundance of body hair." Indeed, I couldn't have said it better myself! I may have noticed the splash as someone dove into the pool. While I was thinking about "an abundance of body hair," I may have watched a light-colored blur glide through the watery distortion of the pool.

Regardless, I definitely noticed when he reached the edge of the pool and shot up out of the water. He was a literal manifestation of what I had just read: chunky, good muscular definition, and an abundance of body hair.

He hung at the edge of the pool, half out of the water, and shook his head to fling off the water. Then, rather to my surprise, he looked up at me and we locked eyes. He knew I was watching; in fact, he expected it. It gave me a definite tingle. Fortunately I was lying on my stomach at the time since my Spandex bikini left little room for misinterpreting my interest.

The moment passed. He bent his arms and their good muscular definition, pulled himself up out of the pool, and reached for a towel. I was fascinated by the water that ran in little rivulets down the abundance of body hair on his chunky, muscular legs and by the glittering beads clinging to his luxurious, full beard.

At first I couldn't decide on his hair coloring. It wasn't brown, certainly not blond, not exactly red but on the coppery side . . . Auburn. That was it: auburn was the color precisely. Oddly, I thought, auburn is a color you don't see much these days, but did hair color go out of fashion? No matter: his abundance of body hair was beautifully set off by green flames in the black Spandex bikini that he wore, much to my satisfaction.

I was inclined to think that the drying-off performance he gave was for my benefit. Witness the way he flexed his shoulder muscles in my direction, how the towel lingered over his buttocks, how he slowly dried his legs by bending over so that I might best enjoy the tensing in his butt cheeks. The little squatting motion he made to dry under his crotch was probably gratuitous, but I wasn't about to complain.

All too soon the exhibition ended and he walked off to rejoin his friends, sitting at a table in the shade. It looked like one other man and two women. Two couples? Two mixed-gender couples? Just good friends on a cruise? Who knew?

Not much later it was time for me to get in out of the sun, find my room, put on some more clothing. I explored the ship for a bit. In particular I wanted to locate the sauna, which I knew would be hidden in some corner near the onboard spa. It was. Then I returned to the upper deck to watch the sun set as we sailed out of port.

You know how, even on a ship with more than two thousand people on it, you seem to see the same people over and over again? It was true this time, too. Fortunately, it looked like my friend with the abundant body hair was going to be one of them, so he needed a name. Sudden inspiration suggested "Max," and suddenly he became Max to me.

I saw Max twice more today. The first was when I was leaving my room for my pre-dinner sauna. As I stepped into the hallway, I saw Max disappear behind a bulkhead. Did he glance in my direction? I was willing to fantasize that he *was* keeping an eye on me.

The second time was at dinner. It turned out that Max and his friends were seated just a few tables away from me, so I could keep a close but discreet eye on him. He could do the same with me: I know I caught him once watching me when I glanced up to look at him.

Now, here's something really kinky. You know how photographers on cruises pop up everywhere to take your pictures, and then how the photographs are displayed in the gallery for your convenient purchase, and where everyone can look at you? Well, after dinner I went to look at all the photos from earlier today of people boarding the ship. Not surprisingly, my eye was caught by one of Max coming on board—a photo of him alone, as it happened. Believe it or not, I bought it for myself! One way or another, it will be a nice souvenir.

That's all for tonight—more tomorrow.

Jay

✦

TUESDAY, 15 DECEMBER

Hi Ron,

Today was our day in Nassau. We arrived sometime in the dark, so when we woke up and looked out our portholes what we saw was a charming, pink town that had appeared magically. I'd done some of the tours before—it was necessary at least to have seen the celebrated marching flamingos—so this time I just took a leisurely walk about the town. On my way I passed the big pink government building, the one across from the Leather Masters store. You remember that picture of me standing under their sign looking suitably butch? Anyway, I had a relaxing walk, saw some very nice gardens with palm trees, and even found an old church to look into.

I came back to the ship for a late lunch, then went to the top deck for my ritual afternoon sun worship. Nothing special happened. I read and turned over now and then, indulging my indolence and making desultory progress with my mystery novel.

I did see Max twice today. At breakfast I watched him enjoy eggs Benedict and half a grapefruit (red). I saw him again later, but we'll get to that in a bit. Oddly, I never ran into him or his friends in my stroll around Nassau. Perhaps they went to see the celebrated flamingos.

I know I've told you before how much I enjoy using the sauna on cruise ships. That and lying in the sun are my two very serious pleasures. There's something primal, or maybe primordial, about sitting in a small, hot room deep in the bowels of the ship. The wood in the sauna creaks slightly as the ship rocks gently

back and forth. At times one can only hear the sound of the heat-
er cycling on and off; at other times one can hear the distant
rumble of the ship's engines. Either way the hot, heavy air mutes
all sounds.

I enjoy the entire experience, so the sauna is a ritual for me. I
do it every day at six for about half an hour, so I can relax awhile
afterwards until it's time to put clothes on for dinner. At that
time of day, it's rare that I have to share with anyone else.

That was true today. There was one hearty soul working out
in the gym, but the sauna area was totally deserted. I got out of
my clothes as quickly as I could, grabbed a towel, and entered
the inner sanctum.

The sauna itself was rather small—with the super hot air it even
sounded small. Just opposite the door was a two-tiered bench that
wrapped around to the left to make an L shape. I stepped up to
the higher level behind the door, spread my towel on the bench,
and settled down. My breathing slowed to match the breathing
of the ship. My muscles and my mind relaxed. My pores opened
and my sweat began running freely.

To be honest, I may have been half asleep and I don't think
I heard footsteps outside, only the soft click of the sauna door
opening and closing. I lifted my eyelids a bit. Imagine my surprise—and delight!—to see Max standing there staring at me. He
wore a towel wrapped around his waist.

As soon as he saw I was awake and looking, he slipped the
towel off and presented himself entire. In that setting it was like
a soft-focus dream. His cock and balls were hefty, as I had imagined from the bulge I had observed yesterday in his swimsuit.
And what a gorgeous tan line! You know how provoked I am by
a well-defined tan line, particularly when it outlines such meaty
thighs and highlights such a nice package. In the dim light of the
sauna, his untanned triangle of skin seemed to glow.

Before I had a chance to say anything Max spread his towel
on the bench before me. He knelt on the towel and put his hands
on my knees. I spread my legs and Max leaned forward, slipping
his hands along my legs and then to my waist. He lowered his
head and flicked beads of sweat off my balls with his tongue,
licking more firmly with each taste. Sometimes there is nothing I

like better than having my balls licked.

Naturally, my dick got stiffer throughout this operation. It bounced rhythmically against Max's beard. At just the right moment, he shifted his attention and drew my entire dick into his mouth, simply holding it there for several seconds. Remarkably, against the heat of the sauna his mouth felt almost cool. It was an unexpectedly stimulating sensation. Soon enough he was moving his mouth up and down, working some sort of magic with his lips and tongue as he went.

He had just found the perfect tempo to get me off, and I was moaning my encouragement. This time, I did hear footsteps. Someone was outside the sauna, preparing to come in. Without much conviction at the point, I whispered to Max that he should stop because someone was coming in. He grunted a negative sound and carried on without skipping a beat.

The newcomer was youngish, tall and slight but muscular; it may have been the guy who had been working out in the gym earlier. Rather than being abashed by our blow job in progress, he seemed inclined to enjoy the spectacle. He spread his towel on the upper bench in the opposite corner, then spread himself out on the towel. His dick was already stiff. He watched and stroked himself. I envied him the view he had of Max's broad, firm ass.

Max maintained his rhythm, the silence of the sauna focusing my attention on the delicate stimulation wrought by his mouth. He soon had me at the edge of climax, where he managed to keep me waiting—and groaning loudly!—for several seconds.

Finally, I grabbed his head and pulled it down on my crotch. You know I can hardly stand to have my dick touched immediately after I come, so I held his head down resolutely and shot several loads down the back of his throat, all of which he drank greedily. I expected him to let my dick out of his mouth, but he continued to hold it there as it softened only slightly. With his face buried in my crotch, he reached for his own dick and began jerking off rapidly.

In not much time, he was ready to come. More than I heard them, I felt his guttural vocalizations through my dick. He exhaled heavily and repeatedly as he shot his come onto his towel. Still, he held my dick in his mouth as his heavy breathing began to normalize.

Our silent companion must have shot his own load sometime along in there, but we didn't really notice. While I sat there with my dick in the mouth of the still panting Max, our friend silently stepped down off the bench, gathered up his towel, and slipped out the door. We heard one of the showers turn on.

Max's breathing returned to normal, such as it can be in a sauna. Slowly, ever so slowly, he pulled his mouth off my dick. Just as slowly, he moved his head down my leg, caressing me with his beard, occasionally planting a little kiss on my leg. Before I knew it, he had gathered his own towel and headed for the shower. Not long after, I followed suit.

I didn't see Max again that evening, which was a bit disappointing since I was suffering a sort of romantic afterglow. Regardless, I think I'm going to sleep rather well tonight.

Do you think this means that maybe he's interested?

That's all for tonight—more tomorrow.

Jay

✦

WEDNESDAY, 16 DECEMBER

Hi Ron,

Today was beach day! This was the day when we visited the sandy little bit of nowhere called Caca Cay, a private-island getaway for me and two thousand of my closest friends. No doubt it's because I'm from Kansas, where we don't have lots of oceans, that I've never been obsessive about being near the water, but I do thoroughly enjoy spending the day lying on the white sand of Caca Cay.

Everywhere there was food, lots of fruity drinks with umbrellas, people riding on skis or hang-gliding or riding the banana boat and, it should go without saying, our ubiquitous Caribbean band playing "I Shot the Sheriff."

To try to escape some of that and pretend that it was my private beach, I went along the paths a way and up a side arm of the island where most people don't go. I found a spot where I could lie in the sun and hear almost nothing except the sound of the waves lapping at the beach. It was very peaceful.

It seemed a little odd to me, with virtually the entire ship crowded onto this tiny island, that I didn't run into Max at all. I might have thought he was avoiding me, except that he found me later that afternoon, just before it was time to return to the ship.

I had gathered my things and was walking along one of the sand dunes when he materialized out of nowhere. I started to say hello, but he put a finger to my lips and slipped behind me, wrapping his arms around me and pulling me tight against his front. We both had on only our swimsuits; I could feel his erection pressing against the fabric stretched across my own.

He turned my head with a hand on my chin and whispered in my ear, "I want you to fuck me. I must feel your dick inside of me or I shall certainly go crazy."

I realized that this was the first time I had heard him speak. He had a rich and resonant baritone voice.

"I will. I want to. I want nothing more, but we can't here. I don't have any condoms with me."

"Must we wait?"

"Yes. For both of us, it's only sensible to have condoms. I'm sure I can get some tomorrow when we're in Key West."

"So long to wait. Tomorrow then."

He turned me toward him, our stiff dicks meeting through the Spandex they strained against. He held my head in his hands and kissed me—not deeply, not yet, just the start of a kiss to be continued. Then he disappeared.

I spent the rest of the day in a haze of lusty anticipation. I'm not entirely sure I remember going back to the ship. I did have my sauna, all alone today. I went to dinner but I don't remember what I ate.

So, I think I'm going to sign off early tonight and see whether I can get to sleep and hasten tomorrow's arrival.

Jay

✦

FRIDAY, 18 DECEMBER

Hi Ron,

Sorry to have kept you in suspense about yesterday, but as you may have surmised I was kept busy until rather late, and I was too exhausted to type. Now that we're docked back in Miami, I need to type quickly before my tag color is called for disembarking.

Let's skip the farcical details of trying to buy condoms in Key West. Right off the ship it seemed every pleasure known to man was available—particularly if it had "Key West" printed on it—but it took me nearly two hours before I found a store with someone who had even heard the word "condom" before! I exaggerate, but only slightly. My frustration was at fever pitch before I finally found what I was searching for. I was so relieved that I foolishly bought two boxes of twenty-four—possibly a bit over optimistic on my part. I did remember to buy lube though.

I made it back to the ship in time for lunch, and then I had to contend with anticipation that was starting to ache. When was I going to see Max? He was the one who had seemed so urgent, but he was nowhere to be seen all afternoon. I went through all my routines with a hopeful eye keeping watch, but no Max.

That evening was formal night in the dining room, so after my sauna I got out my tuxedo and all its hardware to put on. Fussy things, tuxedos. It must have taken me over half an hour to get dressed.

Great was my relief to get to the dining room and find Max sitting at his table. I have to say, he looked really, really hot in his tuxedo. Once during dinner he caught my eye with a questioning look, to which I responded with the slightest of nods. There, that was settled.

Keeping my anticipation in check was a challenge, but I managed. Fucking him right there in the dining room struck me as an ill-considered idea, largely because the condoms were back in my room.

He finished dinner first and left the dining room with his friends, without any further signal between us. How was I going to find him later? Pondering that, I got up from the table and set off for a stroll on the deck to take a last look at the Caribbean night sky and to cool down some.

After probably twenty minutes I felt calmer and headed back to my room. I saw no one in the hallway, but as I pushed open the door to my room I felt a hand on my butt. Max! He pushed the door open, got me through it, and closed it quietly behind him. With desire that matched my own, he pulled me tightly against him, holding my head in his hands.

"You have them, yes?"

"Yes. They're right over there."

He started kissing me, and I started kissing him back. This was serious kissing, fervent and wet. This was kissing that was bigger than our mouths, involving beards, throats, eyelids, even an ear or two.

In the midst of all that, we began the comedy of getting each other's tuxedos off, working our way rather ungracefully past jackets, cummerbunds, bow ties, suspenders, cufflinks, studs, buttons, and zippers. The last bit of clothing I remember was Max's bikini brief, which I slipped down his legs, thus getting for myself a brief taste of his cock for the first time. Yummy, and exactly the right size for my mouth, too.

But Max had one goal in mind and was to be neither distracted nor deterred. He dragged his cock from my mouth and reached for a condom. He lifted me to my feet and again we were at it with the kissing. While we kissed, I felt him grab my dick, incredibly hard by then, and roll the condom onto it. Next thing I knew, Max was lying on my bed, pulling his legs back and exposing his beautiful asshole as my target.

I slid my dick into him with the greatest of pleasure—his too, judging from the sound of the moaning. We had both been anticipating this for so long, and it now felt even better than I had imagined.

This was my favorite position for fucking: face to face. I could feel deep inside him with my dick. I could watch his expression as we moved our hips together, and we could continue kissing as we had before.

We must have fucked like that for over an hour, one position, one pace, exhausting ourselves from the sheer pleasure of it. Without any warning, Max came. No histrionics, just warm come shooting out his dick to glue our bellies together.

I really, really am turned on by a guy who can come just from my fucking him, so that was my signal to fill the condom with my own load. It felt like gallons to me by the time I finished.

We lay there, glued together, for some time. I was so content I may have fallen asleep. Despite that, the time came when Max rolled me off him. He got up and started collecting his clothes, putting on just enough to satisfy propriety should anyone see him. I savored my last look at his chunky, abundantly hairy body, and inhaled as much of his wonderfully acrid, musky smell as I could.

Ready to leave, he leaned over my bed and gave me a tender kiss on the forehead, then he stepped toward the door. He opened it and turned to face me before he slipped out.

"Wait," I said. I felt a bit foolish asking, but "Is your name, by any chance, Max?"

He seemed confused by the question at first, then the corners of his mouth turned up. "Sure," he said, "Why not?" and the door snapped shut behind him.

Ah, they're calling my color, so it's time now for me to get off the ship. My flight gets in early, so I'll give you a call later tonight. Just wait until you see the pictures!

Jay

BERMUDA TREASURE

P.A. BROWN

I NEVER SAW him coming. One minute I'm stepping out of the way of a Peugeot as I try to get a better look at the trimaran out beyond Horseshoe Bay and the next I'm lying flat on my back under some kind of spiky green thing.

Then a dark silhouette eclipsed the spiky green thing and a cheerful voice demanded, "You all right there, boss?"

I tried to sit up. I must have banged my head on the way down. I was hallucinating. How else to explain this vision that bent over me. His skin was like the richest, darkest chocolate, and his smile was as blinding as the snowbound fields around my uncle's Kansas farm. But it was his eyes that arrested my heart.

Could eyes really be that green? Tiny gold specks swam through the emerald pools and I had to tear my gaze away to stop from drowning in them. I let my eyes wander up to his mobile mouth. He wore a thin shirt unbuttoned nearly to his navel. More chocolate silk skin overlay the sculptured muscles of his chest. His nipples were two hard brown knots atop sharply defined pecs and two ridges of flesh flowed down to disappear under the shirt, which was tucked into a pair of cutoffs. At first I thought he was totally hairless, but then I saw a thin line of fine black hair that started just above the invisible navel that carelessly drew my eye until I was staring straight into his fat basket, about two inches from my mouth.

I swallowed and hastily scrambled back, scraping my knee on the road. I welcomed the bolt of pain since it helped reduce my raging hard-on enough so that I was able to stand without terminally embarrassing myself.

"Hey, boss, I'm sorry," he said. "You were moving too damn fast for me."

I looked over at the bike he had tried to run me over with. It barely looked big enough to knock over a flea, let alone run a grown man off his feet.

"Aren't you a little old to be playing with dinky toys?" I asked, standing up and brushing the green stains on my chinos.

"Eeze me up, boss." His grin was easy and sweet and sent a fresh bolt of desire straight into my cock. Fortunately he wasn't paying attention. "That blade be a fine bike."

"You run over tourists a lot?" I looked at the bike. It was blue and squat and looked like the tiny dirt bikes the kids back home rode around scaring cattle with.

He swung his leg over the seat and keyed the bike back on. It chugged and coughed but wouldn't start.

"Damn, she flooded."

He pulled the recalcitrant bike off the narrow road and sat down on the edge of Fairmont's golf course. I looked over his head at a foursome that looked like they were about ready for the nineteenth hole.

I hadn't come to Bermuda for golf. Frankly I hated the game. No, what I wanted to do was get out to some of the famous shipwrecks that ringed the islands. To that end I had already booked my first dive for later on today. The last thing I needed was having to deal with this drop dead gorgeous troublemaker.

Well-meaning friends had warned me when I had announced my intention of visiting Bermuda. I'd hate it, they said. It wasn't very gay friendly, they said. I knew they were right. But I wasn't coming here to get laid. I came for the wrecks.

Then my well-meaning friends told me I never got laid, which I thought was really unfair. I wasn't the hermit they made me out to be. Just because I didn't jump in the sack with every Tom, Dick, and Harry who gave me the eye didn't mean I was asexual. I was just . . . picky.

I knew I was pretty ripped—muscles I'd kept from my military days graced a six-foot frame that had never seen an ounce of fat. Being blond and blue-eyed didn't hurt, either. I know I had no trouble attracting guys, I just didn't act with most of them.

From where he sat on the grass, the stranger was staring at my legs. I glanced down and realized my chinos had been torn during my tumble.

He draped his arms over his bare knees, his legs parted, giving me an unwanted but irresistible view of his tightly packed crotch.

"Sorry, boss." He seemed genuinely contrite. "I s'pose I owe you a pair now, don't I?"

What I really wanted from him I couldn't even hint at, it would get me in so much trouble.

I just wanted this guy gone.

I brushed at my leg. "No, that's okay. It was an accident."

"Sure?"

"Yeah. I'm sure." I avoided his gaze. I pointed over my shoulder at the pink hotel behind me. "I have to get back."

"Oh, sure, sure. That's chilly." He stood, smoothing his hands over his butt before straddling the bike again. This time it started up.

I watched him trundle down the road toward South Shore. His tight little ass clung to the vinyl seat and his muscular legs wrapped around the sides of the bike in a way that was altogether too enticing. I was hard again.

Jesus, what is it with me today? I can admire a hot body as much as the next guy, but I didn't go around sporting a permanent hard-on over them.

Shaking my head at my inexplicable weakness, I began the trek back to my room and a shower. Thirty minutes later I collected my gear and caught a cab outside the lobby. We headed down to the Royal Dockyards.

I spent the cab ride staring out the window at the florid tropical greenery that crowded every inch of open space along the narrow roads, and did my best not to think of a pair of brilliant green eyes and an ass that just wouldn't quit.

I had talked to Eddie Cooper, owner of Marine Treasures Dive Shop a half dozen times in anticipation of this visit. I told him I was looking to visit several of the hundreds of wrecks that ringed the deadly Bermudian reefs. He had assured me he knew just the ones. And he had the perfect dive master to take me down to them.

Bermuda was the warm-water wreck capital. The shallow reefs

that ring the islands are studded with more than five hundred shipwrecks dating from the 1500s. They're unlike wrecks anywhere else, lying in shallow water, making them easy to reach. They fascinated me for their often whimsical history.

Bermudians have a peculiar history of their own. I'm not sure about the stories that they actually lured ships onto the reefs, but they were never hesitant about what to do when one had the misfortune to founder. Everyone packed into their skiffs and promptly went out and looted the unfortunate ship. Usually they let the crew go, but there were stories about some confrontations that hadn't gone well for the foreigners unlucky enough to wash up on Bermuda's pink sand beaches.

I paid the cabbie and climbed out onto the blistering dock. I immediately spotted the *Blue Serpent*, which I had paid through the nose to privately hire for my first dive. Good, it looked like she was all set to sail.

I was still thinking of the little cutie who had knocked me for a loop earlier. Now there was a pirate if ever there was one. Only in his case he probably looted hearts instead of plunder.

I ambled toward the boat, telling myself to focus. This was not the time to be daydreaming about a hot twink I'd never see again.

A figure stepped out onto the deck. I stared. It couldn't be . . .

I saw the recognition in his eyes.

"You!" We both said at the same time.

He burst out laughing. He was shirtless and sunlight gleamed off his sleek form. Suddenly he reminded me of a cat. A slender, deadly panther.

Great. I was hard again.

"What are you doing here?" I snapped, as much tired of my body's relentless response as to his sudden appearance.

He never lost his grin.

"Hey, boss," he said. "You change your mind about those pants?"

"What?" I stopped at the bow, staring up into those electric green eyes. "No. I chartered this boat to go diving. What are you doing here?"

"I be your dive master."

His smile actually slipped this time. Maybe it was the look of horror on my face. I couldn't help it. I was supposed to spend the next four hours in tight quarters with this man?

"You want me to call Eddie?" his voice went suddenly flat and I winced at the abrupt change.

I had already talked to Eddie and he had assured me he would make the best dive master available for my use. I just didn't think Eddie could ever have guessed how I'd want to use this man.

He reached down and snagged his Tee out of his waistband and slipped it over his head. His eyes, when they met mine, were wary.

"It's okay, I go give Eddie the word. You may be a bit late getting out, but he'll find someone else—"

"No, wait." I held my hands up. I hauled myself on board and stood swaying on the teak deck. "Eddie said he'd find the best for me. You the best?"

He was a long time answering but some of his good humor returned and he finally said, "Yes."

I thrust my hand out at him. "I'm Paul McCoy."

His grip was solid. His smile was firmly back in place. "Jhett Kingsley."

"Well, Jhett," I said and hoisted my gear up. "How 'bout you show me where to stow this, then we can get under way."

He led me down three steps into the cockpit where I shed my camera bag.

"Your dive gear be in the stern. You didn't tell Eddie what sites you wanted to visit, so I think we start with Cristobal and Iristo. That fly with you, boss?" he asked.

It was my turn to grin, even as my heart did flip-flops. "Sounds fly."

He pointed out a cooler tucked away in the cockpit. "Got plenty of greeze in there. Help yourself."

"How long till we reach the dive site?"

"Forty minutes."

"Well, what are we waiting for?"

The dive was everything I had imagined. And more. The *Cristobal Colon* had been quite a luxury ship in her day. She had gone down in 1936 and left a debris bed scattered over thousands of feet. Among the wreckage were artillery shells the US Navy had used during WWII.

Nearby lay the 250-foot Norwegian steamer *Iristo*, where I could still make out the undelivered fire engine sitting on her deck.

Jhett hadn't lied. He was a wealth of information on the wrecks as well as the entire reef structure that had trapped so many ships over the centuries. For nearly three hours we drifted from deck to deck, checking out boilers and props, scaring up schools of sergeant majors and colorful parrotfish. I took at least four dozen pictures, including a few surreptitious ones of my companion.

After we came up from the last dive Jhett popped open the cooler and grabbed two beers and a couple of ham and cheese sandwiches. After handing me one of each he deftly maneuvered the *Blue Serpent* out of the dive channel and dropped anchor out of the main shipping lanes. In the shallow cockpit we relaxed and began to reminisce about the dives and what we had seen.

"Bye, did you see the size of that necktie you scared up? I thought for sure he was gonna take a big ol' piece outta you."

"Necktie? Oh, you mean the moray eel. Yeah, he was a big one." I rested my back against the stairs leading up to the main deck. The beer felt good in my dry throat. The sandwich actually gave me some energy back. I felt totally enervated. I was still overwhelmingly aware of the nearness of his dark, lithe body. His green eyes were half closed.

"What time does Eddie expect the boat back?" I asked.

"Don't worry 'bout it," Jhett said softly. "We on Bermujian time now."

"Bermujian time?" I grinned. "What's that?"

He turned to face me, his grin still ever present but a new tension in him. "Late." His hand brushed my bare leg. "We got all the time we need."

"Need for what?" My spit dried in my throat and his eyes mesmerized me. I could feel the heat from his slender body. A pulse started pounding in my thickening cock.

He leaned toward me. "For this." And he slipped his mouth over mine.

I could taste the salt mingled with Heineken on his lips. I opened my mouth and gasped when his tongue slipped between my teeth. Our tongues tangled and danced in hot silence punctuated only by the gentle slap of waves on the hull and our own breathing. He rolled over, pressing his naked chest against mine and twining our legs together. I felt the throbbing hardness at the juncture of his thighs and couldn't resist. I eased my knee between his legs and pressed against his swelling cock.

He moaned in my mouth and broke away long enough to say, "That's shot, man. Oh boss, you hot."

Then he swallowed my tongue again. I slid stiff fingers through his short hair, tangling in the tight curls then slipped my hand down his smooth chest. He arched against my questing fingers. I found a nipple and squeezed it, eliciting more groans from him. He bit my lips and left a trail of fire down my throat.

Jhett's skin was hot satin under my mobile lips. I buried my face in the soft hair of his pits. He tasted of salt and musk and a scent that was uniquely his. I nibbled and kissed the delicate skin then moved across his chest and latched onto his right nipple. His taut skin rippled as I worked it into a hard brown knot with my teeth before moving on to the next one.

His hands slid under my trunks and closed over the firm globes of my ass, pulling me against him. He worked rigid fingers between my legs and stroking the skin behind my balls. I groaned at the wave of desire that swept through me and bit at the skin of his belly.

His hips writhed against the battering ram of my leg. I pressed him down into the deck, sweeping my hand under his trunks, shoving them around his ankles.

I moved down, tasting every inch of his hot silken skin, dipping my tongue into his shallow navel. I leaned back and parted his legs, avidly devouring the sight of his pulsing pink cock head buried inside his thick, black foreskin. With shaking fingers I rolled back the foreskin and exposed the supersensitive skin.

I blew on the pink cock head and was rewarded by a dribble of precome. My tongue darted out and flicked the salty drops clean, swirling around the fat mushroom- shaped head. Wrapping my lips around his thick cock I teased the rest of the foreskin back and took his whole cock down my throat. I swirled my tongue around the marble-hard shaft, feeling its hot pulse under my eager lips. When I came back up for air, I traced the throbbing veins down his cock with my tongue and buried my nose in his tight curls. I inhaled the pure essence of him.

His balls were fat brown sacks and I licked my way around first one then the other, finally making my way behind them. I stroked the soft skin with the tip of my tongue, then pushed his legs up and thrust my tongue into his soft pink hole.

Jhett moaned my name and clamped down on my head with shaking hands.

I probed wetly at his back door. Jhett began to shudder, his whole body wracked with spasms and his breath coming in shattered moans. He reached between us for his cock but I pushed his groping hands away. I reared up over him and held his arms over his head while I attacked his mouth.

"Do you want me to fuck you?" I whispered. Before he could answer I nipped his chin and said, "I want to ram my cock up your ass and fuck you till you scream. Tell me you want me."

Jhett responded by wrapping his legs around my hips and pulling my cock up against his ass. "Fuck me, Paul. Oh bye yes, fuck me."

"You got protection?" I growled.

He reached into what I had taken for a tackle box, pulling out lube and a handful of skins.

I unrolled the latex over my cock, which was already leaking copious amounts of precome. I spread lube over the ridged latex. Then I coated my fingers with more lube and massaged it into Jhett's ass. He squirmed against my touch, whimpering with need.

I rolled between his knees and raised his legs up to expose the pink rosebud glistening with a combination of my saliva and lube. I eased the head of my cock between his butt cheeks, past the tight asshole. Jhett winced and I paused, letting him adjust to my invasion. I flexed my thighs, easing in another inch, then another. Jhett urged me on hoarsely when I stopped again, gripping my hips with his long fingers.

I began to move slowly, rocking in and out, feeling my cock

slip deeper and deeper into his tight channel. Finally I came to rest with my balls against his ass.

"Fucking tight," I murmured against his throat. At his hoarse cries of encouragement I began to thrust, slowly at first until the friction of his tight hole made slow and easy impossible. My control vanished in a wave of lust. I slammed into him and he matched me thrust for thrust.

His cock was drenched with precome. My fist pumped it. Our ragged breathing and the harsh slap-slap of flesh pounding on flesh was the only sound on the boat. The only sound in the world.

I lowered my head, probing roughly past his teeth. I fucked his mouth all the while I ploughed his ass. He grabbed my hips and arched against me, drumming my back with his heels. Our rhythm intensified. He bucked under me, and chanted my name.

His balls tightened, his hips surged up and his ass clamped down on me so hard I nearly screamed at the sensation.

His body convulsed beneath me and ropy come shot out of his pulsing cock, splattering his stomach and mine. The sudden tightening of his asshole sent me over the brink. I threw my head back and shouted as my orgasm slammed through me.

I held his hips in an iron grip and drove into him once, twice, then I froze, my back bowed as I emptied myself into the latex shield.

I fell across him. His arms came up to hold me tight, lightly tracing the damp skin on my back. I pressed my face against his throat and swore I heard the thunder of his heart as it slowed before settling back into a regular rhythm.

We lay like that for several minutes; then I rose up on my elbows and met his brilliant green eyes.

"Wow, boss, that be shot," he said.

I nuzzled his throat. "I have no idea what that means, but back at you."

I withdrew from him, disposing of the condom before rolling back to take him in my arms. I stroked his sweat-dappled skin. "So this is why you run tourists off the road?"

"No, boss." He flicked his fingers across my nipples. "You be de first."

I wasn't sure if I believed him, but I also didn't care. "So, I'm scheduled for another dive tomorrow. You think Eddie can be persuaded to let you take me out again?"

"Oh, I think he do. Eddie like to keep us both happy."

"What about you? What makes you happy?"

"Your dick up my ass make me happy."

"Good." I jammed my mouth down on his and gave him a kiss that left my intentions clear. We were both breathing hard by the time we broke off. "That's just where I plan to keep it."

This time when we kissed, we were both semi-hard when we separated.

"We gotta fly," he said regretfully. "Eddie be wondering where we are."

I sighed and sat up. We both reached for our trunks. Just before he slipped them on over his thickening cock I put my hand over his.

"Have dinner with me tonight?"

His smile gave me all the answer I needed.

ENCOUNTER IN ECUADOR

MICHAEL STEPHENSON

I WAS MESMERIZED by the online ad I had stumbled across. As a high school social studies teacher, I always try to make my August vacation a trip to someplace I will be teaching about in the coming year, so that I have photos and my own anecdotes to share with the students and make the place more "real" for them. Since South American history was on the schedule for the coming semester, I had booked a flight to Quito. I also always try to collect at least a few experiences that I do not share with the students, though, so I had typed into a search engine "Ecuador gay sex." Amid the pages of hits, one stood out: "Rain Forest Sex Plantation." There were photos of the rain forest in eastern Ecuador in territory disputed with Brazil (since the area had not been completely mapped the exact border was in dispute), photos of canoes with native guides, photos of grass huts in the forest, and photos of a myriad guys who would serve as sex toys for the tourists. There were as many guys as there were imaginable types: taller or shorter, blonde or dark, South American or European, thin or muscular, younger or older, smoother or more hairy. Something for everyone. The prices seemed reasonable as well. For about the same per day charge as for a luxury hotel in the capital I could take a boat ride down the Rio Negro (a tributary of the Amazon), get out at the "plantation," and spend one or more nights with the man of my choice. Or enjoy a different guy's services each night.

I spent a couple of days looking at the Web site—after grading the homework each night, of course! (I know what side of my bread gets buttered!) Drooling over the photos, I imagined a variety of scenarios playing out: making out with a blonde with his back pressed up against a banana tree, fucking a dark-haired youth whose ass was firm and round, inside one of the grass huts, getting a blow job from a bearded guy kneeling before me as my back was pressed up against the banana tree. Calculating my finances, I finally decided, "What the hell?! Why not?! This will be one exciting trip to the rain forest—maybe I should take photos for *National Geographic*!" I logged on to the "plantation" Web site and booked a one-night stay (after all, I do only earn a schoolteacher's salary!) in the middle of my trip.

I arrived in Quito after changing planes in Miami. I spent a few days in the city sightseeing and getting acclimated to the elevation (the city is midway up the Andes Mountains) as the guidebooks all suggested. Then I went further up the mountains to the market town of Otavalo to see the famous market, hike the mountains, and see the crater lakes, as well as simply "take in" the local life. The way the natives used various fedoras or other head coverings to distinguish the different tribes and clans was fascinating. After that, I took a very small and very crowded bus down the mountains, along a series of unpaved single-lane roads that hugged the edge of the cliffs; at one point, even half of the single lane road vanished as it had evidently been washed out by a recent rainstorm. The bus driver made a series of moves back and forth, digging a slightly wider channel in the mountainside to scrape along. The waterfall of excess rainwater cascaded down onto the roof of the bus and made me glad I had my small bag under my seat and not tied to the roof with the other larger baggage. Then I spent almost a week in Banos. Banos was a town halfway down the Andes, in the "cloud forest" nurtured by the moisture in the constant fog which never really quite became rain. The volcanic springs, the "baths" for which the town was named, were exquisite. Arranged in a series of pools and mixed with varying amounts of ice water which come down the mountains from melting glaciers, the pools ranged from so-hot-I-had-to-get-out-almost-before-I-got-in to so-ice-cold-my-blood-froze-instantaneously! My favorite, and the largest, was a pool of water so-warm-as-to-be-almost-uncomfortable but so-relaxing-I-almost-forgot-to-keep-breathing. Very nice. And the sulfur and other minerals in the water made the depths just murky enough to allow a few clandestine foot games with some of the cuter but ostensibly married guys there with their kids in tow. Fun. There was even the young dark-haired married guy (but no kids in sight) across the dining room at breakfast I exchanged a few sultry glances with. But I was "saving" myself for the rain forest.

I took a more standard tour bus from Banos down to the base of the mountains, changed into another bus mostly used by locals—complete with chickens in cages under the seats as well as tied to the roof!—to get myself to the rain forest trading post of Misahualli. It was there that I would get the canoe down the river to my plantation.

I arrived late in the afternoon and checked into one of the three hotels in town for my overnight stay in the town itself. The next morning I found the tourist office on the village square, as I had been directed by the plantation managers. I explained that I wanted a round-trip canoe ride to "Los Amigos Settlement" and if the man behind the desk (a handsome native in his mid-twenties with high cheekbones and deep, dark eyes and a whisper of a moustache across his upper lip) knew what went on there, he gave no indication. But it was clearly a name he recognized and said that a canoe was scheduled to take a group out there later that afternoon. I made sure my name was on the reservation list, got directions for finding it after lunch, and left the office.

It was a slightly overcast morning and I spent the few hours I had before meeting the canoe walking along the roads around the town, out among the farms carved out of the rain forest. The only other human being I saw that morning was a young boy driving an ox along the road toward town. The rest of the time I had the world to myself, listening to the dripping water plunking down off the occasional large tree left from before the efforts at cultivation, the occasional song of a bird in the distance, and the crunch of the muddy gravel under my boots. I took a roundabout route back to town in time for lunch at a small restaurant on the square and then collected from the hotel the few things I would need overnight down the river. I arranged to leave the rest of my stuff there in the storage room and booked a night for my return. I then went back to the square.

I found the side road (alley, really) off the square to the left. I went past a dry goods store with small shrunken heads as well as snake and rat skeletons in the windows—things sure to grab the attention of small boys traveling with their families on a South American adventure. There was one such family just ahead of me, the boy jumping with delight at the sight of the windows' attractions while his sister squealed with disgust. The closer we got to the river itself, a few more single male tourists appeared around us. At the river edge itself the family veered off to a canoe on the left and had their luggage stowed on board by a native family who had evidently been hired to take the tourist family to see the wonders of nature. Three other men and I headed toward a canoe to the right of the small "harbor." There were two men staffing our canoe, a father or grandfather (in his mid-fifties, it seemed) and boy (in his mid-teens) who placed our small bags along the center of the dugout ("Los Amigos?" I had tentively asked, just to be sure I was in the right place and the older man had nodded, grunting) and then helped us get our seats in the long, narrow boat. The boy sat in the front (acting as guide or lookout?) and the older man steered with the outboard motor in back. They pushed the boat out into the water, climbed aboard, the motor roared to life, and we were off!

The river was easily as wide as the Hudson back home, flanked on both sides by the lush green trees and undergrowth for which the rain forest was famous. There were several places where native woman were washing clothes along the river's edge, with children laughing and splashing nearby. There was also the occasional fisherman standing on the shore and throwing a net into the water. Sometimes the adults would look up from their work as the boat passed and the children always stopped their playing and waved as we passed. We went down river like this for about two hours, taking in live the sights that I had never expected to see except as part of television documentaries. Beautiful blue butterflies fluttered past as they crossed the watery highway dividing the forest and once a giant green grasshopper-like creature appeared out of nowhere. It was suddenly sitting on the back of the bench in front of me, chewing the wood, large enough that I could see the details of its face—something I had truly never expected aside from much magnified photographs in nature books. Just as suddenly, it was gone, whirring its way across or down the river to its next stop. I was able to get a photo of it just before it vanished. My students this coming semester would be overwhelmed with the number of pictures I had been able to take during this trip.

I also took the opportunity to see who my fellow travelers were. We each took sly glances at the others, though no one actually spoke—whether because we were each nervous about admitting where we were headed or not, I wasn't sure. There was the guy in his late fifties, who was balding, though he had a moustache and glasses. There was the early-thirties guy, a redhead under his backwards baseball cap, whose furry arms extended from the sleeves of his Seattle Mariners' jersey. The other member of our quartet appeared to be late thirties, dark-haired with opaque aviator sunglasses looking for all the world like he wanted to be mistaken for a movie star or famous person. He had a strong chin and a good body from what I could tell under his sweatshirt—a good choice, given the breeze on the river. He easily could have been a leading man traveling to his secret hideaway in the rain forest for a little rest and relaxation.

Suddenly the boat veered into the shore. A group of three local youths—late teens, very early twenties at the most, I guessed—appeared coming out of the woods along the shore. They grinned and waved as we approached.

"Senor McRath," our driver announced and the man in his late fifties stood uncertainly as the boat bobbed gently in the waves. The guys on shore produced a short board which they used to make a bridge to the boat. The driver hopped out and assisted Mr. McRath ashore and the lookout boy handed over McRath's overnight bag. Three guys came to meet him. I wondered if this was the commencement of a several days' visit that I was witnessing. The boys led McRath into the trees, an ecstatic grin of bliss already spreading across their guest's face.

We pulled back out into the water and headed down-river again for about ten minutes before pulling in at the next drop-off point.

"Senor Weitzman," the driver announced in his thickly accented English. The baseball fan was met by a blond athlete in a Speedo and tennis shoes who led the way back to this part of the plantation. The movie star wannabe was next, met a little further down the river, by a pair (twins?) of college-age jocks, their unbuttoned baseball shirts fluttering in the breeze and revealing their sculpted six-packs.

I was the last to reach his destination. This time, I could see a man standing on the shore even before we began to turn toward land. My stomach churned with excitement. This was really like a dream—or, more like a porn film fantasy—come true. My host took my hand to help me disembark and then reached over to get the backpack I had brought from the lookout boy. The driver waved and the boat roared off, making a U-turn in the middle of the river and disappearing around a bend.

The man who had come to the shore to retrieve me was the Viking god whose photo I had chosen from the plantation Web site. A football player's build, tanned and dirty blond, furry and bearded. His curls looped just under and around his ears. The chunky muscles rippled in the late afternoon sunlight that had broken through the cloud cover. His khaki shorts reached just about to his knees and the muscular hairy legs led to Timberland boots on his feet. This vision of masculinity would be mine to enjoy for approximately the next twenty-four hours. I felt ready to swoon.

"Nice to meet you, Senor Miguel," he said in a slight accent (British? Australian?), using the Spanish form of my surname.

"Call me 'Mike'," I told him, shaking his hand. I hardly ever used my first name—that was my father's prerogative. I had gone by this nickname since high school and most of the world knew me that way.

"Right this way, then, Mike. I'm Peter," he told me, pointing out a path through the great overhanging trees. I had remembered that his name "Peter" had appeared by the photo on the Web site but had temporarily forgotten that detail. We walked a few minutes down the path, which branched off a few times. The branch we took ended in a small yard surrounded by three grass and bamboo kind of houses on short stilts. Just like the photos.

"Sometimes each of the suites is occupied, depending on the number of guests we have," explained Peter, gesturing toward the houses. "Or if a tour group travels here together. But we have our privacy today. Just enough guests for one per group of suites. You four timed it right." He grinned at me.

"I set up this suite for us, if that's alright with you," he told me, leading into the one directly opposite the end of the path. We climbed the five-rung ladder into the house.

"Fine by me," I said. My eyes took a moment to adjust to the semidarkness after the sunlight outdoors. Looking around, I saw it was simple but comfortable. Two large beds were along opposite walls, with a chest of drawers by one and a small armoire near the other. A small refrigerator (were there power cables buried out here somewhere?), a small stove, a couple of cupboards next to the stove, and a table with four chairs made the "kitchen area." There were two fairly large-sized windows looking out onto the lush vegetation surrounding us.

"We have a pump outside for water to cook with, bottled water in the refrigerator for drinking, and an outhouse just down the path," Peter said, gesturing toward the direction of each item as he mentioned it. As he stretched his arm and pointed, the muscles were taut and revealed a strong set of shoulders. I also saw the muscles ripple down his back as he turned. The sunlight, lancing across the room diagonally from the western window, caught the silhouette of his nipple and the lush growth of man fur that surrounded it. Another kind of forest, different from the one outside but just as beautiful, golden rather than green. "Just be careful of using the outhouse at night. Animals, you know. That's why the suites are all above ground. Most of the local wildlife will avoid people, but you never know." He set my backpack down on a bed.

"If you want, I can show you around outside before it gets too dark, before I cook dinner," he offered. "Some guests like to see some of the rain forest before—"

I cut him off, reaching my hands out and placing one palm against his erect nipple and sliding the other along his spine. I leaned in and kissed him, sliding my tongue across his lips. I felt him melt into my embrace, his mouth swallowing my tongue as we deeply inhaled each other's musky masculinity there in the humid wilderness.

After a moment, he pulled back slightly, never breaking the

connection between our tongues and the roof of each other's mouth. He reached up and unbuttoned my shirt, pushing back the fabric to expose my torso, and then pulled me into his: stomach against stomach, pecs against pecs. He leaned down and ran his tongue along the nape of my neck and I stretched my head back, giving him as much salty flesh to wash with his tongue as I could. The gentle scratch of his trim beard sent electricity shooting from my neck throughout my body to match the delight of his rough tongue against that same skin. His nose nudged my shirt off my shoulder as he gently extended the reach of his oral caresses along my frame. I let go of his torso, and the shirt fell away as I pointed my arms straight to the ground. He wrapped his muscular arms around me and worked his mouth along my shoulder and down across my chest, pausing at each nipple to tease it with his teeth, nipping and pulling each teat with the touch of an expert. I reached my arms around his shoulders, driving his face into my chest and he nursed harder on my pecs, slurping away as I felt the saliva begin to run down my stomach. I slid both my hands down his back, feeling each fold of muscle and bone, and reached down just past the edge of his shorts. I could feel the beginning of the curve of his firm, round ass and the slight hint that marked the top of his ass crack.

Again, he pulled back just slightly but never breaking the connection between his mouth and my skin. He undid his shorts which fell away and then reached over to open mine as well. Although his shorts dropped cleanly and made a puddle of fabric around his boots, mine were caught up on my stiffening cock and hung there bobbing in midair. He grinned even as he kept licking and running his face along my chest and reached down to free my shorts, which finally collapsed around my feet as well, but without nearly the grace of his. Steadying himself by holding my hips, he picked up each of his feet and with a single gesture shook the shorts away from him.

His tongue ran down the center of my stomach and found the tip of my cock, now pointing nearly upright. He teased my piss slit with the smallest tip of his tongue before wrapping his lips around the head and sliding down the shaft. Then, using his hands to guide my legs, he gently lifted one thigh and then the other, helping me clumsily kick aside the shorts I had worn in the boat (that I had been wearing for the last few days, if the truth be told). His mouth found the base of my cock and I held onto his head to steady myself, both because of the dance involved in removing the shorts tangled around my feet as well as the waves of pleasure rippling across my crotch. His ability to manage all this activity at once signaled that either he was truly excellent at multitasking or that I had actually become part of one of my porn DVDs back home! I took a deep breath and pulled my cock away from him so as to avoid coming too quickly. We walked over to the bed, pushed my backpack aside, and lay down.

It was now my turn to explore his body with my mouth. Finding the taut, erect nipples standing darkly out from the lush fur around them was easy and I licked and sucked at them. I worked them gently at first but bit harder as his eyes closed and he began to moan softly. I buried my face in the deep valley between his chest muscles and traced the cavern with my tongue, letting the joy of this furry crevice cascade through me. I held his skin in my teeth and gently rocked, rubbing my own cheeks against his powerful torso. His moans became gasps and even an occasional roar as I found a new fold of muscle to taste. His salty, tanned torso was probably the most delicious I had ever tasted.

The side of my face slid across his stomach, which though not exactly a stereotypical "six-pack" was nevertheless firm and beautiful, and then found myself looking at the tip of his hard dick. It was like one of the giant trees outside, standing up from the lush undergrowth surrounding it as it found its way to the sky. I saw its last few jerky movements as it became rock hard and totally erect, achingly pointing up toward his chin. His head was by this time, however, rolling from one side to the other, his eyes closed, his mouth gaping open as he panted beneath me. The tussled locks around his head made him look almost like a Nordic male version of Botticelli's Venus rising from the sea while the undergrowth of his beard on the bottom of his chin and across his neck was clearly visible now. In this vulnerability he was even more the gorgeous Viking I had envisioned. Thor was mine.

I wrapped my mouth around that impressive pole of his and

ran my tongue up and down its length and around its massive width. I buried my nose in the fur at its base, drinking in the aroma of his sweaty balls. His boots began to reach for the ceiling as his legs slowly reached up and began to arch around toward his shoulders.

His ass was now displayed in all its glory. I could see the tan line across the small of his back, juxtaposing the alabaster white flesh of his cheeks with the darker golden hues above and below. He reached down and pulled the cheeks ever-so-slightly apart, hinting at the dark mysterious path inwards. I caught my breath at the sight. My cock strained and ached as if it was pulled by gravity itself toward this inevitable destination. I pushed, ever so gently, against the doorway he had so tantalizingly indicated.

He grunted and nodded slightly toward the dresser. I reached over and opened the top drawer, finding a supply of condoms and lube. I pulled one rubber out of its packet and slid it on and then, using a generous mixture of spit and lube, greased both the sheath and the asshole before me. My fingers slid in easily as I reached in and tentatively explored. I felt his massive prostate, throbbing and rock hard. He groaned and writhed, his eyes shut tight in an expression that spoke clearly of intense pleasure and desire. My now-ready cock slid in so easily, I was up to the base in a single gesture and had to catch my breath to keep from exploding too soon. My cock so deep within him, I still attempted to reach up and take one of his nipples in my teeth. He reached forward, extending his chest toward me until I was able to just catch one nipple by the skin of my teeth. He wrapped one of his hands around the back of my head to keep it in place and wrapped the other around his own pulsating cock.

I pushed my dick, not that it could reach much further into him, but to begin that mutual rocking which was set in motion. The bed creaked as we found the rhythm together. I spat down on his fist around his cock, making it easier for his fingers to slide from base to mushroom head quicker and quicker. I realized that I still had on my boots as well, and noticed with the one small piece of my brain not totally overwhelmed by physical sensation, that I had never before been so eager to fuck an ass that I had kept my boots on. I had become the total animal I had always imagined myself in my wildest fantasies.

Our breathing came in rapid, syncopated gasps as well. His ass pushing against me, my crotch pushing against him, his hand massaging his dick, the furry mountains of his chest heaving, my ass flexing with more strength than I had ever experienced before, and then . . . .

And then the explosion came. Thick ropes of come spurted out from between his fingers as I felt the same intense ripping along the shaft of my dick, filling the rubber with seemingly endless wave after wave of steaminess. I couldn't breathe, and held onto both his legs, again in an effort to steady myself. I had lost count of how many times I'd had to struggle to keep my balance in just the short time since I had arrived. I panted. I gasped. He panted. The come splashed across his stomach glistened in the setting sunlight that glanced off his body.

Finally I was able to slowly extricate myself from between his legs. He opened his eyes. I sat down on the edge of the bed, next to him. He reached over and scratched my lower back. "Mmmm," he murmured, closing his eyes once again and flashing his smile.

As the shadows lengthened, I smiled into the darkness, resting my hand on the sticky stomach of my companion. I was comfortable. I would definitely not tell my class about this part of the trip, although I knew it was far and away the highlight of the four weeks I would spend in Ecuador. And my stay on the plantation had only just begun.

PACIFIC HEAT

STEVE ATTWOOD

IT WAS THREE days past Christmas and almost unbearably hot. An unforgiving midday sun poured into the valley. The thin mountain air offered no resistance to its burning rays, and the rocky cliffs bounced the heat back in shimmering waves.

Sweat was pouring down my back and chest, soaking the crotch and ass of my denim cutoffs. My balls were suffocating, trying to find release from the heat of my body and the relentless furnace of the sun.

"Fuck, I almost wish I was back in New York," I thought. "At least there, when it gets colder, you can put on more clothes. I wouldn't be any cooler here if I went stark naked!"

It had taken a lot to get my parents to agree to my first solo overseas adventure. They had finally allowed me to go because they saw New Zealand as a "safe" country—nuclear free, known to be independent of America's foreign policies and therefore not seen as a potential terrorist target. We were also a family deeply committed to the outdoors and conservation, so New Zealand's international reputation for being "clean and green" gave the country added appeal.

So, here I was, hiking in New Zealand, still coming to terms with the fact that Christmas in the South Pacific occurred during high summer.

"It'll do you good," Dad had said, "mature you a little and knock off some rough spots. You might even get to sow a few wild oats." This last remark was added with a wink in an undertone Mother couldn't hear.

Sowing some wild oats was exactly what I had in mind, though not the sort that Dad intended. What I hadn't told my parents was that another reason I so readily agreed to their suggestion of

New Zealand was because it was known to be liberal and have gay-friendly laws. Hell, the country even had openly gay government ministers and a transgender member of Parliament!

Secretly, I'd decided this was going to be my "coming out" trip. In my diary I'd written my goals for the journey:

1. Tell someone I'm gay.

2. Lose my virginity to another man.

3. Get the experience and the confidence to come out to Mum and Dad when I get home.

But in spite of being in New Zealand for just one month, I had not achieved anything on the list, and I was certainly not expecting to during a solo hiking expedition into the South Island high country with its hundreds of thousands of acres of empty land and open sky.

Stopping to check my route on the map I'd purchased at the National Park's visitor center, I reached, for what seemed like the hundredth time, into my shorts to adjust myself, desperately seeking a more comfortable position for my heat-swollen cock.

"Fuck, my balls are gonna melt up here; there's got to be some way to get down and get cool."

Far below the track, the river ran dark and cool, shaded by the high sides of the narrow gorge. The faint sound of cool water drifted up to me. I eyed the steep cliffs. For the most part the faces were vertical rock offering no handholds. But, further on, a small stream tumbled down the sides to join the main river. There the slope was a little less steep and a few spindly trees offered precarious scramble holds.

It was downright stupid to risk such a slope just to get a little cooler, but it was my nineteenth summer; I felt ten feet tall and bulletproof and my hiking experience with my parents gave me confidence. So I cinched my pack a little tighter and committed to the slope. Brambles tore at my skin, flaying my legs with fine scratches that, with blood flushed to the surface because of the heat, bled freely. Soon my thighs were slippery with a mixture of sweat and blood. But the cool water of the river beckoned, promising release from the heat and a balm for my scratches and heat-suffocated balls.

Reaching the bottom, I dropped my pack and stripped beside

a deep pool at the foot of a foaming rapid. My thighs were burning red from the scratches and exertion, the big muscles throbbing in sympathy with the beat in my groin as my overheated cock stretched and luxuriated in the sudden freedom and cooler air.

Through a tangle of sweat-matted hair I caught a glimpse of my reflection in the dark pool and felt pretty pleased with myself. I was in the prime of new manhood; my body fully adult, muscles firm and full, the result of my family's addiction to outdoor activities practically since I could walk. Dark hair fell in natural ringlets almost to the small of my back as I released the band that kept it in a manageable ponytail while hiking. Between my legs my questing cock, thick and heavy, nosed forward in semi-arousal, while a heat-extended scrotal sac banged lightly on my thighs.

But if my body was that of a man, my face betrayed my youth. Although almost nineteen, my chin refused to support more than baby's down and the man's jaw- line that I wanted to be there was, I had to admit, still blurred by the slight fullness of youth, the baby fat not quite gone. I knew my eyes still held an unmistakable air of innocence that betrayed my lack of experience. The legal age for getting into bars in New Zealand was eighteen, but, frequently, during the first weeks of my vacation the bouncers took one look at my baby eyes and downy chin and sent me off with a "come back next year kid." I was continually having to produce my passport to prove my age.

Sexually, I felt I was still a kid too. I had no doubt that I was gay but, apart from some under-the-blankets, in-the-dark fumbling with other guys in my early teens, which I put down to normal adolescent sexual exploration, I hadn't done anything with anyone that I saw as genuine adult gay sex.

After a quick plunge, I pulled my cutoffs back on, shrugged into my backpack and headed upstream, leaping from boulder to boulder above the foaming water. In spite of the cool, however, I was soon hot with the effort. By the time I burst from the gorge into the sunlit high valley, I was once again drenched with sweat.

My goal, however, was in sight. The ranger at the visitor center had told me of a place, just above the gorge, where the river meandered through a wide, lush, alpine meadow.

"It's open country. There's a great swimming hole and you'll be able to fish in the streams above the pool. You won't need a tent, there's an old musterer's hut there, which is still usable."

I stowed my pack in the hut, shucked off my shorts and headed for the pool. As always, physical activity and the heat in my cutoffs had made me horny. My half-erect cock pointed forward, nosing like a hound through the tall snow tussock as if leading the way. A short dive, and I surfaced near the waterfall. The thought of what I was about to do stiffened my manhood even more, until it was throbbing hot, my foreskin stretched back off the swollen glans, precome already oozing from the slit.

I plunged my erection into the swift flow of the waterfall, gasping and arching back as the pummeling water massaged my cock and boiled around my balls. Although ice cold, the mountain stream intensified my lustful heat. It seemed the water would boil to steam as it surged around my engorged manhood.

Turning round, I bent over to present my fuck hole to the water's caress, reaching back to part my cheeks and allow the stream unimpeded access. I probed with my fingers, feeling the warmth of my hand and the rush of cold water enter my ass. With my other hand I kept stroking my meat, twisting and pulling at the foreskin, sliding it over the mushroom tip. Man, this was getting hot enough to boil the stream dry!

At the last second I spun around, plunging my steaming cock deep into the fastest flow. I threw back my head, voicing my lust and release in a primal scream that echoed from the mountain walls as I shot wad after wad of come into the boiling foam.

Knees shaking, my thighs twitching more than they had from the effort of boulder-hopping the length of the gorge, I buried my head into the face of the fall and then withdrew, flinging my long hair so that bursts of spray flew in sparkling arcs across the pool as I waded ashore.

"Oh man, I needed that," I said aloud. "Fuck that was good."

"You're telling me," a deep voice said. "Best performance I've seen in a long time. Made me horny as hell."

I spun around. There, on the rocks above the pool, stood a tall New Zealand native, a Maori, his face split in a wide grin, teeth starkly white against the deep tan of his weathered face. Any fright and embarrassment at being caught in such an intimate act vanished, to be replaced by burning desire, as I sized up my unexpected audience.

A musterer, judging by his clothes—what we'd call a cowboy. He looked to be in his late thirties, handsome in a rugged, outdoors workingman way. A cowboy hat shaded the stockman's eyes, but could not hide their deep, black gleam. I could see travel grit imbedded into the weather wrinkles around the Maori's eyes, and he was darkly stubbled. The face was strong and angular, the nose slightly flared and flattened. He looked proud and strong and was immensely sexual.

A checked shirt did little to hide the broad shoulders and, unbuttoned at the front, only served to highlight the breadth of a well-defined, smoothly muscled chest where a white bone carving nestled. Through the V of the shirt where it plunged into the musterer's snug Levi's, I could see a hint of ripples and knew the man's stomach would be hard and flat.

Lowering my eyes, I savored the man's basket. Hours of horse riding had worn the crotch thin and pliant and the man's sex thrust plainly against the sweat-stained denim, begging for release.

Strong thighs on long legs, feet and calf muscles encased in riding boots, all of it liberally splattered with mud and riding dust, completed the picture.

"*Kia ora*, my young stud," drawled the musterer. "*Haere mai*. I am Hemi, welcome to my valley."

"*Tena koe*," I stammered, remembering some basic Maori greetings from my phrase book. "I'm Rory. I apologize if I'm trespassing, but I didn't think this valley belonged to anyone."

Hemi laughed. "You're all right, son, it is public land, part of the national park. You have every right to be here. I work for the sheep and cattle station that built the hut, where you stowed your gear, before this valley was added to the park. We're still working off the last years of a grazing license over this area. I spend a lot of time here in the summer. More time than anyone else, I reckon. That's why I call it 'my valley'. Though I must say, it is the first time that a handsome young *taniwha* has risen up out of the river to delight my eye and get me all hot and horny."

With that last remark, Hemi caressed the growing bulge in

his jeans, flicking the button-fly open and pulling his meat free. "Reckon you can handle this, boy?"

As I said, I was a gay virgin, but, suddenly, there was too much blood in my cock and too little in my brain to stop and think about the consequences of taking on a guy older, obviously stronger and heavier than me. My straining cock did all the thinking for me. As it swelled to a hardness that surpassed even my previous passion, I answered with actions, not words. Splashing to the bank, I stepped to the foot of the rock, reaching up to caress the Maori's thighs.

"Kneel down," I urged and, as the stockman did so, I leaned forward to take the swinging member into my mouth. Hemi was well-hung, his meat thick as well as long and pulsing with an inner heat that was still stretching the large glans in response to my hot tongue. Gagging a little, but determined to prove myself, I dove on that cock until my lips brushed the worn denim of Hemi's Levi's. Plunging on, I forced the leaking head down my throat until I was nuzzling thick pubes and becoming heady on the odors of man sweat, sex, saddle leather, and horse- hide.

"Ahhh, that's good," Hemi groaned, flexing his hips to add to his pleasure, timing his thrusts with my awkward rhythm. Starved of sex during his lonely vigil in the mountains, the musterer was more than ready and my ministrations, amateur as they were, were not something he could bear for long. His balls, swollen with unspent come, lifted to his throbbing shaft. Sensing it, I increased my pace, reaching at the same time for the man's belt, loosening the jeans, exposing buttocks firm from days of riding and walking the mountain ranges.

I might have been new to gay sex, but my instincts were good. As the heat built in Hemi to bursting point I found the crack in the Maori's ass and dug deep, my river-wet fingers finding the asshole and probing past the sphincter into the soft, warm interior.

That did it! Hemi pushed my face off his cock and aimed at my chest shooting spurt after spurt of hot come, which mingled with the water drops on the my chest and ran down to my crotch, a burning trail of hot man juice that I was experiencing for the first time and just knew I wanted to experience a lot, lot more!

Hemi climbed down and joined me in the pool, splashing the dripping come off his cock and my chest with the icy water, until both our bodies were shivering.

"Boy," Hemi said, "there's a hearth in that hut that needs lighting, and a big thick blanket to throw on the floor in front of it, what do you say?"

In minutes we had branches roaring in the open fire and Hemi was rubbing me down with a rough towel as I quickly chilled from the cold of the pool.

I returned the favor.

"Let me get you out of those wet clothes," I said as I pulled at Hemi's jeans. The Maori's wet boots and jeans were hard to get off and we did a lot of rolling around on the rug to achieve it, by which time we were both warm and horny as hell.

Naked, the tall Maori more than lived up to the promise peeping through the open shirt. His skin, a deep, soft-shining leather, gave off a heady perfume of man sweat and riding leather; his muscles were defined but lean, the natural whipcord that comes from long hours of physical work and days of missed or inadequate meals. A tribal tattoo swirled around his thighs, right up to his crotch and rising up to cover each buttock, where the black ink was a stark contrast to the lighter caramel of skin that was sheltered from the sun by work-worn denims. His cock had a purple undertone to the brown and was a little darker than his inner thighs. Now it was standing tall and proud with precome glistening at its tip.

"How old are you boy?"

"Nearly nineteen."

"You look younger about the face. You suck cock good though and you got a nice pearly ass. Ever had a cock up that ass?"

"No sir."

"Wanna do something about that?"

I swallowed, looking at Hemi's cock, how big it was.

"I think so, but—"

"Boy, if it hurts, I'm doin' it wrong, OK? Just let me know and I'll stop. But I don't think it's going to hurt, I think you'll enjoy the ways I know for opening up a man's ass for a hot pleasurable fucking."

I was so horny by then, my cock was streaming precome just looking at Hemi and thinking about what the cowboy might mean by "ways of opening a man up."

"OK," I said, "let's do it."

Hemi went to his saddlebags and came back with a small black leather zip-bag.

"Like the boy scouts, always be prepared," he joked. "Now lie down on your belly in front of this fire."

By then the valley was in shadow and the fire was the only source of light in the hut. Hemi threw some extra wood on and I could feel the heat blaze up, making my skin glow with its ruddy light.

"Nice," Hemi growled, reaching into his bag and pulling out a squeeze bottle. "Silicon lube. Great for massages but, unlike massage oil, still safe for condoms."

He started on my neck and shoulders, his strong weathered hands kneading into my muscles, so I was relaxing but getting turned on at the same time. Hemi was in no hurry, slowly working across my shoulders and down my back, stretching, pushing, probing with his fingers, finding every knot and not missing anywhere until my skin was glowing and warm, the muscles limp and relaxed. But, just above my ass, he stopped.

I groaned and lifted my ass a little, begging Hemi with body language to continue.

"Not yet, boy, you need to really want it," Hemi growled quietly before switching to my feet. Man that was hot! He squeezed and rubbed his strong fingers deep into my soles before sliding up to work the calf muscles and then ease the tension out of the hard tendons behind my knees.

Soon Hemi began working his long fingers around my thighs, squeezing and probing up toward my white American ass. I couldn't help it, groaning loudly as I lifted my ass again, begging for it, and this time Hemi obliged, his hard flat palms massaging deep into my buttocks, his fingers working the lube deeper and deeper into my crack, searching for the door to my love hole.

"Good," Hemi whispered, "gooood. Mmmmmm, hot wee button you have there."

Hemi's fingers were working my asshole seriously now, gently pushing and probing, working the warm silicon in and around the pink bud. I shifted uncomfortably, my cock was so hard underneath me it was crushing on the floor. It needed more room!

"Wait," Hemi said, and stepped outside for a moment, coming back in with his horse's saddle. He lifted me up and placed the saddle underneath my belly so that it held my ass up in the air, and gave my cock room in the gap underneath to, incredibly, grow some more!

The leather quickly warmed to my body and the smell of it was Hemi's special man smell—of horse and man sweat and leather and the dust of the trail. It was better than amyl! My brain was spinning on this hot sexual perfume. With my eyes closed I just wanted to feel and sense everything, concentrate on allowing my body to be Hemi's instrument.

Hemi eased my legs apart and I heard the Maori shift position and then, wow! there was hot breath up against my hole and a hot tongue flicking at me, probing and tasting.

"Ohhhh fuu u u uck!"

"You OK, boy? You want me to stop."

"No, no, keep going, that wasn't pain, it was pleasure. More. Please!"

Hemi was really working at me now, driving his rough chin deep into my crack, rasping against my hole, and then back with his tongue, his face hard into my ass, driving in there. And then, alongside tongue, a finger, gentle, probing . . . and then in!

"Ah, good, " Hemi drawled, "getting there. Feel good, boy?"

"Yes, ohh man, yes!"

Hemi applied more lube and worked that finger some more and I could feel myself opening up, the tension in my ass melting away, replaced by wave after wave of pleasure as Hemi gently massaged the pleasure button hidden inside my ass.

A second finger and then, quite quickly, a third! I could feel my ass grabbing at Hemi, trying to pull those long fingers in further as I bucked up against the strong musterer's hand, my belly slapping on the saddle as instinct took over and fear evaporated away.

"Ohh, Hemi, fuck me, man, please, fuck me, I'm ready, please, do it now!"

Hemi let me go for a moment and I could hear him tearing open a condom packet and the soft squish of the bottle as he applied more lube. Then he cupped his forearm under my waist and lifted me into a kneeling position, putting my head on the saddle and setting my white ass up high.

He slapped his cock around my hole, and probed some more lube into my ass with his fingers, working quickly back up from one, two to three fingers, probing deeper this time. My cock was drooling pools of precome onto the floor. Hemi scooped some of it onto his fingers and used my own sex juice to lube me up even more!

"Push against me boy, like you're trying to push my cock out of your ass. It'll help open you up."

And then, he was there! I felt his hot head against my hole, gentle, but insistent, as Hemi reached around to grab my cock, jerking back and forth fast.

"Oh, oh, I'm gonna come!" I screamed, bucking back against him as my body rushed toward orgasm. "Fuck this is so good."

And as I bucked my ass against him one more time, Hemi entered my virgin hole, his big cock sliding past the relaxed barriers and deep in, crushing into my prostate and beyond, filling me as I came, copiously, in the longest, hardest, orgasm I had ever experienced. My come flooded onto the floor and I was screaming and Hemi was yelling too, as he came, deep inside me, filling the rubber, his cock hot and twitching, his hard pubic bones slamming into my ass.

We collapsed onto the floor together, with Hemi still inside me, and lay there gasping, fighting to get breath back into our lungs, our sweat mingling and sticking our bodies together, Hemi's arms crushed around my chest, his hot breath panting against the side of my neck.

We lay there for a while, just hugging, and then, reaching down to hold the condom in place, Hemi gently withdrew, tossed the rubber into the fire, flipped onto his back and pulled me onto his body in a fierce embrace.

"Ok, boy?"

"Hell yes."

"Did it hurt?"

"No, I can't believe it, you're so big and you were in so deep but it was all just pleasure man, no pain, just intense, pleasurable, pressure and a feeling of being taken in a way that I know I want to be taken again."

"It's an old trick, taking a man up his virgin ass just as he's about to come. He's not getting all worried and tensed up about how it might hurt right then, his body has other feelings to concentrate on. Later, with practice, you'll be able to take cock sooner and for longer and you can really pound at it, but your ass needed to learn that a cock is pleasure, not pain, and not to be afraid. So, quick, like this, the first time, is all good."

We spent another day at the cabin, talking, fucking. I learned so much. But, eventually, I had to get back and Hemi had range to ride.

"Can I get hold of you," I asked, idly tracing my finger around the swirling tattoo on Hemi's ass as we lay cuddling after our final fuck.

"No, son. I have another life outside this valley. A life that involves a wife, children, the expectations of leadership within my *whanau*. New Zealand might have liberal gay laws, but among my *whanau*, gay sex is barely tolerated. They look the other way as long as I'm not too blatant and have done my duty to produce children to carry on the *whakapapa*, but I can't talk about it, certainly couldn't bring a man home.

"You're young, the world is changing. Even among my people now there are *takataapui*—gays and lesbians—rediscovering ancient traditions of acceptance for gay sexuality that were nearly lost after the missionaries came. Go out there and help change it so one day guys like me won't have to hide. Maybe, then, I'll come find you."

But we never met again. However, I had taken a photo of a tall, naked Maori standing proudly beside a waterfall, his wet body gleaming, the tribal tattoos dark but vibrant against his thighs and buttocks. It's a strong photo, a photo I knew I would show my mom and dad when I got back home, to help tell them the whole story of who, and what, their son is. Somehow, as I watched Hemi ride away, I just knew it was going to be OK.

PILGRIMAGE TO THE MAD MAX CAVES

VIC WINTER

MAN, HE HADN'T expected it to be so hot. Bill wiped the sweat out of his eyes and grabbed his water bottle, tilting his head back and drinking deeply. The water was warm, like everything else, but it was wet and that's what counted. Some dripped down over his chin and along his neck, making him moan, before it was soaked up by the collar of his t-shirt.

He glanced at his directions again, hoping the hotel clerk knew what he was talking about—the road seemed to stretch out in front of him, an unending sea of red sand on either side, broken only by short, browning scrub. It made him grin. This was exactly how he'd imagined Australia would look when he'd come, what he'd been looking for. Sydney had been cool, but so not what he thought of when he thought "Down Under." But this landscape was right out of the movies. Out of the Mad Max movies.

He checked the map again; however there was nowhere to go but straight. Another two miles and he'd have gone too far; the clerk had said no more than ten miles south of Cooper Pedy's town limits. Then there it was: the sign for the caves where they'd filmed *Mad Max Beyond Thunderdome*. Bill slowed and took the turn, marvelling at the rock formations and trying not to bounce.

Mad Max was after all the reason he was here, the reason he'd fallen in love with Australia in the first place, and her rugged good-looking men. Hot as it was, sweaty and glued to the seat of his little rental car as he was, his cock was half-hard at the thought.

He parked in the empty space in front of the caves and grabbed his camera, heading for the cave mouth. He recognized it from the movie as soon as he bent low and walked in. There were drawings on the cave walls, the place just like he remembered from the movie. He started snapping pictures, not quite able to believe he was really here in the place he dreamed of visiting ever since he first saw the movies.

It was cooler in here, the caves half underground. One "room" opened into another; a couple of the openings small and low to the ground, and Bill had to get down on his hands and knees and crawl through.

He had gone through about four and was about to turn back, not wanting to get lost. The place didn't look like it was kept up really; there'd been an "enter at your own risk" sign, and he'd hate to become a permanent fixture. Besides, the air had started to feel a little stale. So he turned and headed back toward the low opening.

That was when he heard it. A moan.

Bill froze, head tilted, breath catching in his lungs. It came again. And it didn't sound like someone in pain. There hadn't been any other cars in front of the little cave. Surely he was imagining things. But no, there it was a third time. Definitely a moan, distinctively male, low and deep and full of pleasure.

Before he could think twice, Bill took off in the direction of the sound, following it through two different caves before he found the source.

There, leaning against the cave wall, was a young man, no more than twenty-five, who looked as if he could have stepped out of any of the Mad Max movies. He wore tan-colored leather pants, his chest bare but for a necklace that looked as if it were made of bones. His hair was blond, curling around his neck and ears. As Bill stepped in, the guy's eyes flew open, proving to be a stunning blue.

Bill gasped. It was like coming face to face with his favorite fantasy.

He was given a grin, the hand moving on the long cock slowing, his fantasy giving him a show. "Tourist?"

"Yeah."

"You like what you see, mate?"

Bill could only nod, thinking he had to be hallucinating.

"You got a condom, mate?"

He nodded again, sure now that this was a hallucination.

"All right, bring it over and I'll give you a private tour." He got a wink, the guy sinking to his knees right where he was.

Whimpering a little, Bill went over, hand digging for his wallet, finding it and the condom inside. Slender fingers grabbed the condom from his hand, warm as they slid against his hand. Not a hallucination then.

He swallowed, cock pushing hard against his zipper.

"What's your name?" he asked, earning a cheeky grin from the blond.

"You can call me Max."

Oh, that was too perfect and if the fingers opening his zipper and tugging out his cock weren't so hot, so real, he would have been even more sure this was just another fantasy. No fantasy felt that real though, one nail scrapping against his slit and making him his.

Max pushed him against the wall and he was grateful to feel it behind his back, to let it support him as Max put the condom in his mouth and slowly slid it down his prick.

Moaning, Bill slid his hands into Max's blond curls, fingers opening and closing as Max's mouth started working him. It was better than any fantasy, Max's mouth hotter than the day, soft and sucking. Max's tongue slid along his cock, teased the tip, and slapped at his flesh. And when he slid in deep, Max's throat swallowed around him.

Groaning, he started to move his hips, taking control of the rhythm, feeding his dick into Max's mouth, watching as sweet red lips stretched around him. Max worked him expertly, quickly, as if at any second one of Aunty Entity's guards was going to come around the corner.

Stuffing his hand into his mouth, he muffled his cry as his hips pushed, his balls drawing up and letting loose his load. He filled the condom with shuddering jerks, his vision swimming for a moment.

As quickly as he'd knelt, Max popped up again, disposing of

the condom as if it had never been there, and tucking Bill back into his pants.

"Good one, mate."

"Uh. Yeah, thanks." He blinked stupidly, feeling melted and more than little . . . well, blown away.

Max gave him a wink and turned, offering a tantalizing view of a leather-clad ass before disappearing through one of three entrances to this particular cave room.

It took Bill a little longer to get himself back together, to catch his breath and get his legs solid beneath him.

He got a little lost on his way out, doubling back a couple of times before the increasing heat let him know he was headed in the right direction. Stumbling out of the cave, clutching his camera, he blinked at the heat and brightness that greeted him.

His rental was still the only car there, and there was no sign of anyone else at all, just the dusty red landscape and the ever present sun.

Bill got into his car, hissing at how hot the seat had become, and started up the engine.

He might still have a week left in Australia, but, real or not, he'd just had his quintessential Down Under experience.

Grinning, he turned the car out onto the road and consulted his map. On to Ayers Rock. Who knew, maybe there was another Australian fantasy to be found.

COMRADES

T. HITMAN

THE BUZZ STARTED right before blast-off from the Bai-
konur Cosmodrome in Kazakhstan. It stayed with Bodie Evans
for the two hundred and fifty miles of flight straight up into
space, and most of the forty-eight hours that followed spent
chasing the *International Space Station*'s orbit around the Earth.
A natural high unlike anything he'd ever experienced, it made
his flesh tingle, his stomach lurch, his balls itch, and his toes
flex. With the Soyuz rocket nearing its vaulted destination, he
realized his cock had gotten hard again and was pressing into the
unforgiving material of his flight suit. The vibrations of the *Soyuz*
transporter's powerful engines steadily masturbated his erection,
and it wouldn't take much, Bodie knew, a few bursts from the
maneuvering thrusters, to push his dick over the edge.

A voice crackled over the helmet's radio, pulling him out of
his trance and distracting his cock from unloading what threat-
ened to be a hell of a mess inside his flight suit. He caught sight
of the station through the vehicle's direct vision port as a tiny
distortion over the curve of the Earth's horizon. The shimmering
anomaly grew steadily larger and more impressive the longer he
stared at it.

"Have you decided what you're going to say?" asked Laird,
the *Soyuz's* American copilot.

"You mean, like 'Big step for Mankind', that sorta thing,"
Bodie answered.

"Yeah."

"First thing outta my mouth's gonna be, 'where's the head'?"

Stoyakovich, the Russian cosmonaut, chuckled at Bodie's
joke. "That will be one for the history books, my friend."

Bodie leaned forward as far as the safety harness would allow. His cock, pinned against his inner thigh by the flight suit, reminded him he was still boned up, still stoked, and now only minutes away from setting foot on the most extreme summit possible. And all it had cost him was a two million dollar donation to the Roscosmos Space Agency in Russia.

The station solidified before them, its solar collectors, trusses, and array of modules pulling free of the black velvet star field. That rush of reverse free fall over a cliff, of dropping up instead of down, began to lessen. Solid ground loomed ahead, a tiny island oasis in outer space, 146 feet from the Zvezda docking port and crew quarters to the *Discovery* module that housed the station's scientific labs. Bodie's natural high soured into the beginnings of panic he always experienced during one of his extreme adventures: would the chute open when he pulled the cord? Would he make it safely down the mountain he'd just scaled? Would the deep submergence vehicle taking him in close for a pass over the wreckage of *Titanic* return to the surface without tangling its tethers on the luxury liner's rusting hull?

Bodie's cock deflated. He closed his eyes, sucked in a deep breath of the oxygen being pumped into his suit, and willed his nerves to steady. Astro-tourism, a voice in his thoughts reminded, was no different than Aqua-tourism or any of the other dangerous adventures he's signed on board for. The station wasn't going to drop out of the sky or get knocked from its orbit by a rogue asteroid. And if it did, he knew the ISS kept an extra *Soyuz* capsule on standby as an escape pod. Ergo, it wasn't so much about the destination as it was the journey, and until he found a way to fly his ass to the moon or Mars, this journey was about as radical as an adrenaline junky could hope to experience.

The space vehicle connected with the airlock and the deep rumble shocked away his worry. As the atmosphere seals cycled into place, a cocky smirk blossomed on Bodie's face. He had arrived!

Cosmonaut Stoyakovich led the way into the Zvezda Module, followed by Laird, with Bodie the last to enter the crew quarters. Thus freed of his space helmet, he sucked in a deep breath of the station's air and found it bitter around the edges with an antiseptic smell, like the air inside hospitals.

The module, he discovered, as was the case with the rest of the station, was smaller than he'd imagined during his grueling orientation at the Roscosmos center outside of Moscow, the space agency that had sold him his ticket. With the module doubling as both sleeping quarters and home to the life support systems, there wasn't an inch of bare space anywhere. It was already crowded elbow to elbow by the time Bodie made it through the airlock.

"We figured you were feeling a little lonely up here," he heard Laird say. Bodie glanced through the tangle of floating arms and legs to see another body blocking the hatch to the station's midsection, the Zarya Module that housed the fuel tanks and propulsion mechanisms.

"*Da*," growled a deep, masculine voice.

"Comrade Petrovek," said Stoyakovich. The *Soyuz* rocket's pilot extended his gloved hand and shook with the fourth man in the module, as Bodie mentally called up the name. Cosmonaut Vaklav Petrovek, until their arrival, had been the station's sole occupant. Laird and Petrovek shook hands, and through the slow-motion effect of athletic male bodies moving in the microgravity environment, Bodie stole a good look at the other man.

At first, he couldn't be sure if it was the tight quarters or the fact that Petrovek was standing with his feet, in clean white socks, anchored into the stirrups bolted to the floor at intervals along the station's deck plates. He seemed tall, a good six feet and probably a few inches more to Bodie's five-ten. The cosmonaut who'd thus far logged over a month on the ISS, the last ten days of it in solitude, was handsome in a thuggish, rugged way, with his mean, rigid expression, cold blue eyes, and short, dark hair, silvery directly above the ears. Cosmonaut Petrovek greeted the delegation dressed in a simple black T-shirt bearing the official insignia of the Roscosmos Space Agency on the upper right chest, gray cotton shorts that hugged, among other bulges, the concrete quadriceps of very hairy legs, and the white socks, all standard space station issue.

"I'd like to present our guest, Bodie Evans," Laird said, taking point.

Using the handrails, Bodie made his way front and center.

"Put it there, comrade," he said, a wide smile on his face.

Petrovek's hard expression grew even harsher, meaner. "*The tourist*," he growled. "On behalf of Russia and the other eighteen countries who've made the dream of a permanent orbital research platform a reality, I welcome you on board, Mr. Evans."

But Bodie didn't feel particularly welcomed by Petrovek, who would be his only other companion on the station once the supplies were off-loaded and his two comrades from the *Soyuz* rocketed back to Earth.

◆

THOUGH IT TOOK a spacecraft two full days of playing tag in orbit to obtain the proper maneuvers to link up with the ISS, the return flight home was a mere three-hour drop back to terra firma after departure, Bodie reminded himself. Not long after Laird and Stoyakovich left the station, part of him wished he'd gone with them.

Petrovek spent most of their first day together isolated in the *Discovery* research lab, which Bodie had been forbidden from entering on the chance he might screw up any number of delicate science projects. Whatever thrill he'd gotten from eating the best the ISS menu offered, like thermostabilized beef tips with mushrooms, washing it down with dehydrated apple cider, and then pissing it into the station's acrobatic version of a toilet, was gone. The simple truth was that after the first day, even floating in microgravity had grown boring. Bodie was now beyond bored, and itchy with a hard-on that refused to let up.

Just after 0:800 hours on the second morning, with Petrovek again brooding in *Discovery* and Bodie's next transmission to his peeps on the ground not scheduled for another five hours, he dog-paddled through the Zarya Module into the crew quarters, his cock teased fully erect by the loose, gray cotton shorts that barely imprisoned it, and the unintentional hand job offered up by floating in microgravity. Bodie was bored, and a sure cure for that, the three-hour free fall through Earth's atmosphere, was still a distant seventy-two hours away. Seemingly, his only option for any sort of fun before getting off the station was getting his rocks off, and Bodie's dick had been more than ready for days.

He strapped himself into the same harness he'd been assigned to sleep in and tugged his shorts to one side, baring the fleshy pole between his legs. In orientation, he'd learned that the lack of gravity in outer space made everything appear bigger. With the push of gravity no longer pressing down upon his shoulders, he stood taller on the station than he did back home in San Diego by several inches. Everything was bigger in space.

Everything.

Bodie ogled his erect cock and muttered an expletive in disbelief. His dick, which usually tented in the seven-inch range, felt more like ten. He shot a look between his legs and was stunned to see something that was so long and swollen, he considered throwing his body into a half-somersault and trying to accomplish one of those rare extreme sports—sucking his own dick—he hadn't yet conquered.

The touch of hand to dick was electric, sparking pins and needles along the sensitive underside of his shaft. A quick fumble of his balls revealed low-g had pulled a similar effect upon them. Thus freed from his shorts, his nuts rolled looser and hung farther away from his root than he'd ever seen or thought possible.

"*Fuckin-A,*" Bodie grunted under his breath, a dreamy smirk on his face. He spat into his palm, lubed up his colossal shaft, and started jerking on his dick. Not long afterward, the itch in his cock reached flashpoint and his balls erupted, pumping out a load that was worthy of the ultra-sized monstrosity between his legs.

Eyes clamped shut, Bodie rode a wave of pure joy, and it wasn't until a sloppy rope of wetness collided with his face that he realized he'd fucked up big time. With the barest level of gravity to contain it, his wad was everywhere, free-floating through the crew quarters!

◆

BODIE SCRAMBLED OUT of the sleep harness and reached for the nearest drops of whitewash. One cluster of thick, white glop splattered across his palm, but the rest slipped between his fingers. Gathering up his nut-juice was like trying to grasp hold of a cloud, something Bodie had attempted on numerous skydives and impossible to pull off. Still, he cupped his hands and pursued—until he looked up and saw that his movements had disturbed the bubbles of come, knocking them around like balls on a pool table and launching the most distant ones out into the next compartment.

"*Oh, fuck!*"

Bodie gave chase. He exited the crew quarters and entered the Zarya Module, only to nearly collide with the very mean, humorless presence of cosmonaut Petrovek.

"What is *this*?" growled the big Russian.

Bodie's eyes widened in horror as he looked toward the object Petrovek had indicated, a string of spunk drifting freely in the air between them. Bodie's heart galloped in his chest. He choked down a swallow and felt all of two inches tall in front of Petrovek's six-foot-plus frame. And as the two men faced off, Bodie shrinking under the cosmonaut's mean blue eyes, more bubbles of come drifted into the module.

Petrovek arched the brow above his right eye.

And then he began to laugh in great bellows that filled the station's cramped quarters.

Fresh sweat broke across Bodie's forehead. "What? What's so damn funny about this?"

Petrovek shook his head, and for the first time since the start of Bodie's adventure, he smiled. "Rich boy who thinks himself so smart, so big that he's sitting on top of the world," he said between gasps for breath, "and he doesn't know first thing about stroking his dick in low-g environment!"

Bodie's face flushed beet-red with embarrassment. "This ain't no laughing matter, dude!"

"*Dude*," Petrovek harrumphed. "I think I prefer *comrade* to *dude* after all." He drew in a deep breath, held it, and then let it fly. "This, this—" Petrovek poked the tip of his finger into the nearest sperm cloud. "This makes us comrades. Come on, my young American friend. I'll help you clean up this come-storm you've unleashed in my space station, and then I'll teach you the best way to do such things while you're here."

Bodie's anguish softened. "You will?"

"Da," answered Petrovek. "And it should ease your conscience to know that you aren't the first man to find himself in this kind of crisis."

Petrovek floated into the *Discovery* Module, but quickly returned with a large, clear plastic bag marked: Organic Specimen. Bodie watched, mesmerized, as the cosmonaut moved around the module like a butterfly collector with a net. In seemingly less time than it had taken Bodie to unleash the gobs of sperm, Petrovek had captured all of them in the specimen bag.

"You've done this before," Bodie said.

Petrovek nodded. "For you, it would be good idea to take your aggressions out on one of these until your Soyuz limousine returns. Dump the bags into trash for garbage module to burn everything up upon atmospheric reentry."

"I'll try to remember that."

Petrovek started out of the module, skidded to a stop, his feet in their white socks continuing to slide another several inches across the deck plates. As he turned around, Bodie caught sight of the lump in the big Russian's loose gray cotton shorts. Like his own over-inflated cock, Petrovek's was impossible to miss, and it seemed to be growing even bigger. "Of course, there is cleaner, better alternative the next time your dick needs releasing."

Bodie forced his eyes off the other man's cock and up into the gravitational pull of his eyes. "Oh, yeah? What's that—"

The cosmonaut released the specimen bag full of his come and shuffled over to where Bodie floated. Fresh fear briefly swept over his flesh as he fell into Petrovek's brooding shadow. That fleeting, nagging register inside his psyche that always sounded the alert bells right as Bodie was about to pull the parachute's rip cord or the roller coaster readied to plunge down a mountainous track began to whoop, when the towering Russian reached a hand toward the floating mass of his cock and balls, which had never felt so eager for action.

"This is how," Petrovek said. His fingers slid into Bodie's shorts. The nagging voice in his head took an invisible sledgehammer to its skull and was gonged into silence by a rush of electric pinpricks that launched his dick back to its gigantic, lowgrav fullness.

Bodie released his grip on the handrail and moaned a breathy, *"Fuck, yeah . . . "* as cosmonaut Petrovek yanked him back into the crew quarters by his cock.

Bodie floated in a daze, eyes half-closed, while Petrovek steadily hummed up and down on his tool, fulfilling Bodie's fantasy of getting a blow job in orbit. He would soon become a member of that most exclusive of brotherhoods: the 250-Mile High Club.

Petrovek's thick, uncut knob was bobbing near his face when Bodie opened his eyes. That, and two enormous, loose balls, wet with his spit. "This is fuckin amazing," Bodie moaned, aware he'd been pushed close to unloading.

The cosmonaut spit out Bodie's cock long enough to order, "Get back on my dick." Bodie did.

He'd sucked uncut meat before, once after a grueling hike up a mountain in the Swiss Alps, another time after banging both knees skateboarding on a half-pipe, but nothing so magnificent as this. The low-grav environment released the luscious folds of Petrovek's foreskin and sent them floating up from around the big Russian's plum-sized cock head. Bodie clasped his lips onto the moist sock and sucked, sucked and was sucked in return, until the Zvezda Module filled with muffled grunts and sealed mouths were pumped full of come.

Bodie swallowed. No mess this time, or any of the dozen other times that Petrovek drained his balls over the course of the next few days.

✦

"I HAVE SOMETHING to show you," Petrovek said. "Come with me, into Discovery."

Bodie raised a hand in protest. "Dude, the rules—I'm not allowed in there."

"I'm in charge of this mission, and as my comrade, I say is okay for you to come into *Discovery*."

Bodie unhooked his body from the sleep harness and released the comic book he'd been reading, sending its colorful pages into a roll. He followed Petrovek into the *Zarya* Module and for the first time, beyond, into Discovery.

He'd poked around near the hatch on several occasions, close enough to see the usual tight quarters and tangle of scientific equipment. But as Bodie entered the *Discovery* Module, he understood its importance, the greater picture of why so much money and hope had been devoted to the orbiting science platform.

It wasn't the brightly-colored collection of plant specimens growing wildly under the effects of micro-gravity, the network of computer instruments, or even the image of the station's powerful robotic arm, but what waited beyond his new comrade that caused Bodie's cock to tingle with excitement, to swell despite unloading twice that morning thanks to Petrovek. It exerted a pull on his maleness that was absolute and undeniable, all-powerful, all-beautiful.

The planet swam beyond the *Discovery* Module's large direct-vision space port, blue and magnificent, more breathtaking than anything Bodie had ever seen. A giant wedge of Mother Earth's southern pole, from the tip of South America to a sizeable chunk of Antarctica along with roiling blankets of clouds, sat visibly beyond the window's reinforced glass.

"*Sweet*," Bodie said.

ABOUT THE CONTRIBUTORS

STEVE ATTWOOD lives in Auckland, New Zealand, where he works as a communications coordinator for an HIV/AIDS and gay rights organization. He lives in a legally recognized civil union with his partner, Stephen, and writes on weekends. A keen tramper (hiker), his story stems from his experience of New Zealand's mountain country and a period employed as a stockman on a high country sheep station (ranch). He has previously been published by Alyson Books in *Slow Grind* and *Best Gay Love Stories*.

JOHN-PAUL BATISTA is a former photographer for a well-known travel magazine, which afforded him the opportunity to experience the world and the diverse men who populate it. He has settled down now, but loves to talk about his many adventures. Originally from Los Angeles, John Paul went to college and spent a few years in Washington, D.C. He now calls Boston home, where he lives with his husband, Christopher, and their two sons, Nickolas and Javier.

P.A. BROWN has lived in Los Angeles, Hawaii, and Canada, and now resides in Bermuda. Writing is P.A.'s greatest love and most evenings and weekends that's what you'll find her doing, while listening to some seriously heavy rock—though that may change once summer rolls around and the reefs and beaches beckon. *L.A. Heat*, the first book in the Chris Bellamere/David Eric Laine mysteries, is now available from www.pabrown.ca.

LEW BULL lives in Johannesburg, South Africa, and has been in a relationship for the past twenty-nine years. Trained as an actor and later as a teacher, with a doctorate in education, for relaxation and pleasure from academia he enjoys theater, travel, and writing gay erotica. He has had a number of academic articles and a language text-book published, and this is his first piece of erotica to be published.

BOB CONDRON made his erotic fiction debut in 1996 courtesy of *Bear* magazine. Since then he has authored two homoerotic novels, *Easy Money* (IDOL/Virgin) and *Sweating It Out* (ZIPPER/Millivres), and has also contributed to numerous anthologies. Most recently he worked as editor on two homoerotic anthologies: *Daddy's Boyz: Tales of Intergenerational Adult Gay Sex* (STARbooks Press) and the forthcoming *Working Stiff: True Blue-Collar Gay Porn*.

ERASTES lives in the U.K. and wishes it was warmer. He spends too much time in front of the computer but enjoys swimming, eventing, and Thai food. He specializes in historical homoerotica because he wanted to read it and found so few books on the subject. He has published several short stories, and *Standish*, his first novel—a gay Regency Romance—will be published in summer/autumn 2006. His blog and Web site can be found at www.erastes.com.

T. HITMAN is the e nom-de-porn of a full-time professional writer who recently celebrated his tenth year writing short stories, cover features, and two monthly columns for *Men*, *Freshmen*, and *Unzipped* magazines. He, his alter ego, their husband, and twenty-one-year-old cat live in a small, very cozy cottage on a large plot of forested land in New Hampshire. When not writing fantasies about hot men, he works as a contributor to a number of mainstream national publications, and writes novels and the occasional screenplay or TV script. "Comrades" is the bastard child resulting from a lifetime of loving classic science fiction shows like the brilliant *Space:1999*, the Japan-ime *Starblazers*, and the original *The Outer Limits*. He also jonesed on the first version of *Battlestar Galactica*, but grudgingly admits he loves the reimagined incarnation just a little bit more.

WILLIAM HOLDEN lives in Atlanta with his partner of nine years. He works full-time as a librarian on LGBT issues.

He has eleven other published short stories and one unpublished novel. He welcomes any comments and can be contacted at Srholdbill@aol.com.

JOHN HOLT is a twenty-something Aquarian who lives in Ireland. Before getting serious about writing, he worked in a variety of jobs, including bookseller, call center worker, and travel agent. He recently returned to university to pursue a few more years of study. In his spare time, he writes short stories in many genres—mystery, horror, fantasy, and gay erotica.

Author/editor **MICHAEL HUXLEY**'s most recent writing appears in these collections: *Van Gogh's Ear 2, 3* and *4*; *Chiron Review*; *Best Gay Love Stories 2005*; *Best Gay Erotica 2005*; *My First Time 4*; *Ultimate Gay Erotica 2006*; *I Do/I Don't: Queers on Marriage*; *Walking Higher: Gay Men Write About the Deaths of Their Mothers*; and *Wet Nightmares, Wet Dreams*.

HENRY JACOBS is an American who discovered a "Sense of Wonder" on vacation in Ireland. This experience inspired him to write the short story. By day, Mr. Jacobs runs a successful dental practice and by night, he writes erotic fiction for gay men. "A Sense of Wonder" is his first published story.

ROB MCDONALD is a gay librarian who lives in Alice Springs, an outback Australian town which filmgoers will recall as the destination of *Priscilla, Queen of the Desert*. He spent the first eighteen years of his life in a place called Wagga Wagga, but otherwise seems fairly rational. Other stories by Rob have appeared in *OutRage*, the *OutRage 1995 Gay & Lesbian Short Story Anthology*, and *CreamDrops: an Art and Literary Journal for Gay Men*.

MORRIS MICHAELS, JR., has traveled extensively. Based in Manhattan, he is an historian who writes and lectures on a variety of subjects throughout the United States and Europe. Educated in the Ivy League, he is not above wallowing in the gutter on occasion and enjoys both cerebral and more intensely earthy pleasures.

MICHAEL MURPHY lives in Vancouver, Canada, where he is an actor and personal trainer, dabbling in writing on the side. His erotic stories have been published in the anthology *Ultimate Gay Erotica 2005* and the magazine *Bear*.

JAY NEAL's favorite flavor in men is "husky," and those best described as "big lugs" are lovingly treated in his fiction, a vocation he was called to late last century. Having held various day jobs as a rocket scientist, he has also published a number of technical papers with remarkably silly titles. Basically a geeky, vanilla kind of guy, Neal enhances his sex life by making up things and then writing about them. His stories have appeared in several magazines and over a dozen anthologies to date. He and his partner are celebrating fourteen years of domestic contentment together in suburban Washington, D.C. Current information is at his Web site http://bearcastle.com/jayneal.

NEIL S. PLAKCY is the author of *Mahu*, a mystery novel featuring Honolulu police detective Kimo Kanapa'aka. A contributor to *Men Seeking Men*, *My First Time 2* and *Dorm Porn*, he is also the editor of a forthcoming anthology from Alyson Books that focuses on gay men and their dogs. He received his MFA in creative writing from Florida International University and is a professor of English at Broward Community College.

SIMON SHEPPARD is the author of the short fiction collections *In Deep* and *Hotter Than Hell*, as well as *Sex Parties 101* and *Kinkorama: Dispatches from the Front Lines of Perversion*. His work has also appeared in over 175 anthologies, including many editions of *The Best American Erotica*, *Best Gay Erotica*, and *Ultimate Gay Erotica*, and he writes the columns "Sex Talk" and "Perv." His next project is an historically-based antho of queer porn. He went to Morocco a long time ago, but these days he's more likely to be found at www.simonsheppard.com.

JOHN SIMPSON is the author of *Murder Most Gay*, a full length e-book carried by Renaissance E-books, and is currently looking for a print publisher for the book *The Virgin Marine*, published in *My First Time 4*, by Alyson Books. John just finished writing another short story called "The Smell of Leathern" which will be shown to publishers shortly. In addition, he has written numerous articles for various gay and straight magazines, and a full-length nonfiction novel.

From Vancouver, B.C., **JAY STARRE** has written for gay men's magazines, including *Men, Freshmen, Honcho, Torso,* and *American Bear*. Jay has also written for over twenty-eight gay anthologies including the *Friction* series for Alyson Books, *Hard Drive, Bad Boys, Just the Sex, Ultimate Gay Erotic 2005, Bear Lust,* and *Full Body Contact*.

MICHAEL STEPHENSON, a Seattle native, currently resides in Manhattan and teaches high school. His students always enjoy the travel anecdotes that enliven their history and geography classes. He enjoys exploring the world and has published several essays in a number of anthologies. An avid reader, he also enjoys classical as well as pop music, and fine wines.

CARY STEVEN lives in upstate New York and longs for California. This is his first published piece of erotic fiction.

JACK STEVENS has been writing gay fiction for some years now and has a published novel about love, death, and drug dealing in the world of hardcore bodybuilding called *Fellowship of Iron*. "Wadi Bashing" was based on real life experiences in Oman.

J. TALBOT resides in the Southwest of the United States with a dog and several houseplants, and still has a day job. J. has a penchant for blank books, gay porn, and men in tight jeans, and can most often be found in coffeeshops and restaurants, scribbling in a notebook and entertaining other diners with loud mutterings.

In his youth, **DAVEM VERNE** fancied himself a wanderer. He has lived in several major U.S. cities, as well as abroad. And where he hasn't lived or traveled, he has imagined. From Berlin to Paris to Tangier, his erotic stories encompass the world and define his literary style as global— but with a hardcore edge. His role model during these formative years was the expatriate author and eternal outsider Paul Bowles, whose self-exile in Tangier in the late 1940s inspired "Tenderly, Tangier." In his own autobiography, Bowles wrote of his Moroccan home "in the night, all around me in my sleep, sorcery is burrowing its invisible tunnels in every direction, from thousands of senders to thousands of unsuspecting recipients." Davem Verne hopes he captured that possessive spirit in "Tenderly, Tangier"—but with a hardcore edge.

Words and snow, silence and long nights, the fall of rain and of silk, and love are some of VIC WINTER's favorite things. To learn more about Vic's writing, please visit www.stemsandfeathers.org/vwinter.